Pandora Inn (the novel)

by Lliam West

Tamarisk

First published in the UK in 2001 by Tamara Publications

This edition published in 2002 by
TAMARISK
16 Lodge Hill, Liskeard, Cornwall PL14 4JP

ISBN 0-9541911-0-2

Printed by Swiftprint, Treverbyn Rd, St. Austell

For Eve, and Theo, and Alice......
and for all who love Cornwall and Devon

Foreword

This second impression offers an opportunity to correct a number of the many mistakes that crept into the first. I was aware of some, several more had to be pointed out .... my thanks to Delia in particular, and to the many others who have helped. Portscatho is no longer Porthscatho (cheers Ralph!), and the Roseland School has regretfully been dis-endowed of its 6th form. Hopefully the spelling and the grammar is improved, and there is the needed clarification as to how McKinley came by the copy of *Slide Rule* that he leaves with Linda in Exeter.

I must disappoint those who have urged me to tamper with the beginning. If I open a jigsaw I expect to find disjointed pieces, likewise when I open a 'mystery'. Clusters of already fitted together bits detract from the challenge and also my enjoyment. Look closely at the fragments and be patient. They do coalesce....honest!

Influential in my storytelling has been the early novel of Nevil Shute, *'Lonely Road'*. For this simple Cornish lad it was by far his best, the first twenty or so pages notwithstanding! I hope that fans of his can accept this tale as my tribute to their multi-talented hero.

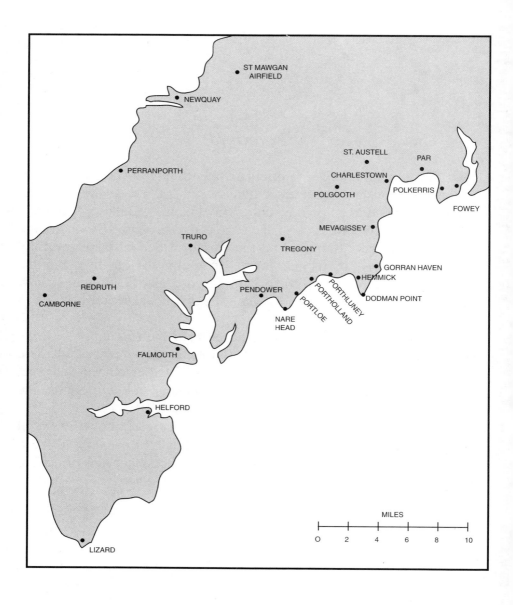

ST MAWGAN
AIRFIELD

● NEWQUAY

● PERRANPORTH

ST. AUSTELL
●
PAR
CHARLESTOWN
POLGOOTH
POLKERRIS

FOWEY

TRURO
●
MEVAGISSEY
●
TREGONY

GORRAN HAVEN
●
PENDOWER
PORTHLUNEY
HEMMICK
PORTHOLLAND
REDRUTH
DODMAN POINT
PORTLOE
CAMBORNE

NARE
HEAD

FALMOUTH
●

HELFORD
●

MILES

O   2   4   6   8   10

LIZARD

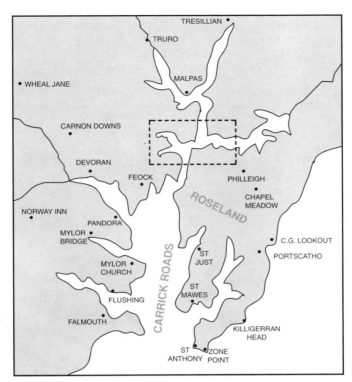

TRESILLIAN •
• TRURO
• WHEAL JANE
MALPAS •
• CARNON DOWNS
DEVORAN •
FEOCK •
• PHILLEIGH
ROSELAND
• CHAPEL
MEADOW
NORWAY INN •
PANDORA •
MYLOR •
BRIDGE
• C.G. LOOKOUT
PORTSCATHO
CARRICK ROADS
MYLOR •
CHURCH
ST
JUST •
ST
MAWES •
FLUSHING •
FALMOUTH •
KILLIGERRAN
HEAD •
ST •• ZONE
ANTHONY POINT

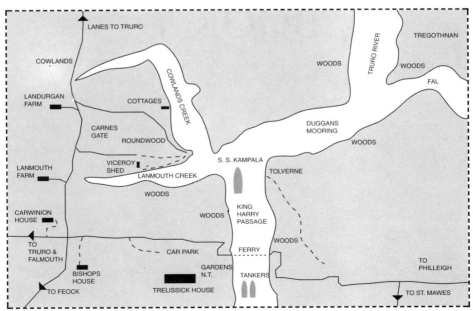

LANES TO TRURO
COWLANDS
TREGOTHNAN
WOODS
TRURO RIVER
WOODS
LANDURGAN
FARM
COTTAGES
COWLANDS CREEK
FAL
CARNES
GATE
ROUNDWOOD
DUGGANS
MOORING
WOODS
VICEROY
SHED
S. S. KAMPALA
LANMOUTH
FARM
LANMOUTH CREEK
TOLVERNE
CARWINION
HOUSE
WOODS
WOODS
KING
HARRY
PASSAGE
WOODS
TO
TRURO &
FALMOUTH
CAR PARK
FERRY
WOODS
TO
PHILLEIGH
BISHOPS
HOUSE
GARDENS
N.T.
TANKERS
TO FEOCK
TRELISSICK HOUSE
TO ST. MAWES

An Airspeed Envoy 1937

BOOK 1

28TH OCTOBER 1931

"........... and I therefore return Mrs Ronald Copeland as the duly elected Member of parliament for this constituency...."

Ida was in, and in with ease. She was the 'National' candidate and, nationally, the sweeping success of the monarch moulded coalition had been widely predicted. Here though, the outcome was less of a foregone conclusion.

The cheer was more polite than it was triumphant, and with composure impressively intact the lady stepped forward to acknowledge the relatively contained acclaim with the customary thanks. The magnanimity flowed. Her platform aides beamed. Those of her stone faced rivals winced.

The young man who stood towards the back of the hall knew most of them by name. For a fortnight, here in the Potteries, he'd been at the heart of the fray. It was time now to get back to that final year of University. He turned to thread a way across to the side door. Outside waited the sturdy bicycle that would take him the forty or so miles to Manchester.

The campaign had so filled his life that he'd almost needed to stay for this the closing ritual, the declaration.... whatever the certainty of the result. He'd met some of the richest in the land, and he'd lived amongst some of the poorest. He'd come to support this candidate and she'd won, of course she had. *'Safety First'* was bound to prevail. There'd been no other practical option.

But what is a student if not an idealist? This was a nation with potential. The people had energy and they had talent. He'd seen this, and they had to be worthy of something better than bankers' caution. There were leaders, real political leaders, with the imagination and the confidence equal to the challenge of the times. Surely they could be accommodated, for they offered hope.... far more than those old stiflers atop the established parties of both left and right.

They were the same, all of them, concerned only to shore up the creaking constitutional structures under which they had, since the war, thrived. Time would tell. So much had been uncertain, at least now there could be an outward unity.

*

NOVEMBER '36

In November 1936 Airspeed Ltd received an order for three new Envoy IIIs from Fritz Mandl, who was acting on behalf of the Spanish Republicans. The deal was betrayed and the first two Envoys were impounded after reaching the Netherlands. The remaining Envoy and five more were then ordered by Air Pyrenees, a small airline created by Auguste Amestoy and other French supporters of the Republic to establish air communication between France and the Basque-Asturian zone. All were delivered. Two were shot down and in one of them Abel Guidez, formerly of the Malraux squadron, was killed while trying to evacuate some Russians from Gijon on 7 September1937. After the fall of the northern zone, the remaining four Envoys were transferred to LAPE (the beleaguered state airline) in the main zone.
One of the directors and senior designer at Airspeed Ltd at the time was N.S. Norway.

G.Howson *'Arms for Spain' p96*

MAY 1937.

"Between 1930 and 1935 production of vacuum cleaners increased from 37,550 p.a. to 409,345. Electricity supply was extended from fewer than a million homes in 1920 to 9 million by 1938.

Many household items were bought on hire purchase, a powerful invention of the inter-war years. Because HP still carried a stigma, firms specialising in such sales promised delivery in unmarked vans."

The British Century. John Keegan's personal view.

Daily Telegraph (Oct '99)

"An' 'ow do 'e 'xpect me t' fetch out me cows with this bleddy thing fillin' the gateway? I got t' bring twenny 'ead through there. They'm wantin' their evenin' milkin'."

"My apologies Mr........"

" ......Carne, farmer Carne, who pays good bleddy rent t' get in an' out of that there 'ole you'm blockin'. If you'm stuck I'll get the 'orse up 'ere t' move 'e 'long a bit."

"Ten minutes and I should be OK. It's these steep lanes......low gear, no speed, warm day, easily done boiling dry. I'm prepared, I carry water. A little time's all I need, just to get the heat down. Cracked block and I'm here a lot longer.... 'orse or no 'orse!"

*

MAY 1937

"We 'ave t' go t'night t'morro' t' Paris," explained the Spaniard who until now had had little to say in his halting English. His van driving was smoother, thankfully, and from the docks they'd made the first one hundred or so kilometres in even time. Now, unexpectedly, they were to ignore the sign for Le Mans and Tours and instead strike eastward towards Bayeux.

To the passenger, a Cornishman, the roads seemed broad and straight. The passsage from Plymouth to Cherbourg had been as scheduled, and he'd been met punctually. They could expect to be in the Capital before midnight.

"An unexpected detour.... your idea?"

"Thees Meester Downes, 'e a beeg nospaper man. 'E know the beeg nems. 'E get their 'elp. They lend to os the speshle, the bes'. We chos from their shops, from the windo's."

The passenger glanced over his shoulder. It was a sturdy vehicle and certainly there was room. What he'd brought over barely filled a corner. It was an enterprising proposition. It warranted a suppressed chuckle.

"And these big names, they enjoy a mention in the papers when the pictures come out. It's a mercenary world. And our Mr Downes, I suppose he gets a take?"

"Meester Downes and yong Meester Sheshle...... t'gether they'ave many schemes. They wan' thees even' t' be beeg. If they are weeth the nospapers then of cos they wan' them t' sell."

"The cynicism though! What'll we hear of next? That they're on to negotiating terms for the bulk stuff.... the ordinary that'll be filling the cupboards and the shelves of the town house, the Costa villa, the ranch out in Canada, and the where ever else the happy couple will be calling their home? I wouldn't put anything past 'yong Meester Sheshle'. He'll have gambled away his share of any commission before it's even been negotiated....let alone secured."

"Sotch ees now the way of the worl' ny frien'. In Spain now we learn thees lesson in the way that is so, so 'ard."

*

RADIO PRESENTER:

This is the National Broadcasting Corporation, serving listeners in every State in the American Union. We open this evening's world news programme with our latest recorded despatch from the turmoil that is Spain. It comes from our correspondent based in Bilbao, the northern port...... capital of the hard pressed Basque province.

Regular listeners will recall that with the fighting around Madrid having arrived at a stalemate, General Franco, the Nationalist leader, has been turning his attentions northwards to where the Basque people hold valuable iron and steel foundries. They also guard the coal deposits

4

further to the west, and command a number of important north coast supply ports......Bilbao included. Listen now to our correspondent:

CORRESPONDENT:

'Good evening America. I speak to you from a frightened city, a city now effectively under siege. To the south there is Mola, Franco's deputy, mustering his considerable forces for a final assault against this town's sturdy defences--the famed 'ring of iron'. His stated vow is to raze Bilbao to the ground. To the north there is the sea and Franco's warships, assisted in their blockade by an increasingly active fleet of German and Italian vessels. There is a long term prospect of the people here being starved into submission, the immediate terror though comes from the skies.

You will have heard of last November's bombing raids against Madrid--the cause of our Embassy being moved to Valencia. Now the Condor legion is aloft in the North. At the end of March a bombing raid against Durango took more than one hundred and forty lives, and at least double that figure perished in a particularly vicious raid against the small defenceless town of Guernica at the end of April. Since then there has been a wholesale evacuation of children from Bilbao, most being taken by escorted ship to France and to England.

The Condor group is meeting little in the way of aerial opposition. You might recall the Spanish ship Mar Cantabrico, *and that furore of early in January when she hastily left New York so as to evade impounding under an imminent Congress embargo. She carried a cargo of aircraft engines. Intended for northern Spain they were, but in fact the ship was intercepted in the Bay of Biscay. Those of the crew who were Spanish were shot. Franco's people took the cargo and it's now being used against those for whom it had been sent.*

This isn't to say that the Government airforce has not been without success in other parts. From a BBC broadcast I've heard that three evenings ago two Republican planes attacked the German battleship Deutschland *as she lay at anchor off the Mediterranean island of Ibiza. A bomb fell on the seamen's mess killing twenty two and wounding eighty three of the ship's crew. The wounded are being disembarked at Gibraltar. The ship is returning to Germany for repairs. The dead are being taken home. Hitler is said to be furious. We can expect reprisals from the* Kriegsmarine.'

PRESENTER:

Thank you to our man in Bilbao. With the situation there as it is we feel unable to divulge his name.

On now to a more pleasant news......and to bring us the latest on this item I can divulge the name of our old friend Mr Ken Downes. He too is in Europe, in France of course, and currently near Tours. He's the most senior of the American journalists covering tomorrow's wedding at the Chateau Cande, that of the Duke of Windsor and the 'woman he loves', our own Mrs Wallis Simpson. Ken Downes now sets the scene...............

*

The *Usk Vale* was now well into her second night out of Falmouth- the port where for the two years prior to this voyage this medium sized freighter had endured a slump enforced lay up. Radio operator Rory Duggan had been stood down from his set at 10pm. It was now past midnight. He lay on his bunk. He needed sleep but it wasn't there for him, even at this hour.

The concern, which had precluded proper rest during the previous night, had been compounded to anxiety by the events of the intervening day. This might be an unfamiliar ship, and a first voyage with this crew and under this Captain, but he was nonetheless a seasoned and accomplished merchant seaman, and certainly no stranger to the vessel's designated route.

She was low laden with timber, a cargo to be discharged at Gibraltar and Valetta on behalf of a government becoming increasingly nervous about the state of dock installations on the way from Britain to Suez and beyond. On such an assignment the vessel could have been expected to comfortably clear the northern coast of war riven Spain but now, from his bunk, Duggan read an angle and a rhythm in the swell which spoke more of France and Biscay than it did of Portugal and the Atlantic.

No less perturbing was the radio traffic, and the order given at the start of the day that there were to be no transmissions from his desk save in dire life threatening emergency. He'd listened, and he'd studied his portholed prospect of the sea, and, as much for his own records as those of his employer, he'd logged. He'd expected a mix of the familiar commercial and the enciphered military, but not such a preponderance of the latter and certainly not such keen, clear and regular communication between vessels of the German *Kriegsmarine.*

Was the *Usk Vale* being shadowed, and if so why? He'd been told nothing. He'd just listened and watched and logged. At 9pm he'd sensed the change in course and suspicion had hardened into foreboding. Could they be manoeuvring for an unscheduled stop? Was there more to this voyage than delivering wood? All was supposition. Maybe they were running guns to the blockaded Basques and had been detected in this mission. Maybe they were a baited trap, a lure devised by the enemy to draw a desperate foe from its coastal cover. Or could there be a spy on board waiting to be dropped singly, or perhaps a team of saboteurs moving in to encourage a fifth column?

And with such a range of possibilities what could he do? What should he do? Who might he warn? Not the Captain of the ship in case all might be according to a hidden plan. But what if it wasn't, and only he, with what he'd seen and heard, suspected this? Was there time and a way to avert a possible disaster? On being given notice -just twenty minutes- of being stood down he'd acted. He'd broken the ordered silence on transmissions and sent out a brief unlogged message.

This done he could only close down and wait. And now, five tense hours later the ship was slowing to a dead stop. The rumble of the screw ceased, and revealed was a deeper more distant sound. Elsewhere at a different time this would have been taken to be thunder, but here and now this was confirmation to Duggan that they were indeed within earshot of Bilbao.

The 'Ring of Iron' was under Mola's hammer. Then came the flap of sailcloth, Basque voices, and the graunch of low wooden beam against steep steel.

English voices joined in, using a halting, grating mix of the Basque tongue and Spanish. The occasional English word dropped into so much that couldn't cohere did nothing to soften the discord. But one, a company name, did confirm Duggan's suspicions. In so far as any British armaments firm could be said to be a household word, this was it. They made it all, the guns, the ammunition, and the vehicles...... whether they rolled, or floated, or flew. Then amidst the creaking of a hatch cover, the whirring of a winch, and the whining wind of a cable two more spoken together words, simple words...... and surely they had to be co-joined, for why else hadn't they been said in basic Spanish? Yes, co-joined, and if so might not this be another firm, one more obscure? And yet it did have a vaguely familiar ring, to this wireless technician. Its operation he would have considered innovative rather than pioneering......for innovative it would need to be, merely to survive. Innovation was key in that field, innovation and solid financial backing. But was there a military application? Possibly, insofar as there might be for anything that was being moved into a zone of total war, but for Duggan this would be a first time at connecting that name with anything that wasn't strictly civilian. He noted it down, as he already had the other.

His ship rocked slightly. Crates were being lifted, and swung, and lowered. They couldn't be more than fishing smacks that were alongside, and for these those crates would have to be compact and tightly packed to be of any consequence, any true worth, for within thirty minutes the transfers were accomplished.

Then the clatter ceased and the *Usk Vale* was once more alone in the darkness. The prop shaft was rumbling again. The voyage was being resumed. At last she was Atlantic bound.

And there was no looking back. What was happening had happened and would happen anyway, despite his attempted intervention. It was full ahead, away from the sounds of land battle but not quite away from the swinging beam of a sea borne searchlight......... nor from the distant rattle of three distinct bursts of machine gun fire.

The voyage was completed without further incident. No mention was made of the events of that night. Rory Duggan was content to stay with the twelve vessel shipping line. The firm was based in Liverpool, his home city and from there he took turns on the other ships, and with the other personnel, always earning high regard for his competence and discretion.

There were other trips on the *Usk Vale*, the last during that desperate early summer of 1940.

*

The SS Lancastria *was sunk on June 17th 1940 while lying at anchor five miles off St Nazaire. There were fewer than 2,500 survivors from a total of around 6000 passengers. This was part of 'Operation Aerial', a desperate attempt by the British to evacuate more than*

150,000 men from western France two weeks after the Dunkirk Operation Dynamo had ended.

The story is one of the worst kept secrets of the war. Churchill slapped a D notice on the press, fearful that the huge loss of life would damage morale. ...... The D notice and the fact that many returning survivors were told they must not speak about the incident created an illusion of secrecy.

............the enemy attack took place at about 3:45 pm. Four high explosive bombs hit the ship simultaneously. One went down the funnel, exploding in the engine room. Another crashed through the hatch of No 2 hold where 800 RAF personnel had been sent. The others smashed through Nos 3 and 4 holds.

Listing steeply to starboard and sinking at the bows the Lancastria took only twenty minutes to go down...... About 1,400 tons of fuel oil was released. It was to prove more lethal than enemy machine gun fire to many of the Lancastria's passengers.

Other ships involved in the evacuation moved in to help rescue survivors.

From 'The Guardian', 17/6/2000 (60th anniversary)
Part of an article written by Pete Bowler ©

Unabandonable equipment, men, and more men, the *Usk Vale* was down to her gunwales. Rory Duggan looked across to the *Lancastria* and he actually saw the bombs falling, he felt the explosions and watched, appalled, as rapid tilt became roll and then plunge. The last message from the shattered vessel was brave........ an exhortation to move out, to get clear. It was sense, and the anchor was being weighed as he pushed along the deck to the ship's boat. Lives could be protected and they could be saved.

He insisted, and alone he was lowered. His ship sailed. He stayed. He would never see her again. The *Usk Vale* took the troops entrusted to her back to Liverpool. Rory, with many of the rescued, would eventually reach Falmouth.

Within two months the *Usk Vale* was in pieces at the bottom of the

Irish Sea. She and her cargo of munitions had ventured within torpedo range of a patrolling U Boat. The crew was shown no mercy.

*

1941

"Nichols?"

"Assistant Director Nichols speaking, sir."

"Mr Nichols, we've just intercepted another '*MDDDW*'. That completes a third exchange in two months.......extremely careless of course, but it's not for us to complain. Have the code people sorted anything yet?"

"Nothing......what they see Sir is a gossipy letter, no more no less. Nothing concealed, nothing faked."

"But they don't know what we know of the recipient and the little dodges being worked by his old friends down there in Nassau. Mr and Mrs 'D'avid 'W'indsor we know to be very concerned about their personal fortunes, particularly as most of it can only be realised in sterling, in pounds and shillings, the ailing currency of his ailing nation. They can't openly go to the foreign exchange, not with the regulations now in place, and even if they weren't it just wouldn't do for them to appear so disloyal."

"But where there's a will there's a way.....eh Boss?"

"They seem to be getting on very well with Mr Wenner Grenn....."

"The Swede, *Electrolux, Bofors*......"

"Some dude, that man. He has a place down there. He likes the spot, fancies it would make a good base from which to take his operation into South America. With sterling looking so sick, and he with a mountain of dollars it's a good time for him to be increasing his share of island real estate. His politics, though, don't help. He's distrusted, people mutter of Nazi sympathies. He's been talked up as a hostile presence, one to steer clear of rather than to do business with. He's getting baulked at almost every official turn."

"Something you've not discouraged Mr Hoover."

"So as to look after our own, Mr Nichols. If the days of 'Rule Britannia' are of the past, then of course we want it to be Yankee corporations picking up the white man's burden. We've got ourselves a useful lend-lease base down there, and that's a start, but commercial development is the thing. Only the dollar wins us lasting control, and actually the Swede is aiding us..... by helping the Windsors in a furtive exchange of sterling for secretly salted mainland greenbacks. Knowing their game, we should be able to bend the Governor and his lady to our will. We can expect the likes of Oakes to be awkward, but not the Duke."

"So that's 'D'ollar 'D'eposits, leaving the 'M' for 'M'iami-- the nearest US State capital? Or maybe 'M'aryland, home sweet home of that dainty little wife?"

"My information is that it's 'M'exico, close by and conveniently outside both UK and US jurisdiction. *MDDDW* ?
Mexican Dollar Deposits for David Windsor......and the how much and the when is somehow encoded within those letters."

"If you say so Mr Hoover."

"I do Mr Nichols. Now the woman here who's sending this stuff, she seems to move around a lot."

"The nature of her work Sir."

"But she is being watched I trust?"

"Closely Sir. "

"Any fascist links?"

"Nothing yet."

"A pity that, but it's still open to us to invent some. They don't have to have been aware of being compromised. You remember Downes, once a newspaper man, now OSS? Above all he's FBI, always was, always will be. He's been telling me about the addressee, the recipient.....says this guy has potential. With careful control and a little of the right kind of support this is one who might be useful, very useful."

*

1943

"So, Private Hayes, it was you who found these?

"Me and two others, a week ago we were down by the creek.......
we were tidying out that store shed."

"But you brought them straight here."

"Straight up, Sir." GI Private Leonard Hayes remained rigidly to attention. This was a brought-in Major, intelligence division. His sort had power. Standard regulations stood to be overridden......with summary effect.

The drawings, dirtied still but no longer damp, lay on the desk. Having reported this find the young GI was wary of appearing too interested in what was clearly a series of technical elevations.

"And what did the three of you make of your little discovery?" The enquirer took a cordial tone.

"Workshop diagrams Sir. I'd say they show a linkage system. At one end you see the word 'rudder' and what you've got is a line of rods. They would move. Stout enough they are to steer a smallish craft." The Major looked down. He nodded, then reached out a finger.

"Here it says 'Viceroy'. Any of you seen a vessel of that name since you've been here, or heard one mentioned amongst the locals?"

"Not yet, Sir."

"And nothing's been found up here in the House. If it had belonged to Carwinion then why doesn't it figure in any of the old paperwork we've sorted? We've looked through photographs, we've looked through repair bills.....boxes of them.... and nothing, nothing at all."

Hayes had no comment. What could he say? What possible use could he be? Why was he here? Clarification was at hand.

"Tell me soldier. How long have you been in England?"

"Just the month, two weeks down here."

"Any contact yet with the locals?"

"Off limits to this group, so far."

"And your home state is.....?"

"Illinois."

"That's good. I'm recommending that you return there for a few months. You can help with recruitment and with basic training. For every hundred we have here now we'll need a thousand by this time next year. Send them over, and when we're ready for the big push you can follow. Get me?"

"Yes Sir. When do I leave."

"A convoy leaves the Port tomorrow. Get to the ferry slip for 8 am. There'll be a boat to take you down. By the end of the week you'll be drinking Milwaukee beer."

"Yes Sir."

*

.........and now come with Pathe News to Persia. This is Abadan, and what you see are the oil installations of Anglo Iranian......Britain's main supplier of fuel oil. Established and developed by the British owned Company, this plant powers our factories and our mines, our lorries and our cars. It stands as an essential part of our post war industrial recovery.

On to Tehran, the capital......and here, commanding the fervent attention of a large gathering of the populace is Dr Mussadeq, their newly appointed Prime Minister. He tells them that in Venezuala and even in other Arab countries Aramco, the US oil giant, is willing to offer the host nation a full half share of the extracted oil wealth. He wants the same from Anglo-Iranian, and should we refuse then he intends to nationalise the installations. They will be seized. The compensation will be nominal, and they will name their own price.

Back now to cash strapped Britain, to London, to Downing St and a more familiar Premier......Mr Attlee. We picture worried faced Ministers arriving at his door, entering, and later they leave looking no less concerned. Under pressure from an outraged opposition the narrowly elected Government is having to consider military intervention.

Hard times bring hard choices. To the British people there is a pledge to maintain welfare provision and to create jobs......for industry, a promise of support for re-investment. To America there is a commitment to the battle for Korea. Any hike in our preferential fuel costs will be critical. Something will have to give, that's what Dr Mussadeq says, that's why he's in place. His people, he says, have already given enough......and look at them again, they certainly agree.

Do we stump up...... through taxes, higher prices, or even a return to prescription charges? Or do we fight? Is postponement an option? Can we turn to America perhaps, does Washington have a responsibility? Might they help subsidise for the duration of the Korean War? Thorny questions! There is just the one certainty. As the answers unfold, Pathe Cinema News will be there.

The car, a well maintained pre-war Rover rolled smoothly on to the parking area outside *The Norway Inn*. The grey cloud, the afternoon drizzle, and the fabric roof served to heighten the gleam of the maroon metal and the elegance in the sweep of mudguard and running board. So solidly built, this was a vehicle to evoke memories of more ordered and certain times.

It was well known locally, as were the two occupants each being a man of reputation and influence. These were acquaintances rather than friends or associates. The younger, the owner and driver of the car, had been born no more than three miles from where they sat. He now lived in Plymouth where, since the war, he had been energetically carving what looked to be an extremely promising career in politics. His passenger, an older man, was a provincial journalist of long experience. Plymouth born, he'd moved to Falmouth before the war to edit the local weekly, *The Falmouth Packet.* He'd made it his own, truly, even to extent of gradually acquiring the controlling interest in the sheet.

Each man dealt in information, information to be given or guarded, filtered, distilled or diluted. There was a mutual respect. There was also a tension.

Two days before Edward Trembath had phoned the *Packet* office and offered to collect who ever had been assigned to report this afternoon's funeral at Mylor Church. This had been agreed, and today he'd driven to Falmouth where to his surprise he'd found that he would be accompanying Arthur Stanaway, the chief man.

The funeral was for one of Edward Trembath's tenants. Rory Duggan had occupied a cottage that was part of a modest waterside estate situated across from and just above Tolverne where the waters of the Truro and Fal rivers joined.

Trembath had covered the three miles northwards from Falmouth in good time. Now they waited, watching for the approach of the hearse.

Having exchanged pleasantries a somewhat cautious conversation was being developed. Each had a regard for his own position and prospects and a matching respect for the other's. There could be opportunities here. There could be pitfalls.

Edward Trembath had recently been selected as the Conservative Party's prospective parliamentary candidate for Plymouth North, and there was every indication that the Labour Prime Minister, struggling against a tide of misfortune with the barest of majorities, might go to the country before the end of another year.

Arthur Stanaway was looking to a comfortable yet still involved retirement. He was ready to sell up his stake in the paper, to hand over the reins whilst ideally retaining a column through which he might dispense the occasional sagacious reflection. Though reluctant to commit resources to renewing tired and worn printing equipment he still cared deeply about his product's reputation for quality -a reputation which owed much to his strategy of giving encouragement and space to young, energetic and ambitious journalistic talent.

There was one former cub now on Fleet Street and at least three with provincial dailies. His current protege, one Francis Cairns, had been rising on this sheltered slip way for two years, the big sea beckoned and there was every indication that a launch might be imminent. Free lance pieces had frequently appeared in the Plymouth papers, morning and evening, and particularly in the weekly *Sunday Independent,* a paper with a readership receptive to his interest in placing on record the parts played in notable wartime events by local people and local places.

Familiar with his writing, Edward Trembath had anticipated that today he might meet the young cub. Instead, now, it was the employer that he was addressing, not the employee.

"Rory is indeed honoured to have you to compile his obituary. I'd have thought this to have been a job for the junior."

"Francis was offered a chance of a few days with a national. If they like him they'll take him on. For me it's a bit out of the blue and certainly inconvenient, but he has my blessing of course. I know he'll impress."

"He's talented. I was hoping to thank him personally for that piece about me that appeared in the *Independent* back in November. It certainly helped with my being selected. He actually went up to the house himself did he, and managed to get the old lady talking?"

"I prompted him. I remembered the piece about you in *The Western Morning News* back at the time of the '31 election. I was with the paper then -a junior reporter myself. He looked it up and from there on the rest was his. At first he thought it a wasted visit. He'd had to do the talking and Ida did no more than listen, but then, a fortnight later, a letter comes to our office containing the ringing endorsement. Without that, the article would have been hardly worth an inch."

The old lady spoken of was Ida Copeland. One of her homes was Trelissick House, the property which neighboured, and comprehensively dwarfed, Edward Trembath's own currently empty Carwinion House.

Mr and Mrs Ronald Copeland were truly wealthy. The family headed one of the largest and most famous of the Stoke based pottery firms. She had been a Conservative M.P. for one of the five town constituencies. In 1931, when her father, himself a governor of the Bank of England, had owned Trelissick she had stood under the banner of the MacDonald/Baldwin 'National' programme and had secured a comfortable victory. It was just that once that she managed to capture the traditionally safe Labour seat, but even now she was fondly remembered by her former constituents, despite in recent years having more and more become a permanent resident at Trelissick.

Locally she'd become known for her reluctance to offer an opinion on any political issue, national or local. But Francis Cairns had ventured, and against expectation he'd gained.

The archived article to which his mentor had referred him told of a young man from Cornwall who was then, in '31, a student at Manchester University. His subject was economics, but alongside this he was fast cultivating a passion for politics. So much so that he'd cycled from Manchester to Stoke so as to offer assistance to the daughter of his distinguished Cornish neighbour in her election campaign of that Autumn. The student was Edward Trembath, the candidate -Ida Copeland.

Now, almost twenty years later, young Cairns found her ready to return this neighbourliness and recommend Edward Trembath to the people of Plymouth. His wife and his infant son had moved to Plymouth in '43. This was when the Americans had requisitioned Carwinion House. At the time he had been serving his country abroad. A sprawling Mannamead mansion had been provided, but Anne Trembath's response to this dislocation had been to throw herself into comforting the dispossessed and the bereaved of the bomb battered city.

Edward had had a good war. Entrusted with 'sensitive' work he'd risen quickly through the ranks. He'd gathered confidence and connections, and then returned to a community in which his name commanded affection and respect. Plymouth had been no more than tidied. Reconstruction offered the perfect scope for his talents. They were exercised and they were developed. To the Conservative Association of Plymouth North he was the ideal man, a coming man, untainted by the failed policies of the '30s yet with comforting links to the pillars which still stood......a plus underlined by the Cairns article.

Ida Copeland had recalled an energy and enthusiasm which was clearly undiminished, and there was mention of the efficiency with which he'd performed his duties when working for the Duchy, and also when later serving with the army. She was impressed by 'a potential for shouldering departmental responsibility'. The sitting member for Plymouth North, an aging 'National' Liberal, had fought his last election, and the nature of the constituency itself had changed as urban Plymouth had pushed towards the edge of the moor. There was all to play for.

The hearse appeared. They watched it pass. The Rover was started and gently turned. No other cars followed the coffin. As they turned up into the lane for Mylor the two-vehicle cortege was complete. Hugh Trembath moved the conversation on to the day's business.

"The list of mourners won't be taking up too much of your notebook."

"He was a private person. It would have been to his taste. Was there word at all of any relatives?"

"No, and I don't expect there to be, not in the light of the uncertain circumstances surrounding his arrival in these parts. We've both of us heard the rumours..... to which, as far as I know, he never offered any denial or explanation. Liverpool he was from, and that's a tight community. To be shunned there is to be disowned by family also."

"So it's left to us to offer our respects", continued the older man, "and if we speak as those around here have found, then we must agree that this man was reliable and competent and careful right to....."

"Not quite to the end," interrupted Trembath. "I expect the Coroner will have something to say about the way things finished."

"You mean that it might not have...."

"I mean that it was an accident that could have been avoided. He'd spent the best part of the day in the bar of *The Globe,* and came away clutching a full bottle of whisky, a third of which had been consumed by the time he attempted to moor the *Viceroy.*"

"But he wasn't operating his service. He wouldn't have put customers at risk. And he was a good tenant, I'm sure. Regular with his rent....?" Stanaway's tribute was calculated. His companion had reservations. The newsman was sizing their breadth.

"Peppercorn that was. Where he was good was with the

maintenance work. He saw to the neighbouring cottage too, the empty one."

"And you'll re-let them?"

"Or sell....... I don't know yet. Either way they'll both need to be properly done up first, and that must wait. The two farms are the priority."

"And Carwinion House?"

"Is at the bottom of the list, unless Uncle Sam gets around to honouring the promise made when he moved in..... to return it as new." A scoff of scepticism broke the owner's reply.

"They ought to be able to stretch. I mean, if they can go fifty-fifty with the Arabs on their oil ......"

The wily old hack was angling. The aspiring politician showed his mettle.

"I'm not going to be drawn on that one, not by a newspaper editor on this side of a general election."

"But you might be asked this at the hustings. Would you threaten force to impose less favourable terms?"

" I would quote the manifesto, and then, if successful, listen to the whip."

A dead bat, Trembath had played. Undeterred, Stanaway looped a googly.

"If I were an Arab I would see it that the principle has already been conceded. If one country can nationalise a coal mine or a railway then another can nationalise an oil well or perhaps a canal. All that remains is the haggle over compensation figures...... and the timing."

"To one waiting on a hand out from the Americans they sound wise words," conceded Trembath.

"But wise words seldom win elections."

"Exactly."

"Isn't there a by-election soon, up in Bristol, where Oliver Stanley was? Won't oil come up as an issue there?"

"I shouldn't think so." And there was a thoughtful pause from the driver.

"Go on," urged Stanaway.

"Three main reasons. It's a safe seat. The nudge from Aramco has not as yet become a push, let alone a shove. And, given the circumstances, we have the ideal man standing as candidate."

" Who is?"

"None other than Walter Monckton, who I know well of course from my time with the Duchy."

"And who we in newspapers know well from his wartime role at the Ministry of Information. I thought he was a top lawyer now. What's he going to do on the opposition benches, apart that is from having to take a hefty cut in pay?"

"This isn't to do with opposition," answered Trembath firmly. "We will win the next general election and Walter will be in place to join the new administration, probably as Attorney General. You know his style and you know Winston's. As a peace time Premier the great man will be needing someone to recognise and flatten out the bumps......before he blunders into them!"

"Yes, it has been Walter's gift it seems, keeping all on board happy...... even those being ushered towards the plank."

Trembath sensed this as an invitation to comment on Monckton's role in the Abdication Crisis of '36, or perhaps on what he had or had not done in the cause of the exiled Polish government during the war....... an issue that might have exploded the Teheran summit had it not been defused, or maybe on the more recent topic of Hyderabad, in India, and its Nizam.... another leading light in his sphere or at least he had been prior to disconnection. All had been brought to realise that to be illustrious was far from being indispensable. The driver said nothing, but the passenger appeared to read his thoughts. The metaphor was pursued.

"I'm not saying he engineers anything. It's just that way of his of seeming to make it easier all round. Baldwin sets up the plank and gets the King out to where it's no return, bound and blindfolded, and the sharks are circling,........ and step up Walter to strap on a parachute!"

"He's obviously now well in with Winston." Trembath was steering away from the contentious.

"But why?" persisted Stanaway. "He was put into the Ministry of Information during the phoney war, by Chamberlain. We reckoned he was there to think the unthinkable -ways of selling to the people the idea of a negotiated peace. With Churchill coming in, and the coalition, we thought he'd be on his way immediately, but no."

"It was more than a year, almost two, before the bust up came," said Trembath.

"And he gets shunted off to Egypt, to the desert, where surely he's got to wither on the vine....but suddenly he's back and going along with the big chief to all the inter tribal pow-wows. Some get dropped as though through a trap door. He seemed to land on a spring board!"

"You've obviously thought about it," responded Trembath, "and no doubt discussed the matter with others in your trade, and they'll know a lot more about the greasy pole than I, a novice as yet. You explain it to me."

The challenge was slightly misconstrued, and perhaps deliberately for Trembath perceived guile in Arthur's response.

" The lurch sideways or back and then the sudden surge forwards is not unknown in journalism. I've seen it, I've heard of it, but only in the context of a smallish outfit being taken over by something substantially bigger.......and more often than not there's a whiff of betrayal to be caught."

Nothing was said as they slowly negotiated Mylor Bridge. The seasoned hack wasn't going to press. Trembath mustered a weak smile before reaching for the anodyne.

"Walter is one of nature's fixers," said the driver. "When we have the opportunity, on a more happy occasion, I'll tell you about when he got me to take wedding gifts across to France in '37."

Now they were at the church. The tone became more sombre as the conversation turned to the deceased and matters more practical and parochial. There was mention of the funeral expenses, which Trembath said he would initially meet as in all likelihood he would be left to administer the meagre estate. He would auction the *Viceroy* and anything saleable from the cottage. He would take his rent and pay any other debts there might be and any residue could, in the absence of any claimant, go to the Duchy with whom he still maintained a close contact.

They parked. The coffin was borne into the church. The two followed. Only five others waited in the dimly lit pews, one of these Jack Butters. He would also fulfil the duties of Sexton.

A young, ill briefed curate read a perfunctory service. His eyes and voice stayed with the written word. To the graveside he took the undertaker with his two burdened assistants, together with Edward Trembath, and Arthur Stanaway. Jack Butters followed, positioning himself at a respectful distance. He watched the coffin being lowered. He heard the soul being commended. He saw the gathering disperse, he could at last step forward..... and begin to inter.

His face dampened. There was the incessant drizzle, and there were tears too. The salt stung in his oil damaged eyes, as it had more than ten years before when he'd floundered in that wicked estuary tide off St Nazaire. His mind went back. The sights, the sounds, the smells, they were vividly recalled, and so too was a remarkable feat of seamanship and courage. He'd been pulled from this hell..... and his rescuer had been Rory Duggan.

He owed the man his life, as did at least sixty others. Some had had to be left in France, but he was amongst those who, with Rory, had been picked up and brought back to Falmouth. His career as a professional soldier, a gunner with the B.E.F., came to an end at his home port.

Then, the hero who'd rescued so many had no name, no face, all being plastered with oil. But Jack never forgot the voice, those gentle Liverpudlian tones. It was the voice he'd recognised when, after twenty further difficult, painful months Duggan came back to Falmouth....... this time to stay.

Challenged, the seaman did reluctantly acknowledge the previous encounter, but he was insistent that nothing of his part in the events of June 1940 be made public...... there was bother enough with the rumour that had trailed him southwards from his home port.

The rumour had driven him from the sea. No longer was there a place for him in the Merchant Service. On coming to Falmouth he'd taken a job in the town, working in the upstairs workshop of a retail electrician. But the rumour came and how it had told. It had told on trade. It was as if people felt that rather than repair, he might in some way infect their trusted wireless sets. But he was determined to stay. He returned to the water, but only onto the harbour where, with a small open motor boat, he taxied people between ship and quay.

This was how Jack came to hear and recognise the voice. Rory was making himself available at all hours to all crew from any vessel, but this was of course another convoy port and on went the whispers, continually gaining currency. There was a tide running. It was relentless, pressing him off and away from the sea.

By then Jack Butters' oil damaged eyes and lungs had recovered sufficiently to enable him to lend skilled assistance to the maintenance of the port's frequently hard pressed defence batteries. There were also guns to service on the increasing number of armed merchant ships using the port. If he had spare time there was also the manage of no less than three of the estuary's traditional 'working boats', the owners having been conscripted. One would later be killed in action, leaving Jack in a position to make an offer. He became an owner himself.

Builders varied, owners modified, and each working boat offered a unique potential and a unique challenge. To be kept up, these boats needed to be used and their performance to be gauged in all conditions and currents, in all parts of the estuary. The local man gladly accepted Rory's offer of help in this task and it was under gaff hung canvas that the fire forged bond tempered steadily to cherished friendship.

Jack was contemptuous of the rumour. His own first hand experience told him a definite otherwise. There just had to have been a misunderstanding, a misjudgement. If only he could be freed to tell of his day on the *Lancastria,* and those hours in that sight corroding water.

But this kind of help Rory Duggan did not want. The man's preference was to be quietly useful. If anonymity was impossible he could still insist on privacy.

What Rory did take from Jack, eagerly, was knowledge of the estuary. Together they went to the furthest corners of every navigable creek. There wasn't a quay they didn't visit, no matter how small or little used and this was how Rory Duggan fell into his niche.

With his own boat he began a three cornered ferry service between Tolverne, Coombe, and the Tregothnan Estate which at that time was hosting a thirty strong detachment of the Women's Land Army. This ended when the Americans came, but even in just those few months of operation he'd earned a reputation for reliability and care. This was a safe pair of hands.

The Americans brought hope, and they brought money. The job was there, and they were up to it. It would be done, though, on their own terms. As anxious dissection of retreat was supplanted by anticipation of advance so new rumours supplanted old. Those who made themselves useful could prosper whatever their antecedents. Those who were a hindrance could find themselves removed.

The Americans found Rory Duggan useful. It was from the Americans that he obtained the *Viceroy.* They liked his skill on the water and his gathered knowledge of the estuary, and it seemed to help also that he wasn't another native. Extended local connections were so often bothersome.

From early in '43 to mid '44 moving through the roads and the lanes to the south of Truro became increasingly difficult. There was construction traffic and armoured vehicles and, all the while, lorries packed with men and equipment. The easiest travelling was by water and Duggan had been at hand to oblige. Carwinion House, being so less prominent than Trelissick and Tregothnan, had been requisitioned as a command centre and it was at this time that Rory accepted an invitation to move into the cottage, his final home.

His boat had been built for the American Navy. She had arrived on the river well before the army, having been brought across on the *Ozark,* an old 'lend-lease' destroyer, early in 1941. Moored just below Malpas, the parent ship had been struck by a wayward bomb, one of a stick directed at a nearby oil installation. She was subsequently towed out beyond The Dodman where as a practice target she endured the ignominy of being sent to the bottom by her own side.

Her tender was reprieved. This was used by the River Patrol and then, on their arrival, re-united with her countrymen. She had a small forward wheelhouse, and room sufficient for thirty passengers, at least half of whom could find weather shelter beneath a stern end canopy. For the Americans she was the ideal water bus, and Rory Duggan made the ideal driver.

They gave sterling service to the occupying force and with the success of 'Overlord' the effort was rewarded. The vessel was left with Rory, together with a crate of engine spares ordered and shipped across from Detroit.

With peace, Rory was set. He had the boat, christened now the *Viceroy,* and the cottage with its nearby quay and storage shed. He had a vessel with the space, speed and the range to offer more than a mere crossing. He developed a service that ran the length of the estuary from Truro to Falmouth and St. Mawes. In summer there were excursions across the bay to Porth Navas, and around to Portscatho.

The *Viceroy* and its master became part of the too long quarantined scenery, part of its considerable rediscovered charm..... but his part was gone now. Rory Duggan was no more.

He was dead. He was almost buried. Jack paused in his task. His musing had brought him to the recent past, to the death itself and its circumstances.

When it was heard that the river had taken him there was surprise, but not shock because it was known that these waters could be unforgiving. Careful competent people had been lost before, and would be again. To those who ventured out alone the slightest lapse could be lethal. An old caution had been repeated. The so far emerged facts did indeed point to a want of care, but Jack was far from convinced.

On that fatal day he'd spoken with the man twice, and this was twice more than most. Each time he'd spoken with a profoundly altered person.

Jack had given that day to painting the rails on the King Harry car ferry. This was one of his cold weather jobs, the ground being too hard for digging graves and the wind too keen for dredging oyster beds. The chain ferry was steam driven. Warmth was at hand.

There'd been no mistaking the distant, deep steady purr of the *Viceroy,* but had he lost track of time? He reached for his pocket watch, screwing his eyes at the vague hands. 10:50 they said. He wasn't out, but Rory was and this was rare. More than that, to his knowledge it was unique........ a departure from what had hitherto been a meticulously observed schedule. From the watch his eyes strained northwards, and see, listen, here was deviation also from the man's normal course through the passage. Today he wasn't straightening to leave the widest possible berth, he was steering towards the ferry, to where it waited against the Trelissick slip way. Rory had seen him. The man wanted to speak. There were no passengers on the ferry and none in the *Viceroy.* Only Jack saw and heard this so much changed person...... one who was animated, urgent, agitated almost.

Bringing the boat around, and holding it on the ebb against the ferry's raised outer loading ramp, Rory's initial concern was to implore his friend to stay with that job for as long as it took him to return. He would not be long. He was meeting his man at noon and it had been agreed that they would then, together, return up river to where the tale might be told in its setting. A large crumple cornered envelope was held up and Jack understood. This man was not in the market for redemption. He never had been. He'd been bidding for exoneration and it was there, literally in his grasp.

He quickly explained. This was information, full information, carefully gathered, compiled and considered, and now it was going to a newsman....... one of local knowledge, who could be trusted, who was able, and who was hungry for a story that could be told across the length of the land. And why hold back? There would be a place for a chapter of heroism, a chance at last for Jack to tell of St Nazaire.

With no time now to waste Rory swung away southwards. Painting on, it was thrill time for Jack. Lifted on a tide of memory, an account was rehearsed, and then revised and re-rehearsed. And in between he speculated. A cautious man had broken from carefully erected and maintained cover. Why now? The information had to be telling, but telling what? And, if it did exculpate, what then? For, as in the way of these things, culpability could emerge elsewhere. He would know soon enough. For the moment what was certain was that on this day as he took the *Viceroy* onto the Carrick Roads, Rory Duggan would be venturing over a personal Rubicon.

From one o'clock Jack was listening for the return. For two hours he listened and with delay there grew a sense of disappointment. It was close to 3:30 when The *Viceroy* eventually crept up to the ferry. Duggan was alone. He was dejected. Hope and optimism had been supplanted by anxiety and foreboding. His man, Cairns he was called, had not shown.......this despite the confirmation which had arrived in the post that very morning. According to the note left at *The Globe* he'd been called away suddenly on "something big". There was an apology and an assurance that when he returned, as he shortly would, his attention would be immediate and full for this, he knew, was a more than promising story. With the note there had been a gift, a bottle of Scotch whisky. It was there on the boat, unopened, standing on the deck by the wheel, close to the envelope which earlier had held such promise.

And that envelope had changed too. It carried the glint of fresh wax. It had been sealed. Rory reached for it, he straightened, and then facing Jack he spoke. The words chiselled into the listener's memory.

"I want you to take this, to hold it and keep it safe. When Cairns gets back I'll come for it. It could be days, maybe weeks, who knows? Should anything happen to me, you make sure he gets it. Don't break the seal, not unless something also happens to him. There's a note for him in there, appropriate to single misfortune and one for you, appropriate to double. Don't be over alarmed. This is just in case."

Rory's tone was insistent. Jack understood. He took the package. No more was said. The *Viceroy* growled away into the closing solstice gloom. In his mind he heard the old wartime saw which had for so long hung about Rory Duggan like a rotting albatross.......Careless talk costs lives.

And now, in this yard scattered with wreaths of holly, he was burying the man. Like Edward Trembath he'd hoped that Francis Cairns would attend the service. He'd brought the envelope. It lay under his folded coat, beneath his pew seat. It would return home with him to its secret place and the wait, Rory's bequest to him, would resume.

And where was Cairns? Jack made enquiries, discreetly, but no one could say. For a month and more it was a mystery, and then, in the second week of February, the Saturday edition of *The News Chronicle* carried the first of his weekly front line dispatches. Francis Cairns had made Fleet Street. He was a war correspondent and on his first assignment. He was in Korea.

Jack Butters bought the paper and saved it, and he did the same on subsequent Saturdays. Studying each issue took days, whatever the pain to those failing eyes. From the reports Jack would learn of Cairns' movements and also learn of the war. And from the rest of the paper there came a fuller understanding of its global context and of the ramifications for Britain and for other nations too.

When he and Cairns met, as he was so sure they would, he wanted to show interest in his work, and knowledge too -and with each issue the interest came and the knowledge built. MacArthur, McCarthy, and Maclean, Bevin, Bevan, and Burgess, Morrison, Mossadeq and even Monckton, when they made the news, then for Jack Butters they made their mark. On he waited, on he read. How those eyes would ache. And then, late in August, after a two month period during which the conflict had commanded progressively less space, there was suddenly no despatch. Was he on his way? Very possibly, and this was exciting indeed..... but for moments only. Turn three pages, and there it stood, the obituary. Francis Cairns was dead.

The jeep had struck a landmine. The driver, a journalist with an American paper, had likewise been killed instantly. The incident had been reported two days previously. The obituary spoke of the energy, the enthusiasm and the fearlessness of one who died doing the work he loved. There was a brief mention of Arthur Stanaway and the *Packet,* and Jack also learned that he'd left a fiancee. Cairns had been planning to marry.

That evening Jack broke the seal on Rory's envelope. He examined the contents. Most had been long held, but not the photograph clipped from a recent issue of an Irish paper -*The Limerick Examiner.* It was far from clear, certainly to his eyes, but with close inspection yes -he understood. He read his instructions and he thought back to '37 and to that month that he and his unit spent with those Basque children at Stoneham. How would they be faring now? He returned to his neatly saved pile of *Chronicles*. Within two hours he'd scanned them all, very closely. There was precious little about Spain.

*

NOVEMBER 1956 - JANUARY 1957

"Over the next four weeks a shabby and humiliating retreat took place. The American government, through representatives such as Dulles and Henry Cabot Lodge, directed the full flow of its fury on the British UN delegates and ministers....... The British leadership, individually and collectively, cut a sorry figure. Monckton, a rare voice of moderation, was sent to the Canal Zone to produce for cosmetic purposes an account of the small number of Egyptian war casualties there had actually been and detail the fastidious care taken by British bombers in avoiding civilian targets. Monckton had been previously an embarrassed critic of the Anglo-French action who had failed to resign.........

....the British stood branded as offenders against international law, if not plain liars. Eden returned almost in disgrace, and still in indifferent health.....On 9 January 1957 he resigned, his reputation in tatters. Harold Macmillan, the hawk turned dove who had been manoeuvring for succession throughout Eden's absence, beat off the challenge of Butler and succeeded Eden as premier.....

Most people did not feel passionately either way as long as Britain's honour retained some kind of credibility and the outcome led neither to a prolonged foreign war nor to bankruptcy......the trauma of Suez, commonly seen later as a major step in the retreat from Empire, did not radically disturb the tranquillity of Britain in this period. In general, the years of Tory rule after 1951 were a time of social balance, with a recovery of morale after the war and post-war austerity."

K.O.Morgan 'The People's Peace' Pp 154-6

Cathedral and College Exeter looks down upon tightly terraced St. Thomas, the urban sump. The district lies beyond the Exe, and behind the second divide of Brunel's raised tracks. The arched hedge supports a modest station. The platforms are necessarily narrow and long. Few wait thereon. The trains that properly stop are the South Devon local services, although an occasional 'up' express will pause if a little early for its platform at far busier, far bigger St. Davids.

In one such train a first class traveller looks up from the book on his lap and craning towards the compartment window he makes a first glance assessment of the grimy suburb below. His is more than a passing interest, and as the express rolls on, over Cowick St., the man stands. He places the book, *Slide Rule*, on his seat and reaches to the overhead rack for his overcoat and one suitcase.

By the time he has gathered himself and has moved out into the corridor the train is gliding into the main station. His suitcase he can leave here in the luggage hall. The book he will take with him.

He'd caught the train in Truro where he'd stayed for two nights in one of the city's better hotels. Whilst there he'd enjoyed an excursion to Plymouth. This was where he'd aquired the book from the man he'd called on there, a nursing home patient. He'd read enough. Hopefully he could now himself pass it on, as that first donor had suggested.

A taxi lifts him back along to St. Thomas in less than four minutes. It draws up at a corner at the end of a parade of modest shops, most of them now closed for the evening. The occupant is told that this is the end of the specified street. The driver offers to wait, but the traveller pays him off. He doesn't expect this to take long, and he can walk back to the main station. The next London train won't be for three hours, and even should he miss this there was a day to spare before his return flight to the States.

He checks the street name and the numbers on the first two houses. He calculates it another fifty yards only to the door he seeks, and in barely thirty seconds he is there.

He is unknown to the young woman who cautiously answers the firm knock, but he knows *her* name and an initial alarm is allayed by an easy American voice that exudes courtesy and a puzzling yet strangely comforting measure of affection.

"Pardon me ma'am, but I'm looking for a Mrs Linda Taylor......who was an Adams before she married and who was formerly engaged to a Mr Francis Cairns."

Two children, both under four, each clinging to an apron string, peer up. They had been expecting their father.....but this definitely wasn't he. The wide brimmed hat, the full-length belted mac, and the brogues, such things are alien to these cloth cap parts.

"You have the right person," replied the mother hesitantly. "And you are?"

"Ben McKinley," answered the tall figure with a respectful bow of the head. "I was given this address by a Mr Arthur Stanaway. I called on him yesterday."

Linda Taylor knew that name. She knew that person. She'd given him her address, it surprised her though that after all this time he should have had it to hand to pass to a person such as this.

"And how is he? He was at our wedding, nearly five years ago now, but I've not seen him since."

"I would say he drinks too much. I fear it'll shortly be the death of him."

"I'm not surprised. When we lost Francis he took it hard. He always held himself in someway responsible, which is ludicrous, but grief can be like that. I came away and, with John, built this new life."

"It can be easier when you're young. And I'm not here to upset things. I'll go now should you wish, if it's getting too much...... ." The American then paused, giving space for thought before adding "it's just that Frank, or Francis, did ask and I did promise, and I've waited and travelled long."

Linda Taylor's eyes narrowed. One hand reached to the hair of the smallest child.

"All Francis thought about was his work, and this is something to do with it and the way he did it which was always so bloody fearless of course, and see where it got him. Look at these children, they are my responsibility now. They never knew him, nor did John my husband. He's got a good job with the telephones, and there's a place at the exchange for me to go back to when these are at school. I know what you people think of this Suez thing, but this government has been good to the two of us. They give us our work, and the health care and for these, next year, the schools. Tell me why I shouldn't keep my head down."

"As I say, you must do as you wish. I must do as you wish. If I leave now I've discharged the promise that I made." There was another pause.

"How long do you want?"

"No more than thirty minutes..... and I've a train from St. David's at 8:15."

"I'll sort these, and get John to see to their bedtime. I'll be in the station buffet at 7:30. I'll listen. I'll then talk to John. He's fair, no less so than Francis was, but he's also level headed. Maybe it's age."

*

JANUARY 1965

The Washington Tribune 23/1/65

REBELLIOUS RHODESIANS by Ben McKinley.

As world leaders gather in London following the not unexpected death of Sir Winston Churchill many will see the occasion of the funeral as a first opportunity to discuss the current international situation with Mr Harold Wilson, the most recently elected of the great man's successors. Less than one hundred days into his Premiership and already concerned at the vulnerability of sterling there can be little surprise at the Prime Minister's rumoured anxiety to speak with President Johnson.

Our Commander in Chief will of course have his own agenda, the first item being his strategy for Vietnam. The President remains persuaded that this war can be won. He sees himself as a player in a numbers game, he only has to find, train, and equip sufficient men, he only has to make and drop a sufficient tonnage of bombs and victory will be his.

Informed world opinion grows increasingly sceptical and dissent grows at home. Time then to call on our partner in the 'Special Relationship'. It will be suggested to Harold that no more than a token military contribution might earn a substantial easing of financial pressure. The answer will be blunt...... 'no dice'. We know the Labour Party wouldn't wear it.

The more interesting conversation could be between Wilson and

Ian Smith, Prime Minister of Southern Rhodesia now for nine eventful months. The self-governing colony seeks full independence. Should it not be granted then they threaten to rebel, much as we in America did. Can they be as successful? No. They might defy the Crown but to deny African nationalism amounts to a very different proposition. This much was apparent to many of the British Conservative Party who at heart sympathised with Smith's vastly out numbered white tribe.

In truth the fracture between London and Salisbury pre-dates Wilson. Mistrust has lingered since 1960 when it was said that the Monckton Commission over reached its powers to effectively recommend the dissolution of the short-lived Federation of The Rhodesias and Nyasaland. By coincidence Sir Walter Monckton predeceased Sir Winston by less than a fortnight. Given Cabinet rank by Churchill, Monckton continued to serve under Eden. In all that Monckton did, and didn't do, he appeared to be remarkably well disposed towards the broad aims of our State Department here in Washington. My view is that the rift that grew between J Foster Dulles and Eden could be traced back to the Geneva summit of '54 and the Vietnam settlement brokered by the latter at that time. Monckton sought to bridge that rift, even as it became a chasm during the Suez crisis. It has been said that in any dispute it was in his nature to seek and where possible to exploit the common ground. As a lawyer his clients included the Duke of Windsor and the Nizam of Hyderabad.... two men who found what they'd assumed to be common ground more than a little treacherous underfoot!

The muffled beat of the dead march filtered back through the square mile. The grim pageant would now be close to the tower. Royalty and visiting heads of state had dispersed and the guard lining their route was now at ease.

Corralled on the Cathedral steps stood a huddle of elder statesmen, former Prime Ministers, each now elevated to his earldom.... Clem, Anthony, Harold. Bareheaded they'd watched the old warrior being borne to the gun carriage. They'd been the inheritors, each aspiring to bring his own shine to the grail, each leaving it no less punitively mortgaged.

It was to see them together as now that Edward Trembath had come to St Paul's and chosen the position he had.

Less than a fortnight earlier at a neat village church in the heart of Kent he'd attended another funeral, one that for him had seemed incomplete....but no longer, for in this day's unique spectacle came the required postscript. It was in their frailty, and in their nervousness of each other, and in a certain helplessness which, with the passage of years, none could for any longer conceal.

The hats were on now and they were being led away. He could leave himself. At the foot of the steps he took a last look up at Wren's masterpiece, noting the time on the towered clock. He'd arranged to meet his son at the end of Chancery Lane. Hugh would be in uniform, having earlier been on parade outside the Admiralty. It was a fifteen minute walk and he had twice that to spare. As he turned again to thread his way towards Fleet Street he felt a hand on his elbow. It gripped. He was being detained. He stopped, turned again, and he was recognising at once the figure that was before him. He hadn't seen the man in twenty eight years, but how little change there'd been.....not least in the voice.

"Mr Trembath, it's been quite some time," drawled the American. It was a cordial voice. The grip slackened.

"Mr Downes," replied Trembath, he was apprehensive. "I was only thinking about...."

".....I can well imagine. And that's why, when I noticed you, I slipped away from our retinue. You're looking well. That's good to see. As ever we've been following your career with interest, and also your son's."

"I'm just on my way to meet him now."

"Well this won't take long," said the American, drawing a newspaper from beneath his coat. " It's just that there's something here we need you to see...." This had been prepared. It was a Washington paper and it had been folded so that an inside page was uppermost, a particular page holding a particular article. Trembath was directed to the title..... 'Rebellious Rhodesians.'

*

Night was yielding to dawn, and for one climbing from the west the turrets and the towers were an imposing silhouette. The Standard, properly at full mast and already taking colour from the east, from this side hung as a black drape. From low in the tall chapel windows there glowed a suggestion of candlelight. The first stage....... the only public stage, was all but done.

Just hours now, and the cancered remnant of the former King would be taken across to Frogmore, there, in the presence of the great and the good, to be entombed with his forebears. It had been a lingering death and the unique ritual that was in hand had been long planned.

Edward Trembath MP, an obvious choice to represent the Commons, had been graced with a discreet invitation. The honour had been respectfully declined. A frail and lonely widow would have to display her grief before those from whom she'd previously known nothing but contempt. It was a distasteful prospect for a loyal Duchy man, and besides he didn't, himself, want to be seen. He had good reason to prefer anonymity, indeed good reason to stay away.

That he hadn't was down to coincidence. The expected death, in France, had been closely and unexpectedly preceded by another.......this in America. And though they'd occurred an ocean and more apart, for Edward Trembath, the first had endowed the second with a gathered significance, enough to soften that initial resolve to stay away.

Two men, two empires..... the one ready made and renounced, the other assiduously self assembled and fiercely, jealously guarded. 'The end of an era,' this was what people said and what many more thought and hoped. Edward Trembath could be counted amongst the latter.

It was to galvanise this hope that he was here now. He'd read the ever grimmer press bulletins, and the report of a last visit by the elder niece, and then the headlines that proclaimed the death. He thought the coverage might be enough, but with all else, no. He had to come, to see for himself. There'd been a personal dispensation. He'd been directed to the side door of a side Chapel, and now it opened. He eased in and behind him the heavy door was gently, securely, re closed. And before him was the coffin, brought down from its imperious main Chapel catafalque in readiness for a last brief journey. Oak it was, plain and simple, with no flag to embellish nor any Royal jewel. A small bouquet of lilies, that was all, a poignant tribute for a one time Prince of Wales, a focus for the pale light that seeped past the weakly stained window glass. There was no colour, even the glow of the candles seem thinned. The tone was simple and it was intimate, and it was uniquely Royal.

Edward Trembath stood, head bowed, for two minutes. The homage done, he then left. He strode away, descending to his car, left at the foot of the hill. The sun was rising, a new day, the new era.

He was looking ahead. There was a figure by the car, and he knew who it was, he knew intuitively, and yes he recognised him now. They'd met just the twice before, the first time all of thirty five years ago, almost to the very day. The hope couldn't have been shorter lived.

"Mr Trembath," greeted the figure, "the long serving Right Honourable Mr Edward Trembath, soon to become a 'Sir' by all accounts. And I hear your son is continuing to enjoy a distinguished Naval career."

"One fully merited," responded the father warily.

"I think I have to agree. It's shame it's going to stall if he tries for a Polaris command. He'll be overlooked, and he'll blame himself....sad that. Unfinished business you see."

"Still unfinished?" said the MP pleadingly.

"You've done well, for yourselves."

"As I've done for your people."

The figure acknowledged the point with a cordial lift of the hand. He'd not come to argue.

"Ted's been a little lax you know. From our side it seems the old relationship's no longer as special as it might be."

"Well what do you expect? He was Eden's Whip remember, and you've got those grand old Republicans in again. Why should he trust Nixon, Ike's old running mate?"

The hand came up again.

"Last time, when we met at.....where was it? Westminster Cath....."

"Outside St. Paul's, seven years ago," corrected Trembath, as if the memory was causing pain. "Westminster Abbey didn't come into it, nor the Catholic Cathedral. The Lying in State had been at Westminster Hall."

"I gave you a name."

" McKinley."

"Well remembered. Did it crop up at all?"

"If it had I'd have sent word as instructed. Still on your list is it? I mean being anti-Vietnam's hardly un-American these days, more like mainstream."

"Which shows how clever and how dangerous his sort are. The Tet offensive was our victory. The Viet Cong, they went for us. We slaughtered them, ten of theirs for every one of ours. We drove them back into the woods. And then, at home, in our news media, our people read and hear of a victory for Ho Chi Minh!"

"And now he's outlived the Boss, and Hanoi is more and more looking the odds on favourite....."

".......we are all the more concerned to keep tabs on them, these columnists, these 'fifth' columnists, and on this one in particular. I'll tell you why....."

*

SEPTEMBER 1980

"Exeter 386317...."

"Mrs Taylor? ......Mrs Linda Taylor? This is Mildred Bruce. You wrote to me a month ago." The voice was elderly, but even through the phone it carried spirit, and no little authority.

"Linda Taylor speaking. Thank you for getting back. Are you calling from your home..... or are you nearer perhaps?"

"I'm using a neighbour's phone. She's a close and trusted friend. I don't want this to be too long, and it's got to be a one off. You say in your letter that you've read my memoirs. I don't hear that too often now. The book's long been out of print."

"It took some finding."

"So you'll know that parcels and letters were for a time my business. I can tell when an envelope has been tampered with....as yours to me was. For me it's not new. We can assume it was done at this end. You needn't feel too alarmed."

Linda Taylor would have been delighted to share that assumption. She couldn't, but she wasn't saying. However brief, this contact was too valuable.

"So can you help?"

"You ask about the company I ran before the war, 'Air Despatch', and about the maker of the planes I used."

"*Airspeed*..... and the *Airspeed Envoy* in particular."

"You're right when you say that these machines were sought after by both sides fighting in Spain. And yes, the account I gave in *Nine lives Plus* was vague...... but necessarily so, and to be fair our Mr Norway would have felt the same constraints when putting together his *Slide Rule*. But he's dead now, twenty years dead, and times change in this country as well as in Spain. I feel I can speak a little more freely, so listen closely. I'll say this just the once, and only for you. I'm putting nothing to paper."

"Go on."

"She was a solid little aircraft, the *Airspeed Envoy*, the equal of anything amongst the pre-Dakota wood and fabric generation. It was an adaptable plane. It could lift up to ten seated passengers, or the fuselage deck could be left clear for a more than equivalent weight of cargo. With us this was parcels and bundled newspapers, for others....... well just hold on to the notion of adaptability. It's a key concept."

"In terms of what went on during the Spanish war you mean?"

"I do that. But going back to before, for all its inventiveness *Airspeed Ltd.* was critically under capitalised. They had cash flow problems.... who didn't at that time? We were able to pick up our four machines for the knock down price of £3000 apiece, this to be paid over three years. The vendor, we know, is celebrated for his creativity, and it's no secret now that this stretched to his presentation of his company's accounts."

"He sailed close to the wind?"

"To the rocks, more like!....But then comes the Spanish Civil War and suddenly there's a queue of customers at his factory door offering to pay double what we had..... on the nail. 'Confidential Agents.....'.

".......interested in a civilian plane?"

"Not quite, for our man with the slide rule had been busy devising a few modifications. Strengthened wing struts and a stiffened fuselage lent scope for larger engines, stronger lift, greater range, more attachments..... larger payload."

"All bringing the maker a considerably enhanced return for

comparatively little work."

"A minimum of work, for provided with the right parts and the appropriate directions these modifications could be effected by the buyer. There was a lop sided arms embargo, far from even handed. The Republicans were really desperate, particularly in the North, but they had the skills there and the workshops. To arrange for a civilian *Envoy* to be flown across the Pyrenees wasn't a bad investment..."

"......particularly if the appropriate modification kits were waiting, or on their way maybe. And your planes were repossessed and sold on to meet this demand.... right?"

"They were ruthless. Just days late we were, with just the one payment, and Norway was sending his heavies down to our hangar at Croydon. One plane we had loaded, ready fuelled for Paris..... the papers were thrown out almost onto the runway and off it took to goodness knows where."

"The knowledge of what was going where, by air, land, or sea being a no less marketable commodity of course."

"There you have it. Those were treacherous times, and the echoes reverberate to this day. Why else would we be speaking so furtively? Did you ever read of the *Mar Cantabrico*? You sound too young. She sailed from New York early in '37, carrying war gear for the Republicans...... ."

"...... and she was betrayed to the Nationalists. I have read some of this, a while ago now though."

"Well that's what it was like on one side. To the other there was Uncle Joe Stalin. At the same time he was culling his top dogs. He had execution squads purging their way across the length and breadth of Europe. Desperate men were seeking sactuary, Russians who'd held high military or perhaps diplomatic office. They wanted protection. They were ready to pay. Information was their currency."

"So by mid '37, to run weaponry to Spain was to run a gauntlet of perfidy."

"Attempts were made and brave people died."

"In his book Mr Norway alludes to *'devious routes...'* "

"........ to which I say look along the shelf, from what purports to be fact to what purports to be fiction. Turn it around just a little. Show it to the mirror...... and tell me then what rings the truer."

*

"That was today's lunchtime radio weather forecast, and this is Robin Knight welcoming you back as you rejoin us for the second part of today's especially extended edition of 'One O' Clock Worldwide'.

Earlier I was speaking to Niall West, the well-known writer on defence and intelligence matters. From him we heard scepticism as to the feasibility of Britain independently waging a successful military campaign in the South Atlantic. Whilst acknowledging that we certainly have the firepower in terms of equipment and trained personnel, he suggests that the very remoteness of the conflict arena could reveal critical shortcomings in our basic signalling capabilities.

His concern is twofold. He questions the quality of intelligence on the Argentine deployments and also the security of the signals passing between the task force and its command centre at Northwood.

Much has been made of our 'special relationship' with the US and the importance of Pentagon help in addressing these problems, but such talk, Niall West suggests, ought to be a good deal less comforting than generally felt. Our war aims are clear enough. British control over the Falklands is to be re-established. What is less clear is whether or not the US administration can offer wholehearted agreement and support.

During the weather break I played Mr West's comments back to our correspondent in Washington. Robert Lock can join us now, live.

Robert, you've heard Niall West making the point that without the benefits of AWAC aerial reconnaissance we are left to rely on American satellites and also their out stations in countries such as Chile and Uruguay for up to date information on the movement of enemy forces. You've pointed out before that Washington makes no secret of its preference for a diplomatic solution to this crisis. What say you to his suggestion that to avert a premature all out war the Pentagon might be feeding to Task Force Command something less than the fullest information available to them in the US?"

"That's a mischievous question Sir Robin. I cannot answer with any authority. What I can say is that the administration here is offering to broker a peaceful settlement and is placing the task in the hands of Mr Al Haig. There are few closer to the President than he and there is a determination that his mission should not fail for the want of a reasonable measure of time."

"We have a general assumption in this country that the President will not want to see the Thatcher Government too deeply embarrassed, but things are not quite that simple...... are they? People here don't fully realise how far General Galtieri and his Junta are nothing less than a product of Washington's foreign policy."

"That's right, and it's only now that even folk in the States are beginning to see this. They've been told for long enough by the liberal press that the CIA has been prosecuting a shameful covert war against popular left wing movements in Nicaragua and El Salvador, but, by and large this has been met with indifference. US soldiers haven't been involved, haven't been killing, haven't been dying. It's been a war by proxy. The foot soldiers have been hired in from South America, notably from Argentina and from Chile. They are cheap, they speak Spanish, and against the people's army style of insurgency they can boast a seasoned expertise. They can be as ruthless as necessary. Last year CIA Director Casey had more than twenty million dollars of tax payers' money to put to the project. In November General Galtieri was here in Washington. It seems that a sponsorship deal might have been struck, for a month later he was back home and mounting his successful coup against General Viola. To sections of the Reagan administration he must represent a valued investment, one that isn't to be so casually written off...."

"Operative Echo Five-Zero answering again from Gibraltar, scrambled and this time we hope unscrambled. Can you copy?"

"Loud and clear at Northwood........ confirm likewise please."

"Pleased to confirm. You have urgent instructions? "

"We've sent a transport from RAF Lynham. You can expect it to land within the hour. It'll refuel. You'll board."

"To be taken to......?"

".......Freetown."

" Freetown? Sierra Leone?"

"Where you'll wait for the *Kampala*. We have an emergency."

"A technical failure? No surprise there.......we had to rush things, as you know."

"No problems there. She's in contact with Ascension, and already talking with the sub Captains. It's a medical thing."

"Still not fully equipped? More personnel?"

"One particular person is ill, a key person, the skipper."

"It's the ulcer is it?"

"There's been concern too over his attitude. He's always been OK about reconnaissance work. We can thank you for that. Involvement in the operational stuff though is something else, especially under that badge. There's been misgivings, so far only privately expressed."

"So he's coming in for treatment, and you want me to work on him."

"He's coming home. You're bringing him home. British India is furnishing a replacement. He's on the plane, suitably vetted, suitably briefed."

"So with Chadwick it's serious. Is there a prognosis?"

"Depends on a lot of things..... on his course of treatment, on the course of negotiations, on the course of the job set for his vessel, on the course of the conflict even. Shouldn't be life threatening, but one can never rule out complications. There's a medical team on the plane, military again. You're to accompany them all back, and to ensure there's no civilian contact. It's a service hospital he's coming back to. He'll have his own ward."

*

21. 3. 1984

10.30 a.m. approximately: Hilda leaves home for shops.

12.00 p.m.: Speaks to neighbour and goes back into house.

12.30 p.m. approximately: Her white Renault 5 seen being driven erratically out of Shrewsbury

1. 20 p.m. Car seen in ditch at Hunkington.

2. 00 -2. 20 p.m. approximately: Running man seen between lane leading to Hunkington, and Shrewsbury.

Mid afternoon: Abandoned car reported to police.

22. 3. 1984

3.00 p. m.: Scott walks through copse, sees no body.

4. 00 p.m.: Dark car seen near copse. Man gets out walks over to copse and returns to car.

Evening: Lights seen in copse.

23. 3. 1984

9. 00 a. m.: Gardener finds kitchen door open to Hilda's house. Light on in kitchen, curtains drawn.

10. 30 a. m.: Car again reported to police. During morning: Red Escort seen driving backwards and forwards along lane near copse.

6.30 p. m.: Policeman calls at Hilda's, knocks and goes away......
....Neighbours say police in house during
evening. Police later deny this.

24. 3. 1984

6. 30 a. m.: Policeman calls at house again.

9. 00 a. m.: Gardeners arrive.

10. 30 a. m.: Rob Green rings his Aunt (Hilda), receives no reply.

10. 30 a. m.: Hilda Murrell's body found in copse.

'Who Killed Hilda Murrrell.' pp 133/4
Judith Cook

"..........so nothing else was found?"

"Not of any consequence."

"And where is it you're speaking from?"

"An M5 service station. Not far from you.....but I'll not call in."

"And the bungler....?"

"........is sleeping like a baby. I'm driving his car, the red Escort. He's propped in the passenger seat, and by now due his next hypodermic. The one more should see him through to his journey's end."

"Which will be where? Mine shaft? Sea bed?"

"It'll be very deep, and very wet."

"Why kill the woman anyway? Did he say?

"Finding him hiding in her spare room she went for him. In the struggle, taking a blow, she passed out. He could have left her, but no. He took a chance. He chose to bring her to where we'd planned to rendezvous, the old airfield. He thought there might be scope for sedating her, keeping her under so to allow her to resurface in Hospital. Her defences would have been down, and with sensitive questioning, and a little of the right kind of medicine maybe you people could have learned something.... something about what he'd been sent to look for and steal."

"But he lost the race against time."

"She came around in the car, her car. He said she forced him off the road. The car was immobilised. That's when he got really rough. He dragged her into the field, well clear of the vehicle, then came looking for me. He knew I wouldn't be long coming down the same road. He was in a state, wanting me to get help. But we were on our own now. I knew that. It was too late for the old lady I'm afraid, and too late for him."

"But you got that letter to the rendezvous. I have it with me now. It pleases me that you remembered the terms of your employment. I have your number, you have your money?"

"I do. Thanks. But what about your ship, is she going to be anymore use to anyone after all this?"

"I'm told she's up for disposal. BI are quietly listening to offers."

"From breakers?"

"From anyone who'll undertake to find a breaker and deliver her to the yard. BI simply want her off their hands. She'll be going cheap."

"So we're finished with her?"

"One can never be sure. You and I, we know it to be a big bad world out there. We've both of us worked with people who've long prided themselves in never missing a trick. For once they were caught out, and they'll be smarting still. They'll be watching very closely."

"I can't imagine any repetition."

"Not the point. Wounded egos I'm talking, and now they'll be wanting to get even ......ideally using that self same vessel and, where safe, as many possible of we whose subservience they'd taken a little too much for granted. 'They've gotten themselves out of line', that'll have been their view over there....."

"....... which means they're going to be thinking of ways to straighten a few of us up."

"So let's get this thing tidied away. Red Escort you say...... and the number? I can keep the traffic division off, as we ought to have done with the old lady's Renault. Drive carefully, that's all."

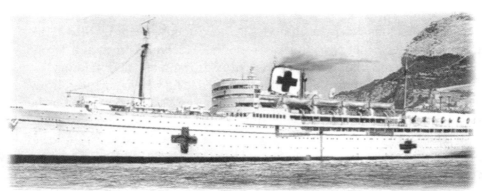

The S.S. Kampala (17,000 Tons)
Sails from Gibraltar, April 1982

BOOK 2

MAY 1985

Unconscious when admitted on the Sunday evening Steve, 17, remained so for the next thirty-six hours. He woke to a murderous headache, blurred vision and the task of re-filing a crashed memory.

The nurse used his name. He responded. The bed head and pillows were adjusted, and from a propped position he slowly focussed on the prospect offered by the ward window

The spire below, with the houses against the hillside behind told him this was Truro. Beyond again, and higher, there were trees and there were fields with their trim of hedge blossom, the vivid gorse yellow and thorn white. This was Cornwall, with May turning spectacularly to June. He lived in Bristol, but he often stayed here with his uncle and aunt during school and now college holidays.

Claire and Grahame Simpson were tenant farmers. Lanmouth Farm was their holding, one of the two that together with Carwinion House comprised the nearby Carwinion Estate.

His parents, they were in Italy where his father was currently working. His mother had flown out for a short stay. The nurse, Kate she said her name was, told him they'd been informed and assured that there was no cause for alarm.

She chatted on, prompting and observing and recording. Recovery from concussion was never straightforward. Stimulation could be helpful, stress was to be avoided. She learned that the boy was a first year A level student at a further education college, and met this by revealing that the partner with whom she lived lectured in a similar institution across at Camborne. Social Studies was his area apparently, subjects that Steve had left behind. He'd done well enough at GCSE, but now his world was of mathematics and computers, here he had flair.

Although she and Jeremy had not long lived in Truro she did know of Carwinion House and its occupant, Hugh Trembath. And of course she also knew of the father....the ageing yet still active Sir Edward.

"I've an old friend staying near you. We went to see her at the weekend." As she spoke Kate reached for the clipped notes at the foot of the bed.

"By the river somewhere?" Steve was making an effort.

"On the river, in sheltered accommodation. *Kampala* she's called, S.S."

There was some hesitation, but the response sought came.

"The old ship, you mean, above the ferry. You've cruised on her have you?"

"Worked on her."

"You mean as a nurse for the shipping line, British India isn't it?"

"As a nurse for Ministry of Defence. Before this job I was with the Queen Alexandra's Royal Nursing Service. I went with that ship to the South Atlantic."

This was enough. Attention had drifted. His mention of the ferry had taken him aboard and he was crossing to the Roseland with his bike. It was Sunday, the last day of this holiday and it was to Pendower that he was headed, for the fourth time in the week. The attraction?......A girl, Jane her name, who was working there at the beach cafe behind the dunes.

Nurse Kate Rogers had done her job. Steve was left to his fragmented thoughts and slowly, between snatches of sleep, order was restored.

At midday he was well enough to take a little food, and in the afternoon, to take a visit from his Aunt Claire.

*

Claire Simpson left the City Hospital at 4:15. She strode down to Lemon Quay where Hugh Trembath had his own chained off parking space. The long wheel base Land Rover waited. Seeing his tenant approach the driver started the vehicle and drew out towards her.

Claire had spent an hour with her nephew. With Hugh giving a lift both ways Grahame had been freed to give the whole of this fine day to completing a mow of silage. Hugh was a good and considerate landlord, always being concerned to help his farmers make the best use of valuable time.

He was an imposing figure, like his vehicle the man was strongly built. The hair was dark, the complexion swarthy and the neck thick. A military bearing was re-enforced by smart yet functional attire. As a young man he'd given distinguished service to the Royal Navy, and the impress would obviously be life long.

Besides managing the estate and serving as an elected member to both District and County Councils Hugh was a part time Auxiliary Coastguard. Also he was a Methodist lay preacher. He had the charm and he had the voice. His words were always well received by the village chapel congregations..... once he'd read a Wesley day lesson at Gwennap.

What Hugh Trembath liked was to know, and to know he networked. In this he was like his father, but whereas Sir Edward's bailiwick was in the metropolis Hugh cultivated influence here, in this corner of Cornwall.

Having paid rent to the man for more than fifteen years Claire Simpson well knew this. She was adept at carefully feeding this appetite for information. She knew how to avoid the man and also how to be available, and how, with no less care, to use his influence as a resource for herself.

It was a brief journey to Lanmouth. With Claire up and settled into the cab conversation started immediately.

"How did you find him then?".... the natural enquiry from Hugh Trembath.

"Awake, sore, starting to remember."

"How it happened?"

"That hasn't come to him. They say it might never. He remembers leaving Pendower and pressing on to catch the ferry. He mentioned playing his Walkman as he went. The girl at the cafe had lent him a tape. He stopped to turn it at the top, where he likes to wait for the cars coming off the ferry to clear the hill. This supposedly makes for a safer descent."

"But not this time. And it's unlikely that anyone coming off the ferry would have seen his plight and acted, and anyone following would have halted the ferry, or at least notified someone on board."

"But no one did," confirmed Claire.

"And yet an ambulance was called, and this was at the Trelissick slip before the crew had everything tied down for the day. And they were taken across, and Steve was there, precisely where they'd been told he would be."

"But alone."

"And that's strange, because someone had checked him over and straightened him out."

"You're the man to get to the bottom of it," encouraged Claire, "and should you be making enquiries with the ambulance people could you ask if they picked up that tape player, it's not with his things at the hospital."

"I spoke with them this afternoon," said Hugh, "and there was no mention of it. I'll have some tea and later go across for a half hour's scout around."

Hugh Trembath would be eating alone. His wife, Sarah, and daughter, Helen, were in London. Helen was 18 and making her debut in society. The eagerly awaited 'season' was under way. Helen was being presented, and her mother had to be there to direct the purchasing of the clothes, and the styling of the hair, and the garnishing of contacts. They were staying with Sir Edward. The London flat, so spacious and so central, had rarely been so useful, and also there were the connections. Sir Edward was still a man of considerable renown.

The expense had been defrayed with the maturity of a purposely-planned savings policy. This left Hugh, so much more comfortable in Cornwall, to enjoy a welcome respite from having to keep up with Helen's local social agenda.....the lifts to here and there, the entertaining of a constantly changing circle of friends, and that wretched succession of summertime gymkhanas.

At this moment Helen was as far from his thoughts as she was from Carwinion House. Into her place had moved that willowy, fair-haired young man, his unexplained mishap, and that mysterious summons for assistance.

He remembered from last summer the boy's fondness for cycling the Roseland lanes. Steve had told him then that he felt these far safer than the wider, busier roads between Truro and Falmouth.

49

During the August holiday, the longest, he'd made frequent forays to distant Portloe where Ralph Bartlett, with his son Joe, operated an eight board windsurf school out of the small sheltered harbour. The wind had been kind, and Steve had been proud of the progress made with board and sail.

But this year, for this last week at least, it was to Pendower that he'd been drawn. To where the same Ralph Bartlett held the near expired lease on the dune screened Beach Cafe. The incrementally assembled structure of wood, asbestos and tin stood in the corner of a small sand strewn car park. Both cafe and car park had this year foregone the annual post winter patching. As a councillor Hugh knew that Ralph had sold his option to renew to the owner of the hotel which looked down onto the dunes through a row of pines. The proposition being put to the planners was that the cafe be demolished and replaced by a modern toilet block, and the car park also resurfaced....the gain for the hotel being a consent to develop a small shop and also a tea room for non residents.

It would go ahead, Hugh knew, and this would be Ralph's last season. Overheads were to be kept to a minimum and he and just one assistant were, during this rather inclement early season period, offering no more than a staple hot drink and biscuit fare. The draw for Steve?........ clearly it was the young assistant.

"It sounds to me as if Ralph has been providing Steve with an interest to rival that offered by his son over at Portloe," said Hugh. "Is that young Jane Byrne that he's got working with him? Has Steve mentioned a name?"

"I've just heard the name Jane, but I think you must be right," answered Claire. "Bright girl that," she added.

"And she's going to need to be, by all accounts," continued Hugh. "Has Steve been told about the father?"

"Not by me. If he knows anything then it's from the girl herself."

"Or from Ralph?"

"I shouldn't think so. He'd be wanting her to make an impression on his customers. A father in prison?.....come on."

"He should have pleaded guilty and offered any information he had. He would have lost his job yes, but on probation he could have been away by now and into a fresh start..... easier on the wife, easier on the child. Instead he's got a three year stretch in Exeter, with his loved ones having to bear the humiliation."

"And the struggle to make ends meet," added Claire. "I saw the yacht advertised last month. Did it go?"

"It did, cheaply of course, but it'll help them along."

"What about an appeal?"

"Not without fresh evidence. He was a solicitor himself remember. All the legal loopholes would have been checked and the evidence was strong. He was the only one on the boat and when it came in it was searched with him there. The stuff was in the two butane cylinders, both adapted for the purpose, just as the excise people had been informed."

"So where did he pick it up?" asked the passenger as the vehicle was turned river-wards at the Playing Place roundabout.

"Only a dozen or so miles out. The cylinders were slung beneath anchored buoys. While not stated in proceedings, I've heard this to have been just one brace out of at least four that were lain at pre arranged positions, spaced and specified, probably at night. Byrne wouldn't have known about the others, but he certainly wasn't the only one out there, fishing."

"So others were caught?"

"More than likely."

"But they would have chosen to bargain rather than trouble a jury."

"It would seem so," affirmed Hugh Trembath. He was pleased to hear his earlier logic being endorsed.

"So who was out there dropping the drug..... cannabis wasn't it? This must be known."

"It needn't be," corrected Hugh. "It doesn't necessarily follow. There's information and there's dis-information and profit to be made in dealing in both. Nothing was seen. A lot of vessels are out there using those waters at night, and what passes between them does so at the very limits of our national jurisdiction. When he came in it was enough that Byrne was the carrier and that it was his vehicle. He carries the can."

"The two cans you mean," said Claire, wanting this to remain light conversation. "How was he able to plead innocence?"

"He claimed ignorance. He would often go out for a solo sail, he maintained, and the cylinders must have been switched before he set out...... but as for the why and the how and the by whom, he was totally at a loss. The law is strict. A jury can only decide on the evidence before it."

"So they had to convict."

"And when they did so the Judge took a dim view of having a lawyer standing before him. Mr Byrne felt the weightier end of the sentence range."

"But he'll behave well surely, and be out within two."

"And then the true challenge comes," said the driver emphatically, "the rebuilding."

On the ferry road now, they were passing the short driveway that led into Carwinion House. Beyond lay the crossroads where Hugh would turn left into the narrowest of the met together routes. It led down to Lanmouth Farm, the first of the two estate tenancies, before rising towards the second.... ridge hid Landurgan.

For the intrepid, the lane went further, to Cowlands and beyond into the parish of Old Kea where it became but one strand in a labyrinth of high hedged byways. Some boasted knowledge of a way back almost to Truro, but rarely could they be persuaded to actually demonstrate this familiarity.

Between the two farms a track branched away from the lane to drop down to Roundwood Quay....... a relic of the busier times of a hundred years before when the mines of the hills to the west fed a heavy world wide demand for Cornish metal.

"What about young Jack Spargo?" asked Hugh as they cut between the Simpson's upper pastures. "I know that he and your nephew became good friends when he worked on the ferry. Has there been any contact this time?"

"Last Sunday they met," revealed the aunt. "Young Jack brought his boat up to the cove below Trelissick last Sunday and Steve was there to greet him. They sailed down to Mylor together. They had some time with the old man before coming back."

Jack Spargo, now twenty one, had acquired the epithet 'young' when, as a school leaver, he'd secured a YOPS placement with the ferry company. Amongst staff and customers it was recalled that back in the mid '50s his grandfather, then near blind, had with sandpaper, brush and pot scratched and painted himself a sort of wage, rail by rail from end to end and back to start again. But that ended in '58 as the dredging and the digging had had to four years previously.

By then the war invalid's blindness was near total. For a further decade there were shadows for him in a perpetual fog, but thereafter all was darkness and to all who knew or remembered him he became 'old' Jack, a man who said little, but one who listened, and heard, and understood more than most.

Steve had been first taken to meet the old Jack back in '81. Since then he'd called regularly at the creek side cottage where the octogenarian lived alone.....at least three times in each year. The host would listen eagerly to the young visitor's snapshot perspectives on happenings at the estate, and in the ferry passage and its surrounds. This would prompt the occasional reminiscence, but his preferred way was to listen.

Positioned between his favourite chair and its nearest wall stood a low table. This supported a radio receiver, compact and powerful. When he had company it would stay off. It was said that when he was alone it was always on.

From his first day with the ferry young Jack, the grandson, had shown himself to be an asset. He was a natural on the water, unlike his father who worked inland as a forester. It was a diesel ferry now, and no aspect of its operation lay beyond either his interest or capability. He was also good with the customers. The friendship with Steve in many ways epitomised his attitude to all.

Earlier, when travelling in, Claire had remarked that had young Spargo still been with the ferry then Steve would have been waited for, or even looked for, before a last crossing. The landlord, a main shareholder with the ferry company had agreed, and this had prefaced a brief airing of the circumstances of the lad's departure.

After three years of full time work an offer had been made to him, the offer of a lifetime. It had been said that he'd been in the right place at the right time.... and maybe that was so, but only partly. The boy's engaging manner was clinching. An opportunity thrown up by coincidence had needed to be grasped and personality it was that had made the difference. The good fortune was earned.

The proposition came from a customer, a ferry user who'd crossed a number of times during the previous August. The man was from London, and to judge from the size and the shine of his BMW saloon he was wealthy. On holiday with his family in an expensively rented house in St.Mawes, his business was investment. He and his two partners had the nerve and the expertise to switch money into and out of shares, currencies, and government stocks with profitable alacrity. The combination of deregulation and new technology offered a limitless prospect, providing that the funds to invest could be kept flowing in.

The challenge was to win savers, and to this end sales associates were being recruited in every city and county in the land. They would take their commission of course, but they would also need close support and this meant more than the intensive training, the glossy prospectus, and the ubiquitous laptop. Also required was scope to play, to entertain and be entertained, be it with client or colleague or both.

For the tyros there could be paint balling, for the less bellicose....golf, and for those to whom it might appeal there could be an opportunity to sail. And, as a starter, what could better the challenge of moving a working boat across the Carrick Roads.

After due consideration and consultation the partners purchased their craft. It was renovated. No expense was spared. True to tradition she would race in the summer, and in the winter be equipped with the dredge and licence. But she would need a master, one who knew the waters, and the ropes, and who had charm and flexibility.

Young Jack Spargo was asked. If he felt he could do the job then it was his, and the boat was too, to look after. He would be retained on what was for the area a generous basic wage, and there would be the tips, and also what he could make from whatever catch he took from the estuary or beyond.

The offer was promptly accepted, and at the end of January a pristine *Flushing Run* was lifted down onto the water. Two months of the dredging season remained, and young Jack never lost a day. Then, in April, he took aboard his first party. The day went delightfully. Conditions were perfect and all vowed to come again, and, moreover, they would spread the word.

And in the district there was unstinting approval. A boat had been restored, but not as a curio. She was being used in the traditional ways, and she had a local youngster at the helm. The capricious local oyster wasn't enough, certainly not at this moment with the bonamia parasite cutting into the yields. To be viable these craft needed to be steered towards new demands, and perhaps this could be a way forward for more than just one of the fleet. And for old Jack Butters, who'd been forced to sell his own boat thirty years before, here at last was a true consolation.

The District Council it was that granted the dredging licences, and Hugh Trembath it was who sat on the scrutinising committee. He'd commended the initiative and was naturally concerned that it should succeed. And so far, as he'd been happy to tell Claire, there was every indication that it would.

The hedges lowered, the lane widened and the Land Rover bounced across the Lanmoth farmyard, splattering for itself a brisk turn.

"He'll be out soon I'm sure", said Hugh, halting by the farmhouse door. "If the plan is for him to stay around here to recuperate then say I'd be pleased to see him up at the house."

"You've been kind," acknowledged Claire, "I'll keep that in mind. And once again, thank you for the lift."

*

Steve had been back at Lanmouth now for three days. This was the first in which he'd ventured any distance on his own. The bike was still at the Truro repair shop. He was walking. He'd reached the ferry and he'd crossed as a foot passenger. For the first time he was inspecting the scene of his misfortune. A week had passed, more than that, and the last part of that doomed descent remained lost to him. Never before had the first part of that final S bend been too tight, he was so familiar with the best line. How could he have found himself on the very rim of the corner..... so precariously as to have toppled onto the dropping bank and so nearly tumbled to the river below?

He climbed down stiffly, pausing for a moment to glance back up at the lip. He would have dropped from sight. Whoever had responded to his plight, it surely hadn't been a motorist. The thought of how long he must have been airborne chilled. He looked down. What he or his rescuers might have disturbed had been brushed out by ten days of vigorous plant growth. A saffron light filtered through the canopy of freshly fledged scrub oak. The river, so close, was screened, but not the hum and the clatter of the steady shuttling ferry, nor the sound of the mainly cars and vans that just about paid its way.

Below this there was a faint incessant drone. Constant, static, this was the on board generator that serviced the two methane tankers which lay otherwise dormant at their twin mooring some two hundred metres down river of the ferry crossing.

People lived on the laid up ships..... the few caretakers whose common round it was to keep their floating homes generally shipshape, and in ocean going trim. In their third year of lay up, these tankers were as voyage tuned as they had been on arrival. Were it winter then someone aboard could have looked across and seen Steve, but not now, and not when he fell either. But somebody did see, and they'd acted. Who was this?

"This is the tree, and this the branch you struck." The statement was punctuated by the knock of knuckle against unyielding bark. Steve spun around, almost losing a still suspect balance. The man was close, within twelve metres. He was standing next to an oak, knee deep in campion and fern. Aged no more than forty, he wore a khaki shirt and a pair of comfortably fatigued jeans. The brown hair was worn long. His face was a friendly smile. Steve didn't know him. He was speechless. "How are you?" The stranger enquired. "Certainly better than when I last saw you."

"Where?" Steve was puzzled, and he was cautious.

"Here, but don't bother yourself trying to remember. You were out of things, completely." He raised a hand. It held the tape player. "I can return this now. I didn't find it until the ambulance people had gone, and the police. Quite a good turn out you had."

Steve stepped forward. Taking the proffered gadget, he looked at it awkwardly.

"It will work," said the man.

"I'm sure it will," said Steve, and then after some hesitation, "I'm grateful of course but shocked, and confused too. What do I ask first?"

"Names? Mine's Alan, Alan Grigson."

"And I'm Steven Clarke. Steve is fine. And you found me last week and called out the ambulance." Alan nodded. Steve continued. "Did you see me tumble? I don't remember. Do you know how it happened?"

"I didn't see, I heard. I think I know what I heard, but it's better that it should come from you. We can be patient." The last words carried authority, and comfort too. The boy had more questions.

"So what are you? Local? Is this part of a job you do? And why this keeping out of the way when the uniforms arrive?"

"I'm not local. My work brings me here, and to your last question......... I'd done as much as I could before they'd arrived." Steve sensed evasiveness. It irked, and he made this known.

"I don't need a guessing game Mr Grigson. We've met and it's been your choice, the time and the place. You could have dropped this in at the hospital." He briefly pressed the fast wind. The whirr and the snap were enough.

"My apologies. How long have you got? Long enough for a sail up to *The Heron* and some lunch?" There was warmth in the invitation. Steve accepted and followed. They stayed on the bank, picking their way southwards through the trees. Eighty metres, and there was a cove, the river cliff having been gulleyed by a side stream. The trees receded, and instead of rock there was a grassy bank. Tied against the bank sat a very tidy all timber sailing cruiser. The canvas was down. The deep red mainsail drooped loosely off the boom onto the cabin roof, concealing most of the bicycle strapped thereon. A working jib lay in similar disarray behind a proudly varnished bowsprit. There was ample tide. They could hoist and be on their way in minutes.

In just twenty a following breeze cleared them across the ferry chains and past the *Kampala*. The fields of Lanmouth Farm could be pointed out, and also the glimpse of Carwinion House. Even with a favourable wind the Truro River was a tight channel to sail. There were other craft and mooring buoys, but the *Speedwell* and her master were undaunted. He'd said sail, and he was true to the word. This was an impressive performance.

As he sailed confidently, watchfully, he spoke with a disarming modesty. He told of his being a writer and broadcaster in 'the smallest of ways'. He compiled pieces about places for colour supplements and local radio stations. Offend no one fare, that was what the ad agencies liked....... sandwich fillers, the blander the better.

He was here to do a piece on the Fal estuary, just as he'd previously done with the Dart and the Fowey. He would make notes, and recordings, and he would take pictures. There would be interviews and observations, and with the notable there would be the incidental. It would be sketchy, and some might say shallow, but it was earning him a living and he liked the way of life, the freedom to rove.

Swinging around the elbow made by Old Kea the *Speedwell* was brought into the wind and anchored. Alan's choice was to dinghy it into the jetty. With *The Heron* being set back from the waterfront and above they had to climb. It was worth it though. The small across the road beer garden offering a complete view of the deep estuary confluence.

Steve was content with a pasty and a glass of orange. Alan preferred a 'ploughman's' with his beer. This was pleasant and Steve was soon talking about himself, and what brought him to the river, and also about the locals that he knew. He thought of the girl at Pendower. She too had got him to talk like this, but not with the same expertise. With her it had taken three or four days to draw as much..... but then she was busy of course, with other customers, and she was no journalist.

This much was coming back now. He might be useful to her. Those were the words, said with a what at the time was a close to alarming frankness. And now here was another who was perhaps sizing him as a potential resource.

Alan went to the bar to refill the glasses. He had such an easy charm, all seemed so comfortably in hand. How different his manner from the girl's, she with the cause that was declared with such purpose and such passion. It was all to her, even on the eve of those fifth year exams. Those words of hers were fast coming back to him, vividly, in all their full intensity.

"What about your father," he'd asked, after explaining the whereabouts of his own parents," what does he do?"

"Nothing." She'd answered, but in a way that invited closer enquiry.

"Sick?....Out of work?"

"In prison." She'd stopped in her tidying task and was scrutinising him closely. Steve recalled the eyes, so brown and so earnest, and the fair slightly freckled skin. The head was up, and the brown shoulder length hair swept back beneath the band. The embarrassment was all his. From her there was not the slightest trace. Seconds of painful silence elapsed, long seconds. He'd had to say something, and he could find nothing that wasn't clumsy.

"What did he do?"

"Nothing....," but again this wasn't an attempt to silence him. He could keep trying. He did.

"What's he in for? How long?" This was better, although he was still groping. Would she open up? It needed to be her or the ground. There was hesitation, and then it was her. She did!

"Drug trafficking. Three years. The case was strong, but I know he's innocent."

"How?" The natural question, but bravely ventured all the same.

"He would have said had he been guilty. I know he never lies to me. He knows I always believe him." It was as simple as that. On she went with the tale of his arrest and his prosecution. Steve listened to strong evidence, but he heard strong faith too...... unalterable faith.

When these exams were done she would start turning stones. There was more evidence, better evidence. It just needed to be found, and she would find it, and, if he was back in July or August then he, Steve, could help. This was why she'd given him the tape, as a kind of keepsake, a bond. It was Ralph's, one of four that for more than a year had waited vainly for the repair of the cafe tape deck. It was of classical pieces, innocuous screen advert andantes, but because it had been from her to him he was pleased to have it back in his possession. This lay at the core of his goodwill towards the affable itinerant who now returned with the second glass of orange.

He would try to phone Jane at the weekend. He'd seen the number in the book. For the moment there were her exams, and his recovery, but she would know soon that there was no need to wait on a July return.

Though he'd told Alan of the girl at the cafe who'd lent him the tape, he'd made no mention of the father's plight. Jane had confided in him. It was a trust to be treasured.

But Alan too had singled him out, and he wanted to somehow acknowledge this. There ought to be a nugget for the man that he could pass, just as a gesture.

Steve settled into the topic of the Carwinion Estate. Alan encouraged him to tell of the Trembath's, father and son, and the boy was ready to oblige..... but as he spoke he was to sense that his companion was hearing nothing that he didn't already know. Something else was required, something special, ideally between them only...... but what, and from where?

Their talk became ever smaller, the silences increasingly stretched. And then it was there, naturally, almost as if fated. The opportunity arrived from the north-east, floating in on the Tresillian River. Alan was first to comment.

"That's one of the estuary working boats, and a handsome specimen too."

"I know her," said Steve, "and I know her master too. I've been out in her....._Flushing Run_." She was turning so as to approach the jetty and the name could now be clearly seen. Jack Spargo was sailing alone. From where they sat the landing was hidden. Confirmation that Jack Spargo had disembarked waited on the sight of him climbing towards them.

And there he was, beneath his arm a package, the outer wrapper of which looked to be a loosely wound black bin liner. Acknowledging Steve by raising his other hand he made for one of the pub's side entrances. In he went, and Alan was suddenly up and swiftly half way towards the jetty and then just as swiftly he'd returned.

In a few minutes young Jack was emerging from the main entrance. He carried a half-pint glass of stout, nothing else.

" 'Ello Steve, lookin' up well you is. They said down the ferry 'bout your tumble...... nasty bang on the 'ead ."

"It was that. Looks like I'm at Lanmouth for the summer. They don't want me back at college yet, not until the clinic's done with me. That'll not be before the end of this term."

"So makes sense to recup'rate 'ere." As he spoke Jack Spargo looked warily at Alan. Grigson looked unconcerned. His attention lay with his food.

"I was intending to give you a call when properly mobile again," said Steve. "How's the enterprise progressing. Had a few clients?"

"Encouragin' 'tis. I'm takin' a group out tomorro'. Wiv t'day 'tis deliv'ries. You know gran'fer guessed it were you who were rushin' for the ferry. 'E knew 'bout it before anyone. 'Eard the message go in to amb'lance control 'e did.... ship to shore 'e said."

"But not through the coastguards?"

"Nor p'lice ev'n," answered Jack.

"And that's unusual?"

"Un'eard of I'd say."

"Maybe some one caught a glimpse from one of those tankers there," said Steve.

"Possible," said Jack," 'cos anythin' is with they ships if you b'lieve the tales."

"Tales?" quizzed Alan, speaking at last.

"There's a legion of they," continued Jack. "When we'm little we 'ave 'm fer bedtime stories. They'm like they ships....... come as tall as you likes."

" My friend here, Mr Grigson, he might be interested in some of that. He writes. Could I bring him down to Mylor for a closer look at the boat, and to have a chat with your grandfather maybe?"

"Whenever 'e likes. A friend of yours is a friend of 'is and ever welcome." With that young. Jack drained the glass and bid them good day. He was quickly down to the jetty again and promptly away and back into view...... beating a course down river."

"Very good young man." Alan's voice had a conspiratorial edge. "You obscured the truth without lying.... impressive that. What was he delivering, oysters?"

"Not in June, he's been out with the line, spinning for mackerel perhaps, or picking up crabs. You've seen the menu in there, it's your guess.

"And this line, he keeps that in the locker at the front end?" Alan was probing.

"Probably, why?"

"Just now I got close enough to see that it was open. I didn't see a line." What Alan had seen was the protruding sleeve of a wetsuit, but he wasn't about to make anything of this now. He moved the conversation on.

"When are you likely to be mobile again? Has the bike been fixed?"

"It has. It's in Truro awaiting collection."

"Who by?"

"By whoever can make time to pick it up. It's a busy time at the farm."

"We could pick it up today if you want Steve. There's room on the *Speedwell*. We could carry it down to Roundwood or to the ferry slip and then it's just a short push home. Phone them at the farm. Tell them where you are and what we're doing. Look, there's a call box just over there."

*

As the phone rang at Lanmouth Farmhouse so another sounded on the office desk at Carwinion House. Hugh Trembath was alone. The call was expected. He'd attempted to contact Colin Toms earlier but the morning was a busy time at Percuil Yard. Toms's marina was a small twenty berth affair, tucked against the back of St.Mawes. So sheltered was its position on the Percuil River that from the main estuary all that showed were the mast tops that peaked up from the larger of the yachts on the the T shaped pontoon jetty.

There was a block with shower and locker facilities, and there was the chandlery. The rest of the Yard itself was given largely to dinghies and their trolleys, and those few yachts undergoing protracted refurbishment. Planning permission for the development had been hard won. Hugh Trembath's interest and support had been appreciated and remembered.

"Colin, thanks for getting back. Things are picking up by the sound of it. Anything new this week?"

"Only more mutterings about these Russian factory ships."

"From local fishermen?"

"No, for they're quite happy. They have an outlet for a lot of substandard stuff. It's the visitors and those of us trying to cater for them. Parked right between here and Pendennis they detract from the amenity."

"A bloody eyesore you mean. Can you tell me anything about a little sloop, wood, blue hull, red canvas?....*Speedwell* she's called." There was a pause. Hugh heard a page turn. A record was being checked.

"She looked in a fortnight ago. It's a Mr Grigson. He writes apparently......., another one of them. He said he was intending to go up river. He's what he says he is. I've heard him on the radio."

"And he's nothing more, you think?"

"So far as any of us can tell for certain. I speak as I've so far found. If he's any length of time on your patch then you'll do likewise I'm sure." There was a hint of irritation in Toms's voice. There was reasonable vigilance, and there was paranoia. He was far too busy to entertain the latter.

"Have you seen Jim Prout recently?" continued Trembath.

"Not for more than a month now. He had some jobs here back in April. He'll be moving around like he does. No phone still ....you just have to catch him when you can."

"If you do see him tell him to contact me. It's more work, tell him. Say I'm on middle watch for the coming week." This last instruction from Carwinion House ended the call. Colin Toms returned to his chandlery counter. He made a note. Should Prout be seen then he would be told, and he would know when Trembath was travelling between Carwinion and Portscatho. The latter had a mobile radio in his Land Rover, the former had the same on his launch. Between the two it was understood that these were the preferred times for making contact.

The call from Percuil was the last that Hugh Trembath was to either take or make that lunchtime. He needed to be in Truro within thirty minutes. He tidied his desk, the papers he needed going into his attache case. It was time to go. He strode out to the Land Rover.

*

The streets of Truro were busy. With so many on the pavements pushing a bike was tricky. Steve and Alan had walked up from Malpas, sparing themselves the bother of finding a mooring closer to the city. Their return from the cycle shop was taking them through an attractive and thriving centre. Steve bounced his wheels over the Pydar Street streamlet, clear in its granite channel. There was life in this town, brisk trade for the shops, and music too. Gospel songs rang out from the Cathedral courtyard. On reaching the corner the pair saw that it was a group of four, three singing, two with guitars, and the fourth, a girl, handing out leaflets.

Alan paused, and this surprised Steve. He leant the bike against one of the courtyard benches and sat, his back towards the dummies that glared from the Marks & Spencer store. He looked across to *Drummond's,* the estate agency at which he would occasionally call with his aunt or uncle. This was where they paid the rent, and to here they also brought the numerous notifications and applications deemed under Brussels directive to need a landlord's endorsement.

There had been growing concern about the efficiency of the firm, but this had been largely allayed with the recent retirement of two of the older partners. Fresher, more up to date, minds had been brought in and the service was markedly improved.

To Steve looking across from the bench there was little outward change, save for a novel promotion that was displayed in the last and least prominent of the windows towards the Cathedral. He wanted a closer look. He rose and crossed.

On offer were holiday bonds. Subscribe and gather points, and with these redeem accommodation bookable at any time in a range of resorts from Bruges to Benidorm. The resorts were pictured, and the accommodation suites too. It was a colourful enough proposition to warrant a harder sell than that given by this cloistered window, but never mind. Previously it had been just interest rates posted here.

A door opened. A man stepped out, and standing in front of him was Hugh Trembath. Steve was taken aback, strangely in a way. This was the landlord, and the firm was his agent. He was often seen here.... and yet, oddly, for a moment the boy was stunned.

"You're not saying hello?" The steward of Carwinion was in hearty form. "A touch of this memory loss maybe......"

"Hello," stammered the boy lamely. He was trying to anticipate the next question. He glanced across to where he'd left his bike. He saw Alan with his back to him facing the singers who'd drawn into enough of a huddle to conceal most of the bench and the bike behind. Was it relief that Steve felt? It was, but quite why he couldn't divine. There was nothing threatening about Hugh Trembath, far from it.

"Good to see you out. Can I offer you a lift back, or anything?"

"No thanks." Steve's reply was hesitant. "I have one arranged." And this was true, so why should he feel that he was being evasive?

"Has that tape player turned up yet?"...... A direct question, difficult.

"I've looked and asked everywhere I can think."......... Neatly fended.

"Well do remember to call in at the House. See the Land Rover there·and I'm never far away. You're always welcome."

"Thanks, yes I'll,....I'll see you soon.".

No more was said. Steve took a firm pat on the upper arm and the fellow was turning to walk briskly away in the direction of the quay. Steve crossed back to the bench and his bike. The singers had dropped back now, closer to the shop window. Alan sat on the bench.

"Was that done deliberately?" the boy asked him.

"Was what done?" Alan seemed puzzled.

"It doesn't matter," said Steve, attending now to his bike. From the courtyard their way took them along the narrow street leading eastwards between *Drummond's* and the Cathedral. After the estate agent's the first door on the right was that of *Conway's*, the firm of solicitors that Jane had spoken of. The offices were upstairs. A door-post carried the name plaques of the partners, and amongst them there was a rectangle of brighter paint. A name had been removed, recently struck off. Here was public humiliation. And if he sensed it as a tingle, how much it must have stung at the daughter.

He might try to phone her later, for there was much to tell. And there could be even more now for as they moved into Old Bridge Street they were hailed from the adjacent short stay car-park by Kate, the nurse. She was out of uniform and she was accompanied, but even so she was beckoning them across with vigour.

Over they went and the man was introduced. This was the Jeremy of whom she'd spoken at the hospital. Courtesy demanded that Steve should introduce his companion, Mr Grigson, who was 'also a visitor to the area.' And they took to each other, did Kate and Alan.

It was instant and it was obvious, and as obvious to Jeremy, her man, as it was to Steve. The two were left looking at each other as the writer and the nurse chatted and quipped for themselves an immediate affinity. The prominent topic was Steve's recovery and this left Jeremy the more distanced. It couldn't be easy. Steve sensed a tension. Relief came when, at last, Alan spoke to all rather than the one.

"Look, I must get this lad home safe and sound. It would be nice to see you again some time."

"Well Steve knows where I work," said Kate. "It's been interesting talking with you." Her companion turned away and she followed. Steve and Alan continued through the car park towards the Travalgar roundabout and across to the road that led down to Malpas.

As they went Steve told an intrigued listener about Kate and her previous job...... and the connection between this and the tired old ship that lay moored just above the ferry.

*

"........and then he put me ashore at Roundwood. I wheeled the bike along the track up through the woods and then down and that was it........ back here at last, and I was done in." Steve had been on the phone now for almost an hour. Jane hadn't known of the accident. When told she'd voiced concern, and had met impatience. It was of today that he wanted to tell.

This Alan Grigson had helped him and he'd listened. He cared, as did Kate the nurse, and he was sure they would take to her if they met. Jane was interested, certainly. She was also cautious. Jane had ideas of her own. It was *her* cause.

"You're expecting to see this fellow again then?"

"He said he'll be at the same place next week, same day, same time. I'm thinking we might go across to Mylor and see old Jack Butters."

"And I'd also like to do that sometime," said Jane in a way that reminded Steve that her claim on his attention had preceded today's encounter. "Listen, I've another week of exams and then we can get down to it. On Saturday week I've agreed to help Ralph at Polgooth. I want you to come along. Ralph won't mind, in fact he'll be delighted to have someone with a bit of strength to help lift."

"Polgooth?"

"It's a kind of fayre, held every year, just outside St Austell. Music, street theatre, craft stalls, it's more for ageing hippies than youngsters."

"And that means grass," said Steve.

"That's what I'm thinking. Ralph sells fruit there, soft fruit......... peaches, apricots, cherries, grapes. He sells it out of the back his van. We're two. One can help him, the other can scout around."

"What for?"

"To start with, just faces. We'll take Dad's camera, it's a good one. It's about having a record of things we might notice, people on their own, or in groups talking...."

"Or dealing may be."

"Possibly, and then later when we're sniffing around these parts that record might offer a scent." The voice was earnest. This girl was determined. To the listener the approach was rather scattergun, scatterbrained even, but Steve wasn't about to demur..... he wouldn't dare. No one was pretending to be a professional.

"And while I remember," Jane went on," have you seen anything of a motor cyclist on your side? The full leather gear, boots, gloves, and the helmet that comes right down, all in black, and a really hefty machine. I've seen him heading towards the ferry and back, but not to any regular pattern. I'm not even sure that he crosses."

"Can't say that I have," replied Steve. "I'll keep a lookout though." Steve went on to ask after her father. He was angry she said, and he was defiant, but this was to be expected. It was a healthy mindset. It was her mother that caused concern. Her belief was less absolute. Yes, she thought him innocent..... but the finding and the presenting of proof, this was a different matter.

There was also the resentment. How could they have got themselves into such a mess as this? In her daughter this was prompting counter resentment. Jane had no time for self-pity.

Steve would need to tread carefully. This was clear to him. Soon he might be meeting this Mrs Byrne, or speaking with her by telephone. She would want him to be a stabilising influence. He attempted a summing up.

"I have an aunt and an uncle. They're busy tenant farmers. They feed and accommodate me. When I'm fit there'll be jobs. We have the landlord, something of a busybody, but he's been helpful, friendly. Then there's Jack Spargo, a long time friend. Less of a Mr Respectable he, but, with his grandfather, no less well up on local happenings. And I can add to these the writer and the nurse...... who looked to me to be just a touch away from getting their own thing going."

"Despite the boyfriend?"

"Possibly it's because. Alan hinted at this on the way back. Mend wings and you can be working yourself out of a job...... occupational hazard he says."

"Hers having been broken in the South Atlantic."

"Quite."

"But that's rough on the guy," observed the girl.

"Yeah, but all's fair as they say. We're not talking criminal injustice now. But that's beside my point. What I'm saying is that if any contact that I have can be a resource for you then take it, use it. They'll hear nothing from me about your father or your efforts on his behalf.

Unless you should instruct otherwise."

"Thanks," said Jane, "that's nice to know."

The call done, Steve hauled himself to his room and to bed. All was so quiet here, with no noise save for that soft perpetual hum of the milk cooler. He was soon asleep.

*

3 days later.

Of all the estuary's waterside inns the *Pandora* had to be held the busiest. One only needed to reflect on the length and sheer bulk of its floating jetty. It was late morning, but still there was ample space for Jack Spargo to bring in *Flushing Run*. Amongst the other craft he'd seen and recognised the *Speedwell,* but there was no sign of the man he'd met three days earlier at Malpas. Alan was there though, watching, keeping low.

Young Jack did as he'd done at The Heron. He was delivering. Carrying a similar package he strode to the attractively thatched pub and entered, again using a side door. Grigson once more moved with stealth. Wet suited, he slipped between The *Speedwell* and the jetty and then under, so as to surface beneath the working boat's bowsprit. No one was near. The lowered jib sail gave cover. He just needed to pull himself up so that he could lean and open and reach and feel, before slipping back and down and under and away.

When Jack Spargo emerged from the *Pandora,* The *Speedwell* had departed. Outbound, she was just about to clear Restronguet Point.

*

Three miles to the north, at Carwinion House, Hugh Trembath was answering his door. The call was expected. It had been arranged the previous day, when he'd seen the lad in the lane.

"Well done Steve. You'll stay for some lunch I trust. How's the head?"

"Much better and yes, I will have something, but only when you're ready."

Steve had been here before. When younger he'd been thought an acceptable playmate for Helen.... but the girl was above that now, she was a world away. And today the boy was much more than an accessory to the dutiful Simpsons. He too was an almost adult, one familiar enough with the locality to move about independently, making contacts of his own. There had to be value in cultivating his good opinion, in winning a blossoming confidence.

Today it could be as if Hugh and Steve were father and son, and that was how they spoke...... man to all but man.

Trembath was not intending to project himself as the 'master' of Carwinion House, nor even as the landlord of the estate. Instead, Steve was about to hear the dutiful trustee. Enhancement would be his theme. Already there were plans out on the table, for new livestock barns at each of the farms. What his father had achieved he'd consolidated and he was building further. The heritage was more than intact. For his successor...... daughter, son in law, or grandchild perhaps, his stewardship would be nothing short of exemplary.

This host was initially minded to talk about himself, and for Steve this had to be encouraged. On farming, though, the boy knew little and he feared he would too soon appear bored. The past offered better scope. In local terms he might be no less ignorant, but in this field there was at least a broad knowledge from which he might intelligently question.

"When was it you came here, from Plymouth wasn't it?"

"I was born here in '38, and lived here until I was almost school age. We went to Plymouth in '43 and came back in '55. I was about your age. Just after my father's second election win it was...... thirty years ago last week. Eden was the top man. My father never rated him, not like he did Macmillan."

"Who took over after the Suez thing."

"Which looking back now seems a total fiasco, but that's with hindsight of course."

"Do you remember anything from the very early days?" The parliamentary career could wait. Steve wanted to know more about wartime Carwinion.

"I remember bombing raids on Falmouth, and a few being dropped between here and Truro. One hit a warship in the river, just below Malpas. My father was on the blackout patrols."

"So he was at home for the first year or so of the war?"

"For the first three years almost. He had land. He knew how to tend it, and how to advise others to tend theirs. Food was a priority. We could have been starved to defeat by the U boats."

"And this linked in with the Duchy work that he did before the war." This lay beyond the son's memory, but he would have been told things, Steve was sure of that.

"Yes, because suddenly there was money for farmers, and labour also. A lot of farms went to rack and ruin in the '30s. Cheap food had been shipped in. It was only the war that turned things around. It was certainly the start of better times for the estate farms."

"How come then, if this was so important, that your father was called up for a foreign posting?"

"Well asked. This was something that for years no one cared to make clear, not even to me. Again though it was to do with the Duchy."

"They didn't need him?" Steve prompted.

"Well yes, and no. It was felt that the Duke needed him."

"The Duke?"

"The old Duke I mean, who was by then not the Duke of Cornwall but the Duke of Windsor."

"So your father spent the rest of the war tending to the needs of his former boss, and the woman he loved..... she for whom he gave up the throne and all that. And where did that take him?"

"To the Caribbean, to the Bahamas where the Duke had been installed as Governor. But don't think this to have been a quiet backwater. The U boat campaign was no less vicious down there, and the counter measures no less strongly pursued. The Americans had taken a lend lease base on the colony and it was when they came here, and the link made, that he was asked to go over."

"By Washington or London?"

"It was a joint command thing. Uncle Sam needed this house. David Windsor needed another minder....... two birds, one stone."

"How convenient," remarked Steve, "and obviously a good career move. Did Sir Edward actually know the Duke from before the war?"

"They had met. When he was Prince of Wales, the Duke was often down here. In '35 he even brought his future wife. They visited

Trebah down on the Helford. My father was introduced to them both. Do you know he actually went to their wedding in '37?"

"As a guest you mean?" Steve was sounding incredulous. Hugh raised his palm.

"He was just on an errand. This is one of his favourite tales, and it's best heard from him. It was Walter's doing. Walter was fun and this was typical." Hugh smirked, shaking his head.

"Walter?" Here was a character being fondly recalled. The boy wanted to hear more.

"Walter Monckton, who was knighted after the abdication, and who became an MP and then Cabinet Minister in '51, and who was raised to a peerage in '57, again just after Suez."

"But who in 1937 was?" Steve wanted, once more, to reel the story back. He was fascinated.

"The top attorney to the Duchy of Cornwall," explained the host. "The office to which my father frequently reported in the course of his work. It was in his capacity as attorney that Walter got involved in the abdication tangle, and so deft was his handling of things that his career was from there on assured."

"And did you yourself actually meet the Duke or Sir Walter?" Steve spoke with awe. The first of the two he knew to have been big in history, and the second sounded to have been no mean player.

"I've met both," said Hugh proudly "The Duke just once, briefly....... Walter more than once."

"You remember meeting the Duke?"

"Not the kind of thing you forget! I was just seven. It was in Plymouth, or rather out in the Sound..... because he never actually came ashore. He was with the Duchess and it was just after the war. My father hadn't been long back. The couple were on the *S.S. Argentina,* travelling from America to France. They would settle in Paris.... you might know that. My parents and I were taken out to the ship in a launch. The audience lasted about forty minutes. There's actual newsreel of this. I've seen it several times on these historical documentary type programmes we often seem to get now."

"Of you, in camera... as a youngster?"

"Of them, waving to us from the ship. We were close by."

"And Walter?"

".......would come down to Plymouth occasionally, after the war.

He'd given up the Duchy work by then, but he still liked to ride on Dartmoor. He was good on a horse. The visits ceased though when he and my father were in Parliament together. He was a Minister you see, and my father a mere back-bencher."

"A bit like officers and ratings," said Steve, forgetting for a moment Hugh's years with the Senior Service.

"But we weren't forgotten. In '56 I was at the Britannia College over at Dartmouth and he visited the place as the then Minister of Defence. He found time to call on me privately. Surprised a few that did."

"Impressive..... for with the Suez thing coming off he'd have had a lot to think about. What did he do back in the war while his old mates were out there sunning themselves in the Caribbean?"

"All sorts. There was a spell with the Ministry of Information. That was early on, during what's now said to have been the phoney war, and in those touch and go months after the fall of France when the unthinkable had to be considered."

"And contingency plans put together?"

"Probably. He was ever the man for sugaring a bitter pill. And then there was some time in Cairo doing similar work when Rommel looked to be a threat, and after that some really high powered stuff. As the allies went on the offensive, so there had to be a series of summit get togethers. After Casablanca the next was in Cairo, just a month or so before Tehran... this last, in retrospect, probably being the most pivotal."

"More so than Yalta?" Steve enquired rather than challenged.

"Because by then Stalin was calling the shots..... from the vantage he'd secured in late '43."

"And your Walter actually went along to these..... as part of the Churchill entourage?"

"To some of them he went," confirmed Trembath. "And for those he was unable to make he was certainly active in putting together the UK agenda."

"Which by the end didn't carry a lot of sway..... busy man though."

"It would seem so, but amongst all this he found time for wooing and winning a series of lady friends. His charm was close to being notorious. And yet when you see him in the old photos...." Hugh was at a loss to explain the man's appeal. While looks are never everything, with Walter they were nothing. This is what Steve was given to understand, and he took his host's meaning with a nod.

"Anyone famous?" he asked.

"There was a West End actress I think, and out in Cairo a quite formidable character who organised the relays of ambulances sent to bring the battlefield casualties in from the western desert. He calmed down a bit when he met his second wife, but that wasn't until well after the war."

"And the first?"

"Divorced, after having parted before the war."

Steve was intrigued.

"So going back to that time yet again, and going back also to the Duke, what should we make of this stuff we now get so often in the papers about his being pro Hitler?"

Hugh Trembath again shook his head, but now he was in earnest.

"Most of this is nonsense, at least that's the view in this house....."

".......which is going to know a lot more than most," acknowledged Steve.

"Our view," maintained Hugh, "is that David Windsor was a patriot. He was well meaning. He had a very unique position in what was a very unique period of history. Many then were naive. Most have since been allowed to adjust their ways of thinking..... but not the hapless Duke. Naive can mean easily used and that's how it's been for the fellow even to this day. You get it with that garbage that we get so often from *The Express* and *The Mail*."

"Used?"

"In the '30s most of the country was pro-Hitler. Certainly the establishment was, and this was a difficult mistake to admit. It still is, and to make things easier it's been helpful to have a few individuals on whom to load the opprobrium. For the Commons it's been Chamberlain, for the Palace it's been the Duke. You see, appeasement has been a hindsight concept. At least until '38 the prevailing view was that Hitler should be accommodated. On his return from Munich Chamberlain was feted on the Palace balcony, and that was by our present Queen's parents! Now look at Uncle David. His great grandfather had been German. He himself spoke the language. He'd served in Flanders during the Great War and seen first hand the slaughter. He was totally, totally conditioned in the task of preserving Empire..... he was a living ingredient in its cement. He knew of its strains, and he knew that with another war it was certain to fragment."

"Czechoslovakia?" said Steve.

Hugh rose to the challenge.

"Again people have spoken since of a Sudetenland, a sovereign territory that was plundered, but then the talk was of a Sudeten people who were of German descent and culture and tongue. A province that might be naturally inclined to choose a future under Hitler by democratic plebiscite."

"Like the democratic process was also championed in Spain for instance." Steve was enjoying this joust, and so was Hugh.

"There again it was accepted that Franco had to succeed because he offered the lesser of two evils. Had he failed the country would have fallen apart and fallen to communism. At the time there was an Anglo German Naval Agreement, the rationale being to cover any excursions that Russian ships might make out of the Baltic and Black Seas. In the context of containing the Soviets the Agreement was regarded as sound policy by nearly all. Part of the deal was a series of courtesy visits by German warships to British ports. We had them here in Falmouth. Our local dignitaries would go aboard and there would even be prayers led by the Bishop, and this while sister ships in the *Kriegsmarine* were dishing it out on behalf of Franco around the coast of Spain. Given that a Red Spain could have offered Stalin bases, on the Atlantic, and at the gate to the Mediterranean, there was much to persuade people that this was acceptable. Even Churchill was on board. His boy Randolph, a journalist then, covered the war from the Franco camp."

"Didn't Philby do the same?" Steve was being mischievous now.

"And that shows how much of a menace the Reds were, and still are." Persuasive indeed was this blend of serviceman and preacher. Steve thought of stirring the mix further with a mention of the recent miners' strike, or of the deployment of American cruise missiles. He wasn't here to agitate though, so he chose to stay with Randolph Churchill.

"Did your father come to have anything to do with Randolph?"

"The enfant terrible? Yes, apparently they met at Cande."

"Cande?"

"The Chateau Cande, at Tours in France. Where the wedding was in '37. Randolph was taking a break from Spain. My father was ....."

"......on an errand, delivering wedding presents," finished Steve, snatching the opportunity to demonstrate attentiveness.

"You have it, and apparently Randolph was another one who was full of fun. Then later their paths drew to a close parallel during the election years of '50 and '51 This was in Plymouth and I was 12,13 and I remember the fellow quite well, and the fuss that seemed to forever follow him. In both years he contested Devonport. In both years he was beaten by none other than Michael Foot, who was quite a firebrand then. Michael was on home ground, like my father was in '51."

"When he first won his seat at..... ?"

".......Plymouth North, the constituency that neighboured Devonport. It was Randolph and Michael who hogged the press and radio. Between polls Randolph had taken a shrapnel wound in Korea, and the young Foot was having to tread carefully. As a true socialist he had an antipathy to Attlee's hikes in defence spending, but then again there were the yardies to think of. Scrapping warships was scrapping local jobs. Even Winston came down to speak. In those pre TV days it made for colourful entertainment."

The exchange naturally digressed towards Edward Trembath's parliamentary career, one distinguished primarily by length. He'd looked after constituents well. They'd looked after him. There'd been no invitation to the front bench. He'd achieved some eminence on the 1922 committee, for a while holding the office of vice chair, but he'd relinquished this in 1972.

He'd always been receptive to lobbyists promoting the interests of farmers, and more recently he'd spoken frequently in defence of the home fishing industry.

As was the way for political survivors Edward Trembath had an unerring feel for the flow of his party's mainstream, meandering as it had out of Africa and then into Europe before seeming to distance itself once more on a flow of undersea oil. Many who were more principled, and in many ways abler, had stood out.... only to gouge backwaters for themselves. Edward Trembath was ever one to avoid turbulence. He knew how to trim, and on he'd bobbed.

Essentially he was a Macmillan man, just as his was still, essentially, a Macmillan party. If asked to define Conservatism he would have struggled. He would have agreed though that misplaced discretion was far less catastrophic than misplaced valour. Accept that Eden had to go, and that someone had to be bold enough to plunge the knife, then for him 'Supermac' might be a sound assessment. The party was held together and the country too. There were jobs, schools, hospitals, and there was a living in the land. And that same ethos still held despite a fashion for 'new right' rhetoric which would for the moment do for the miners and the more profligate of the local authorities. He could live with this, for he was confident that with time the old order would prevail, the well tried post war pragmatism.

Falklands triumphalism would pass, Steve was told. Prior to the conflict Maggie had been cornered, economically, politically. She'd had to fight, a matter of survival, and to her credit she'd earned her second term, a second chance for herself but more so for her party...... A chance to mend social division, address unemployment, which meant more than fighting talk. For there were bridges to be built, a concensus found. The emblematic torch was to be held high, to light a way for one nation. Decline that challenge and others would take it up. See how Labour came back in '45.

Steve pulled him to the present.

"At the hospital, one of the nurses, she went to the South Atlantic on the *Kampala*. It got to her."

Trembath looked askance at his guest. That assessment had been so confidently pronounced. Here was a mature opinion, shaped from interaction rather than in one single concussed adolescent mind. Steve coloured slightly and Hugh eased back. It was a relaxed dialogue he wanted.

"A lot of damaged bodies, a lot of damaged minds," he said gently. "Has she been down to see her? Have you?"
Alan Grigson had taken Steve within thirty metres of the vessel, but the boy wasn't going to say that now, not here.

"She told me she had. Will the ship be here long do you think?"

"Ships brought here are shelved ships, ships without a use....... redundant. For some it's temporary. They're waiting for an upturn in their normal business, or they're waiting for a buyer. With others it can be a wait for a last journey to the breaker's."

"With one last payload to deliver on their way?" ventured Steve. The point stayed in the air. Hugh sallied on

"Sometimes repairs are needed first and they must queue for a berth in a yard. At others the only use is scrap, and again they can be queuing for the yard. After the hospital ship stint she was done up and returned to British India, but then it was back to the South Atlantic as a troopship. I can't imagine anything rougher. Two years ploughing to and fro' between Stanley and Ascension crammed with bored squaddies...... what's she going to be fit for after that?"

"So how many will she have on board now?"

"Six perhaps, no more than eight. I've not spoken to any of them, I've just heard voices, Spanish voices, but that's not so unusual these days."

"Foreign labour being cheaper."

Hugh smiled.

"Look, is somebody paying you to be controversial?" It was a good-natured taunt. Steve took encouragement.

"Now tell me about the Americans," he said. "Give me an opportunity to get truly bolshie." The presence of American military hardware in the UK was very much a live issue. Trident submarines and Cruise missile launching systems were to the fore in the media. Disarmament was being vigorously promoted on both moral grounds and financial.

"As you know, the Americans were here, actually in this house, during the twelve months or so prior to D Day. They took over the area completely. That was how we found ourselves in Plymouth. The war over, they left. We thought they'd forgotten about Carwinion and their pledge to refurbish. Then in the early '50s they were suddenly back in Cornwall. They wanted an airforce base in case they needed to fly bombers or fighters across the pond, somewhere to land for fuel and ammunition. They chose St Mawgan, and they still maintain a corner there..... with warheads stowed away and all sorts. It was when they were doing their place there up that, out of the blue, they were back on our doorstep. Ike stretched his defence budget......"

".......and Carwinion House was once again the family home. End of story, all is straightened out and nicely settled, yes?"

"Except for the Cruise launcher they're wanting to garage in your uncle's barn," quipped Hugh.

Steve found a smile. They'd been seated in the main reception room. Hugh Trembath now rose

"Let me show you this," he said, moving towards a rather handsome upright piano and reaching down to the low, almost matching, chest of shallow drawers that stood alongside. He slid out the topmost drawer and carefully lifted it to the table. Steve stood, expecting to be shown sheet music. That was elsewhere though, for here was a collection of another kind.

There were spent bullets and unspent, there were medals and badges and there were buttons. In an auction catalogue it might have been classed as 'wartime memorabilia'. Hugh explained.

He'd collected almost all of this when as a child he'd been brought to visit the estate by his parents. That was when they'd still lived in Plymouth. They would drive down for the day, and while the state of the House and the farms was assessed he would walk the waterside and the woods gleaning for glint of badge or bullet metal. The winter months had been best, he said, for then the foliage was low and the mud softer to turn. There were still things out there to show up he reckoned, people were still making finds.

"Even of spent bullets?" asked Steve.

"I think they had a practice range," answered Hugh. They must have fired from this side across Lanmouth Creek. I found several in the woods on the other side.... farmwards of that shed over there on the quay."

"And that shed's being used at the moment, is it?" asked Steve. "I've not ventured around there since Easter last year."

"I think it is. If I'm vague it's because I leave it with *Drummond's*, you know, where you saw me the other day. They manage the cottages too. The cottages are offered as summer lets, the shed at no more than two months at a time. The idea is to avoid getting anyone in who might disturb the farming. It wouldn't do to have some one down there running a cash and carry!"

"So who does use that shed?"

"People wanting to store tackle mainly," .... an answer to stimulate rather than satisfy curiosity, and aware of this Hugh promptly served a further portion of history.   "We've always known it as the Viceroy shed. That was the name of the ferryboat run by the poor chap who had the use of the building and its quay during the war and just after. He had one of the cottages too. They were barely habitable then. He used the shed as a workshop. I was always led to believe that the shed took its name from the boat, and that's what I've always told people. It could be though that we've all been misled. This bit I've only found out recently."

"You mention the war, and you speak of 'just after'....... as you did earlier when telling of those memories of the Duke. Can I take it that you can also recall meeting this tenant, and that you feel that he too is amongst the misled?"

"You can," confirmed Hugh. "You've heard me say about our excursions to here from Plymouth. On one of these I actually sought him out. I was eleven, perhaps twelve, and with my boyish curiosity I was trying to find out at least something about what my father had been up to while this place flew a Star Spangled Banner. I've learned a lot since, but at that time no one was saying. My school chums could tell me that my father was making a name for himself in post war Plymouth, and I could tell them of his work for the Duchy back in the '30s and of his early war land husbandry...... but on those late in the war years I had nothing, and that wasn't good. It wasn't comfortable."

"So you thought that this man...."

"....... Rory Duggan he was called, a Liverpudlian, and he'd actually been installed as a tenant by the Yanks......"

"......you thought that this man was the one to know. And was he?"

"He was as much in the dark as I was, but the thing that stuck was his curiosity. On this subject it seemed as active as mine. Strange this, in a fellow who was known for keeping himself to himself. I'd spent days thinking of ways to draw him on the matter, but in the event, once broached, it was like he was wanting to interrogate me!"

"So neither was any good to the other."

"Not then," agreed Hugh. "It was a shame he didn't live for a score or so more years."

"You used the term 'poor chap'. Was this because he met with a untimely end?" Steve was starting to wonder if there might be something in this for Alan.... the human interest angle.

"There was an accident out on the river. Rory Duggan drowned, and when people live on their own, and they go suddenly, like that, it can later seem as if they'd never existed. It happened just a few months later, approaching the Christmas. I wasn't told until Easter when we came down next. By then all had been tidied, the cottage cleared, the *Viceroy* sold. Finding out like that wasn't easy to take. They tried to protect me I suppose........it only made it worse."

"Wasn't there a grave to see? He would have been buried locally surely?"

"You ask these questions and they sound so simple, so natural. I wanted to ask them but I couldn't. It was the way people were then. I did wonder, naturally......a lot at first and then less as the years went on. And then one day, and this was at the ferry where at the time he was working, I heard it from old Jack Butters that this Duggan had been buried down at Mylor. If anyone can be said to have been close to the master of the *Viceroy* then old Jack was he."

"And that boat, what became of her?"

"My father had her auctioned, and she left the estuary. But I did see her again. When I went to Naval College I found her plying between Dartmouth and Totnes, she had a different name but her business was the same. She was a durable tub. She could be there even now."

"The name?....The new one I mean."

" 'Different name' I said. Actually it wasn't new. This is what I've recently had confirmed. It was the *'Ozark'*, and this is what she'd originally been called before she was brought to this country...."

"........from America by the sound of it."

"Yes, she came over on a lend lease destroyer of the same name. She was the ship's tender. Under the terms of the agreement the US names were dropped. In the case of that launch this means painted over. When she went to the Dart the new owner had her stripped down. The old name was revealed, and it was preferred."

"I think I like it better," remarked Steve.

If Hugh Trembath had an opinion he wasn't about to offer it.

"I'll tell you now about Len Hayes," he continued, instead. "This happened about a month ago. I've been on my own since then. You'll be the first to hear."

"Who's Len Hayes?"

"He's an American. He called here unbidden, as I say, about a month ago. He must be about sixty five. For most of the past forty years he's been in commercial refrigeration, in and around Chicago. He's just taken retirement, and forty one years on he's chosen to revisit a few of the places he passed through when on the greatest adventure of his life. He was a part of the Overlord campaign, the invasion and reconquest of Western Europe. Early in '43 he was a member of the advance unit that first moved into here. Their job was to tidy things prior to the arrival of command centre personnel and equipment. He was barely here a month before he was sent home."

"In trouble was he."

"I don't think so. They had a better use for his talents back in Illinois apparently, something to do with recruiting. But they did send him across again, and back here, but that was just a month or so before the fighting."

"Interesting."

"Very. As you can imagine, I was pleased to see him. I showed him around of course, and he was delighted, we both were. But he was intrigued, particularly, by our Viceroy shed, and by the way that name was living on. He could recall the vessel that had originally been the *Ozark*, and he was delighted to hear of the pre lend-lease name having been restored to her. He remembered her as being the *Viceroy* in '44, but in '43 he said she was just an unnamed patrol boat. He'd taken a lift on her down to Falmouth on the morning he'd returned to the States."

"Did he remember the Liverpudlian?"

"Only from his brief second stay. By then Duggan was in the cottage and his name and that of the boat had become watchwords for reliability and efficiency. Already the shed had become the Viceroy shed and it was generally held that that was because there she was garaged."

"Which is what you've said is generally held now. I thought I was going to hear that you'd learned otherwise."

"I was told otherwise by Len Hayes. He said that when they first arrived here in '43, he and two others were detailed to tidy out that shed and that in doing so they came across some old technical diagrams that referred to a *Viceroy* which would have comfortably pre dated Duggan's vessel. From what he saw of them he reckoned it to have been a fairly light craft, one that would have been at home on the estuary."

"Predated by how long?" enquired Steve.

"To before Duggan, who didn't come to Falmouth until '42. To before even the arrival of the lend lease destroyers. They came in '41. I'd say that the shed hadn't been cleared in five years at the least. It sounds like a few people around were asked about this thing, probably including my father- who was away, possibly also his tenants, but this would have gone on while Hayes was back in the States. By the time he returned there was only one *Viceroy*......"

"........that which had once belonged to the *Ozark*."

Hugh nodded. The boy looked thoughtful. "And your father's never mentioned this?"

"No, never had cause to I suppose. Lots of people used that shed before Duggan, lots have since. All sorts have been left behind over the years. Since seeing Hayes I've not had chance to ask him.

"What about old Jack Butters? Asked him about it have you? I could." Steve was trying to be genuinely helpful. He was met by an ill-concealed wariness.

"Jack Butters might be local born, but remember he was away at the back end of the '30s. He was a professional soldier, stationed up country. He came back to these parts in the summer of '40, with the rout of the BEF. He was on the *Lancastria* at St Nazaire. Nasty business that, he was lucky to survive. Thousands didn't. With the injuries he took he was totally out of it for months. When he recovered he took up with Duggan. It's said that he was one of the northerner's few real friends. If Jack had known about an earlier *Viceroy*, then Rory would have too....."

"....and this doesn't appear to have been the case," concluded Steve.

"Let me speak with my father before you go taking this down to Mylor." Hugh was exerting a casual authority. The guest wasn't going to argue. But he had another question ready.

"Did you ask this Mr Hayes about where he thought those drawings might have gone?"

"He told me something like that would have been sent back to Washington."

"Like he was sent back to Illinois I suppose." This wasn't a question from Steve, just a remark, and Hugh was content to let it hang.

There were some sandwiches in the kitchen, 'ready cut,' he said. He rose to fetch them. Steve was left to inspect the drawer of military curios. When the host returned with the food he had a question of his own.

"Have you got that bike back yet?"

"I have, and also my sense of balance, and sense of adventure too. Come the weekend I'm going to be crossing on that ferry and making the most of what's looking like an open ended holiday." Steve was effusive, and this stemmed from alarm. How might he answer if asked how the bike had been collected? Would he be open? Could he prevaricate?

"Pendower again? Your Aunt tells me that that's favourite this year." Steve was pleased to be off the bike, but now the girl loomed. He grasped the nettle.

"Yes, I hope so. You know the cafe there, I was lent a tape by the girl who helps Ralph. She has to be wanting to see me again.......don't you think?"

"Sounds that way, you go for it." Man to man again, but the matiness failed to last. There was a pause, then another probe, "So you found the tape player?"

"I did, it was on the bank where I fell. I went over the other day. I'm still not clear about what happened though."

"It'll come I'm sure." Hugh was relenting. "Listen, this is my month for doing the Sunday shift at the Portscatho station. If you're at Pendower with or without the bike and feel you might be pushed to get back, look across. What is it, five minutes?....The bike can go in the Land Rover. You don't want to be breaking your neck for to get to that ferry. In fact there's a lift both ways should you want. I cross on the 11:30 and I'm there at the station at least until 8."

The offer was acknowledged with due courtesy. The food now consumed, Hugh stood and set to tidying the table. It was a fine afternoon, too fine not to be enjoyed.

They walked across to Trelissick and out onto the sloping meadow that swept down to the head of the Carrick Roads. In the far distance, grey and static in the haze, were the factory ships. Closer, beating towards St. Just under full rig, paced a clutch of working boats, whilst tucked between Mylor Church and Restronguet there swarmed a hive of sailing school dinghies. Trelissick House, so gracefully sited, was behind them.

The Duchy, explained Hugh, was a feudal remnant and Trelissick stood as a totem to the forces which had displaced that old order.....an alliance of big business and high finance. 'Pottery and usery' was his phrase. This sounded glib, but he was under no illusions as to his own modest standing in the scale of these things. The grand House, more than double the size of his, in its Parkland that comfortably accommodated a Bishop's residence, was only a fragment of the total crockery pile. In the context of the whole, Trelissick was but a figurine.

Steve heard that pottery was about clay, an out of the ground commodity which, like cloth, could be cut and coloured and crafted according to need and taste. The product was usefully brittle. Demand was constant and it was world-wide. It had brought real wealth, lasting wealth.

In comparison, Carwinion was little more than mock feudalism, a pocket Duchy purchased on the back of a few boom years in shipping, that run of years just before and during the Great War. Hugh's grandfather had been quick to cheaply gather a small fleet of coasters. The government kept them busy and compensated well the ravages of mine and torpedo.

After the war came the lean years. The fleet was gradually sold. Capital was invested, in the City and on the estate, but there was no return from the land. The best dividend would come from that spent on a university education for Edward. He would need to live by his wits and with the confidence and contacts gained he did.

The opportunist rose. Carwinion survived.....but only just. Had the Americans not honoured their pledge the house could have easily gone the way of so many others. It might now be a country club,or a drinkers' clinic or,... slightly better, a ruin.

And the end game now, for Hugh Trembath and his wife? It was to keep things intact, viable, for it was quietly hoped that if carefully circulated Helen might marry well, or at least well enough, and that a tidily presented Carwinion might count towards such a union.

Carwinion was a challenge, this is what Steve heard. It always had been, and always would be. Its survival waited on marginal considerations, and on events.......on booms and slumps, on elections, on wars and weddings. It had been a compelling listen.

They climbed and crossed to Carwinion. Steve thanked his host and bade farewell. As he strolled down to Lanmouth he thought about Alan and his work. There was material here. What he'd been given he would try to hold in his head.

*

"........then, and this is an intriguing twist, when the Americans moved into the house during the war a job was found for Edward Trembath with his former boss, all the way out in the Bahamas. The Duke had been installed there as the Colonial Governor. Nobody was told of this at the time. The wife and the young child were moved to Plymouth and from the sound of it they knew no more than anyone else. I don't think it came out until after the Duke had died."

Steve was having to lift his voice over the clap of canvas and a fizzing wake. Clear now of Turnaware the *Speedwell* was scurrying southwards under the fresh westerly breeze. They were headed for Mylor and, hopefully, an hour or so with old Jack Butters. Alan, gripping the tiller, watching his trim, glanced back at Trelissick House.

"What about the neighbours up there? How did he get on with them?"

"I'm not sure Alan, and that's perhaps odd given Sir Edward's royal connection and his seat at Westminster. When you talk to his son it's as if Carwinion and Trelissick are on different planets."

"Interesting. What about the local Lord across at Tregothnan, any affinity there at all.......or antipathy?"

"Nothing I've detected. What are you thinking?"

"I'm thinking that the big money and the big titles in these parts may have regarded the man who became Sir Edward Trembath as an irritating little upstart. When those sort of people take that sort of opinion it rarely changes."

"Even after all those years of back bench service?" queried Steve.

"Compliant he's been, certainly" agreed Alan, "and uncontroversial, but remember that what's been orthodox since the war need not have been before. What's the general view on why the Americans chose to requisition Carwinion rather than Trelissick or Tregothnan.....both so much more comfortable?"

"Less of a target for enemy planes....and also, we know now, there was this use to be made of the owner."

"Fair enough," said Alan, now peering ahead. He was working. He had little time for speculation.

They approached Mylor Quay. Steve, steadily learning the ropes, helped lower the sails and then secure the craft against the hard. Alan lifted a bag from the cabin. He checked the contents....the camera, the recording equipment, and the notebook of course.

To reach the cottage they had to follow the creek-side track that went fully to Mylor Bridge. Old Jack lived about half way along. There was no access by car, but it was possible to bring a boat to within fifteen metres of his front door. There was a small quay, but a lot of mud too. Had the tide been more favourable they might have sailed the whole way.

Had they done so they might easily have missed the old man, for as Steve and Alan began the ten minute walk to the cottage Jack Butters, accompanied by his grandson, began towards them in the opposite direction.

Jack Butters had good legs. With patient guidance the track to Churchtown was quite manageable. He would have heard Steve hail them both from a distance, he would have recognised the voice probably, and been interested to hear from his grandson that this time the lad from Bristol was not on his own. It might have been added that this was a pairing seen previously at *The Heron*. It might not, and, if not, maybe this much had been picked up already. His hearing was sharp and it was rare for him to forget a voice, even if heard only on the radio.

With T shirt and jeans young Jack was unmistakably he. Less so was the grandfather. Instead of the customary smock, cords and canvas shoes there was a collar and tie, a tweed jacket and cap, grey flannels, and shoes that shone. Since their purchase there had been shrinkage....in the wearer. The oversize accentuated a frailty, but beneath that cap there was still a shrew like vitality, and it was there in his voice.

"You've caught us on me tie day. You bedderway come 'long too. We'll go back to the cottage later." He moved towards Alan and took a naturally offered arm. "And what is it you do Mr......?"

"Grigson, Alan Grigson. I'm a writer mainly. I do a bit of broadcasting too."

"Thought I might 'ave 'eard that voice. I do's a lot of wireless list'nin'." Both Alan and Steve recalled what the grandson had said at *The Heron.*

"As I've heard from Steve here," said Alan. Even if the old man had his measure, things were best kept cordial. "Is that a regimental tie?"

"I keeps it to wear once a year, an' that's always today."

"Since when?" asked Alan.

"Since 1951, that's 'ow long 'es been gone."

"Who's been gone?"

"Duggan, that were 'is name. I buried 'n 'ere in '51."

"On June 17th, or was that the day he died?"

"I buried 'n in Janree. June 's when we first 'v all meeted. That were back in 1940."

"He served with you then?"

"No 'e were n't no soldier, but 'e were as brave 's any I knew, I'll tell 'e that for certain. On boats is where 'e belonged an' that's 'ow I comed to meet 'n."

"This is good stuff ," said Alan, quite enthused. "If I can hear more of it sometime, and tape it maybe? Was he local this man?"

"He was from Liverpool I think." The answer came from behind them. The following pair had been tracking the dialogue, and Steve it was who'd spoken. Old Jack stopped. Taking his hand from Alan's arm he turned.

"You 'm right enough 'bout that." Confirmed the blind man, and now it was he who was curious. Young Jack passed and walked ahead with Alan. Jack Butters now took Steve's arm and moved more slowly allowing the others to move beyond earshot.

"Some one been sayin' 'bout 'im to you 'ave they?"

"Very recently," replied Steve. "It was Hugh Trembath. He spoke of a Rory Duggan who ran a boat called the *Viceroy*. He rented a cottage and a shed from the estate. He said he died one Christmas when he was a boy, and that some years later it was you who'd told him of a grave here at Mylor. He said you'd been close."

"And 'ow did the talk get on to 'e?"

"I'd asked him about that shed tucked in there between the ferry and Roundwood. The Viceroy shed, he calls it that still. He'd always understood the name to have come from your friend's boat, but last month.... after something like thirty years.... he heard something else."

"From who? From 'is father? From some one local?"

"Far from it. It was a veteran GI, calling at Carwinion for the first time since '44. He'd said there'd been indications that way back before Duggan's *Viceroy* there might have been a previous vessel there of the same name, being built or modified under that same shed roof. Plans had been found. No one could remember it being operated though. I suggested I could ask you."

"An' Hugh Trembath agreed?" It was definitely a question, but Steve fancied it bore a faint note of surprise.

"He said you would have probably been away back then, soldiering. He said he hadn't yet mentioned it to his father, and that he'd prefer to do that first........so don't let on to anyone that I've broached the topic."

"It'll stay under me 'at," said Jack Butters, reaching to remove the same as they approached the Churchyard's waterfront gate.

Young Jack dropped back to escort the blind man through and across to the neatly kept grave. Steve and Alan waited at the entrance. They watched. The grandson moved back against the hedge and Jack Butters stood alone with his memories.... memories of a summer in 1940, of the ten years that followed, and of that drear December day of 1950.

Three minutes was enough. Old Jack was led back to the gate and together the four made back for the cottage. Now the old man was subdued, pensive. He chose to walk with his grandson, little was said between them. Steve and Alan were no less muted. They were taking a lead from the blind man..... all were.

On reaching the cottage the group split. *Flushing Run* rested against the quay, and she became the subject of a discussion between young Jack and Alan. They moved across to the vessel leaving Steve to lead old Jack into his home and through to the favourite chair. Now they were alone, and the old man spoke again as if this were an opportunity. The boy was beckoned closer. Jack Butters was wanting to be sure of Steve's full attention.

"Each year I goes to that grave to re affirm a pledge. 'Tis time now 't were honoured now 'an' you'm the one t'elp see 'tis done."

"A pledge? To do what?" Steve was puzzled.

"A story 'tis, one that needs tellin'. Needs tellin' straight too, an' that's what the waitin's bin 'bout."

"Waiting for me? Is that what you mean?" Steve was even more puzzled.

"Tid'n 'bout you, no. The waitin's bin on events abroad, in Spain to be 'xact, fer that's where 'tis to be told."

"And you think I'm going to Spain?"

"No, but I think you might meet they that is, an' they'm the ones I bin told to use."

"What, holiday makers?"

"Spanish people is what I were thinkin'. I've 'eard there's some on they ships up in the passage."

"So if I run into them what am I meant to say. I've done a bit of French, but never Spanish."

"You just give to they what I give to you, then from our end 'tis all done." Old Jack directed Steve to the fireplace and the cloam set into one side of the chimney. It housed an ageing biscuit tin, one that commemorated the coronation of 1953. Steve was instructed to take it out, and to open it.....but to do this carefully for the contents were irreplaceable.

The tin held scraps of paper. Some were newspaper cuttings. On others there were hand written notes. All were faded with age. The paper was brittle and discoloured.

"And this tells a story?" Steve's question was laced with scepticism.

"Put it in the right 'ands and yes." The answer was sharp. "An it were almost in the right 'ands when Rory was killed. 'E 'ad it ready for a young journ'list who were goin' to run with it. But this wad'n to be, as it turn'd out."

"Because he was killed." Said Steve, meaning Duggan of course.

" 'Ow did you know that?"

"You've just told me."

"When? I said nothin' 'bout Cairns."

"Cairns? Was he the journalist?" The misunderstanding was apparent. "Are you saying he died too?"

" 'E did, over in Korea. I were 'oldin' this stuff for when 'e comed back."

"But he never did."

" 'E never did," old Jack confirmed.

"And since then you've been sitting on this waiting for certain events....... rather than any certain person. And these events...."

"Were set out in there, in a note writ to me by Rory on the day that 'e died. In Spain they were t'appen. I 'ad to wait until Franco were gone, which meant dead, and for there to be proper 'lections, an' press freedom for the people of the north where they 'as their own language."

"And then those people could know I suppose, but know what?"

"They could know that Rory Duggan did 'is very best for 'm, just like 'e did 'is best for me. That 'e were the last person who'd be careless with peoples lives."

"In case anyone should think differently after all these years?" An odd proposition Steve was finding this..... but not one to be taking lightly, for the old man was clearly in earnest. And he had more.

"My promise was for 'ow ever long it took. An' 'mongst they Basque people old mem'ries dies 'ard. Back in '37 I met some of 'm as kids, refugees. They knew oppression alright an' they was stirred. There were plenty cause 'nough then for resentment to last into gen'rations to come."

"And the vicious streak is in this ETA thing. They're busy even now." Steve paused to consider. "They were n't after your friend then were they? Hugh Trembath said his death was an accident. Might there have been more to it? An element of ...."

"..........retribution? No, not retribution. I'm def'nite there."

"So you had this quiet and capable man of Liverpool origin settling here, and obviously making a good impression with the Yanks who came here towards the end of the war. They equip him to run his ferry service, and he does this whilst all though time carrying an abiding concern for the people of the Northern province in Spain, the Basques."

" 'Is concern come to be more for their good opinion, 'n this 'cos 't were 'is last throw t'wards puttin' 'is own rep'tation t'rights, 'is own rep'tation 'ere. If the tale 'e 'ad could be printed in Spain then aft'wards it might be printed in Liverpool, an' 'roun' 'ere too 'course."

"Talk about going a round the houses...! This is 1985."

"In they days people thought Franco were on borrowed time, an' Rory were no 'xception. As 'turned out t'were more of 'n extended credit."

"But what about our own British press......so famously free?"

" 'That were 'is first choice, but only if Francis Cairns were there t'andle it should anythin 'appen. Rory died, Cairns died. I just do's as I were told, an' I'm still alive."

"OK, so you're only following instructions, but why me? This could have been a task for Young Jack, surely."

"Six months ago I would 've asked 'n. 'E were on the ferry then an' it's one of the perks to run erran's for they people up there in the ships. But 'e's moved on now an' there's others doin'it. We got to stay clear 'n' let'n. You 'm alright cos you do'nt belong. You'm 'ere today, gone tomorrow. One off 'tis', an that's the point. Us don't 'ave t'understand, nor do us 'ave t'explain. All we'm asked to do 's 'and the stuff on to they who just might."

"So I'm not to try and piece it together, and I'm not to tell anyone?"

"I've 'ad to tell you. You might 'ave to tell others. It be up to you. Look at what you got there. Get to know somethin' of the man an' somethin' of 'is cause. The more you know the more you'll wish t'find out, 'n not just from me. Do what you think's right. An' if that means you bring it back 'ere 'gain then so be it. I'd just 'ave to try 'nother that's all. I don't want 'e to feel forced. Talk t'others in a careful way an' you'm goin' t' find out more than I've time t' tell 'e t' day, p'rhaps more even than I knows meself. There's more in there than Rory ever fathomed, 'n more than I ever will. "

Young Jack clattered in.... but looking strangely meek, thought Steve, briefly. Alan was behind. Intimacy was broken. It was suddenly a crowded room. Alan's attention was drawn to the radio, and he was quick to engage the host on the topic of reception quality. Then the old man began to tire. All noticed, and when Alan was invited to return any time he wished, either alone or with Steve, the two guests were not slow in following the grandson to the door.

In no time they'd strolled back to the *Speedwell*. Alan had set a brisk pace. If he'd been tempted to question Steve about the tin he'd acquired this hadn't shown. The boy wasn't disposed to explain the contents. For a worthwhile attempt he would need first to consider the whole, and do this alone in his own time. Alan appeared to sense this.

Likewise there was a reticence on his own part to speak, at this moment anyway, of what had passed between him and the grandson whilst they'd been looking over the working boat. There was tacit agreement. They could concentrate on the sailing, on getting the sloop across to Restronguet Point. That was where Steve could be dropped. It would be an easy walk then through Feock, up to Carwinion, and then down to the farm.

As they approached Restronguet Passage a powerful launch emerged from the creek onto the main estuary. It surged across their bow, taking and ruffling their water, its engine growling against the filling tide. It was a substantial vessel, long and low, with a forward wheelhouse. Sturdy, dirty, it looked to be on business, but not that of taking passengers or fish. The helmsman, also sturdy, businesslike, looked resolutely ahead offering not so much as a glance towards the sailing vessel he'd crossed so imposingly. From the stern there trailed a cloud of exhaust. It almost obscured the name, but not quite. It was noted separately by Steve and Alan. Neither had any comment.

Steve was put ashore. Alan took the Lanmouth phone number. He'd be in touch he said. The *Speedwell* was turned. It headed seawards. Steve climbed northwards, making for the farm.

*

Steve was in his room even before his Aunt and Uncle had retired. He made space on the floor, he lifted down the bedside lamp and knelt. The contents of the tin were tipped on to the mat. He knew Rory Duggan already. He intended to find out more.

He learned first that old Jack's role had not been passive. There was more here than he'd been given. Steve could make an initial sort between what Rory Duggan had left and what Jack Butters had decided to add after his friend's death.

In the second category there were definitely two items, both newspaper cuttings. There was one from the local weekly -*The West Briton*. This reported the formal inquest into Rory's death, held in Truro some three months after his death. The other was taken from a National daily, *The News Chronicle*. It was an obituary for Francis Cairns, killed in Korea some six months later.

Most of the rest could be assumed to be from Rory himself. There were two letters type written to him from The Board of Trade. Both had been sent in 1941. They were fastened together by a rusty staple, and this attached also a third document.... slightly smaller it was, and hand written.

It was of letters and figures rather than words. The writing was small and understandably faded, but what was clear enough were two dates.....successive days early in June 1937. If written at that time then of all the items saved this would be the earliest.

The scribe had turned the page through ninety degrees so as to accommodate twelve rows of capital letters, with exactly forty in each. In each of the rows the letters had been marshalled into ten groups of four, and after the second row they were sufficiently spaced to allow a correspondingly grouped line of numbers to be entered beneath each. The first line of letters was prefixed by a swastika. The first line of numbers was prefixed by two lower case letters, a 'u' and a 'v'.

At the end of the bottom most line of figures the word 'VICKERS' had been printed, and immediately beneath that, 'AIRSPEED'.

Two other documents remained, again these were newspaper cuttings, and again from after the war. They might have been gathered by Duggan or by Jack, but as each of them predated the former's death they were probably best regarded as a part of his legacy.

The clearest and most substantial of these was an article from a Plymouth weekly -*The Sunday Independent.* Fascinatingly it told of Edward Trembath, then seeking selection as a Conservative parliamentary candidate for what was later to be his Plymouth constituency. Mentioned too was Mrs Ida Copeland, then the owner of Trelissick House near Truro.... the estate that neighboured the subject's pre-war home.

The last cutting was smaller and much less well preserved. It included a grainy and much faded press photograph. The piece was from an Irish newspaper, *The Limerick Examiner.* It told of the intention of Sir Oswald Mosley, the charismatic and arguably far sighted British pre war politician, to settle in the west of Ireland. There was a brief resume of his closely intertwined political and matrimonial careers, and mention too of his internment during the war and the subsequent time spent in France. The photograph, the article claimed, showed its subject 'electioneering between the wars.'

Alongside the article, inked into a now frail margin, were a few indistinct words. An attempt might have been made to over mark perhaps a pencilled original, but it had been with only qualified success for the ink had soaked and spread to a near blot. There were certainly three words, there may have been as many as five. Also, going by an obvious first two, *'El Hombre......'* they were Spanish. 'The man' Steve knew, but beyond that he could just as well have been attempting to decipher ancient Greek.

This was something for a linguist to peruse under a far better light, or maybe a native under the bright Spanish sun. From what Jack had said, this would surely have been the intention, so what he was holding was the meagrest of covering notes. Clearly Butters still expected it to mean something to someone.... and it wasn't his place to reason otherwise.

It was clear that the package had been assembled so as to tell a story, one that would amount to a refutation, a vindication. That much was apparent from the two Board of Trade letters.

This was another cause, reflected the boy. First the girl's, now the old man's, but with this he had no brief to investigate. He merely had to convey, and he would enquire as to how he might pass these fragments on..... but he would do so carefully. He could expect to stumble upon others with long memories. A generation's worth of years had passed. Much might have been forgotten, but more might have emerged, and even more might yet. He had eyes and ears of his own, and they were young and they were sharp.

*

It had been arranged that Ralph Bartlett should collect Steve off the ferry. The youngster would cross as a foot passenger and climb the near 200 metre turn to the Tolverne slip road. This was broad, having been made so by the American war machine in '43. There was ample room for Ralph's Ford Transit van. He could reverse around and wait.

The first crossing of the day carried a light load. Steve had attempted to linger near the new deckhand......young Jack's replacement. He'd hoped for any kind of conversation that might perhaps have been turned to the ship which stood so quietly above the ferry, a pale shape in the river mist.

But this was no Jack Spargo. This man was curt, surly almost. Foot passengers were unwelcome on the car deck. That was his domain.

Steve had looked up at the *Kampala*. So near she was. There had to be a way, even if not via this ferry.

Ralph had walked down as far as the fateful bend. No one could be more local, more familiar with the vista of river and woods, ships and ferry, and yet even for him it held enduring fascination. They walked up to the van together. They would need to collect Jane and then drive into St Austell to the wholesaler. The fruit, it was explained, would be taken on sale or return, the supplier being pleased to move some of his riper produce before the start of a fresh week. From St Austell it was less than ten minutes back to Polgooth.

The van was briskly up and out of the valley. Down they rattled through Philleigh, past *The Roseland Inn* and the small towered church beyond. Jane lived outside the village almost opposite its remote and now disused chapel. The house, set back from the road, was substantial. There was a paddock alongside, but no longer was there a pony. Like the yacht, it had been sold. Hens scratched around the loose box, and against the far fence, comfortably spaced, sat three touring caravans. Pennies counted.

Jane stood at the gateway entrance, head up, smiling. She was certainty itself. Her father should be out and he would be out. It would happen. She would make it happen. Each new day offered opportunity for advance, and this day's would be taken.

Camera, light meter and film case hung holstered from her shoulder. The freedom fighter was armed. She climbed in, joining the driver and Steve on the bench seat. She and the boy shared the passenger's seat belt, the camera being placed at their feet.

They dropped to the Fal at Tregony and climbed through the length of the village. They passed the Roseland School, the local comp from where Jane hoped to take a clutch of straight 'A's. Ralph spoke of the old school, the augmented elementary he'd attended before leaving at fourteen. It was gentle route filling nostalgia, until he was momentarily stalled by a question from Steve.

"I was reading the other day about a Mr Francis Cairns, a journalist, one of a number killed in Korea. It said that he came from the Roseland. He could have been about your age. Was he at school with you?" There was a pause, for Steve a tense moment. And then.....

"Francis Cairns," repeated Ralph, "now that's a name I hadn't heard in a long while. Fancy you coming out with that one. We were together at what you'd now call Primary School. He was a year younger, but clever, in a lively way. He passed his eleven plus. He went to Grammar, in Truro."

"But you followed his career later on?" continued Steve, sensing interest also from his left.

"I would read his stuff, in the locals and then the national. It's always a shame when someone that age goes, but he was destined for great things. He might even have been big on TV. He had something of the Pilger about him."

"What about family, any still about?" The question was casually put.

"He was an only child and the parents weren't young. They'd be dead now. There was a fiance though and she was local too. Afterwards she went away..... upcountry. Found herself a new chap. No doubt they married, built themselves a future."

Steve was confident that he had the woman's name. The obituary had stated its subject to be engaged and against that paragraph, in the margin, a pen had been taken to carefully print 'Linda Adams.' This would have been Old Jack's work. There was no reason now to mention her, indeed there was no reason to divulge his possession of the obituary. For the moment he was content with what he'd heard. He'd trawled..... modestly, yes, but with significant success. He'd chosen his person well, his moment well, and his place well. The calmly offered morsel had been taken and here was increase at no cost. This was the game. He'd shown himself he could play. He awaited the obvious response and Ralph duly delivered.

"Cairns, Francis Cairns. Where did you find that name for goodness sake?"

"Last week Hugh Trembath showed me around his pile. Along with the guided tour came a potted history of the dynasty. Later I was shown a newspaper cutting. It had been taken from a Plymouth paper, one printed back in 1950. The piece had their neighbour of then recommending Hugh's father to the voters of Plymouth North. I've met Sir Edward, I'd heard of the neighbour, Mrs Copeland. The new name was that of the journalist who'd submitted the piece. It was mentioned that his day job was down here in Falmouth, with the *Packet*."

Steve's words, carefully chosen, casually voiced, implied that he'd been shown this cutting by Hugh. It was a trick. It worked.

"Ida," said Ralph. "Yes I recall her too. I've been told she was an active upcountry politician before the war, an MP even, but after, when she came down here, it was very rare for her to venture into partisan matters. By then her penchant was for honorary roles........ the figurehead thing. She was a top table person for the likes of the Girl Guides, and the Red Cross.... or was it the St John's? Anyway, that sort of thing is about being above the adversarial hurly-burly."

"The good neighbour approach," suggested Steve. "And she's dead now?"

"Long gone," confirmed Ralph, "best part of twenty years. Any other names? Try me again."

"Rory Duggan?" Ventured Steve. "Lived on the estate...."

"....... until that dark, cold evening when he was careless enough to fall into the river." Ralph was happy to relate this as simple fact. "It was him one year and Francis the next, I think."

"So this would have been around the time when the young journalist produced his piece about Sir Edward," said Jane smartly. The girl had been listening. Ralph nodded.

"He was a good man, Rory. Some said otherwise, but I speak as I found. He was certainly good on the water."

"But otherwise....?" Probed Steve.

"There was this rumour," explained the driver. "It had been whispered about, that during the war he'd been drummed out of the merchant service. He'd been a seaman, a radio operator it was said. Experienced he was, and able, but the convoy people weren't having him. There was an accusation that he'd betrayed the position of his ship to German submarines."

"A hanging matter, I would have thought," commented the girl.

"During the war, where proven," responded Ralph, "but this, I think, was supposed to have happened before..... at the time of the Spanish war, and I doubt if it was ever proven. It took about five years to emerge, only coming out when we were really up against it in the North Atlantic. True or not they simply weren't going to risk him."

"But the Yanks had every confidence in him, that's what I've gathered at Carwinion," said Steve. "So that has to be telling us something."

"You mean about Rory Duggan, or about the Yanks?" quipped Jane.

"Or about Carwinion," added Ralph, his gentle chuckle rewarding the girl's attempt to lighten the exchange. Steve had heard enough. He was helping Jane and he was helping old Jack, and if he was to keep any control the causes were best addressed separately.

"Now that's Polgooth isn't it?" He was pointing away to their right, to a derelict ridge top engine house, still some miles distant.

"And that's where we're going," confirmed Ralph, "but first St. Austell."

The twisting Roseland road brought them to Hewas Water and the main A390 Truro-St. Austell highway. As they slowed for the junction their smooth progress was suddenly interrupted. It was an encounter, sudden, and done in an instant.

Without warning a motorcycle, large and loud, swung off the main westbound carriageway. Taking a wide line it was there before them, beneath them it seemed. Ralph, who'd edged to the crown, stamped at the brake. The van lurched to the left. The youngters braced themselves and the inevitable.... did not occur.

There was no collision. Not even did they make contact. The rider had the power there, and using all he'd leant in, and with throttle open he was across, he was clear. For a second they were in a sound box, the van metal amplifying the exhaust, and that was it. For a moment it was all, and then in the next, nothing. It was gone.

Jane swivelled, knocking Steve against Ralph's arm as he groped for the gear to bring them to the halt lines.

"That was him," she said, "I said to you about him on the phone. That's how he rides. You must have....."

"I have seen him, it's come back." Steve spoke through his hands. They were together over his face. "He did this by the ferry, on the bend there, where I fell. No warning, middle of the road, right in front of me, and then away at the last moment, with the noise, that same noise. And then I was on the bend, at the edge of the bend, and before I knew it, over."

"And you were in the middle of the road on that hill?" Ralph's question carried censure. He was on the main road now and back to cruising. This driver was Cornish, and long hardened to the near miss.

"And playing the Walkman!" deduced Jane, correctly.

"But I did wait at the top, and the traffic came up from the ferry, and that usually leaves a clear road," pleaded Steve.

"So if he came over on the ferry he must have been hanging back," said Ralph.

"*If* he came over on the ferry...," repeated Jane, with emphasis. "I've seen him forward and back past our place inside of an hour."

"And I've yet to see him on my side," added Steve. The black clad rider was becoming a man of mystery.

"Milk Tray is it, or would he be delivering Black Magic?" Ralph's humour was again timely. But Alan might have a view thought Steve, because he'd said about hearing something that evening and it had to have been that machine, with that man.

"And he was the one who called out the rescue."
This from Jane, neither statement nor question, was serious.

"I must ask him sometime. I expect I'll be running into him again." Steve had caught Ralph's levity. He smiled as he spoke. The others laughed.

Polgooth stands on what is left of a volcano of tin. This ridge, thickly loded, stream gouged, drew the ancient tinners who having sieved the silt then tunnelled up into the valley sides. Then came steam. Shafts were sunk and deeper galleries driven. A thousand worked here in 1800...... miners, and also surface workers to tend the stamping and the smelting of the ore.

Great Polgooth was the making of St Austell. The drilling and the hosing for kaolin, so prominent now to the north of the town had been then but a diversification. And then the mining for metal ceased, the population drifted away leaving their cottages and mills as quarry for close on a century's worth of scavenging hedge makers and the road menders. A few dwellings survived and now they attract care and also neighbours as they've become the nucleus for the more modern non estate bungalows and houses which now make up the greater part of present day Polgooth.

Above, with its lowered heaps and filled hollows, the Common had become the site of Polgooth's fayre. It was so easy here to set up a stage, indeed several stages, for almost any purpose whether it be entertainment- simple or complex - or just plain selling. There was the gorse and the bramble, and the engine house ivy, and also the hint of gothic in the ruin itself. Beyond, in the distance, were the peaks of shining quartz. Here there was scenery and there was shelter. It just needed imagination, and with some half decent weather an audience would flock.

Ralph brought colour, and youth too. He had apples and pears, peaches and cherries, and strawberries of course, and with all this the two youngsters, and they would be part of his stall, helping to serve.

Ralph and Steve did the first shift. Jane scouted the site. In 20 minutes she was back for the camera and away again, mingling amongst the performers and their watchers, amongst the sellers and their buyers. Every cause was there and every movement in taste too whether this be for food, furnishing, or faith. There was a pot pourri of scents, and likewise of music, all blending gently under the softest of breeze. Harmony suffused the scene. This was more than an event. It was a rite.

Jane was back with burgers for lunch and two films used. It was groups that she'd focussed on rather than individuals. 'Likely liaisons' was her term, that's what she was hoping to capture, but they were having to be taken from a discrete distance and she impressed this on Steve. She gave the boy a brief lesson in loading the camera and adjusting its settings, then he too set forth.

He was drawn to the performers rather than to those who peddled and purchased wares. He'd known Bath during festival week. Counter culture had to be financed. Fringe art was sustained by fringe economy. He watched a theatre group amusingly rework the story of Tristan and Isolde -the local legend of obsessive love, of passion becoming a deadly addiction, a poison. And how well the hero fell, and how far.

And then dancing, to traditional tunes in traditional dress, as it might have been stepped here a century and a half before. He moved along. He gathered leaflets. Come to the flea market at Truro, to the museum at Charlestown, and to the Flambards theme park, 'Come to Jesus' even.

He took the hit as he loaded a second film. The assailants came from behind. The enveloping hug clamped his arms. A palm slapped onto his mouth. He was dragged back and he was between tents. He couldn't breath. The camera went and the film case too. And then he was inside a tent, pushed through a side wall, one loosely fastened, and he was rolling. Too breathless to shout, too shocked to explain, he was helped on to his feet.

He pushed to the door, and he was out and searching, but of course to no avail. The camera was lost. It had been taken, snatched.

He'd failed. What could he do now? What could he say? He

returned to the van. Ralph saw him first and weighed the situation in an instant. These were children, they were in his care.

"You've been mugged son. That's serious. I'll get the police. You're a victim. They must act."

"I'm not hurt," said Steve. He was shaking though. He looked at Jane. He read her alarm. It wasn't at the loss of the camera, nor at the rough treatment he'd taken. "Not the police, not yet."

"But the insurance. You'll need a report for the claim," said Ralph. He and Steve looked at Jane. She would have to answer to her mother. She was shaking her head. "Well I'm going to have to get you back, both of you. Either my advice counts for something or we go home."

"Then take us back." Jane was firm. "If things were different then yes, of course the police, but you know how it is. For the moment we're on different sides."

It was a subdued trio that dismantled the stall. The others knew that Ralph was losing time and losing takings, but there was no resentment. He was firm too. His concern was real. With a sense of leaving a lively party early they wove a way to the lower exit. With the main access still clogged it was decided there that their return should, for the first part at least, be by a different route.

Ralph struck southwards into the maze of lanes behind Mevagissey. By bearing right at Heligan they could rejoin the Roseland road at Fair Cross. On a normal day it would take appreciably longer, but not so on a Fayre day.

Some stretches were narrow. They'd gone no more than a couple of miles when they had to stop and reverse. Where two cars might have slid by, the Transit and a small box backed hire truck faced stymie. Ralph obliged. Jane watched the near side clearance, and as they backed it was only Steve who was looking along the road ahead.

As the hire truck neared he recognised the lone driver. It was the ferry hand, he who'd been so uncharming earlier, Jack Spargo's successor.

Though wanting in width the lane here was quite straight, and as the hire truck drew closer to its hedge a good 150metres of third class highway was revealed beyond. Another van appeared, a Bedford CF in ex Gas Board blue and white. It ought to have slowed and then closely followed the preceding vehicle to and through the passing place into which Ralph was deftly reversing. It didn't though. No sooner had it appeared than it was itself retreating. Its driver was finding a gateway of his own, and needlessly for the CF was clearly narrower than the vehicle it followed. From where Steve sat it was a statement of dissociation. If he was deliberately following then the second driver didn't want the first to know, or he didn't want Ralph to. Why? Steve wondered, silently.

The initial impasse solved Ralph moved forward again, to where a gateway offered the carefully tucked CF and the cautiously moving Transit ample clearance. As they slipped past Steve was able to recognise too the second driver.

"The guy in the Bedford," he said. "Tell me about him. I know he has a boat. I saw him out with it only the other day....over by *The Pandora.*"

"Jim Prout that is," began Ralph, "and the boat....."

".......The *Spartan,*" Jane interjected.

"......is a kind of floating forge," continued the driver. "Mr Prout makes and he mends, usually for boat people, and not only for yachtsmen, for fishermen too, and the tripper skippers. Metal, that's what he'll fix, and if he can't get the part he'll make it."

"Lots of irons in lots of fires," Jane put in again. "Never short of work."

" And based where?" asked Steve.

"He lives over in Devoran and that's where he keeps the boat. He has a van like this and a workshop up on Carnon Downs -near the mine, where he worked for a while I believe. Useful to know he is. I had him over the winter before last. I needed some fresh tin on the cafe roof. He found it, he fixed it fine. Did your father ever use him Jane?"

"Don't think so. I've seen him down at Percuil though."

"So why then the hire truck, and why the ferry hand driving it?" Ralph's question was for both youngsters. They'd been quiet under their weight of worry. He wanted them to speculate. It could be a relief he thought.

The response though was stilted. Where in other circumstances there might have been a torrent of suggestion there was now an excruciating silence. Steve felt for Ralph. The man had meant well, he could see that.

"Parts for the ferry?" The boy's answer was as limp as it was logical.

"And they would be too big, too heavy for his own vehicle," this, from Jane, was better. It was deductive. Steve looked ahead to where water seeping from a hedge had dampened the road. Near side tyre marks indicated twin wheels.

"And he'd be headed for....?" Ralph wasn't letting up.

"St Austell or anywhere east of ," suggested Steve, far from inspired.

"Odd then that we should meet him down here. Wouldn't you expect them to use the main road?" Ralph was making it into a game, but the two were reluctant to play. Another silence followed, protracted, close to being oppressive. Ralph had to break it himself. "And they'll be saying just the same about us no doubt."

Jane let a weary head drop against Steve's shoulder. He brushed her crown with his temple. There were no more words, not until they approached the girl's house. Ralph tried to insist that he should go in with her, but she just wanted it to be her and Steve. They'd made adult choices and they'd erred. A paternal presence wasn't needed. Ten minutes, Jane reckoned, and the boy would be out and needing to be taken on to the ferry. Ralph agreed to stay with the van at the road entrance.

Jane led the way. Steve followed, sheepishly. They entered by the side kitchen door, that to which the caravan clients came for water and eggs. Entering, Jane called to her mother.

But then she stopped........ transfixed. Steve stumbled against her. She turned and glared at him, and read instantly that he too had seen and was no less amazed than she. This was no trick of his, but what then could it be? There on the kitchen table was the camera.

Jane's mother appeared from the inner hallway. Composed, she was and this was as well for the youngsters were dumbstruck.

"Well done, you're back, two of you as well. Pleased to meet you young man, Steve isn't it? I thought I was going to be denied the pleasure. When I saw you'd left the camera I assumed that you'd perhaps rushed off to get that ferry. I heard the door but I wasn't quick enough. Next time though, Jane, don't just drop it here in the middle of the table. Anyone could come in and take it. It's too valuable a thing to leave about."

Jane turned to Steve, speechless still. The relief was tangible. Jane wasn't going to correct her mother, that was obvious, and that suited Steve.

He remembered his manners.

"And I'm very pleased to meet you Mrs Byrne. We've been really lucky with the weather today. That was a first for me, going to Polgooth. It was good to be part of the event rather than just looking on."

"Well there's a ferry in fifteen minutes," said Jane, glancing at the kitchen clock, "and Ralph's very kindly waiting."

"Phone me," said Steve, and he left. To the man in van he looked chastened and subdued. In fact he was bewildered.

It was as much as he could do to thank Ralph on being set down above the slip. Back at the house Jane had checked the camera. All was there, all was intact........ except that there was no film, not in the camera, not in the case.

*

"O.K. Kate, just let me get it straight. You're up at the hospital doing what you do there......... working, and it's in the middle of the night, and this character who we've spoken to just the once breezes into the place and says to you that he wants some help with work that he's got on, and that he thinks that you're the person to give it. He doesn't say what the work is, but he wants you to start right away -this evening, even though you're on the two 'o' clock shift again tonight."

"Yes Jeremy," said Kate, wearing pyjamas still and emerging from the kitchen area holding a mug of coffee. "And I said to him 'yes why not', and he's expecting me, and you've just got to accept that." This was straight talking, and she sensed that it was hurting...... something she didn't want.

She took a sip, and then continued in a softer tone. "Look, I'll be happy to tell you more when I know more. Tonight he wants me for four hours at the most. After that he might not want me again. Or it might be me that decides that I've had enough. Tonight though I'm committed."

"And this is across at the St Erme Country Club........ very select."

"Yes, and there will be a taxi calling to take me there and one to bring me back to the hospital later."

"So what am I meant to do whilst you get tarted up in your finest for that smarmy lot?"

"You can please yourself Jeremy. It's not for me to decide for you, anymore than it's for you to decide for me. But that's not to say I'm not interested, or I don't care, or I'm not grateful. Now it's going to take me a couple of hours to get ready and I don't want that time to be spent bickering. I don't know much more about this Alan bloke than you do. Whatever his game is I'd say he was playing it by ear, and that means I'm having to as well."

"What about that kid he was with, where does he fit into all of this?"

"I'm sorry, again I just don't know. I'm not sure that he even fits in anywhere. He wasn't mentioned last night."

Jeremy Barnes shrugged. He reached for his jacket. He would be in Camborne for the evening, he declared, and maybe for the whole night if he drank too much, and that was as likely as not, given the way he felt. He had friends there from work. They could be relied upon to be accommodating.

With this he was gone, and that was all right by Kate. She would have time now. She would also have space.

Why had she agreed to this? She wasn't sure. She'd half hoped, half expected that this man would come to her at the hospital, and when he actually did, and asked .... it just seemed the natural thing to agree.

*

"What about Ralph," queried Steve. "Might he have had reason to thwart our intentions?"

"Ralph is sound." Jane was emphatic. "I trust him no less than I trust Dad. I can't allow myself to think otherwise." She was now ten minutes into the promised call and only with this did Steve hear her familiar self-sure self. Yes, the camera was there and it was intact, but there were those missing films. This was disturbing, perhaps more so than straightforward theft.

For this was no random mugging. He'd been seen and he'd been selected, and selected on the basis of a particular activity he'd been pursuing, and possibly because he'd been assisting a particular person. Maybe the girl's mother was in some way moving to curtail her daughter's activities? That was a bizarre thought, and one he didn't dare broach, not now.

"I know that you're playing for real Jane," he said. "But when you took me along today you had no idea that the game might get rough. I'm sure of that. You hadn't anticipated danger, but now, after this, you must. Things might get rougher still, that's what you'll be thinking now, and if you want to heed the warning shot and off load me then well and good. Your decision, take as long as you want. Perhaps if we hold back for a few days things might emerge. We might have a clearer picture."

"Well I'm at Pendower tomorrow," said Jane, defiant again at the last. "Come over if you want. You know where to find me."

*

Live jazz, modern, cool, faintly decadent, oozed from the windows of the compact function suite. Outside, looking in, a figure moved amongst the trees. Now he could see her, just a glimpse, and that fragment of conversation was her voice.

She wasn't part of a group. It was just the one man, but not Alan Grigson. This person was younger, smarter. The place was small, it was select, and here was one who was in his element. He was monopolising, and Kate was letting him, seemingly enjoying his attentions. She was at ease, he could see, he could hear.

At a quarter past midnight the pair rose to leave. Keeping to the shadows the watcher moved towards the door. He saw them emerge. Kate had taken the man's arm, and was being guided towards a sleek and gleaming XJ6. This guy had money. He had poise. He had position. It was the smoothest of departures. The watcher felt rough, a sneak.

If Grigson was about then he had to appear now. But he didn't and the figure drew back towards the entrance gate and then away to his own vehicle, parked discretely beyond. He would need to drive past the gate, and he did so without slowing, and without even so much as a sideways glance in. There was someone else there, one who'd momentarily moved out from the even deeper shadows. A second figure........ missed by the first.

*

Steve heard the downstairs clock chime a muffled one. He'd had no sleep. If the girl wanted to be defiant then OK, but it wasn't she who'd endured a week's hospitalisation with a roughing up to follow. The Roseland, hitherto the adolescent's playground was suddenly revealed in a more sinister light. He couldn't share Jane's confidence in Ralph. The whole day had passed without mention from him of Joe's whereabouts...... and this was unusual. Could this mean that he'd been at hand, watching, waiting, and that it had been he who had pounced? Yes, Ralph had suggested that the police be notified, but this would have been the safest of bluffs. Jane was never going to have that.

And then there was the motorcyclist. Another mystery man......a black rider. Steve rebuked himself. What next, trees that talked? He was inventing bogeymen! Yes, he would cross to Pendower in the morning. He would show that he too was undaunted. But he needn't travel alone. Tomorrow was Sunday. There was a lift.

With this resolved then maybe he could at last sleep, but not yet. For outside in the night there grew a sound that was extra to the constant steady hum of the milk cooler. It came from beyond, from out of the distance. It was a motor, and it belonged to a vehicle......one that strained and then idled as if through a narrow uneven lane. Diesel, definitely, and probably a truck, it was moving away now to the north of the farm.

Steve slipped from his bed and crossed the landing to the bathroom. He leant from the window. Now it was clearer and he could see the faint slow moving glow. Hedge shielded it was following the lane towards Roundwood quay, seeking its way eastward along the few hundred yards worth of lane visible by day from this side of Lanmouth Farmhouse. This was more than rare. For Steve it was a first. He'd seen tractors in the lane, and the occasional Land Rover or van, and sometimes in the winter this might be just after dark...... but he'd never known it to be used so deep into the early hours.

It was too much to take in, too much to think about. It was too late, too dark. He was too tired, too alone. All he wanted now was sleep.

*

Incessant rain, beating in from the sea it drummed across the cafe roof. Murky cloud hurried northward. It would be a slow morning. The first customer of the day was, as yet, the only customer. He was kitted for a brisk coastal ramble. He occupied two chairs, the second being taken by a heavy-duty kagoul which dripped raindrops onto the seat and the floor beneath.

A mug of hot chocolate had been ordered, served and slowly sipped. A mid market Sunday tabloid had been eased from the kagoul and a spawn of supplements was spreading over the table. For twenty minutes now he'd been sitting, sipping, and slowly sifting his way into the newspaper. Ralph had left after fifteen and still the customer's eyes were staying with the print, even as he reached for and raised the mug.

Eventually he stood, swilled the dregs and turning away from the counter downed a last sludgy mouthful. The paper he re assembled, but it was not re-pouched. He turned.

"Can you use this?" he asked. "I've carried it far enough, someone else could be interested maybe?"

"I can't insist that you take it away," Jane smiled as she spoke. The smile was returned. "Thank you," she added. "That's kind."

The man approached the counter.

"I'll pay now for the chocolate, and I also owe you for two reels of film." The girl was stunned, embarrassed. And there was trepidation too.

"Who are you? You know something....... how much?"

"Enough to share a belief in your father's innocence. And enough to know that if I let you carry on as you are then there's danger ahead, for you, for your friend, and for others too..... me included. "

"Are you with the law? Can you get him out? Dad I mean?"

"To your first question, yes I am a law man, but not with the local police. It's a bigger set up I'm part of, and more specialist. Their patch is Devon and Cornwall, our remit can take us across the length of Europe. To your second enquiry I've got to say 'not me'. That's a decision for others. But those others can, and they will if they have sufficient good information, and that's what I try to provide."

"Go on," said Jane, the two words being as many as she could muster.

"It's suspected that your father could be mixed up in something a lot bigger, probably unknowingly. We're out to get to the bottom of it all, if we can and if we're allowed to. For the moment the local force isn't aware of our efforts. They don't need to be."

"Then you took a risk yesterday with that mugging."

"Not really, we were assessing you as a risk Jane, and also Steve. Because you didn't report you get the green light. You pass, and today here I am."

"So you know our names then?"

"And quite a bit more besides."

"A bit rough on my friend though weren't you? Snatching the camera off him like that. Necessary was it?"

"You needn't worry too much about Steve. He wasn't hurt, and anyway he and I are already acquainted..... not that he was in on it at all. You can trust him still, it's just that we've happened to have met in a different capacity. Tell him nothing of this. He'll learn what he needs to from me in due course. So long as he's not misused he's happy enough under your direction. Today it's essential that I bring you under mine. He can be useful to both of us then, separately, without conflict."

"He's not stupid you know," asserted Jane.

"I know that, and neither are you. And that means you'll leave it to me to determine how much he gets told, and when. I'm trusting you with this Jane, as you must trust me."

"Can you say how long?"

"How long for......?"

".........for my father in that prison"

"Don't know, but he's going to have to stay put for a while yet. Uncomfortable yes, but safe..... more so than you or I."
Jane took for the chocolate. The films were forgotten.

"So are you going to trust me with a name?" asked Jane as he was turning to leave.

"Alan," he said, "and you'll be hearing from me soon."

*

"Yes, of course I can give you a lift. It's hardly cycling weather. You'll be in the back though this time. Prout's coming across too. While

I'm on watch he'll be bringing the Land Rover back and giving it a touch up. I parked it in Truro the other morning and when I got back there was a scratch almost the length of the driver's side." Hugh Trembath opened the rear door on the driver's side and as Steve moved around to climb in the damage became clear. He ran his finger a little way along the dig. Low and level it was, wheel arch to wheel arch and a little extra towards the back.

"Nasty one ," the youngster commented.

"But not nasty enough to bother my insurer. Prout's got the kit, and the paint's arrived. I know he'll do a good job."

"Not out in this rain surely?"

"He's got a workshop up by Wheal Jane," explained Hugh, stepping up into the driving seat and sliding behind the wheel. There was one last security conscious glance back at the House and then they were away, this time turning away from the ferry and towards Devoran.

"A useful chap to know by all accounts," ventured Steve, seeing a chance of getting an angle on this character before he came aboard. But this time Hugh Trembath wasn't to be drawn. Agreement was conveyed by the briefest of grunts. The boy was deterred, but there was a need for something to say. They would shortly be at Devoran and he didn't want both driver and other passenger interrogating him. A topic of his own he needed, but he didn't want to talk about his accident, or indeed about anything that had happened to him in the Roseland. He didn't want to talk about old Jack, nor about young Jack. The past was safer he thought, but nothing too local, nothing about long gone Rory Duggan or Francis Cairns, and nothing about Sir Edward either, or about the grandees who owned Trelissick....... he had the man.

"Your father's old boss," he began. "Back when he was with the Duchy, the one who became a Cabinet Minister after Churchill got back in. What did he do in Cabinet? What kind of Minister did he make?"

"Walter, Sir Walter Monckton? He was a Minister of Labour, and later a Minister of Defence, and nobody seems to be really sure what to make of his efforts. Ministers, you see, are basically of two sorts. There are those who command a place at the top table because they represent an unassailable strand of opinion within their party. A Prime Minister might not like them, he -or she as it is now- might not even agree with them, but he or she must listen to them. If ignored the

Party can splinter. The other sort are those appointed because the Prime Minister likes them and has a personal appreciation of their talents, energy, loyalty and so on. These the party must accept. The number of each sort, the mix, will tend to depend on the leader's authority over the party, and this is something that can vary."

"And what sort was Walter?"

"The second sort, most definitely. He tended to be given the holding briefs, those departments that appeared to lack clearly thought out and clearly pursued policies. Despite what they might say to get themselves elected, Governments can't be reforming zealots in everything. Sometimes it's as important to leave unruffled as it is to ruffle."

"Wait and see, you mean?"

"I do, and Walter was the man for this. He had the charm to carry it off. Churchill was old, tired, often he was sick, some things he simply didn't want to be bothered with. Walter would keep conflict to a minimum, and that was fine I suppose until the Suez thing flared and a fired up Eden found himself sitting next to a wet blanket."

"But Walter must have carried it through O.K........ I've read that the military did the business and could have easily secured and defended the canal. The problem was the USA, they left Eden isolated at the United Nations and left the pound exposed to the money market speculators."

"Mmm... I suppose you're right in that once unleashed the fighting men were ruthlessly efficient, but actually by then Walter had resigned. This was at the last moment and so as not to rock an increasingly unstable administrative boat he was quietly eased into another cabinet job, the old paymaster post I believe."

"And Eden went of course, totally humiliated..."

"He did, it was a tragedy. His career had been built on the way he'd championed the League of Nations back in the '30s, then, twenty years on, the UN deems him no better than Mussolini. It was put about that he was sick..... nervous exhaustion, that sort of thing. Then he was shoved up into the House of Lords."

"And Walter?"

"He too was given a peerage. He became Viscount Monckton, but not before he was sent across to Egypt to run the rule over the stuff that journalists were sending back, stuff that might have disturbed.........about the mess, the casualties."

"The kind of thing you said the other day he did in the war."

"Indeed, and some of that had been done in Egypt. He'd been there before -and generally that's what he was about. He was acknowledged to be a safe pair of hands. However unpromising the situation he could be trusted to sort things out with a minimum of embarrassment. Butler, a top table colleague, said that Governing the country at that time involved 'an orderly management of decline', and this is where Walter was so good, so useful."

They were in Devoran now and Jim Prout was there waiting outside his house. He was quickly up into the front passenger seat. He clipped on the belt as Hugh turned. Then they were tracking back towards the ferry.

"Morning Jim," said Hugh, "meet Steve, he's a nephew belonging to my Lanmouth tenants. He's off to Pendower. I think he's got a shine for the young lady working in Ralph Bartlett's cafè." The front seat passenger looked warily over his shoulder. There was nothing to indicate recognition. Steve was relieved.

"Hello." The one word, offered somewhat grudgingly, suggested Tyneside born or maybe Wear, and thereafter quite well travelled.

"We 'd just been talking about Suez," said Hugh. "You're a bit older than me and you would have done National Service, were you part of that?" Prout paused for a moment. His answer was considered.

"It was in Cyprus that I did my bit for Queen and Country. Guerrilla warfare that was, conducted by a Greek Gestapo. They stirred up the villages, you had to watch your back at every corner. Suez was a turkey shoot." He spoke in a monotone, his eyes fixed on the road and the rain ahead. "How did you get on to that one?"

"Talking about the performance of Walter Monckton as Defence Minister," said Steve. "What would you say about him?"

"Monckton? In that job? Unmemorable I suppose -for I'd forgotten he ever held it. It's from a bit later that I recall the man. When he was a Lord or whatever."

"In the oil business were you?" asked the driver. "I know he went onto the board of one of the big companies. Drilling was it, that you did?"

"Not exactly. When I came out of the army I did some free lance work in Africa--in what is now Zaire and Zambia. This was in the metal

112

rich Katangan hills. The workings were prized by the European companies who'd developed them......on sweated labour of course, black labour."

"Which is why they were not best pleased when the Belgian Government pulled out of the Congo," continued Trembath. "Those assets were once again up for grabs, and the blacks were looking favourites to take the spoils. Until Tshombe raised the flag of Katangan independence, that was. A breakaway province could only stand with European support and this could only be bought by allowing the mines to stay under white control."

"How on earth did Walter get mixed up in that one?" asked Steve.

"Geography," replied Prout, "Katanga wasn't a heart of darkness. It was a province that hung out from south of the Congo. It was wrapped around on three and three quarters sides by a British territory. Zambia it is now, then it was Northern Rhodesia. Like Katanga it's copper rich. The two territories share the same lode system. At the time Northern Rhodesia was cobbled together in a Federation of colonies with Nyassaland and Southern Rhodesia. The first had originally been a missionary inspired sanctuary from the slave trade. The second was something very different. Now, at long last, it's become Zimbabwe. Mugabe rules from Harare. Then it was developing in a very ominous way. The ruling European farmers were being stiffened by an influx of Afrikaan hard men moving up from South Africa and bringing with them their apartheid ideas. Harare was then Salisbury and Salisbury ruled the Federation."

His memory refreshed, Hugh Trembath took up the history.

"And having seen the direction of things in South Africa the natives, in Nyassaland and Northern Rhodesia particularly, started to get restless. They were hearing talk of Southern Rhodesia and Katanga being linked with a corridor territory that would have amounted to a white reserve. It would have had the railway, the mines, and the hydro schemes. In short, it would have had the wealth, and this would have been retained for the vested interests by an apartheid system stretching northwards from Pretoria. Distrust grew, and denied voting rights the Africans undertook direct action campaigns. Industrial strikes became political, rallies became riots. The prime movers, Banda and Kaunda are still there I believe, despots now themselves."

"That's right," confirmed Prout. They were in the line for the ferry now and he had the others' full attention. "At the time they were outlaws, rebels, but they had the numbers behind them. The arithmetic was conclusive. Even when jailed they knew that in time they had to prevail, just as Ghandi had in India, and the fellow in Ireland."

"De Valera," said Steve proudly.

"Well Monckton could have kept Banda and Kaunda in gaol a lot longer," explained Trembath. "Our Walter headed a Governmental Commission sent to assess the future of the Federation. It concluded that it would be best to allow the Federation to be broken up. Banda and Kaunda could lead their own people. The hard men in Salisbury and Pretoria were thwarted, and Tshombe isolated." Hugh was starting to sound quite an authority.

"Sounds like he came to an enlightened view of things," said Steve.

"He'd become a devout Christian by this time," continued Hugh. "He'd known what Hitler was about, and Stalin, and he'd done what he could to ease the partition of India. In the space of half a generation millions had died just because of their race, and he'd had a ringside seat. He saw what the Afrikaaners were about and yes, he moved to spike their guns."

"Simply by opening the way for the blacks to leave the Federation," added Prout, his sigh hinting at regret.

"Which they did," added Trembath. "OK, apartheid wasn't defeated, but it was contained, as was this ongoing tribal scrap that there ever seems to be in the old Belgian territory. With Moscow sniffing for advantage the two things could have coalesced into an east-west issue. This didn't happen. In the scale of things the two issues remained nothing more than local difficulties."

"So Walter did well," suggested Steve.

"Looking back, I'd say he did with this one," agreed Hugh. "The likes of Tiny soon proved that black rule was no bar to the continued making of white fortunes out of the continent. The Africans were no mugs. If they needed European expertise, financial or technical, they were quick to hire it in."

"So your skills stayed in demand Mr Prout," ventured Steve, attempting no more than to perhaps coax him back into the conversation.

But it didn't happen like that. The man's eyebrows lifted, and he

114

said nothing. Hugh Trembath managed a concerned sideways glance, and it was he that spoke.

"Skills Steve....., which skills?"

"I've been told that Mr Prout was drawn here by the mining operation up at Wheal Jane. That's going to make him someone who's up on mining, isn't it?"

"Fair enough," said Prout, speaking at last. "I was never short of work out there, you're right about that....just as there always seems to be plenty to do around here. It's a fair dig you've had in the side of this bus. Know how it was done?" The question was exclusively for Hugh. Jim Prout had brought the conversation smartly back to the here and now, and this is where it would stay for what remained of their short journey.

Above St.Just they struck westwards to meet the Roseland road. It was a matter of minutes now. They would leave the junction for Portscatho, turning instead into the lane for Porthcurnick Beach.

Steve was set down where the lane started. From here he had a walk of about a mile along the coast as it bent away to the east. The others would need to drive southwards, again for about a mile, along an awkward dead end lane which didn't quite reach the cliff top lookout. There was a space for a coastguard's vehicle in the small lane end car park, but today it was merely a matter of Prout finding room to turn.

It was wet, walking the coast path, but the way granted a welcome stretch of solitude. Hugh's was a full eight hours' watch. He'd no need to rush.

He'd met Jim Prout, spoken to him even, and the man had talked...... but in a way that seemed less than open. Steve glanced over his shoulder, half afraid that the man might now be following him. He wasn't. Of course he wasn't, but he nevertheless wished that Hugh hadn't told the man where he was headed and who he was hoping to see. Not that he'd been at all guarded in his own performance. From the man's reaction there had been something incautious in that mention of his mining work. Why and how he'd overstepped wasn't clear to the boy..... but overstepped he most certainly had and this was now etched in memory.

Steve neared Pendower. If he stayed on the cliff top he would meet the road which curved down to the beach hotel. The tide was low. He took the first opportunity to climb down to the shore. He kept tight to the cliff and suddenly he felt impelled to hurry, but not so as to make his urgency obvious. Where the cliff ended an old concrete pill box overlooked the damp deserted fan of sand that was Pendower beach. This was where he could be exposed. Instinct asked him to creep or to dash. Instead he was circumspect. At a brisk walk, eyes ahead, he was up to the dunes and through, and then straight into the cafe.

Two tables were occupied. Jane was carrying a tray to one. Steve found a nearby third, which was clear save for a newspaper, either provided by the house or left by an earlier customer. Now he wanted to be amongst people. He wanted to hear casual conversation, normal conversation, conversation appropriate to a public place. He might join in. There would be topics in the paper. He began to scan it through, feasting on the actual. He'd imagined enough.... too much perhaps.

And Jane, though busy, was pleased to see him. It was in her first glance. Yet there was a change, an altered demeanour. What he'd anticipated was the next big idea. She would want to show herself to be undaunted, and she would have a new scheme ready hatched. Instead though there was a reserve. It didn't detract from her warmth, nor did it lessen her true conviction........ on the contrary. For she had what he lacked, she had composure. The previous day's initiative had been productive. Action had provoked reaction. What it meant wasn't clear, but they could afford to wait and see, to take stock, and consider.

Steve wanted to know of Joe Bartlett's whereabouts whilst his father was with them at the fayre. He wanted to trust, and he wanted Ralph and Joe eliminated from all that was uncertain. To Jane they already were, and where before she'd been the one to spur, today Steve had a sense of being reined. He made himself useful, clearing and wiping tables, and washing and shelving crockery.

He needed to be patient. Across at Lanmouth he might have a line of his own to follow. Rain had fallen but the deeply cut lane out to Roundwood was tree sheltered. He'd heard a truck. He'd seen lights. There would be tracks, traceable still. Where did they lead? He could find out. This was something for himself.

The weather brightened in the afternoon and between customers Jane was content to talk about examination papers. Steve wanted to show interest and he tried, but his thoughts now turned to his lift back, and where the conversation was likely to be steered.....by Hugh, and even by himself. If it were left to him they would talk about mining. That's what he decided, mining in Cornwall with maybe a mention of this deep drilling for 'hot rocks' that he'd read about. Was it for real this, as a potential energy source? Or was there something in the claim that it might be to do with the disposal of nuclear waste, a feasibility study? This should keep them talking, surely, the two ex militaries, one a technician, the other a politician come preacher.

Ralph returned to tidy up, cash up and then lock up. Steve departed in good time to reach Portscatho before the end of Hugh's watch. He was there with half an hour to spare, and he was invited in to the lookout.

Even now, in summer, the structure felt remote and exposed. But that had to be right. Comfort would have been the designer's last concern. It was a station from which to watch, not admire the scenery. But this hadn't prevented Hugh from likewise ruminating on the morning's exchanges.

"I think you surprised Prout with your knowing about his mining background," remarked Hugh. "Has he been mentioned down at Lanmouth or something?" Steve could have answered yes to this. He was tempted. One simple word, and Ralph and Jane and the eventful excursion to Polgooth might be skipped. But he didn't know that the landlord wouldn't check with his aunt. He chose to be open.

"I was with Ralph Bartlett yesterday. He took Jane and me to Polgooth. He had a stall at the fayre. On the way back we met Mr Prout driving the other way. We had to reverse to let him pass. My companions told me who he was, and what he did. Nothing's been said to me about him down at Lanmouth." This was the truth.

"Sounds reasonable," reassured Hugh, his manner suggesting that he'd detected the slight embarrassment caused by his question. "It's just that I anticipate being asked, and now I have the answer, and that's fine."

The following watch arrived, and looking along to the beach Steve could see that Jim Prout was there with the pristine Land Rover. He was out and waiting by the vehicle. As they walked towards him Steve had his first full view of the man's stocky frame, and his weathered heavily jowled face. The eyes were narrowed, the brows thick and grey. Clad still in his dark overhauls the figure fittingly echoed the subterranean.

Their journey back to Carwinion was uneventful. This time Prout led the conversation. He was content to talk about Land Rovers and the improvements made to them since his army days. Steve had no contribution. None was expected. He was comfortable. This was safe.

Hugh stopped on the road outside Carwinion. He would be going on to Devoran with Prout. Steve could walk the lane down to the farm.

He walked past the farm though. Plenty of the evening remained, certainly sufficient to walk the route of that late night haulier. He climbed northwards to the brow of the spur and looked down onto Landurgan Farm and Cowlands Creek. Below him the main lane to Roundwood Quay ducked away towards the near shore, passing the two estate cottages before following the water's edge around to the quay. That was the way most would take, the easier, wider way, but there was another. It lay to his right, through the woods..... a steeply dropping, almost overgrown extension to the ridge top lane which he'd thought to be now used only by the farmers for getting to the fields or fetching timber. But whatever he'd seen and heard in the night had been using it, and so would he.

Bent grass, broken twig, and tyre track indicated a there and back use. Was it merely to Roundwood though, or had the vehicle ventured further? At the southern end of the main quay there was a gate, and beyond this a track which curled back into Lanmouth Creek. Some 200 metres in, on its own smaller quay stood the Viceroy shed. A notice on the usually padlocked gate proclaimed the track to be solely for the use of persons renting the shed. Steve strongly suspected that it had been used in the night.

The sun was low as he entered the trees. His descent to Roundwood along the packhorse beaten track of mud smothered stone was into a damp gloom. It had definitely been a twin wheeled truck, and emerging onto Roundwood Quay it had turned southward to the gate. He followed the tyre marks. They would go through that gate, he was sure.

He stopped and looked across to Tolverne, and he imagined the truck being guided along here at walking pace by no more than the light of a torch and with its motor at little more than an idle.

The forward two thirds of the *Kampala* jutted from the Passage, she was tied so that most of Lanmouth Creeek was screened from all but the more inquisitive of the river traffic. Steve walked on, again looking down, and yes there were footprints now, just one set and, strangely, another tyre print that was joining from the left and this for a moment was puzzling until he looked ahead and actually saw the explanation.

It stood by the gatepost, a motorcycle. And unmistakably it was *the* motorcycle. It appeared to be unattended. Steve nevertheless backed further under the trees before creeping forwards. It must have come along the main waterfront lane....and the rider? There might be footprints, but he would need to get closer. He would need to step out, and he could, of course he could for he had as much right to be here as anyone.

He strode boldly from the shadows. The gate was locked, but it had been swung, open and shut, for the truck to pass and re-pass. This left a confusion of footprints around the stand propped bike and on both sides of the gate.

Steve had often been down to the shed but not, as yet, this year. He'd been ready to follow those truck tyres all the way, but now with this machine here perhaps it was better to wait......to wait and to watch.

He was next to this bike though, and why shouldn't a lad show interest in such an impressive thing? It was a brute, a Kawasaki Voyager, 1000 cc at least, expansively, sturdily, rigged with a rear box and panniers. This was one to fill a road, as it indeed had, twice, when he'd fallen and again on the way to Polgooth.

As he inspected and admired, his closer attention was drawn to the right pannier, the one that was initially away from him. It was open. The lid was raised. If he walked around he might look into it and see what it contained, if anything. He looked up. He could see no one. He could hear no one. He eased himself between the rear wheel and the gate. He leant forward, peering down and in. He saw a book, a cheap exercise book.

This could be an opportunity. He'd hoped earlier that today he might impress Jane. She'd listened to his suggestions, she hadn't been hostile, and yet, frustratingly, she wasn't sparked. He could tell. But now here could be the chance. There was still time. He could crouch, and reach, and lift, and open, and there would be clues. Just who was this character? Where was he from? What was his business here? Were there contacts? Steve glanced around again. There was just himself, and the bike, and the book.

He decided and he moved. He was crouching now and his fingers had the book. He flicked at the pages, staying low.

Numbers he saw, more numbers! The pages were dated,

successively, with sometimes the same date being carried across more than one page, but never more than three. Once again this was a kind of diary or log. Beneath each date the numbers 1-24 were listed, and alongside each, a time, a block of six figures, and then another number their unit being degrees... from their range, probably of direction.

Steve was acquainted with orienteering. This rider, he would be carrying a watch, and a map, and he would have a compass. These were grid references and bearings. Their pattern brought to mind what Rory Duggan had bequeathed. That had been so compressed, and so complex as to be impenetrable, but there were definite similarities. Steve flicked through the pages. He wanted the last entry.

"You can put that down boy..... right this moment you can."

The command came from Steve's right. Though helmet muffled the accent was unmistakably Welsh. Steve straightened and turned. A tall figure stood in the open, close to the edge of the quay. Steve dropped the book. He vaulted the gate, and he ran.

The track was level. It curved to his right. He could sprint and the trees might shield, at least until he reached the shed. He was there in less than half a minute and only then did he glance back.....and there was no one, not yet. If it was a chase then the pursuer lacked speed.....but where now? This was where the track ended.

He could pick his way along the shore through the marsh grass or strike up into trees towards the fields. Or he could conceal himself here and wait, and if necessary effect a dodge in the failing light.

The shed was substantially built. To allow working space on the quay it was set back, the rear half being snugly slotted into a long ago excavated recess. There was clearance sufficient to allow for periodic pitch painting and a seasonal purge of briar and vine, and this was room now for concealment.

Branches stretched out over the roof. Treading carefully through the leaf mould Steve squeezed himself into what was becoming a wedge of nightfall.

He would position himself at the nearer of the rear corners. He could watch the track and if necessary scuttle up into the wood, or should there be movement up amongst the trees then he could make another fast break, back along the track. He waited. He watched. He listened. Still there was no pursuer. Had he escaped? He had, for what was he hearing? It was the motorbike. It was being started, and now it

120

was climbing through the woods, and out onto the ridge and yes, down to the north and away, away from Lanmouth.

With relief there came fatigue. He could breath now, deeply. He leant back against a corrugated panel....and this one gave, just a little. The overlap should have been pinned, and it had been but it no longer held. There was corrosion around the bolt. He pushed, straining for a glimpse of what was inside. He crouched, pressing with shoulder, hand, and temple too, but it was so dark. What he could recognise was the tang of timber, freshly milled and treated. He reached and he felt, and with his fingers he tapped and he scratched. There was a pallet and on this there was a stack of at least two wooden crates.

He needed light. It was twenty minutes to the farm. He could use his bike to get back and be here in another fifteen. It was becoming darker by the second, but this could be to the good. He would have the lamp.

*

I learnt that Miss Murrell's nephew Rob Green, mentioned in the (New Statesman) article by name, had indeed occupied a key position in Naval Intelligence during the Falklands campaign. I was informed that Commander Green was in a position to know about the receipt and dispatch of signals to and from HMS Conqueror, *and intercepted signals from the* Belgrano *to the Argentine mainland and back, from both British and American sources.......*

The story I am told is as follows......the Prime Minister and ministers close to her were getting very nervy about incessant questioning about the Belgrano *in general and about signals, intercepted signals and GCHQ at Cheltenham, which would call into question their truthfulness to the House in particular. This was pre Ponting.*

Because Commander Robert Green was known to be unhappy about certain aspects of the Falklands War and was known to have wanted to leave the Navy, he came under a cloud of suspicion, wrongly to the best of my knowledge, but certainly under a cloud...... it was thought he might have copies of documents and raw signals, some of the originals of which had been destroyed by the intelligence services.

Just as those of us who have had certain documents have taken the precaution of keeping them in friends' or relatives' houses while we have them, so it was thought that some of Rob Green's supposed records might be in the home of the aunt to whom he was close.......

I am happy to accept that there was no premeditated intention of doing away with Miss Murrell...... only a search of her house when she was out. Alas, on Wednesday 21st March 1984 she returned unexpectedly to change.......

I am informed that the intruders...... were checking the house to see if there were any Belgrano *related documents of Commander Green in the home of his aunt. Things went disastrously wrong....... Hilda Murrell fought and was severely injured. She was then left to die from hypothermia, and the cover up had to begin because I am informed the searchers were men of the British Intelligence.......*

The local police have, I gather, now agreed that the Special Branch was involved and I understand that my praise for the local police does not in all cases apply to the Special Branch. Will the Minister explain what the Special Branch was doing so early in the case of a murder of a seventy eight year old rose grower, if it really was a simple burglary?

Tam Dalyell MP, speaking in the Commons 20/12/84.

Hilda Murrell's death has also brought out into the light of day the activities of MI5's AIA group with its blanket brief to break the law by entering buildings and searching for whatever it is they might deem of interest to them.

Her death has also shone a spotlight on that really murky world of private surveillance agencies and their tie ups with Special Branch..........

Judith Cook   'Unlawful Killing' p128

" You 're going to have to move on.....and for your own good as much as anyone else's."

He'd heard, because he straightened from his crouched position at the water's edge..... but he didn't turn. If at all it was to be a careful response. At last it came, Welsh accented.

"And you're the land owner are you, or his agent?"

"No Gareth, I'm not Lord Falmouth and I'm not in his employ. This isn't about pitching a tent, good place though this is. Handy for the lane, trees for privacy, and a fresh water pond too. I'd stay." The tall figure swayed slightly, but still he didn't turn. He wasn't to be hurried. He had to think. He had to size the situation, and those words...... and then choose his own with care.

"You have me at a disadvantage. With my back turned you creep between me and my tent and my machine. And you address me by name and with a riddle. Tell me first, are you more than one?"

"I'm alone."

"And are you the law, or are you the press? "

"Both I suppose, but mainly the first....... hence my advice to you Mr Hughes."

"The riddle, which I must ask you to explain.... and you have my name. What else do you know?"

"That you are from Welshpool; that you were a Welsh Guardsman, a corporal; that you were sent to the South Atlantic where you suffered grievous injury at Bluff Cove, injury that necessitated the amputation of the lower part of your left leg...... the operation being performed at sea, on the *Kampala*. And then, when got back in less than one piece, you required a series of skin grafts for those facial burns. You were discharged as an invalid, and part of the pay off you put towards the bike. You're still struggling a bit with the grip shift gears, particularly down here on these twisting lanes, but the machine is part of your new life, it's indicative of the persona you've chosen to cultivate."

"Which you characterise as being?"

"Isolated..... and increasingly so."

Gareth Hughes turned. His face was not a face. It was scar tissue, angry scar tissue, and from amongst it glared two fierce eyes. The intruder had been forewarned, but there was shock nonetheless. Gareth Hughes knew. He attacked.

"So just what do you mean by this 'have to move on' stuff, you with your two good legs and your pretty boy looks. 'Advice' you say. Who do you think you are?" His target didn't flinch.

"Alan Grigson is the name. I didn't have to disturb you, but I felt you could be useful to me and at the same time me to you. You needn't listen. If you don't then..... no skin off my nose." This was more than just parrying.

"You're a callous bast....."

"The last thing you want from me is pity," stabbed Alan, his voice raised. "You're meant to tell me that soldiering is a rough game and that you knew this when you joined, and that professionals don't entertain self pity. This is what I want to hear. If I can then I know you can be useful still."

"And you don't think I've troubles enough of my own to contend with?" This was more subdued, more respectful.

"I don't. That's precisely it. You need more in your life. Without it you're going to go on raking over old ground. Stony it is, and sterile. There are other battles you know, battles that are still winnable. The dead are lost. They'll not be brought back."

"Those responsible should be brought to book."

"Proof though, where's your proof? You have your theories, but they'll only lead to a maze of suppositions."

"What do you know about it anyway?" It was the Welshman's turn to defend. "And if I'm wasting my time, why not just leave me to find this out for myself?"

"I know that you have become concerned at a number of deaths."

"The number? The dates?"

"The three hundred and sixty eight Argentinian lives lost with the sinking of the *Belgrano*. That was on May 2nd 1982. Followed by the death of Captain Brian Chadwick, ten days later. And more recently, back in March last year, the death of Miss Hilda Murrell. You would have it that they are all in some way linked, that there's been a hidden hand. And that would be convenient, for next to all this you have your own grief, your own anger. You've lost a leg, a career, an identity. What was is no longer there, not even to greet you in the mirror. You want to pin the blame. It's natural, it's understandable, but only up to a point. Beyond that you're simply hung up, chasing an obsession."

"You can spare the psycho babble. I'm a bad loser. I always was.

And this is England, the country that will always warm to a good loser -someone like Weston." A widely revered name was spat away into the foliage, like spent gum.

"Then think schoolboy rugby. Remember those lessons. You can sometimes run the ball too far, run yourself out of position, and then you're in trouble, and the team too. That's the time to kick for touch."

"You say it like I'm on my own. That's not so. There are others"

"Too scattered and too easily picked off," countered Grigson. "And who do you have who was actually there, either at High Command or in sleepy Shrewsbury? The nephew, Commander Green, he's not talking about what truly matters; and the landowner, Scott, he's a wise, wise, wise monkey."

Hughes shrugged. Alan continued. He had another name to drop. "But that's not to say I under estimate your friend Mr Maura......Alberto, who you met down there in the South Atlantic on the *Kampala*. I know that you correspond. There's mutual support, I can see, but he was patched up, fully, and he was just a conscript soldier remember. The bullet he took didn't cost him a career. He's back doing what he did before.... that right?"

"Works for a haulage outfit" confirmed Gareth Hughes. "One of the larger ones. He helps run a computerised central office. He lost a younger brother. The kid was a rating on the *Belgrano*. That's what he's having to come to terms with, and it's a struggle."

"My point! They like their rugger down there too. He should be hearing, and heeding the same advice. The lost brother wouldn't have wanted two wasted lives, and certainly not three."

"There are other people, people closer to home." claimed the former Guardsman.

"I suppose you mean like M.P. Tam and Clive the whistleblower." The other nodded. That was a mistake. "But I know that you're far from impressed by the Right Honourable Mr Persistent. That actually you think Dalyell to be barking under the wrong tree, having been led to it by the MOD man who was also, likewise unknowingly to himself, being put to a calculated use. You fancy Mr Ponting to be something other than the popularly portrayed 'Boy Scout', that the leaked information was in fact dis-information...and that there are better secrets still to come out." Gareth Hughes wasn't arguing. "But you're too late. If there was an opportunity, it's now lost, gone. You have to let it go....."

".......and instead join you, because that's going to be better for my state of mind?" The Welsh scepticism bordered on the scornful.

"Not the words I would have used, but I think you understand me." Grigson wasn't bending. "And there's also your physical well being to consider, of course."

"Is this some kind of threat. If you're alluding to what happened to Chadwick and the old lady then I'll thank you for confirming my suspicions."

"Easy with the paranoia Gareth. You're down here burrowing, and fine, burrow away. What I'm saying is that the local sub terrain is more dangerous than you might think. I'm in there too, digging for something different. We don't want to be cutting across each other. Work with me and the dangers are lessened." Alan spoke convincingly. Gareth's tone softened.

"So I must understand that you are with an authority that's maintaining a file on my movements, and that if I've been thinking that I've been discretely active, and privately, then I've been sadly mistaken."

"You have been," confessed Alan.

"When did this start?"

"When you called on Miss Murrell, in the week before she died. You were seen and you were remembered. When she was killed the CID initially had you down as a suspect. Then your phone number was found, in the house amongst her belongings. It was realised who you were, your movements were traced, and it was found that you had a strong alibi."

"I was in hospital for the whole of that weekend." Gareth confirmed.

"On establishing your identity the local Force are alarmed. They know you're not the culprit....but could you, in some way, be the cause?"

"Was I? What do you think?"

"I don't think," answered Alan, bluntly. "Not until I know a great deal more than I do now......and I can't see how that'll happen. We keep coming back to this. Did you ever hear from Green?"

"Someone who said he was Green phoned. I suggested we meet. He wasn't keen. If it was him, I guess he was being watched. Maybe he still is."

"I think it pretty clear by now that the man isn't giving. Yes, he's appalled at what happened to his Aunt, just as he was no doubt appalled at the way events unfolded in the South Atlantic, but he won't have the hard evidence to connect the two and that's because at bottom there isn't any. It was to ensure this that things were done as they were. You must accept this, and so must Alberto."

"Maybe." The Guardsman wasn't going to be convinced, not here, not in this encounter.

"So why not join me," persisted Alan. "Others would want you frightened off. I don't. You know a lot, and you're always finding out more. None of it can help Hilda, or Brian, or Alberto's kid brother, but it could help me. My struggle is no less worthy. Make yourselves useful, you and Alberto--I'll sign him up too." It was neither plea nor offer. It was a blend, a proposition, one that for the moment Hughes was choosing to ignore. He fixed Alan with a glare. He had his own question.

"Answer me this first. Who, in your view, killed Hilda Murrell?"

"Some bungling petty crook," replied Alan, looking away as he spoke.

".......who was so inept that he's never been caught." The sarcasm strengthened the Welshman's point. But once made it wasn't pursued. He'd listened. He was relenting, coming around. "So tell me," he went on. "What is your game? How does it currently stand? And where do you propose to play me?"

"I'm calling a team meeting for tomorrow evening. I want you there. You can meet the others. One you might know already........and as an incentive she might well have an angle for you on Captain Brian Chadwick."

*

It is clear now, in 1991, that the two big Colombian drug cartels are bitter enemies. They are at war, viciously so, but this hasn't always been the case......witness this photo. It was taken in Spain in 1984. These two men are in close conversation. All appears cordial, and yet the figure on the left has been confirmed as Gilberto Rodriguez-- a leading light in the Cali Cartel, and that on the right as Jorge Ochoa-- a man of similar standing amongst the Medellin counterpart. At that time wanton violence was largely the preserve of the latter. The Medellin people were ready to assassinate any who opposed their expansionist interests. No one was safe. Policemen, judges, clerics and even nuns, were killed......as were politicians, union activists, journalists, and peasant organisers. The Cali mob tended to be more restrained, but only until the Medellin Cartel were perceived to be a threat. Then, as bad blood grew between the groups, the former became -of necessity- no less ruthless.

But before that, as we see, the two trafficking consortiums were working together. Having been successful with their joint shipments of cocaine to the US, Rodriguez and Jorge were similarly entrusted with the task of setting up export routes into Spain and on to other parts of Europe including the UK.

Foolishly they embarked on a lifestyle of such extravagance that they were bound to attract attention. Posing as Moises Moreno Miranda, Ochoa purchased this eight thousand square foot mansion in one of Madrid's more fashionable suburbs......replete with a swimming pool, a discotheque, tennis courts, and no less than four Mercedes cars. Rodriguez, taking the names Gonzalez Linares, chose to live in this plush city centre hotel...... at the same time buying two large apartments and just the two Mercedes.

By 25 September 1984 the police in Madrid had identified the men and were keeping both under close surveillance. These are police photos. Their phone lines would have been tapped, and their premises bugged. Washington was informed, and on 17 October the US Ambassador requested their arrest.'

ITV Channel 4 'Window on the World' (Special report.) 1991

Wednesday had been the obvious choice. Jane had the house to herself. Her mother was in Exeter. She was visiting. She would stay the night. Steve had arrived at 7. For 45 minutes it had just been the two of them, making preparation. They were well on with the carbonara.

It was approaching 8. They heard a car, the wheels on the gravel, the doors as they were shut, and two voices-one quite familiar, the other less so. Jane didn't look up.

"Can you see to the door Steve while I stir?" The boy went

without demur, and yes, it was Kate with Jeremy a step behind, clutching a bottle of wine and a pack of beers.

"Not too early I hope," breezed Kate. "I'll thank you to introduce us to our host." Steve complied readily. As co-host he could project himself and Jane as an item. He liked that. For a second, as he spoke, he wondered if Jane had met the couple before. Then it was obvious that she hadn't, so basic and so polite were the pleasantries. Steve confidently took and fridged the wine before guiding them through the lounge and out onto to the south facing patio.

He returned to the kitchen, and now here was Alan. He'd just come in, and was looking remarkably at ease, worryingly so. He was looking over the cook's shoulder, inspecting the pasta! No pleasantries here, they'd met -it was obvious. They'd hatched something, this pair. How? when?, and why?.... he didn't know. He wanted to, but now wasn't the time to ask. He would have to wait.

"Is that everyone now," he asked. Jane looked at Alan. He was the one with the answer.

"Just one more person, if he's coming that is. He said he was and......yes I think I can hear him now." Steve listened. It was a motorcycle. The same motorcycle, unmistakably. He coloured. What was he going to say? What could he say?

"I'll.... I'll leave him for you. I'll see if the others want a drink." There was nowhere to hide. Confidence was crumbling. No longer was he the proud host. He was less, much much less.

The two from Truro had ventured onto the lawn. Steve was alone on the patio when Alan came through with Gareth Hughes. Steve could do no better than study his trainers. He couldn't face up. Humiliation loomed. It was unavoidable. He'd bungled, and now he'd be exposed............but not yet. There was a squeal from the lawn. It was Kate. She'd turned, and the recognition had been instant - both ways. The Welshman whooped and brushed past Steve, clattering his way through the patio furniture.

Steve noticed the limp and also the lurch as he stepped down on to the lawn. He was disabled, and this is why there'd been no pursuit when he'd fled. They hugged, and they wept, and again they hugged. The others were left to watch. All could see the face now and the scars. This was plainly a Welshman that they heard, and there was mention of the ship down on the river. These were war wounds, they knew. Jane had emerged to stand in awe with Alan and Jeremy.

No one had forgotten those news pictures. The Welshmen.....that was Bluff Cove where there were bombs and there was bravery and death and horrifying injury. Steve's mind though was adrift, it was crossing to Mylor and conjuring the stones in that estuary side churchyard.

Special they were, these bonds forged under fire, hence the pledge that the old man was still so determined to honour. And how strange that the same vessel that had been on station for Gareth three years before now stood as a possible resource for Jack Butters. Strange indeed, both men had been soldiers, land combatants, and they'd each been caught out of their element...... soft targets the pair. And for both the damage had had career closing permanence. The fortunes of war had been cruel, yes, but the comradeship all the more profound. To see Gareth and Kate together, now, was to see again the blind man standing at that grave.

To Steve it made a quite startling coincidence. He looked to Alan. He'd been there, but of Jack Butters's tale the man knew little. And because no one else here was placed to share the perception it was only he, Steve, who was left to wonder if there might be an obscure something in the cause or the purpose of this evening gathering that was in someway linking the two stories.

Alan sidled nearer.

"No introduction needed there," he quipped. "I think we're eating out here.....if you could help Jane with the plates and the utensils." It was an opportunity to move back inside, but how it rankled to be ordered as if he were the flunky and Alan the host. He had to accept this, and accept also that his star patient status was now emphatically usurped.

As they ate Alan took further control. They were there to speak, he said, and if they heard Jane first and then himself he was certain there would be contributions from others.

Questions were in order, but answers were not obligatory. He hoped they would bond, and that in the light of what emerged they might see a way ahead, a direction that could be taken together as a team.

Steve glanced across at Jane. Having fed her guests she was eager to start. Somehow, somewhere, Alan had won her confidence, much as he'd won his own. All were ushered into the dining room to be seated at the large polished stained oak table. Once settled she began.

She was definite, characteristically. They heard about her father, his job, the crime, his punishment, and her certainty that he was innocent. They heard about her mother and about the job at Pendower, and about her recruitment of Steve to her cause. She spoke of Polgooth, of what they'd attempted and how they'd failed. The camera had been returned though, she mentioned that.... but allowed it to remain a mystery.

Alan had come to the cafè at Pendower that Sunday. He hadn't been told, yet seemed to be aware of her predicament. More than that, he shared her view about her father.

This last part straightened things better for Steve, the rest of course he'd heard before. The questions were predictable. Jeremy asked for the facts of the case, and once again as they came from Jane's lips they sounded as conclusive as ever.

"What about this getting the camera back?" asked Kate.

"At the time I was just pleased to see it," answered the girl. "Steve thinks Ralph might have had a hand in things, probably with his son who knows Steve well enough to have picked him out in the crowd. It's just possible that my mother could have put them up to it. She'd rather I sat back and accepted things."

"Well we can bear Ralph in mind," said Alan. "What interests me more at the moment is your choice of Steve here as a sidekick on this expedition to the fayre. Any reason for this? "

"I like him." Steve looked up. Smiles were exchanged.

"He's nice and he's not local, and he comes to the Roseland from across the river, and though it's only intuition my feeling is that the river holds a key to all this."

"That's fine," said Alan. "Now you'll all hear what I am, what I've been doing, and why I'm unsure as to the safety of this conviction. I do write a bit, and I have compiled pieces for the radio, but all this is largely cover. I work for the Government, for the Home Office. I'm a policeman. I have a specialist role, separate from the Devon and Cornwall set up.

My field is drugs, big boy drugs. Cannabis is small and usually I wouldn't want to get involved but this one, this case, is a little different. I report to London, where I'm based, and it's from the capital that I've followed the trail that's so far brought me to here. I gather information. Surveillance is the term. You know that. I don't attempt to apprehend. That's for others, but to do it efficiently they need me."

At this point Alan hesitated, just slightly, as if to check how well the listeners were engaged. Jeremy it was who urged him on. He continued

"Since just before Easter there's been a new supply of cocaine coming into the big city. It's good stuff, Peruvian probably, maybe Bolivian. Either way it'll have been processed in Colombia, but it hasn't travelled the familiar U.S. of A route. It's too clean, too undiluted. What's arriving is a refined product for a refined market -the silver spoon folk. Everything about it is consistent, the quality, the rate of supply, and the high price fetched."

"This indicates control," said Jeremy. He was thinking as well as listening. Alan nodded, encouraged.

"Which again is unusual," he went on. "A store packed high with the stuff is vulnerable. We can sniff it out, so can rival operators looking to cut in. For this reason most like to unload quickly, even should this entail a drop in price. Not with this crowd though. It's a confident set up."

"Into which you have obviously gained a measure of insight," remarked Gareth.

"We have end of the line informants, and from them we've learned of the mules who are fetching the stuff into the capital. But these haven't yet led us to the import arrangements....."

".........or to whoever's behind it all," added Jeremy. "Which means the last thing you want to do is to move against the mules."

"Exactly," said Alan. "The coke is brought into London by car. The cars are hired. Every time they're sent out it's in this direction. They always come to Cornwall, West Cornwall, proper Cornwall. There are two drivers. We know they vary their routes, and we can only assume that pick up points are varied too. How the variations are decided and communicated we don't yet know. Phone taps and mail intercepts have revealed nothing, but a consistent feature of these runs has been the use of the car ferries at Poole, Dartmouth, Devonport, Fowey, and here at Philleigh. On each trip it's all, but just in the one, westward, direction. Then it's fast road back."

"Intriguing," said Kate. "Would this be a device to foil

followers?"

"Not unlikely," said Jeremy, anticipating Alan. "But it wouldn't do just to dismiss it as such. You could miss something." The others looked to Alan. He nodded, and went on.

"At the back end of April I spent a week looking around Dartmouth, and then there were two days at Torpoint..... quite enough for anyone.... and then, last month, another week spent in the Fowey area. After, it was on to here, thinking that I'd soon be working my way back.....but no, not now."

"You have a lead," said Jane, but a little too enthusiastically.

"I'm not a detective. I don't follow leads. But I do notice and report loose ends. You always get the odd one or two, wherever you go. That's life, if you stand and look at it. But I come to this sleepy Parish and they're all over the place. I'm tripping over the things. And then I'm ducking and diving to keep out of the way of a procession of amateur sleuths. It's like they're almost bumping into each other, literally. One even lands himself in hospital. And it's not just you three." He looked in turn from Jane to Gareth to Steve. "Look behind you and there's Mr Hugh Trembath with his nose to the ground. He comes into the Hospital and quizzes the nurses. Then he's over on the riverbank checking out the scene. Not much gets past that one.... don't think he hasn't noticed you Gareth."

"Should I know this fellow?" asked the Welshman.

"You're familiar with his land," Steve put in, bravely.

"Was he invited tonight?" Kate wanted to know.

"No." Alan was emphatic. "He's too well connected. The coastguards, the constabulary, councillors, clerics even..... get him in and you have the whole reprehensible crew to contend with. That you're here at all is partly because I don't want him being dragged in under my feet, and that's what's likely to happen if I let things carry on as they are. As a team we can go forward with confidence. As loners we're just one indiscretion away from a total muck up."

Steve glanced across at Gareth. Here was a cue for him to mention the encounter on Roundwood Quay. The glance was returned, but nothing was said. A tacit plea had been accepted.... it had been well intentioned incompetence. Alan continued.

"Hugh Trembath owns a couple of farms on the other side of the river. Steve is staying at one. His uncle and aunt are tenants. Steve knows Mr Trembath quite well. The person he doesn't know, and neither do I, is Jane's father..... the owner of this property. We've heard about him just now from Jane. He's in prison. I struggle with that. True, the evidence was there, but where's the motive? He says he was set up, and again the question is why. If he's a victim then the question begged is what is it that's been taken from him." Alan paused, again he was wanting a response. Steve obliged.

"Freedom?"

"True, but a bit vague, a bit abstract. Freedom to do what?"

"To pursue a lucrative career, and enjoy the remuneration therefrom." This was from Jeremy. His words carried that note of resentment so often struck when teachers talk of the relative earnings in other professions.

"Good, so if anything's been stolen from him then it might be his......"

"His job ," said Kate, "and I think I might have met the person who is currently in possession of the stolen item."

"Go on." Jane urged. If there was a thief she wanted him named.

"No, no...." Alan lifted a hand as would a pianist conducting a sextet in rehearsal. "Kate's turn in a minute. Let me finish, and then there might be questions for me."

Imaginations had been sparked. He sensed this. They were all listening now, really listening.

"And there's been another job that's changed hands," he continued. "Hasn't there Steve? But this time bought rather than stolen. You told me about the transaction yourself, you've even introduced me to one of the parties."

"Young Jack Spargo," said Steve "and you speak of the job he had on the ferry."

"So we're looking at his successor," followed Jane. "Anyone know anything about him?"

"Keeps himself to himself," said Steve. "Ex Fleet Auxiliary according to Ralph. Hugh might know something."

"Whoa now!" Alan chided, a chuckle in his voice. "This is what I meant. Hugh Trembath will know something, we can be sure of that, but not so much as we might find out from elsewhere by more discrete means. I've found a good source, one I mustn't yet divulge. It tells me that the new man on the ferry was in Falmouth some eighteen months ago, with an RFA ship. It's said that he knew then that his days with the service were numbered, and that he was expressing a liking for these parts."

"Eighteen months ago," repeated Gareth. "That's interesting. Sounds like he landed himself the ideal job. Do we have a name? Do we know where he lives now?"

Alan wasn't giving a name. He did have an address.

"He lives in Truro, in a terraced house on Campfield Hill."

"So does David Morrish, number 46," offered Kate .

"Which is as next door as you can get to number 44." Alan's show of professional pride was excusable. Certainly it was understandable, but perhaps he'd have done better to avoid the hint of arrogance. Looks were exchanged sharply between Kate and Jeremy.

Steve sensed tension. Alan had been using Kate, this was clear. She knew this and it was fine with her, but less so with Jeremy. If his reflex had been to protect then maybe it was now outmoded. These men liked to control, both of them. The tension would be resolved. It would have to be, but at whose cost or gain the boy wasn't ready to predict.

"David Morrish?" enquired Jeremy.

"The guy who took my father's position at *Conway's*," said Jane. "And it seems there could be a connection between him and the new person on the ferry....."

"...... and perhaps the people who fixed young Jack up with his working boat," added Steve.

"And I think there might be an old lady involved too," continued Alan, "a frumpy old down at heel dowager....."

"........who, if I'm not mistaken, goes by the name *SS Kampala*." Gareth's words carried the confidence of one at last beginning to see how he might fit in.

"In one!" Confirmed Alan appreciatively. "Now we're going to be listening to you, and we're going to be hanging on every word." And they were too. If there had been questions for Alan, well now they would need to be saved. It had been that skillfully done. All were primed to listen, and in Kate's comforting presence Gareth was primed to tell, to tell at last with liberating frankness.

*

The train to Exeter had been packed..... the journey stifling, with delays. Having lost time, her climb to the prison had needed to be brisk. It always stank inside, and today, in the afternoon warmth, the foulness had been acutely oppressive. Her husband, Roger, he'd been heated in mood, in word. She was glad now to be out in the evening air.

A guest house room waited on St David's Hill, only a short walk away, but now she could afford to linger. A little off her route and she was in a small secluded park. There was a cool chestnut, and beneath it a bench. She sat and she leant back. Her eyelids lowered. It was enough just to listen..... to hear the birds out sing the muffled city bustle.

And there were footsteps. Taking a woman's stride, they approached and without a break they passed. Nothing threatened, nothing disturbed, no child, no dog.... it was just that one person going her lone individual way.

And that wasn't so far, not now. Less than a couple of hundred yards and Linda Taylor would be in Velwell Rd, and at her door.

She'd often enough cut through the park at this time, and she was well familiar with the spectacle of a travelled up convict's wife. The odour of gaol was mere confirmation. A glance at the clothes was sufficient. The antithesis of a fashion statement, the garments evinced durability, patience, trustworthiness. This was a uniform, no less than that borne by the incarcerated spouse.

These people were seldom minded to converse. More often they were talked out, and Carol Byrne looked to be no exception. So Linda Taylor strode on....... and it was her loss, for she might have been interested to hear of the Roseland from one who lived only a bicycle ride's distance from where long ago she'd been born, and raised, and schooled.

Indeed, current word of the Peninsula might have been more than just interesting, for there'd been a suggestion from her husband that on his imminent retirement they might sell up here in Exeter so as to buy a smaller, more rural property.... some where in the Truro area, close to where several in her family remained.

This was John's idea. He was quite keen, keen enough to start contacting estate agencies. Linda Taylor wasn't so sure. True, with the way her husband had been treated, it would be good to move on...... but for her, it would be going back. In her past there was pain, a hurt that even after more than thirty years was too easily revived. Cornwall meant

Cairns, Francis, the man she almost married. He that was killed in far away Korea.

Initial information had been sketchy. As details eventually came so the loss became harder to bear..... even with John there, doing his never stinting best, and the children who'd been a blessing. They'd covered the grief, but not fully enough. A burden remained and it was hers alone. To complement the family there'd been the work opportunities, and the good health, and the house, and all told of a rosy progression..... but beneath persisted bitterness. It had outlasted the grown and gone children, to be now compounded by these new tribulations for their father.

He was a proud man, and able. At work he'd given his all. He'd risen, and he'd deserved to rise further. He'd had high hopes. Well warranted they were, but they'd been dashed. The severance of the telephone service from the Post Office he'd welcomed. That was progress, and he'd been active in the subsequent expansion. Now though there was a restructuring in hand, a prior to sell off rationalisation. He was deemed unwanted.

He was taking it on the chin of course, and speaking proudly of the share holding he would acquire.... but what was this? To her, a payoff in rotten parchment bonds! Scant reward for her having knuckled down during those *'never had it so good'* years, even after being made all too well aware of the seamier side of post war Conservatism.

Those loose threads she might have tugged at, but she hadn't. For when they'd said they would be working for a more just world she'd believed them. And in their way they were broadly well intentioned, until they were supplanted by this current lot.....the New Right, in whose hands this dear, dear land was making shameful conquest of itself. And this was being sold to the people as progress, as freedom. What conceit! For the moment she could contain the indignation. She made a brittle vessel though. Tapped at the right angle, at the right spot, and she could well crack.

*

Gareth began.

"I'll take you back to April '82 and the Argentine grab for the Falklands. On Saturday 3rd our Prime Minister announced to the House that a task force was to be assembled with a view to retaking the islands. Washington was displeased. There, the imperative was to find a win-win solution. These were two valued allies. A shooting war was to be avoided......, though of course in a strict sense one had already started."

"With the armed occupation," Alan acknowledged.

"Which was bloodless," continued Gareth. "And while the conflict remained so there was scope for Washington to at least give an appearance of not taking sides. To have to do that was diplomatic catastrophe, a setback for strategic goals either with NATO, or in Central America. Either way it was lose. The answer had to lie in talks."

"Which were in hand," Alan reminded them. "Al Haig was working on it with the Peruvians."

"But talks meant time," said Gareth, "and in London time was of the essence. There was a sense of every passing hour lending legitimacy to the occupation. And for the task force, once mustered, it was strike or stale. London and Washington were at odds. Here the invader had to be driven off whether by action or potent threat. There, it was talk them off, find a face saving formula...... and to this end the Americans were going to use every device available to keep the protagonists at more than swords' length."

"But not by peacekeeping," remarked Jane. "I don't recall a third force."

"Because we out manoeuvred the Argentines at the UN," said Jeremy.

"And because of the distances," added Gareth. "It was in this that the Americans thought they had the trump card. To get even close to having a sufficient knowledge of Argentine dispositions and intentions the British were reliant on US technology. The Americans had the listening stations in Chile and in Panama. They had their specialist analysts in the Pentagon, and linking all this and the high command here they had the appropriately positioned satellites. And it wasn't just one way. Messages had to be sent, situational reports and orders had to go to those who needed to know....... speedily, accurately and securely."

"My understanding is that on our own we were stretched beyond Ascension," said Jeremy, "barely half way."

"Ship to ship messaging was an option," continued Gareth, "but this offered a window to the enemy. We had the firepower, particularly in the subs, but Galtieri had the proximity. We had to keep them guessing as to how our units were positioned. We could do this....."

".......but this meant ceding a measure of control to the Pentagon," said Jeremy.

"Exactly," said Gareth. "In handling the raw signals the Americans gained a scope for manipulation. Messages could be delayed, they could be distorted, they could be leaked even."

"And this happened?" Asked Jane.

"I can't say," answered Gareth, "but early in the game there were incidents that look now to have been decidedly cat and mouse. They involved Naval units mainly. We were still on Ascension. What matters is that at Northwood there was an awareness that this could happen and that steps were taken to ensure that for some orders another route might be available, one that was less likely to suffer compromise."

"Go on," urged Jeremy.

"First consider the *Kampala's* movements. After calling in at Freetown, and I'll come back to that in a moment, she didn't join with the ground force muster at Ascension. She sailed on to move closer to the Naval group, the submarines, the frigates, the destroyers, and the carriers that were lining themselves up on the southern forties. It's been asked why she did this when for the sailors there was sufficient medical provision on the carriers."

"Asked by whom?" challenged Steve.

"Certainly by people in Argentina," replied Gareth. "I still hear from one, regularly. An infantryman, I met him on the *Kampala*. He lost a brother when the *Belgrano* went down."

"The *Belgrano* !" Exclaimed Jane.

"Another vessel, the movements of which we might consider," said Gareth grimly.

"Haven't we had this in the House of Commons?" asked Kate. "That Scots MP, he's been going on and on about it. You're up with this Jeremy. The government is said to have lied. It can be proved that the ship was outside the exclusion zone and sailing away when she was attacked."

"Dalyell," confirmed Jeremy, "Tam Dalyell. You believe he's on the right trail do you Gareth?"

"I don't. I believe him to have been lured into a smokescreen. They've got him floundering."

"Who have?" Kate was sceptical.

"The Government. With their crafty leaks they've got him chasing the elusive signals log of *HMS Conqueror,* the sub that shadowed and sank the warship. With this he can brand Maggie a liar, and a war criminal to boot. But what's this to the Great British public? She's a politician, since when were they expected to be straight? And that was a submarine, for what they cost in taxes it was about time one did something."

"But the civil servant who was put on trial for leaking," Kate went on, "the one who was acquitted, are you saying that it was all a sham?"

"Why not?" joined Jeremy. "If he wanted out of that particular career and fancied dipping into journalism then here was the springboard...... ideal, I'd say."

"And should he tire of facts getting in the way of his more lively stories then he might move on and take a try at college lecturing," quipped Kate, acidly. She wasn't to be so easily convinced. And she was ready to challenge her former patient. "So for our benefits now Gareth, how would you set Mr Dalyell on what you see to be the right path?"

"Our command at Northwood knows the Pentagon controlled signals route to be compromised. We also suspect Washington's game...... delay basically. For starters we like to play along. That way there's reinforcement of the impression that all is under American control. Should we Brits then strike independently, then at first there'll be an erroneous assumption of Pentagon connivance. Reasonable?"

"Not unreasonable," said Alan. "Carry on."

"Whilst doing this, as the warships group and the peace talks proceed, Northwood Command sets itself up an independent line of communication ...... not so much for routine signals traffic as for developing the option of delivering an early knock out blow, a sucker punch."

"Hit one capital ship and the rest will run for port," said Jeremy.

"You have it," said Gareth approvingly. "The hot line is routed through Gibraltar, and Freetown, to Ascension."

"And from there?" asked Steve.

"To a forward post, a floating forward post. A floating AWAC facility, equipped to present Northwood with a truer picture of what is where in the South Atlantic than what was being delivered via the US signals line. And this wasn't just about reconnaissance, remember. Should there be a critical moment for a crucial command then this was the route."

"Is this so controversial?" wondered the nurse. "There was that survey ship down there....."

"Which had been rumbled Kate, and was out of it," said Gareth adopting a compelling gravitas, "Mr Dalyell should be telling of your ship, the *Kampala*, telling of how when she did the schools cruises she spent season after season pottering around the Med. We would hear how many of the Arab countries preferred to keep her away from their waters and certainly their ports. The cruising was a cover they maintained. As well as educating kids she was providing sustenance for Tel Aviv.... in the form of information mainly. As she moved she listened and she reported, gleaning the positions and the readiness of potentially hostile forces. And maybe that was OK as far as it went. We have to tolerate Russian factory ships, they must likewise put up with our trawlers venturing to the north and east of Norway. It's all part of the great game, and if done in the name of deterrence then it's done in the name of peace."

"Arguable that," muttered Jeremy. Gareth continued.

"But then we get this Falklands thing and it's freaky, totally freaky. Every one seems to want to avoid a scrap, but where's the common ground? People fear the worst, and almost as if to partly allay that fear we have the token of the 'hospital ship'. This, with the exclusion zone, gives a Queensburyness to the arena......"

".......which in the context of the distances involved was probably to our advantage," added Alan.

"The Junta were taking on a nuclear armed power," countered Jeremy. "Reason enough there to fear escalation."

"Whatever," said Gareth. "My point is that if a hospital ship was to be included in the South Atlantic palace of varieties then the *Kampala*, with her dormitories, class and common rooms was ideal for the bill. Kate can tell us how the pupils were off loaded at Naples and the ship then brought to Gibraltar for rapid modifications.....the operating theatre, the intensive care wards, and the helicopter pad that she still carries."

"We joined her there," said Kate.

"These things were quite well publicised," continued Gareth, "and to good effect."

"Meaning?" queried Steve.

"That I think there could have been more to this than doctors and nurses, and this is where Mr Dalyell's sleuthing might be better directed. It's been said that whilst at Gibraltar the ship also acquired an additional communications suite, something apart from the medical function, a self contained module, high, towards the front end somewhere. It would have been manned by a specialist team, quarantined from the rest of the personnel...... military and civilian. In effect there were two ships leaving Gibraltar. They shared the same ironwork and the same helm, but not the same business......far from it."

"You're suggesting that her previous SIGINT capacity was enhanced for a posting beyond Ascension," said Jeremy," so that from there she could collect and dispatch home a truer picture of the situation than might be arriving via the Pentagon."

"More than that," stated Gareth firmly, "significantly more. She was at the same time equipped to be the last leg of a command relay, an additional capacity......"

"......through which Northwood could reserve that independence of action you spoke of," continued Steve.

"First I've heard of this," scoffed Kate.

"Naturally," countered Jeremy, scenting conspiracy, ".......strictly 'need to know' of course."

"Because at first it was a contingency," explained the Welshman, "an option of last resort which, in theory at least, could be used sparingly. The idea was to have the measure of Washington should they over meddle. The armed response would be sudden rather than severe, that was how it was argued....... cautionary rather than catastrophic, but enough to secure the initiative."

"But you don't talk theory when it's 'action stations'," said Jeremy. "Whether you're at Northwood command or sat in a sub 8000 miles away you're not going to be inclined to do things by halves, not when the dealing is in high explosives. Go off half cock and you're dead, likewise your cause."

The lecturer won a nod from the guardsman.

"This was how Chadwick argued it, and why at heart he wanted no part," added Gareth.

"Chadwick?" To Jane the name was new, but not to Alan.

"Captain Brian Chadwick," he said. "Kate will remember Chadwick."

Kate took up the prompt.

"Brian Chadwick was the Captain of the *Kampala* when she left Gibraltar. He'd welcomed us aboard. Seemed OK then, but we were hardly on our way when he fell ill."

"Did he have the stomach for it all? This would appear to be the question." Jeremy had been following Gareth's every word.

"He'd long suffered an ulcer," explained the nurse. "We were all under strain. It told on him. There was a perforation. We had to operate. He was taken off at Freetown, replaced."

"That was in the latter part of April, and my information is that he was struggling with what was being asked of his ship," continued Gareth, looking increasingly towards Jeremy. The pair were in dialogue. What Kate had said was incidental.

"The SIGINT role in the Med was one thing......this was something else, something operational. His responsibility for the ship and all on her weighed heavily. Then there was the integrity of the Red Cross to uphold. Made privy to her full function he feared miscalculation, overkill, and retaliation in kind....perhaps even against his own vessel. These were grave misgivings. He wanted them logged, formally logged, just in case. Were this to be denied him then he would make a personal record."

"An attitude which posed a security problem. The ulcer could have been fortuitous."

"Not for Brian Chadwick, Jeremy," said Alan. "The condition proved fatal."

"He wasn't a young man," said Kate. "You can get complications."

"Especially in the Tropics," offered Steve. "Sierra Leone's hardly renowned for its convalescent homes."

"Good point," conceded Gareth, "except that it wasn't in Freetown that he died. The *Kampala* sailed on under fresh command, and by early May his condition had stabilised sufficiently for him to be flown back here, I believe to Lynham. He was taken to nearby Wroughton where there's a secure military hospital. That's where he died, in the second week of May. You'll recall that the *Belgrano* was attacked and sunk during the first week. By that time the *Kampala* would have been well to the south of Ascension."

"I hear what you're saying," said Jeremy. "The mercy mission ship was used to relay the command to attack the Argentine cruiser, the intention probably being to disable rather than sink and slaughter. But slaughter it was, of course, and thereafter Captain Brian Chadwick knew too much. He would have been kept away from the facts and the statistics, but they had to catch up with him some time.....as would the prying journalists."

"So complications there had to be," reasoned Gareth. "For a loose cannon on the top deck there's just the one place......over the side!"

"I don't buy this," protested Kate. "It's easy to play with circumstantial evidence."

"Look at the confusion there's been about the movements of the *Belgrano* and the sub," argued Jeremy. "Here's the explanation..... American meddling, British secrecy. At first it was preposterously said that the Captain of the sub was shooting from the hip, that it was an unsanctioned attack. I can see why now. How else could it have happened? That's what the Pentagon would have been asking. All other possibilities they had covered. That's what they thought."

"And how could they now persuade the Junta that they hadn't connived in this, that they hadn't been double dealing?" Gareth posed. "Only by abandoning Maggie completely, and that they could never do. They had to align with the Brits. They'd been forced to choose. Al Haig, you'd better come home!"

"The Captain was well cared for on the ship," insisted Kate, her manner surly. "And I was there remember. OK you have these theories, but show me proof. Show me that the *Kampala* had a second signals log, that she was talking to the *Conqueror*. For the Captain....... find me a medical record that doesn't point to natural causes."

"There'll be no record," said Alan, "in each case. No record, no proof, I've put this to Gareth already. It might have existed. If so it would have been destroyed....... long ago."

"Gareth?" said Jane. "All safely expunged?"

"Alan's convinced. Me? I'm not so sure, because I don't even think the Government is."

"Not convinced? Explain," demanded Kate.

"You must accept a double premise. Firstly, that having been fooled Washington was then quickly on to what had happened. There

144

was nothing they could do about it, but that's not to say they couldn't work it out. Officially it would have to stay secret. It was either prop Maggie or drop Maggie. The alternative was Michael Foot, a proclaimed unilateral disarmer....."

"So prop it has to be," reasoned Jeremy. "I'll accept that part Gareth. Secondly....?"

"Secondly that there are elements in the US State and Defence Departments that are seeking to disrupt the Anglo American alliance. These might be covert wreckers in the pay of Moscow perhaps, or Libya maybe, or their dissent might be milder in species. Perhaps they feel the special relationship to be an outmoded, overvalued entity, that it may be in the way of a more progressive approach to the Irish problem, or to the securing of US goals in South and Central America. Whatever, the essence is that if these people have the will and the position to embarrass the Atlanticists then all that's required is opportunity. Follow me?"

"I'll buy that too," replied Jeremy. "Go on."

"Once aware of the *Kampala's* capabilities those in the US who were friendly to Argentina would have been quick to warn......but by then of course she'd done her worst. An attack against her was considered but rejected. Any military gain would now be minimal, on the propaganda front there was far too much to lose."

"And after the first land battle, Goose Green, she carried a stock of hostages," continued Jeremy, "your friend amongst them."

"They were well cared for!" Kate was getting angry. "As were you Gareth, and Brian Chadwick too."

"Whilst we were on board, certainly," conceded the guardsman. "It's not that the ship wasn't an effective hospital, it's what she'd been besides......and this still rankles in Argentina. There's much grief, there's much anger. I know something of this. I've lost part of a limb. I've lost my looks, career. And look at you Kate. You're picking yourself up now, down here, but for a while you found it rough ....I can see that. Peace of mind you lost. It's the waste that we rue. We're all paid up members of the same club....the *'how the hell was it all allowed to happen'* fellowship.*"

"There's a lot of us," sighed the nurse.

"And I fancy the membership extends to the topmost departments and the topmost ranks therein," added Jeremy.

"Doubtless," agreed Gareth, "and this rationale offers succour to those whose apparent life's work it's become to bring those who bent the rules to some sort of account, whether this be to assuage grief or merely to make political mischief. I've gathered a personal awareness of this. I strongly suspect that I've been used in their campaign."

"You?" Jane's tone demanded further explanation. Gareth obliged.

"Two setbacks they've suffered. The first, self-inflicted, was to cry foul during the conflict. Their claim then that the *Kampala* had an active military role was too easily dismissed as propaganda. The second has been the way that Tam Dalyell has made such an issue of the movements of the *Belgrano* and the *Conqueror.* He thinks he's being clever. I fancy he's being fooled."

"And those who want the *Kampala's* role more closely scrutinised are being foiled, frustrated," added Jeremy.

"But they are not without help," continued Gareth. " As I said, within the vast battalion that is US Intelligence there will be a few who are quietly wanting them to succeed, and to the extent that they'll be ready to quietly leak. The Americans are avid compilers of information. They will have a database on British Service personnel. It will hold career details, health details, financial details, family details, where and when we've been on holiday, all that sort of thing. They've only to ask and the screen will tell of all who have resigned or been dismissed from the forces since '82. My name would come up. Bluff Cove would be there, and the fact that I was treated on the *Kampala*. There would be mention of my wounds, and also of the contact that I maintain with Alberto. I've never made any secret of that. Asked about it by reporters, I've always told them. You would have an entry Kate. It would tell of disillusionment and depression, and your moving on to here, and the way your spirit has rallied. If you've opened any joint bank accounts they'll have you in there Jeremy. That's how easy it is to be netted."

"Go on," urged the lecturer.

"I just want you to bear the general picture in mind as I give to you another name. It has cropped up in the news, but not so prominently or so frequently as to have made any great impact."

"Try us," said Jane.

"Robert Green," announced Gareth. "Commander Robert Green. Ring any bells?"

Heads shook, Kate's, Jeremy's, Steve's, Jane's, but not Alan's. He was still. For the moment he would say nothing. The former soldier was doing well.

"A Naval Commander," said Steve, "so he would have had a ship, or a sub....one of the carriers was it?"

"He was land based," corrected Gareth. "He held a post at Northwood..... communications officer. The order to attack the *Belgrano* would have crossed his desk."

"And he's on record as having had difficulty with this?" asked Kate.

"Unlikely, but we can't be sure," answered Gareth. "What we do know is that like you he resigned, and again there was disillusion. Here was someone else needing to move on."

"And someone else on that US list," Jeremy added.

"Complete with the customary personal details, including a next of kin, in this instance an Aunt, her name........ Miss Hilda Murrell."

"Ahaa, yes, now you mention the name." As he spoke Jeremy drew himself closer to the table. He seemed to grow in his chair. Gareth primed him further.

"In the file her name will have been somehow highlighted, this to show that here was a character who'd already warranted an entry in her own right, by dint of her own activities. I sense that Jeremy knows something of these....Jeremy?"

"Miss Hilda Murrell was an expert on rose growing. She was also a keen naturalist with an associated concern for the environment. She lived in Gareth's neck of the woods, close to the Welsh border, Shrewsbury."

"And for this she's picked up by US intelligence?" questioned Steve.

"She also didn't like the idea of nuclear power stations," continued Jeremy bluntly. "They were going to be expensive she claimed, more so than the Government cared to admit. There had to be safe waste disposal, and a safe dismantling of obsolete plant. This required public money, at least as much as being asked by the miners to keep their pits alive. The miners' unions liked what she had to say, and she was ready to advise them. She had friends also amongst those who opposed the Cruise and the Trident missile programmes. Protest movements benefited from her donations. On two separate fronts she was mixing with the enemy within. Small wonder that she merited her own file."

"And I think that this file and that of her nephew were scrutinised in combination," said Gareth. "And that details there from were leaked to Argentina, to those whose mission it had become to expose the *Kampala*. They'd had to listen to Dalyell barking up the wrong pile of logs. How frustrating, how galling, to see all that thoroughness and perseverance squandered."

"But here at last was hope," said Jeremy, "a chink of light!"

"It was unlikely to lead to a sworn statement," said Gareth, "but in answer to a sufficiently pointed enquiry a refusal to categorically deny can often be enough. The man was there, remember at Northwood. And if the nephew had the facts, the Aunt had the contacts. She was the avenue of approach. She would know where to be discrete and when to go public. Government mendacity was her theme of course....... but one big problem."

"Which was?" Steve was intrigued.

"Obvious," claimed Jeremy. "If her activism warranted an entry in those US files then likewise she would have been a listed troublemaker over here. That means she would have been subject to a degree of surveillance."

"Not followed, surely?" Jane was asking Gareth rather than Jeremy.

"Not followed, but there would have been phone monitoring and mail intercepts," replied the Welshman. "And this is where I get brought into things. In Argentina it's known that Alberto and I are corresponding, and that there's no suspicion, either in that country or this, of there being any kind of mischief in our exchanges. The fact that I live quite near to Miss Murrell is noted and the idea is hatched that, through Alberto, I can be the one to bring her and her nephew, as it were, into play."

"You were to be an errand boy," said Steve. He knew the feeling.

"That's what I was," confirmed Gareth. "In the middle of March last year I receive a routine missive from Alberto and enclosed amongst the pages is a sealed envelope. It's addressed to Miss Murrell, and I'm to deliver it. What it was about I had no idea, and there was nothing to indicate that Alberto did. What I know now I've learned since. All I had to do was take it round. That's what I did."

"And you met her?" asked Kate.

"I did, at her door. She took it from my own hands. I gave her my phone number...... that's should she wish to use me for any reply."

"And what happened next?" Steve was keen to hear.

"My understanding is that word of the leak from US intelligence to Argentina got back to mainstream Washington. A bit of ferreting, the full implications are fathomed, and then it's panic. That's because Alberto's letter is already with me, and I'm about to deliver the thing. It was too late to intercept. London was contacted and at a very high level the decision was taken to retrieve, as quickly and as innocuously as possible. If the world had come to terms with the loss of those scores of men on the *Belgrano,* the fate of Brian Chadwick was something else. Were a good journalist to get hold of that then the excrement would truly be in the air conditioning."

'Cairns,' Steve thought. Why? There were parallels. There'd been another ship, and she'd had to endure allegations, again concerning signal transmissions, again irregularly logged. And there'd been another old salt who'd met an untimely death......and another sealed envelope, one that had survived for thirty years, to fall now into his own hands. He said nothing. It was Jeremy who spoke.

"Hilda Murrell is dead. I've read about this. I've seen programmes. She was killed unlawfully, murdered it's said.........by burglars?"

"It's what the police say," responded Alan. "And no one's come close to proving otherwise."

"How soon af......."

"Just two days Jane, two days after I called."

"And did you hear anything more of that letter?" asked Jeremy " Did anyone find your number and call back?"

"Someone did phone me, a man. He said he was Robert Green. I was very wary, and he was too I sensed. We were both angling, and neither of us biting..... and that was that. I've been following the story in the press, local and national. I've been sending cuttings back for Alberto. And in the course of our correspondence I've gathered more and more on those suspicions about the *Kampala* .... still mere suspicions, alas."

"The police in Shropshire," joined Jane. "How do you rate their performance?"

"Inept," answered Gareth, with dismissive bluntness.

"How surprising," scoffed Jeremy.

"Why the irony Jeremy?" Jane wanted to know.

"Because everything points to a certain type of perpetrator," explained Jeremy. "And this type are what they are by virtue of being well nigh impossible to identify individually, and well nigh impossible to properly control."

"And this type?" Kate was quietly insistent.

"Are known as 'temps' to those who seek their services." Jeremy paused, only for Alan to urge him on.

"Don't stop, let's hear what *Guardian man* understands by this term."

"They're crooks. Crooks hired by crooks. The hired will typically be a serial offender. Adept at small time breaking and entering he'll have been caught convicted and imprisoned more than once. For most it will be the only life they know. A few can claim to be making a legitimate living on the proceeds of a business. They might deal in used cars, or scrap metal. They might have a garage, or command a retinue of hire out bouncers. What they aspire to is a territory, a personal parish in which they can operate with a minimum of harassment from the law and a minimum of competition from their kind. Sometimes a local constabulary will connive in this, their maxim being that it's better the devil you know."

"And the hirer?" encouraged Alan.

"Will be a big time crook, really big time. Think Nixon. In an ideal world our politicians wouldn't dream of breaking the laws they are pledged to uphold. We live though in the real world. We have a Prime Minister who talks glowingly of those Ministers and senior civil servants who bring to her solutions rather than problems, and this appears to have been a key to advancement in recent years. Temps offer a solution, usually a quick fix solution, and that would appear to be what was required following your call, Gareth, on Hilda Murrell."

"Killing the woman though.....?" said Kate.

"A practised house breaker won't necessarily be a practised killer," replied Gareth. "This was a mess. She probably disturbed him and took him on, bless her. It looks like he panicked. The chief problem with the device is control."

"And the advantages?" Could there be any? Jane was asking.

"Deniability," said Jeremy, authority in his voice. "If they're caught then they're on their own. That's the deal. Should they renege and attempt to squeal then by their records they'll be wanting for credibility. Proven liars they are. A good job will be well rewarded, cash in the hand, further opportunities. A foul up and the punishment can be severe. Loose ends are intolerable. A 'temp' will be recruited and supervised through a middleman. The cash comes down from the man in Whitehall and that helps, but essentially he controls by fear. He's the gang master. Think in terms of a mercenary captain, and think too in terms of the associated hardware. He'll be proficient in its use. He's ruthless. He has to be to survive."

"So if in their hearts," reasoned Steve, "the police know their culprit to be already sporting a set of concrete galoshes, then they're bound to appear inept, half hearted." He shrugged. Old Jack's tale of Rory Duggan had brought him a measured perspective. Those likely to know anything were no less likely to be lying low. Such things might take a generation or more to emerge.

If the words were neutral, not so the body language. Kate read the boy's despair, a mood she was conditioned to counter.

"Too much of this is supposition," she stated flatly. "In fact all of it is. If what came via Washington was dis-information then who's to say it wasn't calculated to deceive those listening on behalf of the enemy? If challenged, that's what they would claim. You would need to find documents."

"The *Kampala's* South Atlantic log.....?" suggested Jane.

".......will have been laundered long ago," said Jeremy, "and likewise the Captain's medical records. If there was a smoking gun then it's been reloaded...... in readiness for the next person deemed to know, or even suspect, a little too much. Mr Green will have every right to be cautious, for the sake of other relatives as much as for himself. Maybe it's been admitted to him that what happened to his aunt was a clumsy mistake, and on that understanding he's found a measure of forgiveness. We don't know."

"And meanwhile the trail goes cold," said Alan. "Another year and every jail in the country will have its queue of privilege seeking convicts telling that the deed was done by this individual or that, that gang or this. The thing gets even more muddied, and this of course is what the man in Whitehall wants. It was a long shot. It misfired messily. Tough...... but no one need know. And what can we do?"

Gareth answered.

" 'Let it go,' Alan will say. And that's why I'm here. It's more than muddied, it's become a mire, a bog that can swallow you whole, that's what he means. And he says I'm worth better, he says 'join me', and so here I am."

'And you can join me too,' thought Steve.

"Kate?" Alan's tone confirmed that Gareth's piece had been said, that he was grateful, and that now it was the turn of the nurse..... from whom fact might be preferable to speculation. She wasn't about to disappoint.

"A smoking gun and a dripping syringe, that's what you want and that's what you won't get. The *Kampala* didn't carry torpedoes.... and believe what you like about what might or might not have been relayed through her aerials, no one on board would have given orders to fire. Serviceman or servicewoman, you're there to follow orders. Things can go wrong, as they did for your unit Gareth at Bluff Cove. You can feel betrayed, but you don't whinge. It's not about fairness. It's for others to reason why. Loyalty demands that we desist. This is what loyalty means. If conscience intervenes then it fails the test. If you don't like that then you get out....."

"As this Mr Green has," said Jane.

"And when 'out' then you shut up, " continued Kate. "Mr Green is not in the business of attacking former comrades, and neither am I ..... certainly not on the basis of hearsay and enemy propaganda."

"So your having come out," posed Steve, "has that become a matter of regret?"

"No. I'm happy enough now as a civilian nurse working with accident casualties. Keeps me busy, keeps the past in its place. Jeremy's helped me. We've helped each other. We can't re-fight the Falklands conflict any more than we can re-fight the Spanish Civil War."

It was just a quip, an affectionate throw away dig at her partner and her partner's profession maybe, and Jeremy had smirked.....but not Steve. The past wasn't to be dismissed so easily as she and Alan might have wished. There might be opportunity here, a hobby horse that could perhaps be put to work on Old Jack's cause.

Kate continued, mentioning Steve's fall and recovery, and Hugh Trembath's close concern. And now it was on to her meeting Alan in Truro and how he'd subsequently looked in at the hospital and sought her assistance to find out more about one David Morrish..... the name from earlier.

He was a solicitor. He was single. He was a member at the country club over at St Erme where he would often enjoy an evening meal, occasionally with a client, sometimes with professional associates, but more often alone. Should he be on his own, and should there also be an unaccompanied lady then she would not remain so for long. He had a winning charm, one that she had given full opportunity for him to wield.

She'd ventured to the club with this purpose. It had been Alan's idea and it had worked. The evening had been fruitful. She'd learned his address of course, and also of his expectation that this sojourn in Truro was unlikely to be protracted. London he'd come from, from the city, and there he wanted to return, to a practice in which he could take a share of the profit. For the moment though, *Conway's* suited him.

"Did he say why?" said Jane, almost pleading.

"I'm afraid he had me doing most of the talking," said Kate. "Sign of a good technique I suppose."

"So what did you tell him?" asked Gareth. Jeremy moved uneasily.

"Well I gave him my phone number, and I told him I was a nurse, and that a lot of nights I worked ......" Jeremy sighed and looked up at the ceiling, ".....and I told him that I had a live in partner," the others chuckled. "But I tease you too Jane. My best listening was at the start when he came in. I was at the bar and this other guy was too. Morrish knew him and they got talking. This was before he noticed me. They talked about their jobs, or rather an aspect of their jobs where there was this overlapping interest. The other character was from the Estate Agent's which neighbours *Conway's*. It seems they're hawking one of these holiday bond schemes. You pay in, you get points, and you can redeem these by spending time at a variety of attractive locations. The impression I got was that Morrish does a lot of the legal work on behalf of the company running the plan, and that this could be starting to stretch him. The scheme's being sold all over the place. It's catching on."

"And this might be why the gentle routine of a Truro practice might suit him," said Jane.

"And he's living right next door to the chap who started on the ferry at near enough the same time," added Steve.

"And in his professional capacity he'll be receiving and sending on monies paid in for these holiday points," said Jeremy, with a glance across to Alan. That glance was loaded. The recipient's eyebrows lifted. Tacit speculation was being tacitly endorsed, encouraged even. "I'll call in and pick up some brochures for this scheme. Find out more about it if we can, perhaps see who the directors are?"

"Do that Jeremy, I'd be grateful," said Alan.

"And next time I can maybe make a better contribution," muttered the lecturer.

"Don't belittle what you gave us earlier," said Alan, "and you've been listening, I've noted that. Keep listening. When Steve's done his piece I'm going to ask what you make of it all. Now Steve..."

Steve looked at Gareth. The soldier hadn't mentioned Roundwood. He was indebted. How much of this should he himself say? And what, if anything, of Old Jack? He was nervous, hesitant.

*

Hugh Trembath was rarely hesitant. Here was a man of decision. With Alan, information was to be relayed. For Hugh it was to be acted upon. He'd completed his Portscatho shift and there was time to spare before the last ferry. It gave a chance to drive southwards onto the near enisled parish of St Anthony. The ridge offered an unofficial station, one for looking in rather than out. There was a quiet lane, and as it dropped on the Percuil side of the brow there was a hedge gap. He could pull in, and he could look down and across to the back of St. Mawes.

Percuil Yard was to the fore, with its chandlery and also its proprietor. Through his binoculars he could make out Colin Toms, scouting his waterfront, checking his berths, making sure all were up to date with their dues. Colin had told him of the *Speedwell*, but he had nothing there now to resemble her description.

At a further distance, in the mouth of the river, he could see *Flushing Run* turning in towards the harbour town's main quay. Jack Spargo had five aboard. It had been the ideal evening. They'd be back, and they'd be telling their colleagues and friends. It had been a good initiative.

The coastguard checked his watch. Prout knew he was on shift today and he might yet contact him on the vehicle radio. It was worth waiting a while in case. He was placed to get a strong signal. He had the channel open..... and this was him, speaking from Devoran he said. Responding call sign for call sign Trembath fine-tuned his reception. He was ready now for the main message:

"Word from the passage. The *Speedwell* is at Tolverne, on the jetty, unattended. Grigson has taken his bike, but not across the ferry."

"So he's on the Roseland somewhere."

"Somewhere," repeated Prout, "and something else..... the boy. After we'd given him that lift I said that I'd previously seen him about. Then, I couldn't say where and you asked me to put some thought to it."

"And you have?"

"Twice, I now recall seeing him. Most recently it was with Ralph Bartlett, in his van, with Byrne girl."

"And before that?"

"With Grigson, on the *Speedwell*. They were headed up towards Restronguet, keeping to the inside of the Churchtown moorings."

"As if to have come out of the Creek?" suggested the Coastguard.

"Very likely," confirmed Prout.

The exchange was closed, and Hugh Trembath could this time take food for thought. The boy and Grigson had become acquainted, and the upshot was likely to have been an introduction for the latter to Jack Butters, and maybe also Jack Spargo. And why not?...... The old man had the memories, the young man the working boat. Prime material this was for one in Grigson's line, and Steve of course was ever helpful, ever useful.

*

Steve began by turning to Kate.

"These South Atlantic experiences, yours and Gareth's, only so much were you prepared for. For all your professionalism, the pair of you have had to adjust. I can see how former certainties were

155

shaken, that there's having to be a period of adjustment. And I can see, Kate, that you're working through it, but for Gareth it's less straightforward..... if that's the right word. For you are able bodied. You can get the job, you can do it, and that's helped see you through. You've said as much. But how can you say 'best foot forward' to someone injured as Gareth is, or 'look to the future' to someone with wasted sight?" The boy paused, summoning courage, summoning the right words. "Maybe it's not so easy for them, and maybe we should respect this."

"By leaving them behind, to sniff and hobble their way along blind alleys?" Alan wasn't mincing.

"I don't know," said Steve "but isn't that sometimes preferable to despair."

"No, for this is a symptom of despair," countered Grigson. "One we cannot afford to indulge. The challenge to all is to find a positive alternative. Which is why Gareth's here. He's said as much. If you think me insensitive it'll be because you don't know that he and I have already had this conversation. It's your turn Steve. We're waiting. It's the here and now we're concerned with." Alan's words were all the more brutal for being gently spoken. Gareth had been invited here, not ordered. He hadn't needed to show. If he did, then it wasn't to hear someone condescend to complain on his behalf.

Steve continued, chastened but resilient.

"Obedience," he began. "I know what's expected of me. Jane first and then you Alan..... you've wanted an extra pair of eyes and ears and hands, and you're not only ones putting them to use."

"Like who else Steve?" asked Jane .

"Like Hugh Trembath. He's been curious about my contact with you, Jane, and curious too about how I came to be taken to the hospital. You know what he's about Jane, and you've met him Kate. He likes to know what's going on. If I start avoiding him then the more he's going to wonder. He'll have noted your presence Gareth, and if he hasn't already he'll soon work out who you are."

"Best to tell me more about him then," said Gareth. Steve obliged.

He related how the young Hugh had been brought up in Plymouth after the family had been moved out of the house during the war. How he'd attended boarding school and then the Naval College at Dartmouth before following a distinguished career in the senior service.

156

On retirement there was the stewardship of the estate, the coastguard work, the local councils and the local preaching.

Steve explained how he'd been welcomed into the impressively renovated Carwinion House, and even how he'd been proudly shown Hugh's relics from the requisition collection, the buttons and the badges and the bullets. Mention was made of the well-connected wife, and a daughter for whom there were lofty aspirations. And where were they? They were in the capital with his father, a Sir, a famous Sir, a renowned Conservative MP no less.

Jeremy leant forward. Westminster, politics, once again they were moving on to his territory!

"And you've met this eminent figure Steve?"

"Not this year, yet, nor last, but before that fairly often. That was when I was deemed a suitable playmate for his grand daughter. His scene is London, like his son's is here in Cornwall."

"And he became an MP in....?"

"........ '51, the year that Churchill won for the Tories." Steve was proud to answer so informatively.

"The year of Mossadeq. That was the jolt for Attlee." Jeremy was into his stride. "Wonderful idea nationalisation....until it caught on with the Arabs that was. Then it was do as I say, not as I do. And it was the Yanks of course who put them up to it."

The others were looking puzzled. They looked to Alan, half expecting him to rein the lecturer, but he was to surprise them.

"Remind us Jeremy.... ," he said, "......and briefly if you can."

"These days the political buzz word is 'privatisation'. First the telephones, next off it'll be gas. Back then the fashion was the other way....... 'public ownership', and not just for the old lame ducks, the trains and the pits. A road haulage network would make profits for the country, as would bus and coach services. Essential to all this though was a continued supply of cheap oil, and this would come from British owned installations in the Persian Gulf, notably in Iran. But the Americans queered the calculations. They offered neighbouring countries a better share of the takings and they encouraged the Iranian leader, Dr Mossadeq, to demand no less from Anglo-Iranian. The company resisted and found itself facing a compulsory purchase, the shareholders having to accept imposed compensation. It wasn't too well received."

"Amongst the 'Rule Britannia' brigade," said Kate.

"Which at that time was most people," Jeremy reminded her. "The general view was that Mossadeq was a re incarnation of the Mahdi and, by jingo, that he should be similarly sorted. In retrospect he was just another in the post war procession of nationalist leaders who were impatient to call our progressively transparent bluff. It had been done in India, and in Pakistan and Burma, as it would be later in Cyprus, at Suez, and throughout Africa. Dr Mossadeq was just one more to tweak the lion's tail with impunity. Over did it though....went on to upset the Americans, the power that had effectively put him in. He was showing an inclination to stray offside in the cold war game. He was soon subbed off."

"A lesson that could have been heeded in Buenos Aries more recently," remarked Gareth.

"But returning to '51," said the lecturer, "the prospect of dearer oil squeezed Attlee out of business. The Americans were already extorting more from us in Korea....... the price for not nuking the Chinese..... and the combination meant a service charge on the best of the bargains struck with the voters in '45 and '50......the welfare provisions."

"Do I detect a strain of anti Amercanism in this?" asked Jane.

"You do," ho-hummed Kate.

"It's just this cant about a 'special relationship' that gets to me," protested Jeremy. "When Washington needs a credible ally against the Reds they'll get behind us, but only to that extent. Beyond, and we're just another industrial competitor and back in '51 we were still on our knees. Aramco, General Motors, Boeing, they were placed to take the lion's share of the future. Morris and De Havilland would have their place, but no longer was it top table. If we were to be assisted to our feet then it was to be on no more than crumbs. Helping ourselves to cheap Arab oil was no longer on."

"Anyway, back to Cornwall," said Alan. "How did Sir Edward get to be an MP Steve? What did he do before?"

"Before the war he had the estate of course, but also he worked for the Duchy, and he must have been well thought of because during the war he was sent out to the Caribbean to assist his old boss. That was the Duke who became King and then gave up the throne to marry the American lady."

"That would have been the Bahamas," said Jeremy.

"And clearly this was a good move," observed Alan. "Edward Trembath, still a youngish man, came back to Plymouth brimming with confidence and connections. He helped piece the place together and it was an easy step then from local into national politics."

"Sounds like a good man to ask," said Jeremy. There was mischief in his voice, of the playful nature.

"Ask what?" Steve said.

"An Aid de Campe to the Duke of Windsor? war time Governor of the Bahamas?........One question only." Jeremy was winding them up.

"Which is?" yawned Kate.

"Who killed Harry Oakes?" said Jeremy, his tone suggesting that the question should have immediately been on everyone's lips. "It's a mystery still. There was a trial, but the accused was famously acquitted."

The others looked amongst themselves. All save Alan looked bemused. Kate voiced a general reaction.

"Now it's a whodunnit from fifty years ago. Do we really need this?" The exasperation was genuine.

"Perhaps not," conceded Jeremy, "but what an opportunity. Steve could be speaking with a guy who was actually there, so, so close to events."

The boy, though, was looking utterly puzzled. He needed priming on this one, and the say so was with Alan. Should Jeremy be indulged?

"Well perhaps when the two of you are together by yourselves at anytime," suggested Grigson tactfully, but not all was being shifted to a back burner. "We'll leave Harry Oakes for now, but not the Duke....not yet. Tell me Jeremy. Why was he, a former Monarch and still a HRH, chosen to fill a political job? The Governorship was an *efficient* post. This was a colony still under Westminster. He was accountable to the Colonial Secretary, and sackable in the event of a mishandling. There were figurehead posts elsewhere, titular Governorships, why wasn't he found one of these? Merely by taking the Bahamas he was distancing himself from the Palace, where all had to be strictly *dignified.* "

"That it was even contemplated amazes me," replied Jeremy, whose tone veered then towards near apology. " I know some of you think me tiresome in this vein, but I'm ready to again suggest this to be about US string pulling."

"But why would they want him there?" scoffed Kate.

"Because he was some one they could control. The FBI would have had a file on him, a good ten inches thick. All the juicy stuff would have been collected, the sexual liaisons, the financial dealings, the outmoded political inclinations,......all sorts of dubious connections which were best kept under wraps."

"You could have made a brilliant historian Jeremy," sniggered Kate "it's just that you were lumbered with this imagination."

"Too dismissive," chided Alan. "In my job it's what you sometimes need."

Steve was sympathetic to this gentlest of rebukes. The Americans had featured in his last conversation with Hugh Trembath. He couldn't share Kate's scepticism.

"Sir Edward's wartime posting to the Caribbean was an American initiative," said the boy. "Hugh's told me this. It was arranged when they took the House. They wanted him and the family out of the way. For him it was a job out there, for the wife and child it was Plymouth."

"There," said Jeremy. "Thank you Steve."

"So how did the Duke perform in his job?" Gareth asked Jeremy.

"Generally quite well, considering that he had to learn as he went along. But then came this murder of the Mr Big and the copy-book gathered a few blots. It was a crime that warranted a special investigation by a specialist team. One could have been summoned from Scotland Yard or perhaps even Washington. Instead the Duke opted to whistle over a couple of City Police detectives from Miami."

"And they were incompetent?" This was Jane.

"I think they were shown to be crooked. They managed to destroy as much evidence as they found, and then when some one was brought to trial it was shown they'd attempted fabrication. It was a fiasco. The accused was acquitted and the thing remained unsolved......conveniently for some."

"And the two clowns went back to Miami leaving the Governor dripping with egg," said Gareth.

"Which might have been easier to wipe off had he first cleared his actions with the Attorney General in London. That's what he's there for after all."

"So the Duke didn't go by the book, is that what you're saying Jeremy?" asked Steve.

"Because important people in the States wanted the waters muddied," anticipated Kate sarcastically.

"As they've shown to have been muddied following the Kennedy thing," snapped Jeremy.

"And as they've much more recently been muddied in Shropshire," added Gareth, pointedly.

"Stretching things there, Gareth," murmured Alan. "But staying with Sir Edward and his wartime exploits, our question to him is not 'Who killed Harry Oakes?', but 'Did the Duke, under pressure from Washington, connive in a cover up?' You might remind the former Duchy employee that his master could well have been vulnerable to top level manipulation, the FBI having been almost certainly furnished with information pertaining to the Governor's own shady dealings in land and currency."

"A shade impertinent!" chortled Jeremy. "You'd be shown the door in an instant. Imagine, if the redoubtable Sir Edward had been leant on too, to go out there and assist with these fun and games."

"Imagine, imagine, imagine ..." Kate was impatient. "Indulge your imagination and we're going to be sat here all night. Steve... is there anything else of note in Sir Edward's early career, or can we at last get back the here and now?"

It was an affectionate exasperation. Steve responded, but not before a brief tease.

"There was another little thing, and there's a story that goes with it which apparently he's fond of telling. It's something else that's been suggested I ask him, and this one I will. Before the war when he was working down here for the Duchy they got him to travel over to France to help set things up for the Duke's wedding. It was at a Chateau near Tours and by the sound of things something of a rush job. Edward's mission was to gather and take over a presentable selection of wedding gifts. I think he came up with the goods, but quite how came to be source of many a colourful reminiscence..... especially when later he got together with a guy called Monckton. He was a Duchy man, and he was entrusted with making sure the event was at least vaguely recognisable as a wedding."

"Walter Monckton no less," said Jeremy. "Now there's a mystery figure..... was he dove or was he carrier pigeon?"

"Dove or carrier pigeon?" Alan repeated. "Enlarge please."

Jeremy obliged.

"Let me tell you of two politicians, and of two humiliations...... one apiece. The dissimilarities are obvious, to the point of almost obscuring the parallels that lay beneath. The more recent episode I chose as the subject of my final year college dissertation. Then, in the early '70s, it was very recent history. Much has been unveiled since, and more will yet."

"And the earlier episode, you've also made a close study of that?" enquired Gareth.

"No, this was undertaken by a fellow student, a then close friend. He'd chosen it for his research project."

"So your episode, Jeremy, was....."

".......it was the '56 Suez fiasco Steve, with Sir Anthony Eden taking the central role. The man miscalculated. Without firm indications to the contrary he assumed that Washington would support his bid to retake the canal by force."

"Where in fact they were to oppose him," added Alan.

"At the UN, of all places," said Jeremy, "the forum where previously he'd won considerable renown. The troops had to be brought home, and the canal effectively ceded. The humiliation was complete and it was public. Eden had to go.... in disgrace."

"Hasn't it been suggested that he might have been manoeuvred out by US State Department people, that they'd found him difficult to work with, particularly over Far East issues, Indo China, Formosa, and all that?"

Gareth's question was gratefully taken up.

"This was the main thrust of my enquiry. Clearly, as the crisis brewed, there'd been communications failures, warnings that hadn't got though, that sort of thing. It had to be asked, though, how much of this might have been contrived. A question mark will always stand over the conduct of Macmillan, then Eden's Chancellor....."

"First in, first out," quipped Alan.

"......and there were others besides. One was this man Monckton. He was Defence Minister, right up until the 'eve of invasion'. At that critical moment he resigned. It can be argued that this began the erosion of the Premier's standing. His power base in Cabinet was undermined, and then in the House, and then in the Country."

"The inference being that this might have been at the American's bidding," followed Kate, the same dash of mockery in her voice.

"Hard evidence is there?" asked Jane. She was in earnest.

"Desperately little," answered the lecturer. "Much went by word of mouth, beyond earshot of the minute scribes..... but you only need see the gaps in Mac's diaries, and in the papers that Walter gathered and normally saved with care."

"So again it's what's left to the imagination." Jane's scepticism again, but softening with a realisation of how closely Alan was listening.

"Which will in some way be fuelled by the earlier episode and the work done by your friend," said Gareth. "Another politician you say. Another Prime Minister is that?"

"Sir Winston Churchill, no less... from November 1956 we go back exactly thirteen years and across to Persia, to Teheran."

"Churchill was at war," said Steve, "and by then he was winning it."

"But was he?" challenged Jeremy. "Some have argued that he was about to lose it." Steve was suddenly looking puzzled, and so too the others. Jeremy led them forward. "We went to war in '39, against Germany, on whose behalf?"

"The people of Poland," answered Gareth confidently. Jeremy nodded.

"When their lands were seized. The exiled Government came to this country, as did a good number of their soldiers and airmen. They joined the fight of course, and were we and they to prevail against the invader then they expected to be restored..... an expectation fuelled by Churchill's stirring early war rhetoric."

"And come mid '43 Hitler was as good as defeated." Gareth was well versed in military history.

"So, in diplomatic terms Germany was no longer the problem," said Jeremy. "Instead it was Russia. The Red Army might have heroically turned the tide at Stalingrad, but that hadn't erased Uncle Joe's part in the carve up of Poland that began the shooting match. Though now they were the deadliest of enemies, in '39 Stalin had been Hitler's accomplice.... to the degree that, for the first eighteen months of the war, Russia's material aid to Hitler far outweighed that received by Britain from the US."

"And the Katyn corpses," muttered Gareth grimly.

"And to cover this and a host of other horrors Stalin badly

needed his own men, puppets, to be keeping a firm hold over post Nazi Poland," reasoned Jeremy, "and this meant no place for those whose cause Winston had been honour bound to champion."

"But the British and a few thousand exiles were never going to retake Poland," said Gareth. "Without the Yanks we would have been hard pushed to re take the Channel Isles!"

"But with the Yanks it could have been a different story," argued Jeremy. "And this is my point. Here is the parallel. If the British and the Americans were making common cause, why shouldn't this have extended to them adopting our guarantee on Poland?"

"Because they knew that without Stalin's efforts against the German's eastern armies, just getting so far as Paris looked a murderous prospect," Alan was speaking with authority.

"Exactly," confirmed Jeremy. "Roosevelt knew that. Churchill knew that. But was this enough to stop the latter from attempting to recruit the former to the cause of the exiles? Teheran, Winston argued, was the place for he and the President to present a united, principled front against Stalin."

"And did they?" asked Jane.

"Nothing like it. If anything, Washington sided with Moscow. And having been snubbed by Roosevelt, Churchill was then cruelly, mercilessly ridiculed by Stalin. The likes of Mr Philby would have been keeping their spy masters well informed about the Prime Minister's abortive scheming. Churchill came home a chastened, dis-empowered man. Teheran was a personal defeat."

"But what about Roosevelt?" said Steve. "This would hardly have enhanced his image."

"Unless the option of confronting Stalin were in some way revealed to be dangerous and self defeating......... and this is where our item of interest crops up. The Teheran three power summit was in November '43, and just a few months before that word had filtered from neutral Stockholm that Russian and German representatives had met in the capital to discuss the possibility of a bilateral cease fire! Mooted between them was a second partition of Poland, this allowing Hitler to re-deploy his Russian front armies in the west. They might stiffen the Atlantic Wall and perhaps even recapture southern Italy."

"This helped the American President?" queried Steve.

"In that whereas previously the President might have appeared too pliable in the hands of Stalin, now, in the light of these purported shenanigens, his strategy looked to be common sense. As things were going, with the Red Army punching their weight, FDR could at least be reasonably sure of securing Rome, and Paris, Brussels and Amsterdam, Copenhagen and Oslo. By contrast Churchill's taste for squaring up to Moscow over Poland looked to be risking all."

"But it was bluff, surely," claimed Gareth. "Stalin was never going to shake hands again with Hitler. By then they were in a fight to the death. With the Georgian tyrant knowing he'd gained the upper hand he wasn't about to relent."

"Maybe," allowed Jeremy. "But it was suiting Roosevelt that the threat of a repeat Molotov-Ribbentrop pact be taken seriously, and if bluff it was that it should remain uncalled..... not withstanding the concerns of his vast Polish and Jewish diasporas. The Italian campaign was tough enough, and he had soldiers dying in the Pacific too, don't forget."

"And this was your friend's view....?" checked Steve. ".... the fellow student."

"He went further. He entertained a third possibility and, on consideration, came to find this the more persuasive. That consideration included more than a passing interest in my project."

"A third possibility that related to Suez..... to do with Eden was it?" It had to be, thought Gareth. But the lecturer had a surprise.

"His third possibility held that rather than bluff, what had emerged from Stockholm was dis-information."

"Which is the substance of bluff, surely," challenged Steve. "Aren't you talking the same thing?"

"Not if the dis-information was laid by Washington, by powerful people who'd learned to be wary of Churchill's gung-ho streak. Unlike he, they were in no mood to tangle with a rampaging sharp clawed bear."

"Of course, an American ruse," sneered Kate. "One day Jeremy you'll really surprise us!"

Alan ignored her. He was still listening, enquiring even.

"And the connection with Suez?" he asked.

"Is the British envoy who happened to be in Stockholm at that critical time, and who reported what was supposedly going on back to London. Step forward Walter Monckton."

"I see," said Steve. "You're saying that as later, in '56, the man was instrumental in undermining the standing of his Premier."

"Because Washington wanted it so," added Kate, her voice oozing a re-gathered scepticism. "Any hard evidence?"

"Not really," conceded Jeremy. "But that's not to say none will ever emerge. Few have looked. The most successful subversives always cover their tracks. Then there's an initial leap of the imagination that's required. Most are deterred. Walter has gone, but his family, they were well looked after. Children and grandchildren have assumed powerful positions, made influential connections. It doesn't do to upset such people."

"Certainly not if you're building a career in the Armed Services," reflected Gareth, the old soldier. "Did you say that Hugh Trembath rose quite high in the Navy, Steve?"

"Rose pretty high, pretty quickly," confirmed the boy, "but not all the way, now you say it.".

"OK," concluded Alan. "We're now back to where Walter came in. He had an association with Carwinion. He and Sir Edward had both worked for the Duchy pre war, and both found a post war niche at Westminster. Steve, if you find yourself in there with either father or son, or both, I don't want you raising what Jeremy's told us head on. That said, if they want to talk about the Duke, or Churchill, or Eden, or the Americans, then you encourage. You listen very closely, and you remember."

"So can we at last get back to present?" asked Kate, adopting mock relief.

"Yes, and to one that's all the more interesting for Jeremy's contribution," rebuked Alan. Gareth grunted his agreement. Jeremy was silent. He merely raised a palm. The appreciation was acknowledged.

"And we are still listening to Steve," Alan reminded them, "and yes, it is time to move him up to the more recent past. Tell us Steve, these past few weeks, across in your neck of the woods, anything unusual... suspicious?"

The boy hesitated. Jack Butters and the late Rory Duggan would have to wait. Too much in the past they were. That shed though, the Viceroy shed, he could mention that and link it to the last of his series of encounters with Gareth. He drew a deep breath.

"Well there's been this motorcyclist. Twice I've met him on the road. The first time I came off the worst, then it was his turn to almost kill himself. Jane, you were with me, we were passengers in Ralph's van. Then I stumble across his unattended bike. It was on Roundwood Quay. I take a chance, thought I'd have a closer look....."

"....at what I carried in the panniers." Gareth was making light of the incident. Steve could relax.

"And I was almost caught in the act," the boy continued.

"He ran....," said Gareth, the derision being censure enough.

"Yes...... thinking I'd be hotly pursued. I can see now why I wasn't, I couldn't know then. I followed the track that turns into Lanmouth Creek. There's a quay there and a shed. I ducked behind it. It's an estate building, often let out. I think people take it on a month at a time arrangement. I stayed low until I eventually heard you ride off, Gareth."

"Being used now do you know?" Alan's question was casually put.

"It is. I'm not sure by whom, but from the farm I've heard a truck headed that way in the dead of night...... and I've seen the tyre marks on the quay. I've looked inside the shed. Later I took a lamp to where the galvanised gapes just enough. I made out a stack of wooden crates. Long and flat, they looked small enough to have been placed there by two pairs of hands. I do know that the shed is let through *Drummond's*. All Carwinion properties are and this means that Hugh Trembath won't necessarily be acquainted with the tenants, or their business."

"But that wouldn't be like him, would it?" stated Jane, boldly.

"On these crates," probed Alan, "was there any mark, something that might indicate what they contained, or where they'd come from, or where they could be going?"

"All I could see were sides and ends, not lids. There was nothing save the three letters that make the word 'Fal'......

"........which is where they've now arrived," finished Kate.

"But that shed can't be anything but a temporary home," said Gareth. "Those crates are awaiting collection, and by what else than a vessel coming in to that quay?"

"I looked down there again this morning," continued Steve. "It was the quay I wanted to check more than the shed, and I did, and yes there were paint marks on the stone against which a boat might tie..... and above this, actually on the quay, there was worn ground and bent grass, signs of coming and going."

"Good information Steve." Alan was pleased. "Could be useful. For now it's enough. I don't want you going back down there, nor you Gareth. Apart from we here does anyone else know you've been sniffing around that quay?" He was taking a firmer control.

"My Aunt and Uncle are used to me exploring that way, there's never been a stay when I haven't. And then there's the landlord. Whilst showing me his relics the other day Hugh Trembath actually went so far as to recommend that side of the creek as a good place for finds. He said there'd been a practice range down there."

Steve paused. The others were attentive. He was encouraged, he could feed them more. "It was by following the truck made tyre prints of the previous night that I came across Gareth's machine, and then Gareth himself. Now I reckon I might have seen the wagon during the previous day. Together we were Jane, you and I, returning from Polgooth in Ralph's van. It was in the back lanes between Tregony and Mevagissey. We met a hire truck, the sort with the twinned rear wheels and that was the kind of tracks left."

"And the firm?" asked Jeremy.

"Roper," answered Steve.

"A national firm with at least two depots in Cornwall, and that probably means there was about thirty similar such vehicles chugging around Cornwall on that same day." The lecturer was dismissive. "You can't just pluck out the first one you see."

"I hadn't, not until this evening. What might be significant is the person who was driving the truck. It was our Mr Friendly, the character who's working on the ferry, and living next door to Mr Morrish the solicitor. Tenuous I know, but there's a possible link through the neighbour to *Drummond's,* and through the agents to the shed.... and this is how I'm only now thinking it might be the same truck."

"So was the driver on his own in this truck?" asked Alan.

"He was, and he wasn't," said Jane, cryptically. "There was someone following in a second van."

"And perhaps trying to follow discretely," said Steve. "Jane knows him as an odd jobber..... name of Prout. I've met him. Hugh was using him just the other day, on Sunday, for a touch up job on the Land Rover. He lives in Devoran."

"He has a boat," added Jane, "does a lot of marine work."

"So who's ready to speculate as to what's in those crates?" challenged Gareth.

"Vacuum cleaners?" offered Jeremy, directing his stab towards Alan. Alan shrugged. He wasn't to be drawn. He was the professional.

"Right sort of size," said Steve. "A consignment for the local Trago Mills maybe.....next month's loss leader?" The boy was sincere, and Alan was approving. That innocence, it held such charm, it could be so useful. Vacuum cleaners they would stay. Alan again turned to the Welshman.

"The ship Gareth. We know what she was to you. We've listened to what you've had to say on Brian Chadwick, on your friend Alberto, and on Hilda. We hear you, but all that relates to the past. Leaving it there for the moment, I want you to tell us what you make of the old tub now."

Gareth made no reply. Watched in silence he hauled himself from his chair to limp stiffly to the door. Through he went, and on to the outside leading kitchen door. Alan sat motionless, palms on the table, head raised, eyes closed. He could have been at prayer, he might have been. No one dared move. Had offence been taken? Had there been a question too far? No one was asking. All were waiting. The second door opened. A draught swept through. The evening air chilled. Was he gone? They would hear the Kawasaki, as Steve had at the shed. That would be confirmation.

But there was none. The outside door was closed---from the inside. Gareth was returning. He limped into the room. Under his arm he carried a zip fastened leather pouch. Still no one spoke, not until he was back in his seat with the pouch before him on the table, opened, with the contents revealed.

Photographs, this is what he'd fetched. There were packs of them, at least eight, and there was also a notebook.... this Steve had seen before. The subject of his camera work was the ship, the *Kampala,* as she lay at her Tolverne mooring. She'd been snapped from every angle. Some caught her in her entirety, others, many of them telescopic, focussed closely on particular parts, decks, cabins, fittings.

"These were for Alberto," explained Gareth. "They still can be of course, but if they can do anything for your father Jane then they're for you too. That ship's less than she was three years ago, but to the end she's going to be more than she seems."

"Habit of a lifetime," remarked Alan.

"All the prints are numbered," said Gareth. "For each I've noted the date and the time, and there's also a two and a half inch OS reference to fix the stand point. Look at these and maybe we can come to a joint opinion as to what she might be now." Gareth passed a pack to each. Alan's was slapped onto the table in front of him, the gesture confirming acceptance of the invitation extended at Lamorran. The Guardsman had been recruited.

*

Jack Butters reached forward from his chair to switch off the radio receiver. He'd tuned himself some interesting radio traffic, enough for one evening. In a moment his grandson would be through the door. From outside he'd caught the familiar jolt of the boom being lowered, and the locker clatter as the canvas was stowed. The boat was ready to rest. It was almost secured, and old Jack was ready to hear of its day's work.

*

"So what actually are we looking for?" asked Jeremy, joining a jigsaw like assemblage of close ups, all taken from the Tolverne bank.

"Anything that grabs your eye," answered Alan. "People on board, people passing by, you might even see me in the *Speedwell*, you could even see Steve on board. I took him for an upriver sail one day."

Three or four minutes elapsed as each searched quietly. The first observation was Kate's.

"I've a number with what appears to be members of the crew.

They don't look too English any of them."

"Good for them," muttered the Welshman under his breath.

"I've been told they're Spanish," said Steve, and all assumed that this would have been by Hugh Trembath. It was the kind of thing he could be relied upon to know. They looked Spanish these people, and it was accepted they were.

"How many individuals?" asked Jeremy.

"Four," answered Kate, but then after a pause she corrected herself. "And here's a fifth, distant and blurred, but he certainly looks a bit more Anglo Saxon." The print was held towards the others. Steve was first to respond.

"That's our man on the ferry, and I'll warrant it was taken fairly early in the morning. Delivering to the ships is one of the perks of his job. I've made the rounds before with young Jack Spargo." The print number was checked and the log, and yes, this was so.

A back calculation confirmed this to be the Monday morning that Steve lay unconscious in the City hospital.

"Whatever his errand on that particular day, this guy appears to be at the heart of a good share of the general manoeuvring," commented Jeremy. "This ship is booked into the river and up crops this opportunity for young Jack as you call him. And his place is taken by our friend here who happens to make his home next door to Mr Morrish, who's also fallen into a tailor made little number in sleepy Truro."

"So let's keep looking," urged Alan. Each pack was passed on so that the prints were re-scrutinised by a further pair of eyes. Kate passed hers to Jane. Spurred by that further mention of Morrish the girl gleaned each print from edge to edge. And then she was on her feet.

"Ah ....ha," she exclaimed, and was promptly out of the room, up the stairs and quickly down again. She had a calendar, a complimentary wall calendar provided by Percuil Yard. It was the tide chart she was wishing to consult. She had two successive prints, and they were of successive days. And during the intervening night there had been a high water..... in the early hours. She explained this to the others and then turned the prints towards them.

"Now look at these, and look at the hoist at the front end of the ship. When not in use it comes down flat over what must be a hatch cover beneath. That's how it is on one day, but then on the next, early in the morning, here it is still up, at an angle. I'd say that that hoist had been used during the night."

"Good one," said Steve, "and the significance of tides....?"

"......is in what might have been hoisted aboard, and from where. That quay in Lanmouth Creek, you're only going to get in and out to that around high water time...... and there you have it. High water was at 2.10 am."

"Impressive," said Alan. "Now look at the boats. I want signs of one having been lowered."

They were all on their feet now, heads huddled over a spread of prints.

"This one I'd say," said Kate. "One of the smaller boats that's kept slung up high between the bridge and the funnel. Look, on this one you can see those things you can drop the oars into to stop them slipping about."

"Mmmmm ...rowlocks," said Alan , "and two each side, which with one oar each means four to do the job. "

"I'll check that quay again, those paint marks," said Steve. "If I can scrape some off you can get the colour confirmed."

"You don't go near that quay," Alan reminded him firmly. "I'd have thought you'd learned your lesson with Gareth." The boy coloured. Mercifully Alan moved on, again turning to the Welshman. "You're coming up trumps boyo, just as I'd hoped. Now what do you know about where this ship has just come from, and where she's likely next to be going?"

"There would have been a last trip from Ascension to Stanley and back, but thereafter I'm not wholly certain. Gibraltar is my bet, and that's where the charter contract with the Ministry of Defence would finally have expired. But it's possible, of course, that British India sold her for scrap whilst still in harness."

"Boxered," remarked Jane.

"Or they could be holding on for a better price," continued Gareth. "Either way, those characters on board would have been engaged through an agency, specialists in ship storage and delivery."

"So are we talking 'temps' again?" enquired Jeremy.

"I think we could be," said Gareth. "And if I get the drift of this we're talking temps with the nerve maybe to stash away pallet of cocaine right under the noses of the MOD." The choice of idiom drew a chuckle from Alan.

"Yes, you do get the drift," confirmed Alan, "but if this is the game then those on board are only small players. They're the mules, expendable mules. We don't want to disrupt their routines lest the big boys take fright. This is where the real watching begins."

"And my father?" asked Jane.

"......is, for the moment, in the best place," said Alan." You just have to be patient there."

"OK, but can you clarify please how his involvement in all this might have been contrived?"

"All we can do now is advance theories, hypothesise, and as Jeremy's the best at that we'll listen to him. What can you give us Jeremy?"

"Just say," began the lecturer, "just say we have Spaniards on that ship and, with them, cocaine from South America. We can go maybe to Peru, to the Andes and a group of peasant farmers in the Huallanga Valley. They can grow and gather a couple of truck loads of Coca leaf and for this they'll be happy to take the equivalent of two or three hundred pounds. The buyer knows that if carefully refined, transported, and sold, his purchase could fetch maybe five million amongst fashionable London society. For the bother of the refining and the getting it across the Atlantic he's ready to accept two and a half from anyone on this side ready to pay him up front in clean money. Some one from Spain would be ideal."

"And for this the second buyer takes the product, and the risks, and the rewards of the next phase of the operation," summarised Alan.

"But he's wanting clean money himself," continued Jeremy. "So he sets up a holiday bond company and there'll be real sites out there on the continent, and real holidaymakers, but scope for a lot of phoney ones besides. He finds a group of City wide boys.....likely lads, part of the scene. If they play along they can pocket a million between them. All that's needed now are the mules. It's a risky job and it can be expensive, but there's a group that's ready to do it for a knock down £100,000 provided they can be paid in kind, and as they're Basque terrorists that means in the form of small arms.... 'vacuum cleaners'. Maybe it's Kalashnikovs they like, and so a Yugoslavian resort becomes an ideal venue to include in the bond scheme. Delivery's no problem, not with a fleet of Russian factory ships roving the western approaches. My figures might be slightly out, bigger mark ups probably, but it's this kind of thing I envisage."

"Thank you Jeremy again," said Alan, "plenty there to mull."

Steve was speechless. 'Vacuum cleaners' had suddenly become automatic rifles and if this was to be believed he'd stood within inches of the things. And what else had he heard? ...Basques, for goodness sake. It looked like old Jack Butters could be spot on. But that had to be co-incidence. Whatever his sympathies back in the '30s, surely the old man would never knowingly assist or condone a modern day terrorist campaign. But there were those factory ships. They weren't far from Mylor, and those ever-listening ears.

Jane was reborn. It would take time, yes, but from here on it was surely downhill. What she'd heard was vindication. Parts may be inaccurate, but that was only detail. At the core of things her father stood as an innocent victim of a conspiracy.

And Gareth had gained, indeed he'd gained the most. It suffused his whole being. No more was he old Noah's raven picking through debris of the past... old sores, old scores. He could be part of a better future, he could be instrumental in a mending. Kate was taking the same fix, drip fed, at City casualty. With this one dose he could be up with her.

And that wasn't all, thought the soldier, not if he could help it, not now. There was an angle in this that appeared to have escaped Jeremy and certainly Steve .....escaped Alan though? He didn't know, he couldn't be sure. It was only a possibility, but one that would have occurred to any soldier of the British Army...... or of the Argentine, come to that. For the moment it was one to keep to himself.

Kate had a question. It was for Alan. Jeremy's scenario was neatly woven, but for her there was a loose end.

"This chap who works on the ferry," she began, "we see him on the ship. He's living right next to my friend. He's been seen with a hire truck. It sounds like everything's passing through his hands, money, drugs,... vacuum cleaners. His role is so pivotal, he must be more than just a mule. At the same time he can't be the Mr Big. Once rumbled he'd be too exposed. How do you see his role Alan? Can you offer a profile?"

"His role will be crucial," replied Alan, "and that's why we don't give him any cause to suspect that he's been rumbled. Clear?" There was no demur. He could expand.

"It's likely that there's two identical bags. One comes down from London stashed with cash. Another waits on the *Kampala* stashed with the dope. The driver crosses on the ferry. He pays his fare. He gets his ticket. Also he gets a note. This specifies a one-time rendezvous point. It could be anywhere. In some ways the busier the better, Trago Mills down at Falmouth, or even up at the big one near Liskeard. Woolworth's in Redruth would do just as well. Say a time, say a counter, get in the queue, switch the bags. Away goes the coke to London, while the cash comes back to Campfield Hill. There it's passed through the garden fence, less any deductions due."

"The empty bag goes back to the ship," continued Jeremy. "The cash goes down to *Conway's,* and into the client account as holiday bond money. It goes abroad and into real estate, except for the top slice diverted for the purchase and delivery of the 'vacuum cleaners.' "

"And a profile?" repeated Kate.

"Outwardly reputable," said Alan. "He'll have performed well in a number of responsible positions, so well he'll be considering himself underpaid, under promoted."

"Ralph said something about the RFA," remembered Jane.

"The Fleet Auxiliary," said Gareth. "I know they've been looking to make lay offs in that section."

"And this one could well be feeling a need to boost his pension fund." Alan had money at the root of this. "His lump sum has had to meet the mortgage perhaps. Maybe he's maintaining an estranged wife and kids. A couple more like this and he can tidy all that up and lord it with the best of them, move abroad maybe."

"So with him the deal is all to do with cash," said Kate, "nothing ideological, embracing separatism in Spain, or International Marxism. I heard you mention Kalashnikovs, doesn't that suggest Moscow sponsored terror?"

"That was Jeremy, stabbing a bit wildly I'd say," said Gareth soberly.

"But weapons of some sort," persisted Jeremy. "You can agree there, Gareth."

The Welshman nodded. It was Jane who spoke.

"Vacuum cleaners were mentioned. I don't get that."

"It's a book," explained Jeremy, "Alan knows it, he would have challenged me otherwise." The other nodded. "It's an old story. I read it when I was about twelve, a Nevil Shute novel, *Lonely Road*. It was written before the war. A film was made I think."

"The only one of his I managed to finish," remarked Alan. "I enjoyed it. Too much perhaps, for the others never started to match up, not for me anyway. I was only thinking of it the other day, when coming along the coast. I do every time I sail this way."

"As I think of it when I've a National Trust talk to do at Cotehele, up on the Tamar," said Jeremy. "They have one of those old sailing barges up there, restored to how she might have been back in the early '30s."

"I still don't see the vacuum cleaner connection." Jane feared digression.

"Jeremy?" prompted Alan.

"If you can just be a little patient," the lecturer gently admonished. "The business of a best selling author is to paint the world as his readership wishes to see it. Forsyth, Higgins, Seymour, Follett, they're all masters at this. Most of what they write is pure tosh, nine pages out of ten, but it panders to popular prejudice, to the comfortable myth. That's where it strikes the chord, and that's why people buy."

"Because it articulates the dominant ideology," sang the Welshman.

"And the other one tenth?" enquired Steve.

"Is brilliantly researched fact. Accurate to the most minute detail, it can be, entertainingly so too. But that's not its main purpose. The exactitude lends credibility to the rest, and that's what the audience truly hungers for. It's a well tried formula, and in this respect each of those modern men would have to admit a debt to Nevil Shute."

"So the tosh in *Lonely Road?*" Asked Steve.

Jeremy obliged with a brief synopsis

"Guns are being smuggled into this country. There's impatience with the seeming helplessness of our democratic institutions in the face of commercial stagnation, and a right wing group is planning a putsch. The weapons are being landed on a remote beach in this corner of the country and then being hauled, by road, to secret urban arsenals."

"In readiness for the uprising," added Gareth, jokily. Jeremy grew more earnest.

"And what he affirms for his readership is that comforting

fiction peddled by the likes of Arthur Mee and Arthur Bryant. A fiction swallowed by young and old alike, that Britannia had, after her victory in The Great War, renounced things military so as to become, once more, the green and pleasant land of Blake's vision. This was how those either privileged or lucky enough to have been taught to read wanted it to be. Set in our silver sea we were quarantined from the wicked politics of that wider world out there, where ignorant armies clashed by night. Avuncular King George, avuncular Stan Baldwin, avuncular James Ramsay Mac, they were monkeys of infinite wisdom. As the banks ground at the organ so they danced, and the mother of the free could just about look the part.... to those who'd never think to lift her skirts, that was."

"Which hid....?" prompted Jane.

"In this context a traffic which was flowing, almost totally, in the opposite direction. Across the globe, from the Chaco to China, there wouldn't have been an armed incursion or insurrection that hadn't at some point been attended by a sales agent operating on behalf of a British weapons manufacturer or stockpiler. In these wares this country was the mail order capital of the world. By roads not adopted, by woodlanded ways, the loaded wagons were constantly rolling....but rather than from, it was towards the quiet quay and the secluded cove that they went. Bringing weapons into this country? Tosh! Coals to Newcastle."

"Now tell of the other 10%," urged Gareth, "where, in your opinion, the writer could have been spot on."

"The baddies are foiled in their dastardly designs by the hero and heroine fortuitously stumbling against the weakest link in the operation, this being the transport arrangements, the use of lorries. And this is fact. In those days they were small, they were unreliable, and, more often than not with just a canvas canopy to protect the payload, they were open to casual inspection. To these difficulties we can add the roads. Rough, twisting, steep, they taxed driver and vehicle to the full. Breakdowns and accidents were frequent, and these incidents would tend to draw the attention of a local constabulary. Canvas would be lifted, lamps would be shone, and questions asked. Where these pertained to the contents of a certain size and style of crate then 'vacuum cleaners' became a stock answer...."

"....of the sort that can be made all the more acceptable when proffered with a £5 note," added Alan.

"And if there were pistols rather than rifles then the hand held hair drier no doubt came into its own," suggested Gareth, now more serious. He could imagine all this. If the police could be bought now, in Shropshire, and forty years ago in Nassau, then why not fifty years ago by the side of a dark high hedged lane. "So how does this story end?"

"With a chase along the coast of Cornwall," answered Alan. "Shute must have sailed it himself. It's vivid. There's a storm. There's a gunfight. Then we have the rocks. I like it. The man was fond of Cornwall and Devon...... that's clear enough, and I am too. That's why it works for me perhaps. But this is enough on the merits of Mr Nevil Shute as a writer. We've covered a lot tonight. You've listened well, we can go forward together. We'll meet again soon. You'll hear from me. There'll be tasks for you all. In the meantime keep those eyes open, keep those mouths closed."

*

" .....*the financiers of Europe and America not only expected the Nationalists to win but desired them to.*

......*Five tankers of the Texas Oil Company were on their way to Spain at the time of the rising. They received orders to deliver to the Nationalists on credit. These shipments continued. After the US Embargo Act, some were made by declaring they were bound for France. The Texas Oil company was fined $ 22,000 for this. It made no difference; 344,000 tons of oil were delivered in 1936, 420,000 in 1937, 478,000 in 1938, 624,000 in 1939. The bill was paid and credit renewed.*

Hugh Thomas   'The Spanish Civil War' p 350

178

"Surprised me that one," whispered Jeremy, "after all that 'keep well clear' stuff, suddenly to hear less than a week later that we're going aboard."

It was late afternoon. He and Steve had found a spare table in the County Council Schools' Library, barely a stone's throw from the City Hospital where, earlier, the two had met. The rendezvous had been Steve's idea. He'd suggested it could coincide with the last of his out patient visits and Jeremy had been eager to comply. Carwinion had caught his imagination. And now there was also this prospect of actually getting on to the *Kampala.*

They both thought this a cunning stroke. Steve suspected Alan and Gareth of hatching the scheme together. OK'd with Kate the ploy had gathered its own momentum. So neat it was, not least in how Alan was left to edge back to his cover.

It was Kate who'd gone to the Radio Cornwall Studio and personally expressed a wish for a last look over the ship. Meanwhile Steve had gone to Carwinion House and revealed the identity of the motorcyclist who'd been the cause of his mishap, he who might have then anonymously summoned the emergency assistance. Steve's account was that they'd met since, down at Roundwood, and in talking he'd learned who the fellow was, what he'd been, and also of his previous acquaintance with the old ship.

Steve said he'd been asked if the *Kampala* had featured at all in the local media, for if it hadn't then this veteran was saying that he wasn't, himself, averse to participating in a radio interview if that could help him get up onto the ship one last time.

Hugh listens. He phones Radio Cornwall and the little station, ready primed, has its scoop.... a reunion between one of the nurses, and one of the nursed, and the ship itself. And maybe it could even be done on board. The name 'Trembath' carried influence. Sir Edward knew the top people at British India and they'd been contacted. It was coming together so naturally, all were hopeful, they just had to wait for a date.

"Subtle stuff from that Alan," said Steve, "I only hope we don't disappoint him."

"He'll be content with a few more photos, more than that and he'll be delighted. He wants me to tell him what part of Spain those crewmen come from. Kate's told him that I can speak the language, and speak it well, well enough to pick out the main regional dialects. That's what's got me my invite for the party."

The word 'Spain' was Steve's cue.

"Last week you started talking history, that's what interests me. There was mention of the war in Spain back in the '30s, and of the Basques. I've got some stuff here, just old scraps, I'd like to hear what you make of it. "

With him Steve had a supermarket carrier bag. Reaching into it he produced an A4 envelope. He eased it open and spread the contents.... just a few of the items entrusted to him by old Jack. All that related to Francis Cairns he'd left behind. What lay before them were the three early documents, still joined, and also the odd newspaper cutting, that taken from *The Limerick Examiner.* The cutting drew a smile from Jeremy.

"You can start with that one," prompted the boy. The article is clear enough, its subject is famous.... or infamous perhaps, but I don't get how it might fit in. The inked in Spanish that's so blurred though and faded...... I'm hoping you can help.

" *'El hombre'*, " began Jeremy. "You know that...."

" 'The man'," offered Steve.

"And the last word tails to either *'izquierda'* or *'izquierdas'*...... and that'll mean 'left', as opposed to 'right'.

"In the political sense you mean," said Steve.

"For me, looking at this now, no other sense could be meaningful. Tell me something of who wrote it and in what context. Then ask me again."

"And those faint blobs that sit between the two main words.....?"

"...... have to be *a la,* or maybe *de la.* And this man was to the left, or of the left should you prefer. Sir Oswald had been a radical minister in the '29 Labour government, the first the Party formed on the strength of a clear majority. This is fact, and we can stay with that." He put the article aside, choosing now to peruse the two typed letters from the Board of Trade and with them the attached plain side with its faded hand written tabulations.

To start he read to silently, but was soon moved to voice a passage from the earliest of the letters, the one of October 1941.

" '...... *and having given due consideration to the information recently laid before this department, concerning the interception of a*

180

consignment of weapons off Northern Spain in June 1937, a decision has been made that you shall be removed from the list of qualified radio operators available to all merchant vessels engaged in the war effort. We understand that these events took place over four years ago and much has changed in that time. We ask you to bear in mind that the relevant information has only been available to us since the entry of Russia into the war in June of this year. You will appreciate that with the struggle that lies ahead there is a National interest in carefully working, wherever possible, to retain the goodwill of equally hard pressed allies.......'

He was thrown out, wasn't he? The poor sod...."

Jeremy stayed with the page, taking in the remainder silently, his brow furrowed. And then,

"That's some knock. But he wasn't taking it lying down, that's clear enough. For he'd saved this record, some kind of log. It must relate to the circumstances that surrounded the alleged indiscretion. And he must have submitted a copy of it to this authority by way of an appeal........ probably referring them to the formal entries that he would have made at the time into the official log, which should have stayed with the shipping company."

Jeremy was looking now at the hand written page. He grunted, as if he were making some kind of sense out of the letters and the numbers grouped thereon. He stood up, scanned the shelves and then returned with an atlas.

"This is about the codes," he explained confidently. "What I see here is information about a voyage, and probably the same information written twice. That's what this Mr Duggan would have thought, though he'd have had no way of being sure of course."

Jeremy pointed first of all to the lines of letters. Seemingly chosen at random they offered not the slightest clue as to any meaning they might convey, the one concession to order being in their having been marshalled into those groups of four.

"These are signals, transmitted in Morse and intercepted by our Mr Duggan reading the same, but only after being mechanically encoded into these groups of letters. To be properly read they would have had to have been mechanically decoded....."

"....as they would have been by the intended recipients. They would have had the necessary machines," reasoned Steve, before concluding with the obvious question. "Is this about those German

'Enigma' machines with the key board, and the rotors and the plugs which could be set and reset in mid message? "

"Looks like it," replied Jeremy. "Beneath each line of letters there's a line of grouped numbers. These would have been ordered by Duggan. They're not in code. I'd say that the first group gives us a time, and look at the second and third groups. In each case that's latitude and longitude. Then there's a two digit group that remains fairly constant...."

".......speed ," said Steve.

"........and finally, three digits for a compass bearing. Rory Duggan is telling us about his ship's voyage. We can plot it roughly on one of these maps." Jeremy started to thumb through the atlas.

"And his logging of this would have been prompted by these intercepts? " asked Steve.

"Because they would have been very loud and very clear, in fact he might even have seen the vessels transmitting the calls, or seen their aerials and their periscopes."

"A submarine?"

"U Boat was the term, and several I'd say..... 1937...... June......, and this course, right into the angle of Biscay..." Jeremy had found a map and it was lending authority.

He leant back. He knew enough about Franco's rebellion to think of the war in terms of episodes, and this would have been not long after the wretched bombing of Guernica by Hitler's Condor planes and then the Government retaliatory air strikes against the German surface fleet. A graver tone entered his voice.

"Before that summer the U Boat was rated a useful rather than a decisive weapon. Only the battleship could truly do the business. That's how things were still seen at the top, but beneath the waves there were people who felt otherwise."

"And they were right."

"It's so obvious now, but less so then. The capital ships and their bases were vulnerable to the bomb and the torpedo, and if it was about starving nations into submission the sub was going to be both cheaper and more effective. This had been evident in the Great War, but the people at the top were still to be totally convinced There's always rivalry within a Navy, and reluctance among some to accept the new, so with the bombing of.... I think it was the *'Deutschland'*.....the under-sea boys got cracking. They would drive home their message with a few hard statistics, and where better to demonstrate the effectiveness of a U Boat enforced blockade than in southern Biscay? With the Basques being garrotted in their own 'ring of iron' the U Boat would help turn the screw."

"So they were attempting to sell themselves as the weapon of the future......."

".......by developing and demonstrating their team play, much to the discomfort of vessels attempting to run the blockade off Spain's northern coast. Duggan's guess was that the coded signals were reporting the course of his own ship......the *Usk Vale* it says here in the official letter, the *'u.v.'* on his log. Their voyage was being monitored by a pack of U boats, that would have been his suspicion. There had to be a reason, and that would have gradually become apparent with an unexpected course alteration maybe, and the Board of Trade here speak of an order to maintain radio silence. An order that was breached."

Steve picked up the second letter from the Board of Trade.

" He was anticipating a rendezvous. That's clear from this letter. And with what he knew, he feared for who ever was coming out to meet them. It was starting to look dangerous."

"Too dangerous to do nothing," Jeremy concurred. "And yet, at the same time in a different way, almost as dangerous to act, particularly as it must have been just he that was aware of the menace. To anyone needing a scapegoat he was presenting himself, gift-wrapped. Is this fellow still alive? He'd be getting on a bit now."

"He's been dead for more than thirty years, but he's alive in the memory of an old friend who lives in the district....... very much so. But tell me more about these codes."

"Let's look at this second letter." Jeremy silently scanned down so far and then again read aloud.

'......we reject your claim, based on the enclosure you sent, that you recorded in the ship's radio log a series of coded transmissions which you purport to have been made by German U Boats at that time active in the Bay of Biscay. The log you refer to is with the shipping company. We have examined it. There is no trace of any of the entries you claim to have made.

It can only be assumed that you fabricated this document in the vain hope that the true record may have either been lost when the ship was sunk last year, or subsequently destroyed.' "

"I don't quite understand that," said Steve. "You don't think this fabricated.....do you?"

Jeremy hesitated. He looked again at the hand written page.

"I think this the true record. I think with their second letter the Board of Trade are lying.... and look at it, they're doing so with all the ruthlessness they can muster. He's being also accused of attempting to exploit the loss of his old vessel, probably with the death of some of his old shipmates. He'd have been angry at that for sure. These things always get out. There would have been rumour and other stuff would've been pinned on him and.......I don't know, he'd have been wounded and crippled worse than Kate and Gareth put together. He didn't kill himself did he?"

Steve could only shake his head. He was choked. The valour at St.Nazaire had gone unnoticed, and instead there was this. A hero had been betrayed by King and Country........ but not by old Jack Butters. The youngster was genuinely moved, and alive to this the lecturer responded.

"But it wouldn't have been done maliciously. All options were invidious. This would have been deemed the least. Other lives were at stake. By '42 the survival of the country was on the line."

"Because of something that happened five years earlier?" Steve was sceptical.

"Yes.... in the sense that the advocates of the U Boat who'd made their point at that time, were, five years later, coming perilously close to proving it ....against this nation."

"The Battle of the Atlantic...,"

"........which was a close call. The U Boats almost prevailed. That they didn't owed much to our hard won ability to read their coded signals. The Enigma settings were constantly under adjustment, then an extra rotor was added. We had machines to process their signals and an army of analysts and clerks but there was always a time factor, and the assumption in Germany was that with constant innovation this lag could be kept sufficiently stretched to preserve the system's security."

"But they were wrong, weren't they?" Steve was starting to understand. "I've read about this and its been on TV. We did crack the codes, but as we did so it was essential that an impression be conveyed that we were never anywhere near being up to speed."

"Exactly, and the game was at its most cat and mouse during the spring of '42. In fathoming Enigma no stone would have been left unturned. The evolution of the system would have been traced back to '37, and probably before. The quirks of individual operators were even picked out. Months and years of Merchant radio logs would have been trawled for unwitting contributions, and no doubt Rory Duggan's original record would have been picked up and filed. It would have become just a tiny piece in a jigsaw which by '42 was almost complete."

"And once used like this, for the nation in top secret war work, it thereafter had to be denied. No matter how important it might otherwise have been to any one individual." Steve was reasoning confidently. The tutor was good at his job.

"You have it," said Jeremy. "What's one man's reputation when the survival of the nation's at stake?" There was no answer to this, but it still seemed hard. Steve found another question.

"But this delay in his being denounced....why was that? If he was such a security risk how come he wasn't thrown out his job two years earlier, in '39?"

"Because the initial information had been gathered abroad, possibly by a Russian ship, possibly by a communist cell active in that corner of France or Spain. It would have been passed on to Moscow of course, and the people there would have sought and gained fuller information from their British based informants. A watch would have been kept on the shipping firm, and also any sister ship. Individuals would have been put under scrutiny too, officers, crew, shore administrators, and what came back they would have sat on. Remember that in '39 the Germans and the Russians had agreed to co-operate. We had this the other night. They both took a bite into Poland. That was what the war was about then, and when nations acted on their pledges of support for Warsaw then the Russian line was to obstruct them..... their game then was to make things easier for Hitler. In Liverpool the communists were setting up dock strikes, sabotage and goodness knows what else all in the name of the infamous pact brokered between Messers Molotov and Ribbentrop. In this context, to denounce our Mr Duggan would have been an own goal. People forget that this is how things were before 'Barbarossa'. After that of course it was ' all change'."

"And it became our game to pander to Uncle Joe Stalin," remarked Steve ruefully. "But what about after the war? Couldn't things have been put right then?"

"The code breaking expertise continued to be useful after the war. It's still useful today. It all had to stay secret. It's only in these past dozen years that we've started to get some idea of what it was all about. And then you've got to think of how, in the scale of things, this would have been just a minor cover up. There were many a lot bigger....with bigger persons involved, and sometimes even populations. Lift the corner for just one and how do you smooth it down when the others start to twitch? "

Steve took the point with reluctance. He pointed to beneath the seventh line of numbers, Duggan's last. Two words were printed. As with the letters above, they were in block capitals.

VICKERS

AIRSPEED

"Any ideas on this?"

Jeremy shrugged. He could only speculate.

"If they were delivering guns, as would seem likely in a rendezvous at sea, then the *VICKERS* might refer to a brand of British made machine gun......"

".......and the *AIRSPEED* would be the name they'd travelled under in this country," ventured Steve, light heartedly. " 'Airspeed' being as excellent a name as any for a make of vacuum cleaner! Philips Airspeed, get it?"

" Or Electrolux perhaps," returned Jeremy, a shade less lightly. Steve's amusement grew.

"Perhaps we should be consulting the collected works of .... What was he called? That writer, Nevil.....?"

".....Nevil Shute," said Jeremy, niggled slightly by the boy's flippancy. He didn't have time for adolescent silliness. That he'd ever mentioned vacuum cleaners was becoming a matter of regret. "If they were machine guns," he continued, sternly, "and of a kind devised for mounting in an aircraft, then airspeed would have been a critical measure. If air cooled, as they'd surely had to have been, then efficient use would demand a certain speed lest they should overheat and seize."

Chastened, Steve moved again to the newspaper cutting.

"So what might connect that with this character. How might Sir Oswald Mosley be linked to the Battle of the Atlantic?"

"I think he was in prison by then, interned. He would have been kept well away from the code-breakers, that's for sure. This was put out by the paper late in 1950."

Jeremy lifted the cutting, bringing it closer to his eyes while angling it towards the close-by window.

"And I'd say it was cut out and saved by this Duggan. What's written along the edge looks to have been originally in the same hand as that one page log. Beneath the ink one can still trace the impress of a finer point, probably a pencil. Fearing it might fade, someone else has inked over it. That would have been later."

"By when the paper would have aged and thinned to a blotter," added Steve, knowing that there was also the significance of his old friend's fast failing sight to consider. "So can you make better sense of Duggan's Spanish now, now you know vaguely where he was coming from?"

"I have to stay with what I said earlier.....'*de la izquierdas*', of the left, in the political sense. And it's a valid message, for most in 1950 saw Franco as a leader living on borrowed time. Democracy had to be coming to Spain soon, and the people would surely choose a leftist government. Duggan is saying 'beware'. Men of the left can veer towards despotism no less than those of the right......and witness here Sir Oswald."

"But Franco wasn't going, was he?"

"He wasn't. Propped by American cash he held sway until he died, twenty five years on! But that doesn't make the warning any less timely. Look at Mosley-- progressive Labour Government Minister in '29, New Party candidate in '31, and then, within four years, a Jew baiting pseudo Fuhrer."

Steve was puzzled. "But why look at Mosley in '75 or now in '85 even, when it was more than fifty years ago that he was on the stump?"

"It's one of those warnings that'll never be obsolete.....any where, and especially not in Spain now they've put this Gonzalez fellow in charge. "

"And he's their first elected Prime Minister since the '30s." Steve was thinking of Jack Butters. The man could indeed be acting strictly as instructed.

"Actually he's the second under the new post Franco constitution, but he's the first to head a party returned with a mandate to implement a declared programme. What they had over the first elected assembly was a kind of temporary caretaker. He held the ring whilst the members sorted out where and how far they were in agreement. Where there was common ground, parties started to emerge."

"And this Gonzalez, he's a man of the left?"

"He is," confirmed Jeremy, "and with no little charisma. Power was handed him on a plate. You might remember, a couple of years back a handful of gun toting Generals tried to turn back the clock.....shot themselves in the foot, the right was totally discredited." It was clear that Jeremy wasn't yet entirely convinced by the Gonzalez administration. It was as if he felt it more proper for the left to have come into its own in the course of struggle rather than by default.

"So they have free elections now, and independent courts ....what about the newspapers? They would have been Franco controlled." Steve was angling, shrewdly.

"They're going back into private ownership, and regional papers are being revived for the likes of the Catalans and the Basques. This said, there's just one central news agency and this remains government controlled."

"And you're of the view that young democracies can be adept at reserving some dictatorial powers?" Steve's question prompted hesitation from Jeremy. He was choosing his words with care.

"A cynic would say that even mature democracies are adept at reserving dictatorial powers, and even more adept at exerting them in subtle ways, this in many ways accounting for their longevity......but back to Spain. You mention the courts. It's said that short cuts are still being taken there, particularly against suspected terrorists. The task of the police should be to apprehend and bring to trial, but I've heard that there are units out there assuming all the roles, judge, jury, and executioner."

"Street justice, a shoot to kill policy you mean? Do I hear sympathy for ETA terrorism?"

"You hear sympathy for Basque activists wrongly suspected of terrorism," answered Jeremy. "Those people had it rough under Franco, particularly in this year." He tapped the page of coded signals. "And a lot that are grown up now were kids then, evacuees, some to this country where they arrived convinced that they'd left their parents fighting to the last person, the last breath."

Steve again thought of old Jack. He'd been involved in the care of those children. He'd heard him say.

"You want to speak with my friend. As a young soldier he helped with some of those kids. There was a camp set up. He said it was Southampton way, not far from his base."

"And I'd hear again that it's in the trauma and the dislocation of such camps that the seeds of terrorism are planted. It's the old perennial. Look at the Palestinians. But getting trigger happy isn't the way, if anything it just makes it worse. The rougher the justice the sharper the resentments. It's a downward spiral. When people get angry they want to fire guns. Others are looking to get rich by selling the things. So more weapons get pulled in, pushed in......"

".......and it's more truck loads of vacuum cleaners," quipped Steve. "You think that this is what's going on down on the river. Weapons, probably of Russian origin, are headed Basque wards."

"Strong possibility," confirmed Jeremy. "This is one of the reasons Alan's wanting me to go onto the ship with Kate. She's told him I'm good on Spanish dialects. I've travelled the country. I speak the language, and more than that I've studied it and taught it. I'm on there to listen for clues."

Steve nodded. It made sense, but was it going to ease or complicate his own task? He couldn't be sure. He looked down again at the faded picture of Mosley.

"This, then, you think was saved by Rory Duggan merely to illustrate a general point, an observation on pre-war British politics that might bear relevance to post war, post Franco Spain. You don't think it to do with the specific incident involving the *Usk Vale*. After being dropped from the convoys Duggan was ever followed by a rumour that he'd betrayed a shipment of war materials bound for northern Spain. I've been told that he was anxious to disprove this and to an extent he might have with the signals log, but that was never going to identify the true culprit......"

".........and you were wondering if this might be offering a lead in that direction." Jeremy understood, but he couldn't be encouraging. "Bear in mind that Sir Oswald was no more than a high profile light weight, just as David Windsor was. In their day they had a lot of press, the pair of them, but neither appealed to or led a substantial body of opinion. There was no real party about them, and that's how they came to be so easily marginalised. But this isn't to say they didn't have their uses, then and now."

Steve had heard something like this before, at Carwinion House. He hadn't quite understood Hugh then, nor did he Jeremy now. This time he wasn't going to let it pass.

"Now?.....With both long dead?"

"It's how they're painted these days in the popular press, and on TV and radio too..... drama or documentary. They have to be demonised it seems. They were the ones who dabbled in Hitlerism. The rest of us knew better and rejected all that, and this is why we rejected them, and that's what makes us such good, good people. And this is 'tosh' of course, but people swallow it by the spoonful. They love it"

"So what should we be reading and watching?" asked Steve. Jeremy sighed.

"Sometimes I'll open the *Express* or the *Mail* and there'll be page after page of shock horror revelations about the Duke and his dealings with the Nazis. The same old pictures will have been trundled out...of the Duke being greeted by Hitler in Germany in '37; of Bedault and Wenner Grenn, the swastika tainted friends; of Ribbentrop and Count Ciano, and the guy here.....Tom Mosley. You get the full rogue's gallery. But then they're all dead, as you say, so why worry too much? And in the meantime I'll be thinking to myself 'isn't this supposed to be a newspaper?' Why can't just a few of these copious column inches be given to what's actually happening now, in places like East Timor and Chile? This is present day Hitlerism and it's being condoned, and in some places encouraged even. We like to think the dragon was slain, and exposés on the dabblers in chief can help us do that, but it's alive, and we know it's alive because in places we're feeding it, deliberately."

It was impressively put. Steve now understood fully. Jeremy's point was that the Duke and Sir Oswald made useful scapegoats. They were still attracting opprobrium. Others could quietly get away with murder.

"Scapegoats," he murmured.

"And this is where this particular picture is a little unusual," said Jeremy, turning the cutting so that both had a clear view of the photo. "It's probably to do with it being an Irish paper." Steve only had to offer a puzzled expression. The lecturer was continuing

"In this country, since the war, photos of Mosley will usually have him strutting about in Black shirt gear. This despite the archive having easily as many takes of him doing what he's doing here.......pursuing the normal business of democratic politics. You don't see these now though. If not suppressed then they're deliberately ignored."

"Because the fascist regalia is more usefully wicked?"

"That, as I've said, and also there's a cross party movement to minimise any risk of guilt by association. Mosley started as a Tory. Then it was Labour, and then his own New Party. He lurched across the full spectrum, there and back, and at the time there were others who were adrift. Many of those earlier pictures caught him in the company of persons who most would now prefer to view as renowned parliamentarians."

"Such as?"

"Lloyd George, who'd won the Great War; and Nye Bevan, who pressed the NHS into being. To this day, these people and their achievements are celebrated by their Parties. In this context, that they even chose to debate with Sir Oswald is best forgotten. That they might have shared a platform at one time......God forbid!"

Steve wondered. Could there be something particular in this photo. It held out for Jeremy an opportunity to air his own high minded philosophies...... but was there something more?

"So looking at the gang of hangers on he's collected in this one.......any that look familiar?"

"Too faint, too faded," said Jeremy. "Without what's written beneath I'd have been hard pressed to identify the principal."

"The year? The place?" persisted Steve.

"He was never more *'de la izqierda'* than in '29, but from the cut of the coat and the angle of the hat I'd have to say '31. Which means it could be anywhere. He was Party leader. It was a General Election. He would have been travelling the length and breadth of the country, not that it did his candidates too much good. The New Party was hammered out of sight, himself the only exception. He didn't win, but at least he competed."

"Where was that?" Steve wanted to know.

"I don't know. We could find out I suppose, but it's hardly going to matter in Spain. I don't think it ever did here. It's enough that, when put to the people, his ideas were rejected...."

"....and that he took that rejection rather badly," said Steve, and then he paused. He felt frustration. This was all too abstract and too distant. There had to be a personal dimension to this, and something of parochial significance. He felt this through his own personal knowledge of Jack Butters, and through that relationship what he'd also learned of Rory Duggan.

This, he reflected, was where Jeremy differed from Alan. In his intellectualism and in his liberal opinions the former was close on conceited. Alan might have concluded similarly on this out of Ireland snippet, but not before seeking out he who'd so quietly, and for so long, kept it to himself. He'd have made it his business to hunt down a common thread between something or someone hereabouts and this photo, however remote a phenomenon its subject might now appear.

And for Steve there was a strand, a character who Jeremy himself had mentioned just a few minutes earlier, even in the same breath as when speaking of Mosley. David Windsor was the man...... and the something local? That was Carwinion...... the someone?.....Sir Edward Trembath.

Steve favoured caution. He was indirect.

"Tell me how you view claims of a link between Sir Oswald here and the Duke of Windsor?"

"It's overdone," replied Jeremy. "They might have become chums after the war, but that was because by then they were very much in the same boat, neighbours in exile, over in Paris. It suited everyone that, so much so that it might have been arranged."

"Don't tell me.....by the Americans," taunted Steve, grinning wryly. "With our man Sir Walter facilitating the arrangements with his unique tact."

" 'Many a true word', " responded Jeremy. "It's recorded by their biographers that as the tide of war turned Monckton did indeed visit both, the Duke in the Bahamas and Sir Oswald in Brixton Gaol. Why else but to discuss their dollar pensioned post war roles?" The lecturer sounded in earnest. Steve sat up, but then the other winked. It was a retaliatory tease. Of course it was. But even so it introduced another common strand, another person, and one whose association with Edward Trembath was revived after the war when both found their ways to Westminster.

Steve was more respectful.

"Is there a book about Monckton? Did he rate a biography?"

"He did," answered Jeremy, his authority almost professorial. "And very readable it is too. Written by Freddie Birkenhead it was. I've only sampled parts, and that a good time ago. I've told you of my college project on Suez.... it was then. The book was fairly recently out, but disappointing none the less. It was good on the getting out of India and Africa, but no one was giving anything on Suez..... not then, and I don't think ever."

"Which for you is a challenge."

"As it should be for any historian," countered the lecturer. "After your mention of the man the other evening I went down to the Public Library, in the city. I ordered a copy. It should be there by the middle of next week. I want you to collect it, and for homework you can read the wartime chapters. It's an intriguing phase in an intriguing career. See what you think."

This was almost another errand. Steve was ready to comply though, and he was ready also with a request of his own.

"I can do that, I'd be glad to. And you can do a little something for my old friend, he that passed me these things. He knows there are Spaniards on the *Kampala*. He wants them to have this story. It's to do with a promise he made to Duggan personally. It was important to his friend that his name would at least be cleared amongst the people who were most damaged. It's got to go to the Spanish media, but because Franco over lasted, and because the tale was so long asleep, we need I think to send with it an explanation of the sort you've today given me. I'd like it written out in Spanish though..... the same things, about the codes, about Mosley, just a couple of sides and in a way that's going to excite a newspaper editor. We want it to catch on over there."

"I'll do that," agreed Jeremy. "I'd be delighted to." And he most certainly would, for there were possibilities here for himself, he could see that. He reached for the letters, the log and the cutting, but Steve had them already. He was returning them to their envelope. If the lecturer had attempted to conceal his disappointment, he'd failed. And Steve wasn't about to bend.

"I'm afraid I'm trusted to keep these until I get up onto the ship," said the boy. "Just do your best from memory."

He'd been rationing the man, and of course he was wanting more. This was to be expected, and the youngster was ready with a counter, a stalling device prepared and saved for this moment.

"In the meantime there's something you can help me with, " he continued. "Tell me about that murder out in the Bahamas, back in the war. You spoke of it at Jane's. It was too far in the past to interest Alan much, I can see that, but I could have listened to more. It's something else I might be able to sound knowledgeable on when in Hugh's company, or in Sir Edward's even..... the name, Harry....?"

"Harry Oakes? Harry was one of the richest men in the British Empire. Of the many who'd ventured to Canada and dug for gold he was one of the few who'd struck rich...."

"...... rich enough to retire to warmer climes......"

"....... where, like the Wagnerian dragon, he'd sat on his hoard and become himself the quarry of treasure seekers. It's been said that there might have been a Mafia involvement in his death, and that those concerned with the investigation had been leant on."

"And that would include the Governor?" asked Steve.

"So many have been led to conclude," answered the lecturer.

"And this happened in....?"

"The summer of '43, just prior to the US led landings in Italy. That was in September."

"You speak as if that might in some way be significant," said Steve.

"You heard me speak of a fellow student, and the study he made of the Polish question. He maintained that attitudes in Washington were at that time being largely shaped by the challenge of pushing an army up through Italy, of keeping it supplied, and covering its rear. He even went so far as to suggest that with their performances in Stockholm and in Nassau both Monckton and his old boss, the Duke, realised a useful dividend for the Yanks."

"In Italy, how?" Steve was confused.

"It's well documented that Washington sought and gained Mafia assistance. Sweeteners were required........"

"....... and one might have been the removal of Oakes," reasoned Steve, without looking entirely convinced. "I get it. Now implicate Walter."

"Until Tehran the Polish army in Britain was largely being held in reserve," explained Jeremy. "Its time would come when the way was open for a thrust across a near beaten Germany. They would liberate the homeland..."

"...... but not after Tehran they wouldn't, that was to be a job for Stalin's chaps."

"And where were the Polish Brigades sent instead? They were sent to Italy, and at Cassino, under American command, they were worse than decimated."

Steve half expected a 'QED'. Though still far from persuaded he was none the less nodding, content to have pulled the man away from Spain and Biscay. Rising now to leave, he was confident enough to venture more than an ounce of mitigation.

"I suppose though, across in the Pacific, the GIs were facing a Jap held Monte Cassino on every island group."

"Good point," conceded the lecturer, and each was happy to leave it there and depart now with his secured profit. Steve had sought assistance. It was promised, a 'translation' was in hand........ and for his pains Jeremy was taking a nugget of information that this youngster appeared to want to overlook. Steve was sparing with his old friend's tale, that was obvious, but perhaps not as sparing as he thought. A certain detail was telling more than the bearer had seemingly heard. The blind man would have noted this long ago, but on the boy it seemed not to have registered.

For the moment Jeremy was choosing to play along. Like the others, Steve was tending to underestimate him. Let them. He could live with this. Indeed, it might be preferable

*

This same hour had Gareth sitting alone in the *Rashleigh Inn*. Polkerris tucks itself neatly between Fowey and Par. It has its own stone pier, a soft sandy crescent of a beach, and it has the *Rashleigh Inn*. That Gareth should have been here at all was indicative of his changed outlook. A week ago and he would never have countenanced entering a place so public.

Before him lay two sheets of paper....behind him, four hours of frustration. He'd been to Par first, the shallow water port, and then across to Fowey where the deeper draught ships docked. At each he'd gone to the harbour office and been given what he'd asked.

He'd been here now for forty five minutes and he'd carefully scrutinised both lists. Both ports were about china clay, all was to do with loading. The ships came in empty. They left full, usually returning to from whence they came. He was looking at two month's worth of comings and goings. There were British ports, there were Irish ports, and there were Russian and Polish ports. There were ports in the Mediterranean, in Portugal and even in Spain itself.

He was disappointed. for he'd been hoping for something else, particularly around that remembered set of dates. He was undeterred though. He had another throw. He would be seeing Steve tomorrow.

Leaning back into his seat he considered the team. He'd led platoons before, and he saw Alan's role as similar. There were tensions, but such was the nature of any small operational group. To a competent leader they might be a resource, and Grigson, so far, looked to be competent. He reviewed his other first impressions. To an extent they had to matter, for as well as his own there were the perceptions and the reactions of others to be considered.

Jane was the youngest. She was bright, but could be emotional and this was natural of course, given the circumstances. She had a tendency to glaze whenever Jeremy theorised, but this might be a useful brake. She was the one local. She brought a native intuition.

Steve was a little older, and he was the true innocent. He was so compliant, and this made for an openness in others. That ingenuousness was key. He could blunder his way into a bank vault. It was he who'd brought word of those mystery crates. At Polgooth there had been a performance no less abject, with a pay-off no less impressive. Indeed, hadn't it all started with a tumble? What would any of this had been without that?

Kate was much as he remembered, but it was clear that between times she'd known dislocation. The trauma had been endured, it was being overcome, and now, clearly, she was hitting things off with Alan.

And this left Jeremy, with his suppressed chagrin and his more problematic contribution. Where before he'd enjoyed a monopoly of Kate's affections he was having now to compete, merely to maintain a

196

dwindling market share. But there was compensation. He carried much learning, and in the group context this was winning respect. The academic was seen as an asset, definitely, so long as he wasn't lingering too long in the too distant past. On a number of points Alan had turned to him and tactically this was sound. All needed to feel involved. Neglect breeds frustration, breeds resentment, severance, and that's when the loose cannon can start its roll. A loose cannon had crushed Hilda, and Brian?...... maybe he'd been one, threatening such high level havoc as to warrant pre-emptory disposal. He had to be pitched off, and was.

As for himself, maybe Alan had been right. He'd needed to feel useful, and now he did he was feeling better about the world and better about himself. He was back with the living..... the old soldier, with an old soldier's perspective, one not too easily out-witted.

*

Jeremy wasted no time. By mid evening he'd composed the best part of a first draft, initially in English. That the documents had stayed with Steve was of no matter. What they'd told was fresh and sharp in his mind. Mosley was a side show, he always had been. The main action was in those Board of Trade documents and in that log. Steve felt the same. The boy had stressed this when speaking of the Spanish media. If the story made an impact over there then it would come back to these parts, south Cornwall, and the local broadcasters and press people would be looking for expert comment. He wanted to be in on that, to be first in line. A little local research now could, in time, be the making of a local reputation. Well handled this could even run to national interest.

How much of what he'd been entrusted with was Steve keeping close? It would help to know that, as it would to know of its nature. This elderly friend, the one who'd actually set the errand, he was using the boy. And if he was using one, then why not two. If he could meet the man, if he could offer himself....this might be a way forward.

Jeremy re-read his draft. The wartime letters from the Board of Trade had been for merchant seaman Rory Duggan, the radio operator who'd kept and saved those Biscay signals of '37. Duggan was dead, long dead. He'd lived in this district during and just after the war, and in that time had attracted rumour. It was said that back in '37 he'd betrayed a shipment of arms meant for the hard pressed Republican forces in northern Spain, and when this emerged during the war he was, as a consequence, deemed too much of a risk to be kept on convoy work.

The documents suggested an injustice, and before he died he'd expressed a wish that they might one day be circulated amongst the people of northern Spain. His hope was that if his reputation could be restored amongst those who suffered then it might ultimately be restored amongst his native community. After he died this wish was remembered and now it was to be honoured, with Spain once again free.

There was more to do. He would need to expand a little on 'Enigma', and those Kriegsmarine signals. Intriguing they were...look at the very first, for instance.

And Mosley...so faded and frayed? The image would have meant more had Franco been ousted in the 50s, reflected Jeremy but, as he'd told Steve, there was an essential lesson that was timeless. For every Pinochet there was a Castro no less contemptuous of individual liberty.

*

".........anyway, I told the lad that when I was a boy I found entertainment in scratching around the Lanmouth banks for relics of the requisition, and you know what we've got here....... the buttons, badges and the bullets. Well yesterday I pass him in the lane between here and the farm and he hails me to stop. I do and from his pocket he produces a bullet. No cartridge, it had been fired, or somehow knocked out, and it was grimy, freshly prised out of the track which leads along to the Viceroy shed.

He wants to know what it is so I take it from him and bring it back here to clean and size up against the others. I said I'd be in this afternoon. I'm expecting his knock at any minute. He'll be wanting to hear what I've made of it. I've sorted it. I'm sure I can send him away happy.....Look, I can hear him at the door now. I'll try to catch you later....Take care."

Hugh Trembath replaced the receiver. He went to the door and Steve it was.

"Come in come in young man, we have two things to speak of. Your find of course, and I've just this moment taken a call from Sir Edward. We have the necessary permissions and we have a date. Be ready to go on board next Tuesday. I just need to get back to Radio Cornwall. I'll do that later."

Steve was guided through to the study. The relic drawer was on the table. Next to it lay an opened book. On the book rested the bullet. It had been cleaned and polished, the shape all the more sinister for being revealed in its dull leaden hue.

"There you have it, and it's a good start. It's a classic." Hugh picked it up. He gave it to Steve to handle. "It was fired by an M1 Carbine. Made by Garand they were standard issue to the American GI. You can bomb and bomb all you like, but in the end wars are won by the advancing infantryman. The Garand was his tool. They took on the Japs with this, it's what got them off Omaha, it was with this they held Bastogne. Show me a picture of a GI in action and I'll show you a picture of an M1."

"So it's not an unusual find," said Steve, his first words almost since arriving.

"I've got several. That can be your first." Steve was grateful. He took it and pocketed it, but it wasn't his to keep.

"If you've a scrap of paper I'd like to write that down," he said. Trembath obliged and as Steve noted down the make his host returned the collection to its accustomed place.

All tidied, Hugh was ready to move on.

"Tuesday morning, 10 am.... we'll have an hour. They'll be lowering a boat and coming across to the ferry. They'll be expecting six, me, Jeff from Radio Cornwall, yourself, the soldier, the nurse, and her boyfriend. It's going to be up to you to contact the Guardsman." The host was brisk. This was almost an order.

"And I'm thinking of bringing a camera ....is that OK?" asked Steve.

"You can do that."

"And I thought something for the crew, some local strawberries, perhaps with a bit of cream."

"Nice thought," said Hugh, "but I'm not sure how well they speak English."

"We'll have Jeremy with us, Kate's companion, he knows a little Spanish, he could pass it on."

Hugh was amenable. Steve was pleased. It was working out. He went on to ask after Helen and was duly given an up to date report on her progress through her season. She'd attended Wimbledon, next it was Henley. Her grandfather though was feeling the pace and he'd be down soon for a much needed breather....... probably within the next fortnight.

"Is there a chance I could come up and meet Sir Edward?" Steve's question was casually put.

"Why not," replied Hugh. "He'd certainly like to hear about our *Kampala* re-union. Maybe by then we'll have some photos, and the tape. He's met you before of course, a while ago now, but there's little wrong with his memory."

"Good," said Steve, seeing his opportunity. "I'd like to hear more about the old Duke...hear the tale about the wedding gifts."

"He likes telling that one," said the son, nodding. Steve was encouraged.

"And also anything about the character mentioned the other day in the Land Rover."

"Walter eh? .....some character. Could fill an afternoon on his own, that one."

A pause followed. Steve was taking a deep breath. Then in he plunged.

"Tell me about the Suez thing. How do you recall it. You would have been ...what 17?"

"18 I was, and at Dartmouth, and, I tell you, the whole thing was wild. Being an officer is being in a chain of command. You wanted to follow orders because that was the job, but where were they coming from?....The Admiralty? Number 10? NATO? Washington?

Then the Russians went in on Hungary and the £ into free fall. Some were being ordered out while others were still being ordered in! I saw a political party, the party of government, lose its collective nerve, and then, amazingly, survive in power. At the party conference we heard a bulldog. By the turn of the year we'd seen it was a poodle. My father went with the flow and that meant with Macmillan. 'First in, first out,' people have jibed, but like Mac he went on to prosper. This is why it's *Sir* Edward. People soon forgot Egypt and thereafter it was year on year defence cuts, and where once we'd had colonies it was independence for all."

"And people weren't cross with Washington?" asked Steve.

"Who could afford to be?"

"So Eden went, the Prime Minister, and Walter did too. Wasn't Monckton's instinct to protect this 'special relationship' we hear about."

"See Walter as a kind of electrical fuse, one with an unequalled capacity for transatlantic diplomacy. It wasn't limitless though. There was overload. There was burn out...."

".......and Eden lost power. Kate's friend teaches recent politics. He's read plenty on Walter, and where you say 'fuse' he asks 'dove or carrier pigeon?' "

"Bit of each perhaps..... something else to ask my father."

"Jeremy said there was a biography, available from the Truro library apparently."

"We had a copy. I think it went to the flat in London. He's got shelves of books up there. I can't remember it saying much about Suez, some good pictures though, and this astonishing tale of a promiscuous Rector. This was before the war. Walter was amongst the legal team hired by the Bishop of Norwich to establish the wayward cleric's unfitness for office. The consistory action succeeded. The poor man was defrocked." If doubts there were as to Hugh's commitment to the cause of Cornish Methodism his intonation of the term 'Rector' dispelled all.

"But you get that sort of thing all the time these days," said Steve. "Not like this one," snorted Hugh, relishing the moment. "He met a most unfortunate end, C of E or no, but I won't spoil it for you now. Not that Walter was far behind the Rector of Stiffkey in the field of dalliance. You go down there and get that book out. A little later, as you get into the war, you'll come across the extra marital ladies, the lovely Leonora.......theatricality personified, and then the naughty Mrs Newell...... his piece out in Cairo. Freddie Birkenhead might be sparse on Suez, but he got that pair in. Get down there Steve. Read it for yourself."

Hugh rose, and Steve was ready to leave. He was led to the door.

He had what he came for, the bullet, and with it he was taking much to think about.

The wartime chapter, it seemed that both Hugh and Jeremy were wanting to guide him towards that same episode. Could there be something in this? Steve wondered.

*

Jeremy was proud of his completed composition. So proud that earlier in the day he'd phoned Steve from the college. He'd been rusty at first, but now, glinting from three days of polish his piece had attained the strained for sense of drama....not least in a final paragraph, which warned of unchecked left-wing zealotry and the latent dangers therein.

He liked it. This was relevant. He didn't want it wasted, he wanted to see it through. Steve had told of his call in at Carwinion. The *Kampala* arrangements had been confirmed he'd said. He knew when they were boarding and what they could take, and there was mention too that Sir Edward might be in the district within the next fortnight. That was a bonus.

Spurred, the lecturer had contacted an associate at Exeter University. He'd obtained names, and addresses, of two prominent Bilbao based newspapers...... *'Egin'* and *'El Correo'*. He'd then purchased two large stout envelopes...... this a contingency.

He'd spoken well at Jane's, impressively, plausibly. He'd been asked for an interpretation, and he'd ventured one, there, on the spot, and it had been allowed to stand. The others had listened without demur, even Alan. But he knew that he'd ventured nothing more than unproven hypothesis. Founded on mere supposition it could fall at its first real test, on Tuesday, on that ship.... where then for this intriguing errand? Into these envelopes, that's where. This was his fall back.

Steve had no such misgivings. He'd disclosed selectively, and, he thought, cleverly. Success beckoned. The story would go to Spain and it would break there just as its subject would have wished. And then it would get back to these shores, of this he was certain. There would be media interest, local, maybe even national, and that's when Jack Butters would tell of St.Nazaire.

This was youth. Optimism was a right. He was 17, of course he was untutored. Supposition wasn't to be merely entertained, it had to be fondly embraced.

This was how he approached the weekend, a self styled go-between with influence. He had the bullet to return, a book to collect, and, most importantly, that errand still to perform.

*

Gareth held the bullet up, slowly turning it in front of his eyes. With his other hand he raised and looked at the note.

"M1 .... Garand ," he murmured. Both items were then zipped securely into one of his many jacket pockets. "That's fine. Thanks."

"And you can agree with that?" asked Steve.

"Why not, he'll have seen a lot more of them than me." As he spoke his eyes scanned searchingly across to Roundwood Quay and then beyond, into as much as was revealed of Lanmouth Creek.

They were at Tolverne. This had been Steve's choice, and it was apt. Where else west of Slapton did GI endeavour linger with such redolence? It was even said that the famed Ike himself had called at the waterside cottage just days before the great Overlord embarkation.

"Talk to Hugh Trembath and he'll say the M1 won the war," said Steve. Gareth nodded a qualified agreement.

"From this side perhaps. I'd urge him not to forget the small matter of the Russian tank."

"And urge him you can," said Steve, "for an opportunity will shortly be at hand. He's looking forward to meeting you, I know."

Whilst not averse to the prospect Gareth showed little outward enthusiasm..

"Tell me about Jane," he said, abruptly moving from Carwinion. "How did you find her today? She's not going to be part of Tuesday's thing. How's that going down?"

"It's getting busy over at the cafe. It's not like a month ago when there was time for standing and chatting. She's going to be at school on Tuesday of course, but even so she'd have been ready to stand apart. 'I'd only clutter the outward agenda'...... those were her words." And Steve was approving, for how much had he fully divulged? Only as much as he'd needed to, enough to slide things on their way, no more. It was why he'd left nothing with the lecturer. It didn't do to invite complication. He saw that, so did Jane.

"Shrewd girl," said Gareth, "much to admire there, but as you've had a busy day I'll not detain you longer."

"Until Tuesday then," said Steve, mounting his bike.

"I'll be there," promised Gareth.

The boy went on his way. Just minutes and he'd be on the ferry. Already it was within earshot. The Guardsman chose to linger. He looked across to the *Kampala*. Yes, the lad had done well. So well that this hunch which last week had taken him to Par and to Fowey was fast hardening into something firmer than suspicion.

He would go back to these places, but not yet, and not too often. The quarry would be watchful, as would others amongst the chasing pack. That's why he'd spent much of the past week touring. He'd been to Mevagissey, and even so far as Looe. He'd been across to the north coast, to Padstow, where coal had been brought in during the miner's strike. All were ports, but for this sort of business, of the furtive kind?... No. For their quays doubled as public car parks!

He'd also been down to St Anthony's Head, where more than once he'd trained his lenses on each of those factory ships. More film he'd used. That would please Alan....... but there'd been nothing to shake him from that first hunch. There it was, a gut feeling, inexplicable, undeniable. Maybe Par, maybe Fowey, it had to be one or the other. It just had to be.

*

Tuesday dawned, cloudy but warm. The finest of drizzles asked for a garment extra to the blouse or the shirt, something light, something damp resistant. They were to muster in the Trelissick car park. From there they would together walk down to the ferry slip. Jeremy and Kate called for Steve. They'd picked up the strawberries in Truro, four good sized generously filled punnets. They rested on the car floor, behind the driver's seat. Their scent filled the car. On the rear seat there waited a standard sized carrier bag. Already it held two pots of clotted cream. It could take the strawberries, and there would be room too for the documents.

This was mentioned as Steve climbed in and he was quick to slide his envelope into the bag. There were parts, of course, that Jeremy hadn't yet seen...... and he needn't. The lecturer's own contribution waited on the dashboard. That would have to go in, and the sooner the better if the cover of gift giving was to be adopted with true purpose.

Jeremy knew this. He reached for his own two stapled sheets and turned. He wanted to see them go in with the others, and he did....and he wasn't fooled. Steve coloured. Nothing was said. It was as well that time was so tight.

The interviewer, Jeff, and his sound technician were already there in the car park, equipped and waiting. They had their own final checks to make. Next to their car stood Hugh's Land Rover. He sat at the wheel. He'd obtained some notes on the ship's design and its history. He'd also obtained a deck plan. This was the Naval man, ever prepared.

The notes were still in his hand as he stepped out to greet the arrival of Jeremy's car. And then Gareth arrived, swinging into the car park from the west. He hadn't used the ferry.

Steve helped Hugh with the introductions, he more than helped. With his clumsy starch bending charm any residual regard for service protocol that might have hung between Hugh and Gareth and Kate was soon dispersed.

Hugh led the procession down to the river. The road was steep. It was narrow and it was dank. As cars were starting to climb from the ferry they had to keep to single file. This suited Steve. He was wary of Jeremy coming up on his shoulder. This lessened the risk.

Reaching the slip they were beckoned across the ferry deck by young Jack's successor. Only Hugh spoke to the man. He was courteous and he was brief. He used the name 'Baz'. The fellow was efficient, and he was close to silent. Irregularity was being made to look routine. He wasn't looking to create an impression, but on one of the party he did, immediately. He was recognised. Likewise he'd skulked in the past, somewhere, on a different shore, as part of a different life..... but here, now, it wasn't to be said. That would only disturb. The recognition looked to be the one way, and it was desirable that it should so remain.

Two men brought a lifeboat across from the *Kampala*. Though plainly heavy, the steering, the fending and the tying were accomplished well. In the currents and the confines of the passage the men showed themselves equal to an exacting task. To each other they spoke in Spanish. Jeremy listened intently. Steve gripped the bag, watching him and willing him to understand every inflexion. As they boarded from the ferry ramp Hugh offered a salutation, one barely acknowledged by the helmsman. As they moved out, the others were watching the looming vessel. A flight of permanently lowered steps hung close to her stern, dropping to a narrow pontoon. Steve determined to pass the bag as they climbed. The less the lingering, the less the scope for Jeremy to too closely scrutinise the contents.

Steve manoeuvred himself accordingly. In they came, and up they went. On reaching the main deck that first transfer was done. The bag went to Jeremy. He was the mailman.

A sour smell lay about the vessel, a queasy blend of engine oil, musty upholstery, and weary disinfectant. Sea air she needed, and the warmth of fired up engines. Instead she was staling amongst the trees and the low water mud.

They'd arrived well aft, where the main deck supported an enclosed observation lounge. Acquired during a mid life conversion from passenger and cargo carrier to cruise ship a formerly trim rear had been made thicker, more matronly. The addition was roomy though, and it was safe. When a school ship this was the pupil's common room, its roof offering a sports deck. On conversion to a military hospital it became the main recovery ward, with the roof widened and strengthened so as to enable casualties to be brought by helicopter.

The landing deck had been re fitted for the ship's last two year task for the Defence Ministry, that of ferrying troops and supplies between Ascension and Port Stanley prior to the completion of the fortress Falkland's airfield. The platform remained, and this was where the party was now being led. They had to climb again and they emerged at the forward end of the landing area close to the davits from which the last of the port side lifeboats..... the one in use...... had been lowered.

The two crewmen who'd fetched them remained here. The other two stood similarly on the starboard side. The use of that particular lifeboat, together with the positions adopted by the hosts gave little chance for snooping. In fact there was no chance. A camera was produced, it was handed around, but angles were limited. In this respect the excursion promised little that hadn't already been obtained from the shore. Steve wasn't too bothered. He had other hopes..... pinned on Jeremy.

The genuine broadcaster was a genuine professional. Others might have been tripped by restricted time and access, but not he. He'd talked with Hugh, that was obvious, and also he'd absorbed enough of his personal research to express a close and relaxed interest in the experiences of the military nurse and patient.

Kate was asked about her introduction to the ship at Gibraltar, about the conversion work, and the preparation, and even about the attitudes of the civilian crew. There was mention of Captain Chadwick, of his illness, of his on board operation, and of his subsequent death. With Gareth the themes were the wait at Ascension and then the advance, of complacency at Bluff Cove and then heroism.

By sowing facts he was reaping feelings. His piece would be more than informative. It would be moving, and it was veering towards the controversial. Gareth was primed, and he was tempted.......

He'd been damaged he said, irreparably so, but many had given their lives, many from the UK, and many more from Argentina.....with the loss of the *Belgrano* for instance, so many in that one initial stroke. Kate was shaking her head. Steve held his breath. Those ghosts, Brian and Hilda, they were restless, but if this was the place it wasn't the time, it couldn't be, Gareth had to know that......

And he did. Restraint prevailed. He backed away, and was talking now about the shipboard treatment of Argentine casualties, and in general terms only. He invited Kate to take up the story because, at the time, with the drugs, he'd been so out of it for so long. And Kate was quickly in with her statistics, the number treated, the number of operations. She spoke of the problems of language and segregation, and of the arrangements for offloading casualties, the comfortable and the critical.

Steve turned. He'd been listening, and Jeremy had crossed behind him to the two starboard side crewmen, the other two. They were having to whisper. The technician had insisted.

What was being said? Steve watched. Jeremy reached into the carrier. A first punnet came out, and then a second, one each, and then a pot of cream to share, and all was well received, but as yet.......... no envelope. Was it still there in the bag? Or had it already been passed to the other two...., even with Hugh standing so close by?

Steve glanced across. Each held of them held a punnet, one with a pot of cream. Neither had the envelope. Where was it? Steve's eyes came back to the bag. It was in there, still. He could see from its shape. How was Jeremy playing this? Was he going to leave it on the boat as they returned to the ferry? Or was something awry? Whatever, he could only wait.

The principals were being ushered towards him. Kate was telling how the seriously hurt were lowered by lift to a deeper deck operating theatre, and then, when patched, how they would be moved into its adjoining intensive care facility, previously the ship's smoking room.

Little trace now remained of these arrangements. They were in Kate's memory and in her words, and through the skill of the interviewer they would need to be conjured in the imaginations of those who listened. They climbed back down to what had been the main recovery ward. With her Red Cross work done the *Kampala* had been rewarded with a full refurbishment. A return to educational cruising was anticipated, but the business was no longer there. Instead it was back to the MOD, and back to the South Atlantic. It had been a nice gesture, the prettying up, but now there were to be two years of truly hard labour, two years of being a floating barrack. The roughest of cargoes and the roughest of seas were going to leave their mark, and it was apparent to Gareth that his 'Sea View Ward' had borne the brunt.

He peered in. He recalled Alberto, prone. This was where he'd met and befriended the Argentinian. Here was something for his next letter. But he was due to receive one first, and it could have arrived and be waiting for him at home. He'd been promised an account of the ship's final return through the southern seas, information for which he was now more than ready.

The same two men took them back, but this time their timing was less exact. They had to wait in mid river as the ferry dragged itself onto the slip. Between Steve and Jeremy it was the former who now had to suffer. The lecturer had the bag, there on his lap. It should have been just the bag, empty. Both knew it wasn't. Extra time, and without possession it was suddenly, for the boy, a very much tougher game.

They were disembarked. Thanks were expressed to the hosts, and gracias were proffered in return. They'd liked the gifts, the treats. But why had they been denied the Duggan's long saved testimony?

Jeremy hung close to Hugh. That was shrewd. Steve was going to have to be patient, and the more so in the light of Hugh having invited all back to Carwinion. The sandwiches were ready he insisted, and who could refuse? None, not even the pair from the radio station.

But at least this would be to Alan's liking, of this Steve was sure. The cover beneath which they'd boarded the *Kampala* was stretching to allow Kate, Jeremy, and Gareth into Carwinion. To go with Steve's there would be a second, a third, and a fourth opinion on Hugh Trembath at home.

And Jeremy too read it this way. He was keen of course, predictably, transparently. His lady though looked less comfortable, but to the attentive this had been noticeable prior to the invitation, and particularly when they approached and were on the ferry deck. She would have been struggling with unpleasant memories, that was what Steve thought..... but only for a second, for like Jeremy he'd become preoccupied with that bag.

Reaching Trelissick the lecturer went to his car, but only to place the bag on the driver's seat. He re-locked the door saying they would walk across to Carwinion, and then, later, he could run Steve down to the farm. This was coolly played. The boy was wrong footed. He might have insisted on being taken straight to the farm, there and then. That he didn't was down to momentary relief. He'd anticipated worse. Jeremy might have been straight into Carwinion House, then straight to Hugh's bathroom, and there, closeted, straight into that envelope.

Gareth took the bike. Hugh rode in the radio car. As the other three followed on foot Kate at last talked. Had they made the most of it? That was her outward concern. She'd wanted to please Alan, as she'd pleased him before at the country club, but now she had doubts. She hadn't expected the run of the ship, but she had hoped for more time. There hadn't been a spare second in the whole while they were on the water.

"Fear not," said Jeremy confidently. He was striding with purpose. "We are in profit. We have a dividend, a return. For the moment it's with me. Later we'll share it, but not until we're clear of the media. Alan will be pleased, rest assured......and there's something here for you too Steve."

He was alluding to the errand, Steve was sure, and this was far from comforting. Steve's purpose had required Jeremy as a mule, nothing more. This mule had assumed, and was now flexing, an irritating measure of discretion.

Kate though was heartened, and with spirits rising the buffet went well. For the host, with his best hopes handsomely realised, all was unmitigated success. Gareth was even responding to his mention of chapel. Hugh was due to preach down at Penryn the following Sunday morning and he'd ventured to suggest that the Welshman might help him by reading a lesson. To the surprise of the others Gareth had given there and then agreement.

Jeremy was showing a preference for the hallway, and the main stairs. He was absorbed in a series of framed black and white photographs. Of varying sizes they were clearly selected and ordered so as to chronicle Sir Edward's political career. He was pictured with a succession of Tory Prime Ministers, the beaming Ted, the lordly Sir Alec, the inscrutable Mac, and then Churchill himself, on his visit to Plymouth during the '51 campaign. Eden?....'There had been one,' said Hugh, it was probably in one of the bedrooms, and there was even another with Maggie, but taken prior to '79, when she'd led the Opposition.

Of the visible, only two photographs pre dated that of '51. In one, Edward Trembath, gabardined and bowlered, stood with a group of onlookers as King George VI, great-coated, studied an umbrella canopied plan..... Plymouth again, just a few years earlier, shortly after the war.

The other had a date.......1932. A youthful Edward Trembath posed proudly in cap and gown. His hands held the scroll. This was his graduation ceremony. It celebrated the award of a B Sc in economics from Manchester University.

Of the years in between, when he'd worked for the Duchy and for its Duke, there was nothing to be seen. Jeremy was minded to explore further, but thought better. He was a guest of course and he fancied there to be a chance of a further visit, with maybe even an audience with the man himself......not a prospect to jeopardise.

A concerted chuckle drifted from the reception room. The occasion was brewing quite adequately without him, and this was good, for if he were to slip out for a few minutes he wouldn't be immediately missed. The poster in the Trelissick car park had told of a touring theatre company. In a month's time they were to stage an outdoor performance in the Gardens. Tickets were on sale now at the office. He could slide across the road and be back inside fifteen minutes. If he were challenged on his return the explanation would be simple, he would have the tickets.

Out he went, along and across the road, pausing just once at the car park entrance..... just to ensure no one followed.

"Oh there you are!" Said Kate on his return. And that was all, a mock scold. No one was accusing, not even Steve... that watchfulness having eased. The boy was huddled with Hugh, and the sound technician. Together they inspected a map of the estate.

The boy glanced up momentarily, but Jeremy wasn't giving eye contact.... he might look as smug as he felt, that was his fear. For the boy it had to be continued frustration.

First to leave were the Radio people. Hugh saw them to their vehicle and through the gate, returning then to corner Gareth. Already his thoughts were running ahead to Sunday's chapel service. The guardsman's readings would be of his own choice, but they would need to relate broadly to the address so there had to be some pooling of theme. An attempt was made to persuade Kate to attend, but she had work she said, and with this Gareth slipped in his only reservation. He hoped to attend, and would certainly assist if he did, but it wouldn't be until towards the end of the week that he would know for sure.

Amongst the four guests there'd developed a tacit understanding that all would leave together. Accordingly a group exit was smoothly effected some twenty minutes after the departure of the local broadcasters. Gareth rode off, leaving the other three to be escorted across to Trelissick by Hugh. They were almost to the car before Jeremy at last heard the hoped for largesse.

".......and you know you're welcome at any time," said Hugh.

"Perhaps then when your father is in residence?" enquired Jeremy, as if without forethought. "From what I've heard from Steve here, and seen from your hallway photos, the man's a walking archive.

Would he mind much being gently interrogated by a humble teacher of social sciences?"

"I'll see how he is when he comes down. It should be quite soon. I'll ask, and then it'll be up to him.....should be OK. His strain of Conservatism tends to be derided these days, not least within the Party itself. A sympathetic listener would be well received I'm sure, and well rewarded."

"Thanks for the tip," said Jeremy as he opened the car. The bag was where he'd left it. Kate handed it to Steve as he settled into the back. Dazed he was, from sheer relief...... to the extent of neglecting to acknowledge Hugh's hospitality. But Jeremy was alive and he was quick to voice a fulsome appreciation. Then they were on their way.

Within minutes Steve was at the farm, scrambling from the vehicle with the bag firmly in his clutch. Jeremy wasn't lingering. There was to be a meeting that very evening. Kate would be working, and there would be nothing yet from the camera, but no matter. Alan wanted them at *The Pandora.*

He wanted impressions, freshly taken. Reflections were never the same. Steve was to cycle down to Restronguet Point. There he was to meet Alan and Jane. They would be sailing across from the Roseland, the idea being to collect the boy and cross to the Inn together. Jeremy, by car, and Gareth, by motorcycle, would each find his own way. Six thirty was deemed a reasonable time. Jane was rarely home from school before four.

Steve made for his room. Everything came out of the bag, it was spread across the bed and closely checked. It was there, all of it, even that last note in Spanish prepared by Jeremy. Did he need to take any of this down to *The Pandora,* he wondered. No, he decided. What he'd hoped Jeremy could do, which he hadn't, was something apart. There would be a reason, but to hear it he must wait. Steve didn't want the others involved, he didn't even want them being curious, not now. These things could go back to Mylor, tomorrow or the next day. He'd tried with them, but the attempt hadn't worked...... and that would have to be that.

*

Accordingly, Steve arrived at Restronguet with nothing save sufficient coin to finance a gentle evening of sipped lager and nibbled crisp. He was early. He could see the *Speedwell* way out in the Roads, an exaggerated tack to the south taking her clear of a group of boldly rigged working boats. The colours of the high gaffs gleamed against the distant Roseland. Between the blue of the sky and the water he was looking across at a belt of brightly studded green, an enchanting spectacle. This was good, he had nothing now to hide.

So why then was he shrinking back into the tree shadows as the *Spartan* ploughed in from the direction of Mylor Churchtown and through into Restronguet Creek? They'd met, he and Prout. They'd spoken. There'd been no antipathy. It had to be that one sighting, on the road returning from Polgooth. There was a connection between this character and the deckhand, Baz. He was sure, and this was why he was keeping back now, and regarding Alan's slight delay as fortuitous.

On motored the *Spartan,* and then in nudged the *Speedwell.* On leapt Steve, and across they sailed. Jeremy and Gareth waited and in seconds the craft was secure at the end of the pontoon. Jeremy stood the first tray of drinks. To Steve he looked worryingly composed.

Being just the five they were able to stay in the cabin....... just about. The sitting space amounted to two facing bunks. Steve and Gareth took one, Jane and Jeremy the other. Between them the narrowest of tables rested atop the even narrower casing that housed a retractable keel. Alan sat on the steps that dropped from the stern cockpit, presiding in the manner of the Commons speaker. It was claustrophobic, even with the cabin doors and the sliding hatch above left fully opened. It made for a floating den. There was little room for vacillation and none for evasion. Jeremy knew this, and straight away he was setting the tone, dictating the pace, pushing his agenda.

"Right, listen to this. You all heard what I had to say last week over at Jane's. I was asked to give an interpretation, I did my best with the information available."

"And it figured," added Jane supportively.

"But I'd presumed things, too much, because we were short on fact. My interpretation was untested, but from today we know better."

"In what respect?" asked Alan.

"For a start, this crew..... we were told there were four, rightly, and we were told that they were Spanish speaking......."

"....rightly again," followed Steve, puzzled. He was looking to Jeremy for explanation.

"And thereon it's assumed that they're from Spain, from northern Spain moreover. We allow ourselves to believe they're Basque people even. Why?... because we want them to be. Today I spoke briefly to all four. Each had a few words for me. Also I listened as they spoke with each other, and I heard enough to leave me convinced that not one of those on that ship actually comes from Spain........far from it."

"From where then?" asked Steve.

"Certainly from beyond Europe. The two who stayed on the *Kampala* throughout, their Spanish was as pure as any I've heard and to me that marks them as Colombian. From the other two I was hearing something less equatorial, more tropical, more Gulf of Mexico than southern continent. I'm less certain with these."

"But your best guess would be?" prompted Jane.

"For the moment, Cuba," plumped Jeremy. "Forget about Basques. We're a world away from that. I'm sorry Steve but you're going to have to tell your old pal that he's been way off beam. That was a fool's errand...... but I've got some ideas for him if he's interested."

Steve was stunned. He'd no reason to doubt Jeremy. The man was a well travelled academic, one who would be familiar with a range of dialects. Jack Butters had only a basic knowledge, simple words and simple phrases. He'd never pretended otherwise. He was a proud man though, circumspect, sagacious, and usually so certain in all he said. Steve had never known him to be so utterly wrong. The prospect of having to correct him disturbed.

It was as well that he'd recruited Jeremy, thought Steve. The errand could have so easily miscarried. Now it was a matter of backing from a blind alley. Tact would be required.

"But the racket is essentially the same, surely," insisted Jane, "and it still ties in with this Morrish character and the holiday bonds, and whatever it is being loaded onto the ship at night."

Alan nodded.

"Worry not," he said. "I'm still assuming that your father's been stitched up. In the run of things Jeremy might only be slightly wrong. Forget about Spanish middlemen in the cocaine trail and Basque terrorists as customers for guns and we're left with something simpler. We have the Colombians dealing direct, seemingly with the help of a few friends in Cuba. I like that more. I'm impressed Jeremy. I'm still listening. Last time you told us a little about Colombia, now tell us more. Tell us about Colombia and Cuba."

"Colombia has a pleasant climate. It has pleasant scenery. It could be a thoroughly pleasant place, that's if it weren't so dangerous. You get nice people there and you get people who are very, very nasty.... so nasty that those who look to make names for themselves are soon faced with a stark choice...*plata o plomo,* silver or lead. Either you are bought or you are shot. Offering the choice are the cocaine barons based in Cali and Medellin. A few years ago these were separate cartels, at each other's throat. Now they work together and between them they have the government departments in Bogota in their thrall. It doesn't do to cross them. They maintain private armies, and their own gun law. Justice ministers have been shot, also Judges. The power of the Barons derives from money. The return on sugar, coffee, and bananas is nothing against that from cocaine. It buys better schools and hospitals, and even football teams. It also buys weapons and training in their use. Leftist guerrilla movements are traditional to any South American country. Colombia's only an exception in that there these 'people's armies' have been bought out by the cocaine industry...... the FARC famously so, more recently the M-19. They're weaned off terrorism, as we know it, and given a well paid role in maintaining a kind of controlled anarchy. They have to be vicious, that's their meal ticket."

"And the Cuban involvement?" asked Steve.

"Probably two fold," explained the lecturer. "The prize customers for cocaine are in the States, and Cuba sits solidly across the stepping stone supply route. Coming back, Cuba also offers convenient access to weapons and ammunition, eastern bloc stuff.....no questions asked."

Gareth had been listening closely, and he wasn't about to let this slip by.

"So it's still Kalashnikovs you think, in those crates? And you're thinking that when the ship goes, it'll be back through the Caribbean?"

"Or to a mid-ocean rendezvous with another vessel headed that way." Jeremy was making sense. His revised interpretation was being received with approval. It didn't matter that he'd been wrong about the Basques, in fact this helped. It was down to him, his rigour and honesty, that the error had been detected. Conceding it had enhanced his authority. Alan appeared impressed, it was just Gareth who was wary.

"If the weapons can be got from Cuba then why not pick them up on the way past? Coming all the way to sleepy Lanmouth sounds what it is..... far fetched."

Welsh accented, those last two words carried more cynicism than intended. Alan countered on behalf of Jeremy.

"Don't forget, there's more than two hot potatoes here. If there's drugs, and if there's guns, then we'll also be hearing the slush of dirty money...... and this can be hardest of all to handle. Find a way to launder that at a preferential and for the rest the distance factor won't matter. A key thing in this is that holiday bond ploy. It doesn't yet extend to the Caribbean. If it did then yes Gareth, you'd have a strong point"

"You're the expert," shrugged the guardsman.

"And there's something else to bear in mind," continued Alan. "The US government is under pressure to do something about the inflow of cocaine. They know it can't be stopped, but there's been moves made recently to show that at least some kind of effort's being made."

"Like......?" asked Jane.

".........last Autumn's military take over of Grenada. The strategic context was the containment of the Colombian big boys. They have two main export routes into the States, the isthmus trail through Panama, and the stepping stone trail mentioned by Jeremy.... along the West Indies. The first makes for New Mexico and California, the second for Florida. Grenada guards the southern end of this second route. The idea was to dislodge an administration that was becoming increasingly Cuban friendly, sovereignty counting for little of course in America's back yard."

Yankee hypocrisy! Alan had kindly wheeled in Jeremy's favourite hobby-horse, more than that he was urging him to climb on and tilt. And of course the lecturer was only too ready to oblige. The oppressor identified, the rest was reflex. In an instant the cabin became a village hut in beleaguered Guatamala, and he was going to rally these poor fruit farmers with every argument he could muster. It was all so unjust. And added to this there was the drug issue, and this was compounding the iniquity because........ *and at this moment another possibility was crystallizing in that analytic mind.* Just a possibility, no more, no less, but enough of one to persuade him to hold fire with his customary invective.

216

They could hear that another time. This was a moment to just sit back for a while and listen. He needed someone else to speak, and Alan it was again, now addressing the boy.

"Steve, help me. We've heard what Jeremy's had to say. He's given us much to digest, but something sticks and I must ask. There was mention of an 'old pal', one said to be 'way off beam'. Isn't this something I should know about?" All turned to the boy. He was trapped. He was going to have to say something. He knew this, and Alan did, and so too Jeremy.

"The 'old pal'.....that's Jack Butters across at Mylor. I took you to see him Alan, the one who's blind. At the time you were wearing the guise of freewheeling journalist and the *Kampala* was no more than another curio along the way. How things can change. You were with the grandson when he spoke to me about the ship. Like us he'd heard that the men on board were Spanish, and he'd been waiting for something like this. He had this errand. It had been left to him, now he was entrusting it to me. The main man was long dead, but there had been a pledge, and hope was that at long last it might be honoured. Had those crewmen been Spanish then there was a small package to deliver, papers mainly."

"Entirely," corrected Jeremy. "But they weren't Spanish up there, as I've just explained. The package we took, we also brought back."

"And now it's at Lanmouth," continued Steve. "It'll go back to Mylor tomorrow."

"And you didn't think to inform me?" rebuked Alan. Cornered, Steve surprised himself...... so spirited was his own response.

"Jack Butters had the opportunity to do that. He didn't. He wished for it to be kept to as few as possible. And I respected that, just as you would want me to respect the very similar wish expressed by yourself. Think about it. It was to me that this was entrusted, and I took it on before you dropped your disguise, and before we looked closely at Gareth's snaps of the ship. He's nobody's fool, Old Jack, particularly in his own cottage. He has a sharp nose for duplicity."

Alan was taken aback.

"Fair enough," he conceded, contrition in an altered tone. Steve glanced across to Jane. He'd been true to the old man and he'd be no less true to her. He wanted that to register, and it probably did, but she wasn't looking to dwell.

"We saw young Jack out on the Roads. Another scratch crew by the looks, but going well all the same. He called across as we went by. 'If you see him remind Steve that my grandfather's waiting for another visit.' So consider yourself now reminded."

"Shame I didn't bring my bike across," said Steve, "I could have nipped around there this evening."

"I'll take you round." offered Jeremy, so alert. "And I'll get you back to your bike, no problem. I'd like to meet the old fellow. As I said, I've an idea or two for him to consider."

"And perhaps you can let us know how you get on," added Alan sharply, his authority directed no less at Jeremy than Steve. The intervention was telling. An awkward offer became one that was impossible to decline. The pair were going to Mylor together because as well as Jeremy, Alan too willed it.

Was this calculated? It was.....to the extent that Alan was noting that Jeremy was on a surge. Kate wasn't there to curb him, that was his concern. There had to be a different check, and where better than at Mylor. With Spain now seemingly a non-issue, here was a low risk backwater where Jeremy could wade around in the past to his heart's content. Old Jack had to be the man.

And how this suited the lecturer. Getting where he wanted to be was too simple. He could sense Steve's unease, but of course the poor lad was helpless.

Ever impatient, it was Jane who moved things on.

"So where do we go now, if we assume a Colombian connection stretches right to our doorstep?"

"We just carry on watching," said Alan. "It's not for us to move in, and neither is it for us to say when others might. We merely inform. We don't decide. We should be looking for peripheral figures now. The ones who know the most are those seen the least. They'll have cover, just as I have, and as my superiors do too. It might be that a senior of mine is working now in this pub, ostensibly as a barman or a cook perhaps. You never know, and that's why we are to watch rather than challenge."

"A rule that was broken in my case," Gareth reminded him.

"Only after getting clearance. It was a matter of getting you, Jane, Steve and me into step. We could have been tripping each other."

"And Kate, and me?" joined Jeremy.

"I took a risk," answered Alan, "like you have to sometimes, and so far it's paid off well. Let's hope it can continue to. I know what you want Jane. You want a bust, a seizure, because that's what's going to get your father out. For us though there are others to be put in, and for this we'll need fuller information. We know about the drugs, where they've come from, where they're going. We know who's handling the money. Now we want to find out more on the weapons aspect."

"And this sounds all the more likely to be Red if there's a Cuban involvement," reasoned Steve. "Any connection established yet with those factory ships? I suppose I could ask Old Jack what he makes of them."

"Too loose," Gareth was emphatic. "We've come too far, and done too well, to start throwing it open as a guessing game. The old boy's had his go, it was good try, we've done our best to help, but he got it wrong. He just needs to be told. Say that these Spanish speaking gentlemen are of the new-world variety, yes, but after that I say it's up to us to get on with things ourselves."

All looked to Alan. He was happy to agree. Not that that meant letting things rest or drift, he was ready with a strategy.

"To me," he began, "the whole thing seems to pivot around this character who works on the ferry. He's the one visible individual who looks to be touching everything, the drugs, the money and the weapons. He's a key man. That's obvious, maybe too obvious.........in the sense that he can't be the one who's behind it all. He's too much out there in the middle. He's a lieutenant, trusted and no doubt competent. He's also a sensor, an alarm sensor, and that's where we need to take the utmost care. I repeat. We watch, we don't disturb."

"Which is why you wouldn't have wanted me near the ship this morning," said Jane, "even had there been no school. To that man my jailed father is out of sight and largely out of mind...."

"Meaning that your presence would of amounted to heat, unnecessary heat," confirmed their host. "You're learning. This is why I insist we keep well clear of Lanmouth Creek, its quay, and its shed, and also Roundwood Quay. And now we've been on that ship we can leave her alone too. Just watch. Listen. Is that ferry hand, Baz, really short with everyone, or are there people being favoured with a little more time or courtesy? I want to know."

"Jim Prout," said Steve. "There might be a connection there, an acquaintance even. I saw him just now as I waited for you at the Point. He came through the passage with his boat. He lives in Devoran. I guess he was making for home."

"I thought it was him," said Alan. "It looked like he'd been doing business at Mylor Chuchtown. You'd expect him to find a bit there, plenty of yachts." He turned to the girl. "Jane, you're the one from these parts. Give us what you can on him. How long he's been doing what he does. What people say he did before......that sort of thing."

"He's been coming with the *Spartan* to Percuil Yard for at least ten years. That's how long we've been keeping a boat there, until recently that is. But he's not local. He's northern, you can hear that in his voice."

"Despite a name which sounds so local........could have been adopted I suppose. Do we know anything about a former life? Has there been word of any crimes?"

"On the contrary," said Jane. "He's renowned for being straight. 'Typical tyke', people say, blunt but dependable. He's trusted with valuable equipment, which means he's rated for both competence and honesty. What also goes down well is his distaste for gossip. My father used him when we had the boat. Ralph's used him with the cafe roof......"

".....and Hugh Trembath used him only the other day," remembered Steve. "There were some scratches and dents to tidy up on his Land Rover. It was done during that day Hugh brought me over to Pendower, the day that was so wet. We picked him up en route so he could get on with the job while Hugh was doing his watch."

"Which means he must have a good sized workshop somewhere," deduced Gareth, "big enough to take a Land Rover One Ten in out of the rain."

"Up past Carnon Downs apparently," Steve informed them. "I think he's using part of the old Wheal Jane complex. I've been told that it was the mine that brought him down here. This would have been when Consolidated tried to revive things back in the late 60s, early 70s. Sad that was. The price just wasn't there."

"So it was just to do with tin," said Gareth. "Some say that a lot of this modern day drilling and pumping has had more to do with testing out possible sites for storing nuclear waste."

"Thank you Gareth," Alan patronised. "Hilda would have been proud of you I'm sure. For the moment let's just say that information pertaining to that issue might have been a useful by product. Whatever, I can't imagine that Mr Prout would have been hired for anything other than his mining expertise. I don't see him as a nuclear physicist."

"Strictly drilling," conceded Gareth with a fading voice, "and pumping.......and explosives."

It was a muted parting shot. One Alan chose to ignore. He had questions.

"You were in a car with the man Steve. That must have been the best part of an hour. And the journey would have included a ferry crossing in each direction. What did you learn about him, and about his relationship with Hugh Trembath? And what about the way both acted towards the ferry deckhand? Was there any familiarity such as might bear out the acquaintance you suspect? Or perhaps you thought it deliberately concealed. Would this have been solely for your benefit Steve or for Trembath's too?"

"The deckhand kept himself to himself, nothing out of character there. The Trembaths have shares in the ferry. They go across free. It was raining so the windows stayed up. I'm sorry, I've nothing more sinister."

"And how were Prout and Trembath together?" asked Jane.

"They're about the same age, but from different ends of the country of course, and whereas Hugh chose a Naval career Prout was just a National Service conscript. He went into the Army. This came out because of a mention I made to Hugh of Walter Monckton. Prout was almost involved in the Suez action. Only got as far as Cyprus apparently...."

"....... and even to this day he's wondering why they weren't allowed to finish the task," murmured Gareth. Steve nodded. "Well there's a lot of his sort," continued the Falklands veteran. "I used to listen to them, and even sympathise.....no longer though."

"Indeed, why sympathise?" Jeremy concurred, "for to have been in Cyprus for any length of time would have been to have seen action aplenty."

"He would have, indeed" said Gareth quietly, as the youngster continued.

"Anyway, as the in-car conversation developed it came out that after his stint in the Army he went back to mining and this took him abroad. He went to Africa on free lance work, mostly in what I think is now known as Zambia. It was while he was there that our man Walter happened to feature in his life. Although long retired from being a Minister he was apparently sent across by Macmillan to sort out the best way of moving that territory, and the others grouped with it, towards independence."

Jeremy helped.

"Northern Rhodesia, Southern Rhodesia, and Nyassaland were federated colonies. The blacks didn't like the arrangement, and understandably too. It brought them under the control of the Southern Rhodesian whites who were in turn falling increasingly under the influence of Pretoria and all that that implies. The Monckton Commission facilitated the break up of the Federation. Nyassaland then became independent Malawi, Northern Rhodesia became independent Zambia."

"And Hugh's opinion is that, with his work out there, Walter did much to avert a bloodbath."

"I wouldn't argue with that Steve," said Jeremy. "The prize was the copper ranges, not only in Northern Rhodesia, but in Katanga as well..... Katanga being part of the old Belgian Congo. Conor Cruse O' Brien is good on Katanga, I'm not sure what they call it now. The whites were looking to ring fence the mineral rich areas and sustain them from the south. There's this rail link across the Zambesi that was central to the plan, but the idea never got off the ground. Things moved too quickly, largely thanks to Mac and to Walter. This was the 'wind of change' era. A strong body of Tory back-bench opinion was defied, and this is another area where Sir Edward could well entertain with some tasty recollections. What mattered of course was front bench opinion, a front bench still sore from the caning administered by the Americans and the UN in '56."

Gareth had a question for Steve.

"We know Prout's opinion on '56, did he offer one on Katanga in, what was it, 60/61?"

"He didn't."

"Did he give a view on Walter? Was he approving?....... disapproving?"

The answer from Steve would have been 'neither', but he was

given no time to say. Alan intervened.

"You're on to something aren't you Gareth? Spill it."

"I'm wondering about this 'free lance work' that was mentioned. The boy's been encouraged to think it was to do with mining experience, but there wasn't actually a great deal of that.....was there?" Gareth looked at Alan and then at Jeremy. He'd set them thinking. Steve was puzzled. Jane was starting to look bored.

"Go on," said Alan.

"Between leaving school and joining up he'd have done precious little underground. The experience that counted would more likely have been that gained in Cyprus."

"Mining?" queried Steve.

"Not mining," said Jeremy. He looked to the Guardsman for unspoken encouragement, and yes, it was there. "Gareth's suggesting that what was being hired was his soldiering skills......because of what was happening in Katanga at that time."

"What was happening in Katanga, Gareth?" asked Steve.

"Jeremy will tell us, he's obviously read O' Brien." All turned to Jeremy. He took a deep breath, and this cabin which he'd earlier imagined to be in Central America was now offering a U2 overview of Central Africa.

He reached to the forward end of the narrow table and slapped the hefty mast socket.

"This is where our leg room ends," he said, "and that's because it's braced by a waist high transverse bulkhead. Beyond the mast this supports the front-end stowage shelf. Look at that and you see the old Belgian Congo, now Zaire. See this table that we sit around as part of that, joined, roughly the same level, and narrowly tailing back into the cabin where we all but surround it on three sides. This table can represent the richly loded province of Katanga. Our end of the cabin then becomes Northern Rhodesia, now Zambia. Much of this is remote wilderness. The border is long. It's poorly policed. The Belgian Government no longer want their Congo, but their mining companies and those who have invested therein are loath to see Katanga, their 'milch cow', fall into the wrong hands."

"Meaning the wrong hands of Patrice Lumumba," added Alan, "who appeared to many to be a little over receptive to overtures from Moscow."

"Their preferred inheritor was Tshombe," continued Jeremy, "A puppet African who, if he could be helped to establish a breakaway state in Katanga, might then be trusted to look after the considerable Western interests therein."

"But the UN determined that there should be no breakaway state," joined Gareth.

"Which wasn't going to stop Tshombe and his backers from striving for at least a degree of autonomy," continued Jeremy. "A UN army campaigned southwards in an attempt to destroy Tshombe and his separatist movement........

" ....only to meet a Katangan force considerably stiffened by fast moving, hard hitting, well trained, well paid mercenary units, " explained Gareth. "The wind of change was to become a gale, but these were early days. It was thought that Katanga could be screened, and for a while it looked as if it might work. Hit and run was their tactic. As the UN force probed into the province it was vulnerable to cross border attack from mercenary bands based in Northern Rhodesia....."

".......much to Macmillan's embarrassment of course," added Jeremy, "for this was a British territory."

"And amongst the mercenary armoury would be British made equipment, as well as plenty of Belgian origin of course." The last phrase of Gareth's was calculated. It was a tester, something dropped just to see whether any might pick it up. But no one did, and for the moment that was to his liking. He was ready to move away. Jeremy could help him. He turned to the lecturer. "And the American stance in all this?"

Jeremy bit.

"The last thing Washington wanted was a triumphant Lumumba," he chimed, "so they found themselves a Colonel Judas in his army, encouraged him in a successful mutiny, and had poor old Patrice delivered bound to his foe.....in whose gentle hands he was put to death. And the Colonel who made his mark in this manoeuvre was none other than Mobuto, the current top man. From that time to this the key to control in that country has been the army, US supplied, US trained, US directed." Jeremy was again into his stride.

"Whilst not their ideal, the mining interests could go along with that. What they'd feared was democracy and it was clear now that Washington wasn't going to sponsor that......not for a long time. Katanga would go back into the fold. It was just a question of maintaining a critical measure of tension thereabouts, sufficient to render the country as a whole to be 'unready yet for democracy'---for as long as possible!"

"So political oppression and economic exploitation still run hand in hand," declared Alan with a sarcasm that Steve missed.

"And wherever complaint might be voiced this can be dismissed as Red inspired," added the boy grimly

"And met with vigorous counter measures," continued Jeremy. "Mobuto stepped up from king maker to king. He's been ruling Franco style now for twenty years and looks set for another ten at least. He'll out run the Iranian Shah, I'm sure, and Pinochet won't make half that."

"So what happened to the UN, weren't they for the people?" This was typical of the boy.

"Steve, you can be so naive!" shot Jeremy. "We talk Realpolitik. The UN, with their 'peacekeeping', won Washington the time needed to find the right man. After that they were dispensable... in fact any arguments and they were disposable. Look what happened to Hammarskjold!"

And look what happened to Chadwick, thought Gareth, briefly....... and then Jane was at him.

"I thought I was about to learn something about Prout," she said, querulously. "You're saying, Gareth, that he might have been soldiering in Northern Rhodesia. What does this mean? That he was helping to police the border?"

"I'd go as far as to say he was mercenary material, that he was working for Tshombe and the mining cartel. If he was out there guarding the installations then in extreme terms that's not so far off what he's been doing recently down here." As he spoke Gareth looked questioningly at Alan.

"Jeremy, I liked the other night's profile of the 'temp'," said Alan, taunting no more, indeed verging rather on the deferential. "Now sketch for us another, one for a retired mercenary."

"I don't know that they'd ever completely retire," said Jeremy. "It's that kind of game. Get into it and someone's always going to have your number. And there's always going to be the call with the offer of a little job to do, the sort of offer that can be unwise to refuse. He'll be familiar with small arms, particularly those brought to such refinement in Africa during the '60s and the '70s. Gareth will know of them, particularly those Belgian built automatic rifles. After saving Katangan ore for the west they secured Nigerian oil, and after that, for a brief vicious pointless while, helped sustain the hard pressed Portuguese in Angola and Mozambique."

Gareth eyed the lecturer. What did he mean by this? Anything? Was there something to infer? Whatever, it indicated the direction of the man's thinking...... and this was close to that of his own. The Welshman still fancied himself ahead, though of the measure of his lead and how long it was going to hold he was no longer so sure. If and when Jeremy knew more then he wouldn't be holding back...... or so Gareth thought, and eight hours before he would have been correct. But people can see things, and they can hear things, and they can change. They can become more guarded, less forthright. They can become ambitious. Jeremy spoke on.

"And he'll be no less familiar with the enemy hardware, the Russian made equivalent, and not only in terms of how it's put together and operated. He'll know something of how they're moved to the trouble spots, and that'll include the more recent ones. I'm thinking in terms of the supply to the likes of ETA, the IRA, and yes, even to these FARC people, and that other gang of thugs who are stirring things up in Peru."

"The Shining Path," Alan put in.

"He'll be well aware of the delivery services offered by Mr Gadaafi of Libya and Mr Castro of Cuba, and even if his fighting skills are now a little rusty his specialist knowledge in these matters will be eagerly sought and well remunerated by those concerned to counter these flows."

"I'll wager that he's a popular visitor in Ulster," remarked Gareth, moving to broaden the lecturer's drift, "amongst those whose holy mission it is to defend the province for the Crown."

"And look, throughout it all there runs a persistent theme of anti communism," continued Jeremy. "And this is the key to his 'temp' style usefulness to the security services. Just say that Cornwall really is being sized up as a granite vault for nuclear waste, and that since the closure of the mine something really sour has been placed deep below Baldhu just to test what might or might not leak out, and this is being done 'unofficially'. You'd want someone to stay behind just to watch over the site, take the dial readings......that sort of thing. Who better than the likes of Jim Prout?"

"And at the same time he can keep a watch on the estuary, particularly when the factory ships come a calling," said Alan.

"So are you saying this character could be doing the same sort of job as yourself?" asked Jane. "Is that efficient? Why can't you and he get your heads together?"

"Let's just say that we must entertain a possibility that our work could be overlapping. And this is where it's essential that we take care. My trail, like my parent organisation, is concerned with drugs. He could be coming at the other aspect, the clandestine traffic in arms. Possibly he's stumbled over something we've not yet sussed.... perhaps a link between the Russian fishing vessels and the Kampala. And maybe he's keeping his own close watch on the one we know as 'Baz' down on the ferry. It's important that we both keep sending what we know upwards, that we don't disturb each other's cover. If liaison is appropriate then it can be initiated at that higher level. They'll have the fuller facts. Until then a good surveillance man will stick strictly to his own remit."

The loose abstraction hardened to firm instruction. "We keep clear of the man. We don't snoop around his boat, or his house, or his van, or his workshop. And Steve, if through anyone at Carwinion you get drawn into another conversation with the man then steer clear of Africa, and mining, and also fishing. Try tourism!"

"......and the weather ," smirked Jeremy.

With this quip Steve identified common cause between Alan and Jeremy. While he was himself projecting Prout as a sinister presence, from them there was a joint concern to cast a character in a more positive light. It was true, he had seen Prout in his van, seemingly attempting to follow Baz and the hired truck at a careful distance, but his own reading was that the pair could be in cahoots. He still thought this the more likely. But he wasn't about to argue, even though he sensed that Gareth and Jane might have lent support. For the moment this needn't matter. Whatever..... in practical terms Alan's instruction was going to be the same. Keep well clear!

"And Jeremy," said Alan, no less firmly, "did you bring a brochure from *Drummond's*?"

Jeremy had collected one, but with so much else in this day it had slipped from his mind. It was back at the house. Suddenly he was a found-out schoolboy, diminished, the smirk was no more.

"Give it to Kate can you? Then I can collect it at the hospital."

Alan split his two sentences with the faintest of tuts. Jeremy was stung, and he was resentful, and he was silenced.

"Gareth, if you're away to Welshpool tomorrow you can leave me with the counterfoil for collecting today's photos. You're coming back for Sunday is that right?"

"I've told Hugh Trembath that I'll be at Penryn Chapel for his morning service. I'm invited to take part."

"And Steve and Jane," continued Alan. "You two will have enough to do with school and the farm, and there's the cafè at the weekend. Within the next ten days I anticipate another exchange, coke out, cleaners in. The tides will be right, and if it happens then as far as we can see to it I want all to go without a hitch. I want them to feel secure, to feel that they're getting good at it. We'll have another get together when it's done. In the meantime I'm back in my writer-broadcaster guise."

"What about what's been recorded today?" enquired Jane. "When's that supposed to be going on air?"

"Thursday evening they said ," replied Gareth, "and that's an excellent reason for me to be well out of the district!....Record it for me some one."

"You'll have a tape," Alan assured him, "and I think we've been closeted for long enough. If no one's got anything else I think we can go up and enjoy something of the evening air."

The skipper turned and climbed, leading the others out onto a very different scene. All was casual cordiality, a contrast to the below deck intensity. *The Pandora* was a honey pot. Gareth's aversion to the buzz was understandable. He was quickly on his way.

Steve wanted time alone with Jane, but this would have entailed leaving Alan and Jeremy to each other, something that both seemed concerned to avoid. Alan had tasks for Jane..... ropes to tug, canvas to tuck. Jeremy hung close to Steve. He was ready for Mylor, and the boy had to be content with Jane's promise of a next day phone call. He could keep the lecturer waiting no longer. The car park was tight. Jeremy had to shunt for a way out. He did so with impressive technique. The tension of the morning had dissipated. In terms of the errand the *Kampala* had been a let down and the discrepancy between what Jeremy had and hadn't needed to know was no longer such an issue.... that's what he thought. For the papers were back at Lanmouth. If the man was about to learn more then it could only be from Old Jack himself.

The octogenarian was sure to be in, and Steve's best hope had to lie in presenting Jeremy as a prudently chosen asset, someone who was well acquainted with modern Spain and whose knowledge might help, particularly with this simple errand revealing a task more complex.

"So you've not brought what we took onto the ship," said Jeremy as they crested the dividing spur between Restronguet and Mylor Creeks.

"Because it hadn't been my intention to come this evening," explained Steve.

"Reach behind your seat," instructed the driver, calmly. "With your right hand, feel along the floor."

Steve complied, twisting and stretching with his left hand. "You should have your hand on two large envelopes, each as bulky as the package you took onto the Kampala."

Steve did. He straightened, drawing the items up and forward between the seats, bending them slightly as he negotiated the handbrake. "They're for your friend, if he wants them."

"He's blind. He can't read, I've told you that."

"What you have in those he read long ago, save for the small piece added by myself...at your request."

Lifting an unsealed flap Steve reached into the topmost envelope. He partly drew out the contents, and he was looking at photocopies of the documents he knew to be back in his bedroom at the farm. Nothing had been omitted.

"How did.......?"

"There's a copier in the admin office at Trelissick. The staff there were delighted to be of assistance...... as people can be when proffered a little paper inducement." Jeremy dripped self-satisfaction.

"And these addresses on the envelopes....."

"Are of newspapers, Spanish provincial newspapers, each based in Bilbao and circulated to a mainly Basque readership. You can tell your friend that you still have the original, and why, and you can offer him an option of having these copies mailed to where he perhaps hoped the original might have been taken. You can say too that if he doesn't trust the postal service I'm ready to drive him, with you as well if you want, down to Newlyn. There's hardly a day that passes down there without a Spanish trawler calling in."

Steve was speechless. An attempt to gull had shockingly recoiled. His errand had been hi-jacked, and what could he do now but comply? Indeed it was best that he should. Jeremy hadn't had that much time, and all that he'd copied was perhaps still awaiting his perusal. If the copies with their envelopes could be presented to the old man so that he could either send or hold them then maybe Jeremy's involvement could be contained.

Holding to this possibility Steve said little, beyond directing Jeremy to the appropriate place to park. He wasn't wasting words. He wasn't wasting time. With the envelopes tightly to his side the boy was quickly out of the car and striding for the creek side path. Jeremy needed a moment to lock the car. He had to jog to catch up. There was to be no inspection and no discussion.....not until they were in the cottage.

The door was wide. Jack Butters was within.....ensconced.

"Sit 'e self down boy, and whoever 'tis with 'e. And don' say 'tis who 't were las' time cos I know 't idn't. Footfall idn' the same. "

It wasn't that he didn't trust Steve not to attempt a deceit, it was more a concern that the stranger should know that this man listened very closely. Jeremy was suitably impressed.

"Do meet Jeremy, Mr Butters. He's been helpful to us and he's been waiting to meet you.

"Good Day, Senor Butters," said Jeremy, negotiating a smooth handshake.

"He teaches over at Camborne College," explained Steve. "He speaks Spanish, and he can write in Spanish too. Today he and I were on the *Kampala.* I'd told him something of what I was attempting on your behalf, in fact he's actually written a short piece to go with all which we hoped to pass on."

"An' all the lod'v it were passed on t'gether?"

"It wasn't I'm afraid," replied Steve, "because Jeremy here spoke briefly to the people on board. They did speak Spanish, but in his expert judgement they weren't actually from Spain. He reckons......"

".....Central America, Caribbean," Jeremy put in, pre-empting any attempt by Steve to be more specific. Steve studied the old man closely. He expected to see frustration..... but if felt, none was shown.

"Then we do 'ave to be grateful to 'e Mister. 'Ave 'e brod 'n back fer me then boy?"

"I've left it at the farm. I wasn't meaning to come here when I set off this evening. I was only going as far as *The Pandora.* Alan Grigson was there. He'd been hailed by your Young Jack. The message was that you were waiting to see me. Jeremy had his car. He suggested that we might call."

"I remembers Mr Grigson alright. What do 'e say 'bout what I bin askin' 'e t'do? "

"Nothing," answered Steve, "because I've told him next to nothing, and anyway he's not much interested in the past...... unlike Jeremy here."

"So whadavee writ 'n this 'ere added bit?" the old man asked Jeremy.

"Steve showed me what your old pal Rory saved from his voyage across Biscay back in '37, and with it those two letters received from the Board of Trade during the war. The only other thing was the newspaper cutting from Ireland.......that piece on Mosley." While Jeremy was painting himself as a passive presence, he rightly sensed that he had the old man's full attention. "I've heard what you told Steve about Rory's death, about the instructions that he just had time to leave, and the pledge that you made. A long time ago it may be, but I nevertheless think it an intriguing tale. Put with the right newspapers it's going to attract a lot of interest, certainly in Spain, and quite possibly in this country, here and in Liverpool. Injustice sells, so does wartime code breaking. Put the two together and......."

"Wad it's 'bout is they 'nigma machines we 'm now startin' t' ear of," broke in the old man. "You only godaliss'n on your wireless for a week an' you get summ'n to do with it all." This man was clued up, more so than he'd earlier cared to show.

"And that's what I think I've successfully explained," pronounced Jeremy. "Your friend's reputation was sacrificed. Had he known why, then maybe it might have been easier for him..... but he couldn't be told of course. No one could. War winning work was in hand. It couldn't be compromised, not then. But now these Basque people can be told. They weren't so friendless after all, and it's ironic that they might now be suffering at the hands of an elected leftist government. What prescience the man had to include that cutting of bad old Sir Oswald..... he who was so impatient of democratic process."

"So you'm makin' thad out t'be a warnin' as t'ow they'm needin' to be watchin' theyselves with their votin' now that that their Franco's gone on ?"

Jeremy nodded, but slowly. The old man's rising, questioning tone was sufficient to lodge a seed of doubt.

" 'An thad other thing 'e saved out of the Plymouth paper, wad 'ave 'e got t' say 'bout that?"

Jeremy looked at Steve. Steve's heart sank. He couldn't have been sure either way, but he'd chosen to believe that the Cairns piece about Edward Trembath with its quote from Ida Copeland had been included after Duggan's death, gathered he imagined by Butters himself together with the report of the inquest and the Cairns obituary. These things he'd kept back from Jeremy, they amounted to the substance of the discrepancy. How was the lecturer about to respond? Had he had time to check what he'd copied? Had he had time to think about it even?

"I've not shown him that," blurted Steve. He was anxious. Such grip as he had on this situation he felt slipping. "I thought it something you put in, just so people might recall who Francis Cairns was."

The name was out now, that was careless. Further in the mire he was, and there was another attempt at repair. "Actually we've brought photocopies, two complete sets. The idea is to give you an opportunity to post them to Spain. They're in two separate envelopes, each addressed to a Basque newspaper........ that's thanks to Jeremy. If you want we can leave them with you."

"Or alternatively I can take you across to Newlyn," offered Jeremy, "I'm surprised you've not thought of that yourself.... plenty of Spaniards calling there these days."

What Old Jack wanted now was information.

"So your friend 'ere ain't 'eard nothin' from 'e yet 'bout Cairns," said the blind man, "an' no one else 'as either?...not bin speakin' with your uncle, or your aunt, or their landlord, or any other person else?"

Steve had to come clean.

"Only with Ralph Bartlett, you know..... he runs the cafè over at Pendower. I've not shown him anything. We were in his van going to Polgooth, and he got on to talking about his school days, and I just slipped the name in just to see, and yes there was a recollection. They'd gone to the same primary school where Cairns had shone before sailing through his 11+ and away to grammar school. Roseland people were naturally interested in his career. There was a local girl, a fiance. He was

232

bright, he was young, when he died there was shock and there was grief."

"Well we bedderway leave it at that fer now," said Old Jack. "Leave us they env'lopes, I'll see they gets sent off. My thanks to you Jeremy, I'll be 'appy to tell 'e all I knaws 'bout the boy Cairns, but all this 'as to come out in Spain first. That were what was promised."

Jeremy had stayed calm, not pushing for information. He'd been listening though........ very, very closely.

"Glad to have been of help," he said gently. "That story's sure to make a splash in Spain, and the ripples will reach Cornwall. We must be ready."

Steve was relieved. Things seemed to be working out for the best. They were on the way those documents, and this was down to quick thinking Jeremy. He was proving useful.

They were talking now about the Basque people. Jeremy spoke of Guernica and the coastal blockade, Jack of the evacuees brought to Hampshire in the summer of the same year. On the ETA campaign of violence there was agreement. The weapons might be imported, the bitterness, the enmity, that was home grown.

Old Jack entertained them for a further twenty cordial minutes, and then, unburdened of those envelopes, the pair could enjoy a relaxed stroll back to the car. The morning post had brought Steve notification from the Library. The ordered book, Birkenhead's 'Monckton', was awaiting collection. This became their topic of conversation as Jeremy drove the dozen or more circuitous road miles from Mylor Bridge to Restronguet Point. Jeremy guided the conversation towards India and the challenge posed by the Princely States to the independence arrangements and the Hindu/Muslim partitions. It was a long way from Spain, and that was suiting both.

*

Wednesday

It was an early start for Gareth. If he could beat the Exeter traffic he might reach Welshpool in less than five hours. He headed directly for the A30, and he'd crossed both moors before nine. He planned to return on Saturday, leaving time to check out Par and Fowey on the way. He could leave Cornwall behind, but not those two ports. Between them they'd cornered a section of his mind.

Another corner belonged to Alberto. There would be a letter, of that he was sure, and it would be informative. They always were. What would it tell him of the *Kampala,* he wondered, of her departure from the southern seas and her journey back to home waters? And how might this sit with what he already knew..... and what he was beginning to suspect?

*

Jeremy had a full college morning. It was lecture, tutorial, lecture...... back to back, no break. He was good. Normally he would cope comfortably, today though he was struggling to perform. He was distracted. He wanted time, but since dropping Steve the previous evening he'd had none. There had been Kate to collect from the Hospital, and then she was anxious for an account of the gathering at *The Pandora.*

He'd shared what had been said aboard the *Speedwell*........but not what had been said in the creek side cottage at Mylor. He was playing Steve's game, disclosing only selectively.

The originals of the documents he'd had copied at Trelissick were back with Steve, at the farm, so the boy had said. Two sets of copies were now with old Jack, each in an addressed envelope. Kate knew of these, but he'd not told her of his third set. They lay in the boot of his car, concealed beneath the mat that covered the spare wheel.

He was a professional historian. This tale that he'd stumbled upon was a find. It would make the papers in Spain, and word would come back. He was sure, and he was determined to be prepared. Gourmet fare he had, a local delicacy to serve to those with a refined taste for the past. It was an opportunity to establish for himself a lasting cachet. It could get him onto the screen, but there was Grigson to consider. He would need to move carefully. He would need to be patient.

*

"...... Thank you Mr West for those impromptu comments on the jury verdict reached earlier today in the Clive Ponting trial and its implications for those whose task it is to from time to time invoke Section 2 of the Official Secrets Act. We can move on now to the topic you were expecting to be talking to us about on this afternoon's 'Today PM' programme, the subject of the latest of your many, many books on intelligence matters......the so called 'Venona' project.

Niall West, tell the listeners please, what was this all about?"

"Venona was a top secret American initiative. Dating from the early days of the last war, the operation continued for a good dozen years or so. It's about code breaking. Much has been written about the successful Bletchley based British assault on the German's mechanised 'Enigma' system...... in many ways this was to become the Cold War equivalent. The Russians were the enemy, their encoded radio messages were the target."

"Machine encoded?"

"No. It was a one-time pad system, and that should have made it unbreakable. In fact there was duplication, and that was careless. It became a more than one time pad system, and here was the way in......"

"......the crack in the door?"

"The crack in the door, and never really more than that. As machine became the measure of machine the Enigma code break offered the widest of windows. Intelligence on enemy intentions was prompt and it was comprehensive. Venona, Mr Redpath, was a far more laborious and time lengthy sift. Hostile intentions were more often enacted before they were read."

"So it was of limited use."

"It was useful in a different way. Its achievement was to throw up the identities of many of Stalin's most deeply burrowed agents in the West. The agents were given cryptonyms, disguised names. One of the most renown was 'HOMER'. In 1951 a message from 'HOMER' to Moscow sent in 1944 was finally deciphered. It told of his having journeyed to New York to visit his pregnant wife. A number of personal histories were checked and one particular British diplomat fitted that bill."

"And that was?"

"Donald Maclean, and likewise 'HICKS' would emerge to be Burgess and, much later, 'STANLEY' to be Philby. Venona nailed the

atom spies, Fuchs and the Rosenbergs. It also confirmed that in America the likes of Alger Hiss were far more dangerous than they could openly be proven to be. The charges against Hiss looked to be trumped up, and that was because the more persuasive evidence had to be kept back. Venona was too valued a resource to be squandered in any public hearing. For a long time it was kept strictly to a top level few, drawn from the Armed Forces Security Agency and the FBI. It was kept even from the OSS and the CIA. J Edgar Hoover was in the know......"

"......and the knowledge was power."

"Very much so, for on his informed recommendations careers could be made or broken. World War Two had enhanced Hoover's pre-eminence in security matters. The Cold War and Venona left him unassailable. For a while, nothing was above his scrutiny, not the Presidential retinues, not even their households."

"So he became mole hunter in chief?"

"In his mission to cleanse he would be the identifier. The exterminating, the turning, the feeding to them of dis-information, all this he left to others."

"And it was a home ground operation."

"Initially, but then it was felt that the Kremlin challenge was best met on foreign soil. Burgess and Maclean hadn't parachuted into Washington. They'd had a free pass, courtesy of a trusted ally, us. We'd allowed ourselves to be subverted, that was the perception. To the likes of Hoover, we were a source of infection."

"And the antidote?"

"Counter subversion, Mr Redpath, orchestrated from Washington."

"Fire with fire."

"If you like."

Brian Redpath speaking with Niall West on *'Today PM'*
(BBC Radio 11/2/85)

Gareth sat at his table, before him his helmet and gloves, and next to these a pile of letters. One envelope had been opened, that with the Argentine stamp. Alberto hadn't disappointed, indeed he'd delighted. His friend's contacts had been active and with their help he'd diligently compiled an impressively full record of the old ship's last voyage home.

She'd left Port Stanley on Thursday 4th April. There were no troops aboard, the Defence Ministry's charter being at an end. Her customary course would have brought her to Ascension, but this time she was headed for the corner of Brazil, the more direct course to Europe and the UK.

There was surprise therefore when she was next sighted sailing between Trinidad and Tobago, and heading westwards into the Caribbean. Two theories were offered. The first held that British India had sold the ship for scrap immediately she'd been paid off, and that she was headed for a Far East breaker's via Panama. The second, that she was returning some of the equipment used in the construction of the new military airfield at Stanley to the Americans, who were now engaged in a similar project on Grenada. If she was making for the Pacific then this answered why she hadn't quietly slipped around the Horn.

This view was strengthened by a whisper from Washington that there had indeed been a brief stop off on Grenada. Next came a sighting off the Guajira Peninsula, the most northerly tip of Colombia, and she'd been flying the St Vincent and Grenadines flag..... indicating a re-registration. With only a further five hundred miles to the canal a report from Panama had been expected imminently. But none came.

The next five hundred miles covered were instead in a northerly direction. She was spotted off Haiti, and off Cuba. She was taking the Windward passage through to the open Atlantic. Either there'd been a change of plan or the ship had effected a pre- arranged detour. As to which and why, Alberto and his associates had this time declined to speculate. They only made the point that if the vessel was now in the hands of a ship delivery company then they might have been concerned to install their own crew. Flying men off and on would have been an easy matter in the Caribbean area, the ship being appropriately equipped to receive a helicopter, one dropping across from Panama perhaps, or maybe Caracas, or Maracaibo, or Baranquillo.....or Santiago even?

How much of this would Alan know, he wondered. He didn't have to know any of it. He was paid to know and to notice other things. But his bosses, the higher ups in his department, they would be briefed surely, and what would they be making of it all?

*

Jeremy returned home at 4pm. He knew Kate was at work. At last he could sit with a mug of tea and closely examine that which for more than twenty four hours had lain concealed in the boot of his car. He retrieved the copies, purposefully locked the vehicle and strode to his door. In he went and straight to the dining table. Soon it was close to being covered. Jeremy at last had a sight of the full hand.

The 'cards' he arranged in order of date, a process that was simple, seemingly innocuous. He wasn't to know that what he pieced carried an explosive potential, and that a lethal volatility was but one catalytic ingredient away.

Jeremy went to the kitchen, to the kettle. He took with him the obituary to Francis Cairns. He'd read it before the tea was even brewed. He thought back. He was himself of the baby boom. He could remember Vietnam from his teens and his student days. That was more than ten years after Korea and by then it was the television reporters who told the story, the Pettifor types who actually went, and the studio newscasters.

Just two years old he'd been during the winter of '50/51, and at that time not many had televisions. For pictures that moved people went to the local 'pit' and there took a measured dose of approved newsreel. And to find out more of the story it was go to the news stands and the papers with their despatches sent by front line war correspondents. He couldn't have read these at the time of course, but he'd sampled them since and had concluded that it was in Korea that this kind of reportage had made a final and distinguished stand.

Had the old man in Mylor saved any sample of such work from Cairns? Jeremy wondered. If not, then no matter. He knew where it could be found. And he did have this other piece, saved from *The Plymouth Independent*. The young hound's contributions to this paper had been mentioned in the obituary, and also his start with the *Packet* back in post war, bomb battered, Falmouth.

The obituary and the tea came back to the table. Jeremy sat to read the piece taken from the Plymouth weekly.

Almost immediately he was up again, on to his feet. It had been the name.... 'Edward Trembath'.

In fact there'd been no particular reason for Steve not including this with the rest that he'd first shown him, but after that joint performance when they'd put out to the *Kampala* this wasn't to be a natural conclusion. The item had been purposely kept from him, that's what he thought, and this after he, more than any of the others, had shown interest in Sir Edward.

And this decision was unlikely to have been Steve's on his own, he wrongly concluded. It would surely have been at the insistence of the old man who maybe knew something about Sir Edward that, in some way, back in '51, could have helped the people of Northern Spain to a better appreciation of Rory Duggan. Perhaps it was to do with an insight that Sir Edward had then enjoyed, for there appeared to be nothing at all in Cairns' piece to question the man's integrity..... on the contrary.

Jeremy read it through, twice. It was respectful, almost bland, hardly the kind of thing to catch the eye of a Fleet Street editor. At best, to one wishing to be positive, it was resourceful. Francis Cairns had produced a warming story of good neighbourliness, a tale which he'd managed to adorn with an enterprisingly won verbatim quote from an old lady, who close to twenty years before had won the seat of Stoke on Trent for Baldwin's National Conservatives. Her words stood out. They'd been underlined in ink.

"Had it not been for busy campaigning by the likes of the then young Mr Trembath, and his fellow activists, then I have little doubt that my seat would have been retained by the Labour Party, even though it was in such disarray at Westminster."

What an endorsement! How it rang across the generations. But what could this do for Rory Duggan, even while he was alive. What had been underlined were the credentials of an aspiring politician and an aspiring young journalist, both relatively unknown. Both had been noticed, and were to be selected, and were to then make their mark nationally....the second with tragic brevity. What anyone in a newly free Spain might make of this Jeremy was at a loss to imagine.

They would seek a common strand, he thought. And if there was one then it had to be the locality, this locality. The *Usk Vale* had sailed from Falmouth in '37 and it was to Falmouth that Duggan had chose to return in '42, and where he'd died in '50. Mrs Copeland had a home by the estuary as did Mr Trembath, and Francis Cairns was the local boy making good.

What was odd, in the sense that it seemed to offer no local connection, was the inclusion of Mr Mosley. He'd made a kind of sense of this to Steve when they'd met in Truro, and what he'd said there, and later written briefly in Spanish, had been accepted when sketchily re-iterated in front of the old man at Mylor. But somehow, now, this part was failing to convince. Within a whole that was very much a personal plea such an explanation was too theoretical, too doctrinaire.

While the copier had attempted manfully to reproduce the Irish newsprint, the faded original wasn't to be retouched. The article and the picture caption might be clear enough, and even that inked note along the margin, but that now enlarged photo was little more than a shadowy smudge.

'El hombre de la Iizquierdas?...... a la izquierda?'.

Whatever, and relevant still or not, there could be no doubting the message's intended destination. These things were going to Spain, a firm decision had been made, and a firm promise was being kept.

So why the wait for Franco's demise when this local journalist had been to hand, and clearly attracting Duggan's interest? The young cub was clearly ambitious, and that meant busy of course, but that wouldn't have made him inaccessible.... would it? Not until his work took him away and he was killed.

"Taken away and silenced," Jeremy muttered to himself. When that happens to a journalist, he thought, it can be because they've been deemed a little too talented, too percipient. Was this being preposterous?..... paranoia again? He recalled Duggan's signals log. It told of his ship leaving Falmouth and then being shadowed into Biscay, and there was this other point that it made.

Cairns may have picked up on this. It was time perhaps to make a few enquiries. Not with Hugh Trembath, not with Jack Butters, they weren't to be disturbed. Alan said that and so did he. But there were others who would remember that lad.

Jeremy glanced again at the obituary, and there was something too that he'd heard Steve mention to the old man whilst they were together down at that cottage. He glanced at his watch. It was too late now. Thursday afternoons he had free. He would go tomorrow.

*

Thursday

Claire Simpson's Lanmouth Farm larder happened to be well stocked. She would go into Truro, as she always did, but this week with an abbreviated list. She just needed the one hour's worth of pay and display at the Old Bridge Street 'short stay' and this left her nephew having to move smartly.

To the old Passmore Edwards Library in Pydar Street it was less than five minutes. There was a queue at the counter though, even with the book there on the reserved shelf a full quarter of the parking time had elapsed before the boy actually had the thing open before him at one of the reading area tables.

A brief scan through would be about as much as he could attempt. He flicked through the thirty or so photographs that were spread through the volume. The monochrome tended to project an austere, charmless image. The greyness of it all was so at variance with Hugh's personal recollections, and those colourful stories passed down from father to son.

Two plates in particular caught the eye. One had Walter standing with the Duchess of Windsor at the wedding in '37, the other showed him seated with King George VI on the occasion of the monarch's visit to the Ministry of Information in '41. In each instance the regal figure looked totally at ease. It could be believed that these parties were estranged but Walter clearly retained the confidence of both.

The major episodes, the ones mentioned by Jeremy and also by Hugh, shouted from the chapter headings. The abdication, India, Cabinet office, Africa...... there was an evening's read on each. The great issues of Crown and Empire had to be for another time. Here, now, he would merely dip.

Steve remembered Hugh's anecdotal vignettes. There was the tale of the advocate who'd helped with the action brought against a promiscuous Rector. What was the cleric's fate, he wondered? Then there was that of the wartime ministry mandarin whose own appetite for the ladies extended to a tasteful West End actress, one being of international renown. Maybe the book carried detail enough to fill these spare minutes.

Steve went to the index, first to the letter R, R for Rector and yes, there he was...... the Rector of Stiffkey. Steve found the page and he read what was a rather sad tale of 1930s Britain. A wayward priest being deprived of his orders, and his living, then lost his senses. And he was allowed to make an exhibition of himself at a seaside circus, sharing a cage with a lion. The beast killed him. It was as cruel as it was tragic. This was geek fare. He needed relief, and the actress would surely offer a sweeter tale.

Back to the index he turned, this time to the letter C. He remembered the name, it had a theatrical ring, 'Corbett', and there she was ...... .Leonora Corbett, pages 184-5. Steve turned back, and fine, again it was just two or three paragraphs, the ideal moment sized morsel.

He learned that Leonora was indeed an actress of international repute, one who'd trod the boards on both sides of the Atlantic. During the war she was in the States working while Walter was at the Ministry of Information. Steve read on, and then, suddenly, he was looking at this page, this passage, with a wide- eyed astonishment. He went back to where it began and read again, this time actually speaking the words, as if to convince himself they weren't imagined. He then closed the book onto his hand, checking the cover to see that it was the same author, the one mentioned by Jeremy........and it was of course, Lord Birkenhead, he did have the right book.

Jeremy had been almost dismissive when speaking of the work. From the lecturer's tone Steve had inferred that it was hagiography. He'd 'just read parts', that's what he'd said. He might have looked a little more closely at this section, thought Steve. He read it yet again.

'Two of these who found Walter irresistible at the time were actresses of beauty and distinction, and in his letters to one of these, Leonora Corbett,, who added sharp intelligence to great physical attraction, we can read much of his life in the first nine months of 1941. Leonora was in the habit of addressing Walter as MDDDW, meaning "My darling, darling, darling Walter'. 'Walter's attitude to Leonora Corbett,' said one of his intimate friends, 'was naive. He was dizzy with the glamour of this lovely creature,' and he certainly made her the repository of close confidences, some of which he would have done better to keep to himself.

At the time of his letters to her, Leonora was in America. Their affair, after her departure there, was to die a painless death, and it was a tribute to his marvellous tact that when it was over she was to remain a loyal and devoted friend. He now told her all the details of his daily life; he wrote of anxiety, success and failure; sent her notes he made for her memoirs, including his account of the Abdication which he regarded as so secret that he refused an offer of a hundred thousand pounds to publish it during his lifetime.

We shall see him soon visiting the Middle East, and when he did so, a copy of his diary was always sent to her. He described his progress at the Ministry (of Information) finding relief in pouring its daily problems into a sympathetic ear..........'

The author might have preferred to put a benign construction on this relationship, but the stated facts spoke loudly for themselves. Monckton, the Director General of the Ministry of Information, the highest non elected official in this most sensitive of departments, was leaking like a sieve, and what's more, leaking to an individual who was, at that desperate time, enjoying the protection of a foreign power, the US of A.

Steve had read of 1941 America. The whole northern continent had been in two minds. Decision time it was. The slide towards war had to be made a positive step or it had to be reversed. There was alarm at Hitler's successes, his defeat of France and the alliance with Mussolini. At the same time there was a wariness of military adventure, of joining the fight for democracy on foreign soil. Against those eager to launch their crusade there were as many who preferred to embrace isolation, and between stood a silent majority, waverers, the yet to be persuaded. The contest for hearts and minds escalated into a fierce propaganda war. It raged the length of the northern continent, from Canada, through the States, and Mexico, to the Caribbean Islands.

The US intelligence agencies were put and kept on high alert, and overseeing so much of their operations stood Mr J. Edgar Hoover, Director of the FBI, the Boss. For this character, with his coast to coast legion of listeners and watchers, wire tappers and mail snoopers, the likes of Walter Monckton and Leonora Corbett had to be the softest of touches. Naturally he would have been tailing the Duke and the Duchess of Windsor, and in their files Walter would have been prominent. Now, as letter on letter went to his repository of close confidences he would surely have rated a file of very his own.

Two blossoming careers, both bright, both brittle, and perhaps initially just the one minor indiscretion, but enough to bring ruin to either were it to be allowed to get back...... that would have been the lever. The Ministry of Fear is mobilised. There's a little leaning, the threat of disgrace, but also a way forward.... on Washington's terms. Co-operate Walter, or else. He does. And now the net closes. He's been turned. There's no way out.

When was this book published? Steve checked...1969, during the Nixon years. Hoover was still alive, still in place. The writer could only hint at J. Edgar's methods, at the ways by which the powerful, the useful, and the simply foolish were bent into his service.... explicit details emerging only since his death, and then only at a seep.

Steve was elated, and justifiably. It was speculative, this find, but it would do Jeremy, he was sure. He went to the photocopier. He wanted this page now. He would ask his Aunt to drive past Jeremy's door, and he'd drop it in, through the letterbox. The copy came out. He folded it once, and borrowing the pen that lay on the counter he addressed it to 'Jeremy' and beneath the name scribbled briefly... *'Carrier Pigeon, I'd say! One for J Edgar's loft',* and below this just *'Steve'.*

The pen returned, Steve dashed back to market. He was in time to help carry the bags to the car. One had room for the book, and in it was slipped. Their road out of the city took them almost by the flat, only a short detour was required. The note was delivered. What was going to be the response? With luck this should ease the lecturer off and away from the Basque business.

*

A showery midweek afternoon would often bring Ralph Bartlett the odd solitary customer, one whose preference it was to linger at one of his cafè tables with a mug of tea and a book. It would usually be a paperback. Today brought something a little different. This fellow was immersed in what appeared a scholarly tome. As he brought the beverage the proprietor caught a glimpse of the title...... *'Labour in Power 1945-51'.* Morgan was the author's name. The period fell comfortably within Ralph's memory. Attlee, Bevin, and Cripps, nationalisation, rationing, austerity, he could engage the man on this, and he might stay longer, spend more.

"Interesting period that," he commented, casually wiping at the surface of a neighbouring table. The table was in fact already clean, it hadn't been used for the day. Aware of this, Jeremy was pleased. His ploy was working.

"Bit before my time," he answered, barely looking up. "We could do with a proper Labour Party again."

"Old Footie's hanging in there though isn't he?" Ralph wore a gentle smile. The '83 election had obviously been a cruel experience for the veteran leader, but he'd held things together. Few could have managed that, and the man deserved credit.

"Don't you worry, they'll be back bigger than ever inside the old firebrand's lifetime, and mark me, he'll be fondly remembered long after this gang of four who they talk of now are forgotten. Same thing happened back in the '30s, before my time that was. The party was humiliated at the polls. 'The end,' people said, but then look what happened in '45. Those who'd kept faith were rewarded. Those who'd either sold out or walked out had to take the opprobrium. Nowadays for Mosley read Owen....same sort of ego. Mind you there's always going to be the one thing that Michael Foot and David Owen will have held in common."

Ralph was posing a riddle, and an obscure one...too obscure he thought, but wrongly. His customer was equal to it.

"They both won and then successfully defended the Plymouth Devonport seat," responded Jeremy with an impressive if slightly smug immediacy. Ralph had touched on Sir Oswald, but Jeremy wasn't here to work that one. Plymouth North was the desired destination for this conversation, and it was almost there. "Now you've mentioned Plymouth," he went on, "I have something in here which might take you back."

Jeremy turned deeper into the book and from between the pages drew the now folded copy of the Cairns piece from the *'Independent'*. He passed it to Ralph to read. The proprietor did, speaking only when he'd reached the end.

"You know it's amazing, but I was only talking about this fellow just a few days ago."

Jeremy knew he'd hit the right seam, but it was still best to dig gently.

"About Edward Trembath...?" asked Jeremy, the ingenuousness artfully contrived. "I'd imagine him to be quite revered in these parts."

Ralph duly delivered.

"No, about Francis Cairns. You see his name at the top there, the journalist who wrote this article. He was a local lad, I went to school with him for a while. There's a youngster who sometimes comes and helps here at weekends. He's sweet on the girl I've got working for me. It's a pity he's not here now. He asked me about Cairns after seeing his obituary."

"So he's just died has he? Shame....Couldn't have been that old." This was cant, but Ralph wasn't to know. For him, the enquiry was being made in good faith, and he answered likewise.

"Thirty four years ago he died, 1951. This youngster, Steve, must have got hold of a newspaper which was that old. How and where he didn't say. I didn't think to ask. I was happy to drive along talking about our schooldays. Not often I get the chance!"

"So he died young."

"Tragically so, in Korea, doing war work for a national." Ralph grew sombre. "It had been his big break. And he was due to be married and all."

"What about parents and siblings, any of them still living locally?" As would a trowel-hoeing archaeologist, Jeremy was carefully working closer.

"An only child to elderly parents, both now dead," answered Ralph, grimly. Jeremy was so near to securing a name. He would need to sound inquisitorial now and that was a risk, but one he thought worthwhile.

"And the fiance you speak of. Was she local? Was she at school with you too?"

"She was local, and slightly younger. She was an Adams, Linda Adams I think it was. What she is, or where she is now I don't know. She wasn't long in finding someone else to marry and to move away with."

"But the wedding would have been in a local Church or Chapel?"

"In Portloe it was, at the Chapel."

Jeremy had scored. He could ease up on probing for fact, and wind down by gently drawing opinion.

"And how did you rate Francis Cairns as a journalist?" he asked.

"I'd rated him to be far better than anyone might think from what you have there," said Ralph emphatically. "Given his head I'd say he could be brilliant. Getting into Trelissick and talking with the old girl warranted a lot better than this. Look at it, it's shallow, it's sentimental. That wasn't Francis Cairns. Too much of the old blue pencil in that, and too much of it also in what he sent back from Korea..... but I guess that's war."

This was bonus. The sincerity of the man was compelling. The opinion of a school chum had to be worth a lot. Jeremy had listened closely. What he'd heard would stick.

*

".......and I know why you've seen less of him up on your stretch of the river. It seems he's taken up a permanent residence down here on the Percuil. He has this fascination with the factory ships, and with what he refers to as an 'interface' between the Russian and the Cornish ways of doing things. He was in the shop yesterday, talking about it."

"Jim Prout's seen him out there too," said Hugh Trembath. "Does this mean he's been tying up at your yard?"

Colin Toms stood up, in doing so taking the telephone cord to almost full stretch. He leant towards the upstairs office window and looked down.

"The boat's out there now, the *Speedwell*."

"But not the Master?"

"I think he said he was going over to St Anthony. He'd have used the ferry. He likes to get up on the headlands. He can get a good angle on the factory ships there, and also watch what's coming in and going out."

"And has he spoken of anything else?....Like when he might be moving on?"

"He was speculating about the weather for next week, and talking like he was intending to go back along the coast, past the Dodman. You know the chart I've got hanging by the counter, well he was looking at Mevagissey."

"And that was this morning?"

"Quite early. He'd been in for the night," confirmed Toms.

"Thanks for that, you've done well. Anything else, you phone...... any time."

"One other thing," remembered the chandler. "We've had this gospel group down here for the past week or so........songs, readings, leaflets, all out in the open. They've been over on the harbour quay and up by the castle, across at Porthscatho, all around. An old camper van they've got, with a tent as well, and they've been given a pitch by one of the farmers up the back here. They looked in this morning, saying that they were ready to move on across to your side, and they asked if I knew of any sympathetic landowners who might find a spare corner for them in one of their pastures. The radio was on in the shop, and I was listening to that piece about the *Kampala,* and the soldier, and the nurse, and I heard your name crop up a couple of times. There was even a plug for a service you've got coming off at Penryn Chapel. As this was while they were with me I told them how to find your place. They could be calling on you over the weekend. I said that even if you weren't placed to accommodate them you'd at least point them towards some one who could."

*

The name Adams comfortably fills two columns in the Cornwall and Isles of Scilly phone book. Jeremy was listing those who lived within fifteen miles of Truro. Already he had thirty numbers. Too many, he thought, to call them one by one. That would be too hit and miss. Many would be related, and word of his interest would run ahead. He would lose any advantage of surprise. He completed his list and slid it into the folder that held all that he'd copied two days before. Also within was the note that he'd found on his doormat when he'd returned. He drew this out. He'd seen who it was from but not, as yet, given it any real attention....so eager had he been to follow up on what Ralph Bartlett had said.

Jeremy hadn't lost interest in Monckton, with Francis Cairns though he was fascinated. He was building an affinity with the character, partly because he had himself considered starting with a local newspaper as a chancy alternative to university. He played safe, as it happened, but always fancied that he could have made his mark in the way that this lad was so clearly doing at the end of 1950. At that age, at that time, he would have been young and energetic, idealistic and fearless. And then he'd died, died in action it seems, possibly because of these qualities.

If, after all these years, Ralph Bartlett could be so scathing about that piece from the *Independent* then surely at the time Cairns himself would have been no less disappointed, no less eager to see his name above better. And perhaps this is where Rory Duggan came into it. Duggan had a tale that could have been the something better. Duggan knew this and was confident that Cairns would think the same way and truly go to town. Was that the rationale? It was possible. And no less possible was it that there could be more to that piece on Edward Trembath, prospective Member for Plymouth North, than met the eye. Duggan had contacted Cairns, that was known, but was anything of the tale conveyed? This was another question. One to take to Linda Adams, if she was alive, if she could be found.

He checked his teaching timetable for the next day, and also that of the train services to London. He then phoned an old college friend living in Kentish Town. It was arranged. He would drive to work as usual and then at 2.30pm, after his last class, take the train from Redruth. He could return there on Monday's early train back, his first tutorial not being until after lunch. All that remained now was for him to tell Kate.

*

Friday

Gareth sat by the Severn. He had Alberto's letter in his hand, but his thoughts weren't for Argentina, neither were they for Colombia, nor Cuba. His mind wasn't even on the Roseland, but it was in Cornwall.

Again it was shuttling between Par and Fowey.

Just one sighting, that's all he needed, one of those ships, that one van, or just one of those two individuals. It was important though to be inconspicuous..... to be off the stage, to be of the scenery, lest Alan's work be put at risk of course. Not that Gareth was totally happy with all he'd heard the guy say. Why for instance should it follow that a white mercenary of the Congo era should be without question consistently anti Red? On this Jeremy and Alan were in agreement, but in his own experience the notion of 'mercenary' ran against any ideological stance. And he wasn't happy either with that presumption that this Prout character was also conducting undercover surveillance. This was far too hasty a conclusion, or far too convenient.

To the guardsman the man was simply a killer, and if he was in with the villains he could be doubly dangerous. In a scam such as theirs there would be cut-offs in place, fast escape provision for the important should things get a little too hot. Prout was unlikely, he thought, to be amongst the so privileged. By the terms of his hire he risked being left on the wrong side of the fire proofing. He could be cut adrift, the loose cannon...... and then he might be doubly lethal.

Alan, he was sure, was concerned to keep all well clear....... but what if Jeremy was like himself, nurturing a personal initiative? He would need to step very, very carefully.

Gareth reached down, searching with his right hand into the same side pannier. He'd brought the map, and also from a box in his loft a coverless and some what dog-eared tourist guide, a musty relic of a dampish fortnight spent in a tent just outside Newquay back in the late '70s. The guide focussed on the attractions of the county's surf capital. It had nothing on Fowey, but it did have a map which stretched to take in Par,....... the railway junction there being the start of the Newquay branch. There was a page or two also on St.Austell and on its own old port, the pocket sized dock basin at Charlestown.

His map had indicated the harbour to be a museum, a heritage project curio for the summer visitors. If they were lucky there could be the added interest of a film or television company on outdoor location. Turning the guide book pages he found a picture ....and maybe this impression leant by the map was partly false. To the fore in the chosen print was a three-masted sailing ship. That figured of course, but the photographer had also caught part of another ship that lay in the background, against the quay that stretched along the far side of the dock.

If Gareth wasn't mistaken, and he'd seen plenty of these by now, what he was looking at was a modern shallow draught coaster, one of the kind that frequented Par..... from here, less than three miles to the east.

The cleft of the basin into the hillside enabled vessels against that side to be loaded from above by lorries. They could come to the edge of a high wall to tip their china clay into either of two purposely-devised folding chutes. In this picture, taken not so long ago, the chute over the freighter was lowered. The ship was taking clay.

So this had been a working port up until quite recently, and perhaps it still was...... and it would be without the gates and the fences and the floodlights which restricted unauthorised access to the quays at Par and Fowey. That was interesting, very interesting, promising almost. Tomorrow he would take a look.

*

Steve had persevered and at his fourth attempt the phone was at last answered. He wanted Jeremy. It was Kate who spoke.

"He's not here Steve. He's taken the train to London.....said he'd be back on Monday. He told me he had some research to do. He said something about a note you'd left, and he wanted me to thank you if I was the one who spoke to you first.......so 'ta', that's from Jeremy. I presume you know what it's about?"

"Only history," replied Steve, trying not to sound as disappointed as he felt. He'd been anxious to tell Jeremy that he'd just that hour passed Carwinion House and he'd noticed Sir Edward's Jag parked next to Hugh's Land Rover. "Have you seen Alan at all?"

"Briefly, at the hospital," replied the nurse, slightly defensively. "He said the photos we took on the ship hadn't offered anything profound, they might though come in useful with establishing identities."

"So where's the *Speedwell* at the moment?"

"Across at St.Mawes. He was talking about another full meeting at Jane's on Monday evening, prior to his making a midweek excursion back along the coast."

"Were you thinking of going to Hugh's service on Sunday?"

"I'm having to work. Jeremy's going to be away, and with Alan and Jane staying clear it looks like it'll be just Gareth and you."

*

It was always well filled, that Friday evening train to the capital. There were few empty seats and for those passengers who could find one, a strictly limited share of table. Jeremy kept the folder beside him, there not being the space to even start to spread the contents.

He had a notepad, and while that could stay in front of him the other documents would have to come out singly. First up was the note that Steve had posted through his door. In Kate's presence he'd played this down, as he'd been doing with this on-the-spur chase to London.

He'd been vague, deliberately, in anticipation of returning with a truly firm lead, one that he might then present with maximum impact. It would impress all the more for being unheralded and, moreover, purely his own work. This was no minor concern. Kate was taken with Alan, he could tell, but this time he would be matched, more than matched perhaps. Underused, his skills had been underrated. People were about to see otherwise.

Folded once he opened the sheet to reveal the two facing pages taken from Birkenhead's book. He read them through, and yes, this could well be significant. He looked again at Steve's scribbled note.

'Carrier Pigeon, I'd say! One for J Edgar's loft.'

He recalled his quip made at Jane's. It had drawn a response, one to both gratify and intrigue. He'd used this book before but he'd missed Leonora. Steve hadn't though.... clever boy! He could see the youngster's point. Walter might well have been pressed into being useful to Washington, for it was difficult to see any alternative...... only ignominy, in no small measure, and, for a lawyer, ruination.

He thought back. The Boss had still been firmly in place when he'd last seen this book. The man had been venerated, likewise David Windsor. How times change, he thought. Hoover had gone first, a sudden death, and then the Duke, no more than a month later, a protracted, painful death. And it hadn't been long before the re-assessors of reputation set to work. Cupboards that had long offered the whiff of skeleton could be aired. Facades were ready for demolition. Each had bequeathed an industry.

In this context Birkenhead had maybe been a little too soon off the mark. If the noble Duke attended by his faithful attorney had made an attractive tale for the end of the '60s, in the grittier '70s he might have honed something a lot sharper. The romanticism cloyed. If only Walter had lived another ten years! But would that have been allowable, he wondered, when the man had been privy to so much....... and he heard Kate in his mind's ear, rebuking.

But this was indeed a neat find. It was pithy. It was pertinent. It was persuasive. It was common knowledge now that Hoover had been watching David and Wallis Windsor very closely, and there was no reason to think that Walter would have escaped similar scrutiny.... particularly as his stock had grown within the Ministry of Information. Those indiscretions noted by his biographer, was there any way they could have escaped the attentions of the FBI?.... unlikely, very unlikely.

And Hoover was big, and growing bigger through the '40s and the '50s. The VENONA decrypts crossed his desk, for clearance to only his chosen, his trusted. And in this country, back in 1950, they wouldn't have been many. In his assessment the UK was a sad, sad case. If there was a 'special relationship' then it was due for re-negotiation on his terms, and wherever possible with his own personnel to the fore.

But could all this hold some relevance to Rory Duggan's predicament, and his fate? *There* was a question. A vast realm of speculation beckoned. Jeremy had to be professional. Discipline was required. He could easily wander and stray.

The name Monckton....... would this have held any significance for Duggan? It was unlikely. But Cairns the journalist, towards the end of '50 he would have noted the Bristol by-election occasioned by the death of Oliver Stanley, and Walter being privileged with the safe seat candidacy. Maybe he knew something too of Leonora Corbett, a renowned actress. But he would never have connected the two, not then. The liaison was kept veiled until the late '60s, just as the Enigma work was until the '70s. As some things are buried with time, reflected Jeremy, other things can be revealed.

Jeremy pulled out a notepad. At root he'd gotten himself involved in the tale of two ships, the *Usk Vale* and the *Kampala.* The two were linked, tenuously perhaps, but they definitely were, if only by virtue of that shed down in Lanmouth Creek, the Viceroy shed. Duggan, formerly of the *Vale,* had once been an occupier. The current occupier was handling a clandestine cargo for the one-time floating hospital.

The names of the two vessels went one apiece into the top corners of a fresh page. Below, in the very centre, the lecturer wrote *'USSR'.* He did almost the same on a second page, save for writing *'USA'* instead of *USSR.* From each hub he was hoping to mind map a spread of connected ideas, a web. With the two to compare, he would see what was potentially the tighter sieve, the more likely to snare an identifiable miscreant.

He turned back. He would start with the Red scenario.
'Factory fleet' was a confident opener, entered below *Kampala* and slightly to the right and above *USSR.* Below again he wrote *'FARC'* and *'M19',* two groups who might be supplying the drug and who were hungry for weaponry. A ring went around both, drawn large enough to also include *'Cuba'.* And for the moment that was as much as he could derive from the first vessel. It didn't look a lot, but those factory ships...... they were strong, strong enough to merit a double exclamation......*'Factory fleet!!'.*

'Usk Vale' stood in the other upper corner. What had she been to Moscow, he pondered. Very little, apart from that post Barbarossa denunciation of Duggan, acted upon by the Board of Trade. That had to be worth an entry. *'RD denounced '42'* went in, and that again was about as much as he could think of. He wasn't aware of any Russian units having been encircled in the '37 Ring of Iron, or Russian ships contesting Biscay; and those names VICKERS and AIRSPEED, they were hardly to be associated with a Soviet arsenal.

Jeremy went to his second page. He could centre now on the *'USA',* and he could indulge, he could flow. Directly beneath this *'Kampala'* he wrote *'SIGINT'* , Gareth's contribution, made with the help of his friend Alberto. *'Belgrano'* would have to go in, the actual sinking plus the suppression of the facts about how she was sent down..... implications here maybe for the very survival of the *'Thatcher'* government. The rationale held that at bottom she was indispensable to Washington given the critical state of play in the NATO/Warsaw Pact cold war, Central American politics notwithstanding.

'ANTI RED' could be printed in, an invitation for his brain to storm on. This was 'Prout's' line they'd determined, and whether he was tracking 'Baz' the ferry hand or they were in cahoots the name was going in, beneath 'Kampala' .... as was 'Lanmouth/Viceroy' which merited a double entry, here and beneath 'Vale'. For on that side of things, Duggan's craft had been US built and had been brought across as a part of the lend-lease deal, an arrangement that had granted to Washington military bases, one to be established in the 'Bahamas'. And that's where 'Sir ED' had been sent, to assist the Duke of 'Windsor', with whom 'Walter' kept in regular contact, and over whom Hoover kept a close watch.

And of course the 'US Army' had requisitioned 'Carwinion' for the duration of their war, 'WW2', in which Hitlerism was vanquished, but not Stalinism. In the post war world there was now a Red Menace to contend with. There was an 'economic' front, concerned with the regeneration of western capitalism, and there was a 'military' front...... in global terms a simmering stand off, but with localised flash points, the foremost being in 'Korea' where in the winter of '50/51 a Chinese offensive had supposedly brought the US to the brink of re-opening its nuclear armoury. '50/51', when 'RD died', and 'Cairns too' had gone to Korea from where he would never return. In the meantime Walter and Sir Ed became MPs, eventually part of the Churchill led 'Tory majority', Trembath having had the assistance of Cairns. The reporter had gone to 'Trelissick' and spoken with 'Ida' Copeland. He'd reported her good opinion of Sir Ed, but to Ralph, an old school chum who'd been following the young cub's career, the 'Independent piece' hadn't impressed.

Placing his pencil aside Jeremy considered his second page. How much fuller it was than the first. A jumble of jigsaw pieces it was, but they looked to be of the same puzzle and this was counting for a lot. Some corner bits would be useful, he thought, pieces to give brim to the picture, to curb his free ranging imagination. With eyes shut he considered remote places and significant times. Korea '50/51 could be one corner. For another why not Westminster 1931-85? More than fifty years of Parliamentary history encompassing Ida Copeland and Tam Dalyell? Stand here for the British perspective on the Spanish war, on

World War Two, on post war India and Africa, and on the conflicts over Suez, and the Falklands.

For another perhaps Colombia in the '80s, and for the fourth Washington, again to the present day.... but from how far back?

J. Edgar had been there in '31, but it was stretching things to credit him any role in the Ramsay Mac stitch up. By the same token '41 was starting too late. Lend lease comfortably pre-dated Pearl Harbour.

So why not '37?, he thought. Significant for Duggan on the Usk Vale, it was also the year of David Windsor's marriage to his American bride. Moreover it was the year that had started with another arms shipment to Spain, another betrayal, that of the *Mar Cantabrico* .... an episode indicative of where mainstream American sympathies had truly lain during the Spanish Civil War.

The corners offered a framework both broad and sturdy. All that he'd heard and read of this since that first meeting with Grigson and the boy in Truro might be accommodated and to a degree, sorted. If he could just locate and then position the key pieces, then the rummage that he'd gathered would largely fall into place, the full picture would emerge.

Just one item remained problematic.... that article on Mosley. Published in 1950, by then its subject was a good ten years beyond his political sell by. He'd become an oddity, a colourful misfit who few took seriously. With the rest perhaps pointing to something altogether more insidious, grimmer, and more permanent, there looked to be little place for bad old Sir Oswald's up front pantomime villainy. Despite what he'd told Steve, this more than ever looked to be one for the discard pile.

Yes, he'd told the boy that this former Labour minister stood as a caution to post Franco Spain, and he'd been in earnest with this. But on reflection this might be a view too much coloured by a personal scepticism towards Senor Gonzalez and his country's shiny new constitution. Having alerted the youngster, he had himself gone and bought the dummy!

Enquiry was his way forward. He knew who he wanted to contact. This was why he was travelling and with a little luck he could be returning on Monday with something truly impressive to assemble.

*

"He's in London Alan, he went by train earlier this evening."

"And said he would be back when, Kate?"

"In time for his Monday afternoon class. Is that a call box you're using?"

"It is, and I'm fast running out of change. When do you finish shift tomorrow?"

"2 pm."

"Come out on the water for the evening. I'll be at Malpas for 4 .... meet you there?"

*

Jeremy rose early. His hosts, in deference to an intensity he'd brought to the house, were inclined to keep clear. He could come and go as he pleased, and this morning that meant immediately....But which way? On the journey in he'd entertained two options. It was now time to decide. Emerging onto Willes Road, he could turn left and take the one hundred and fifty metre walk to Kentish Town tube, or he could turn right and walk the five times that to Chalk Farm.

To choose the first was to opt for the Central Registry of births, marriages, and deaths. A southbound Northern Line train could take him into Charing Cross, and from there it would be but a short stroll along The Strand. He looked at his watch, paused briefly, and instead turned right.

Chalk Farm was also on the Northern Line, but on a different fork. It was the first station on the Edgware branch. Charing Cross trains stopped there too, but for the moment that was not his intended direction. Choosing Chalk Farm meant choosing a northbound train to take him out into the suburbs beyond Hampstead Heath. Just six stops and he was at Colindale, and there, across the road from the station, stood the British Library's newspaper archive. It was possible that what he sought was there, if not then he could try the West End later.

It was a forbidding building, but not unknown. He'd used the library before, in the course of academic research. He had a card, and he was familiar with the procedures and the regulations.

He checked in with his bag and his coat and found himself a reading desk. His initial request was for three years' worth of the Truro based weekly, *'The West Briton',* 1950, '51 and '52.It was a broadsheet then, and up they came bound in six correspondingly sized volumes.

Rory Duggan's death was reported and, very briefly, his funeral. Jeremy learned a little about the *Viceroy* and something of the service that man and boat had given on the estuary. It was also told that the man was a tenant of the Trembaths, renting both his cottage and the Lanmouth workshop from the estate. Later there was the small report of the inquest, the same as saved by Jack Butters and copied by himself.

The first and only mention of Francis Cairns came with his death in the late summer of '51. The report also spoke of the local fiance, and a name was given, the same name remembered by Ralph Bartlett....... Linda Adams.

For early '52 Jeremy opened the fifth volume. Weddings, that was his concern now. He went straight to the first week in April, and thereafter through the whole month, and then the whole of May, and then there she was on the second Saturday in June. She'd married one John Taylor, and here in the paper was the kind of write up for which he'd hoped. As well as the husband's name there was the address where they would settle, an Exeter address, and also his employer.....the GPO telephones division. All this was useful of course and he would pencil it down, but what he'd hoped for were family details, and yes, here they came.

She'd had brother, Raymond. He was already married. He'd had two children. They were lads, Gerald and Terry, each a page boy at their aunt's wedding. Jeremy took out his list of mid Cornwall Adamses. For the moment he ignored the 'R's. If he contacted Raymond then he could be going a little too close. There were six 'G' s and five 'T' s. He listed the numbers of all. Of the eleven only four had a Roseland address. It was on these that he would start. He left the building and crossed to the station newsagent's. Facing this were two phone booths. He purchased a cheap pen, and furnishing a £5 note asked for his change in silver. The assistant obliged. A payphone was free and in working order. He made his choice from the list, a 'G', and dialled.

A woman replied. It was an elderly voice. The accent was West Midlands rather than West Country. She knew of no Gerald Adams, and neither did anyone at the first of the 'T' s he attempted.

Jeremy tried a second 'G'.

"Hi, 37724, Jennifer speaking."

It was the voice of a teenaged girl.

"Hello Jennifer, I'm not sure that I have the right number but I'm trying to contact a Mr Gerald Adams."

"My father's a Gerald, but he's not in at the moment. He plays golf on Saturday mornings. He's usually back before 3. Can I take a name or a message?"

"If it's the right Gerald Adams then you might be able to help. The chap I want has an Aunt called Linda. She would be a sister to your grandfather."

"That's right, she was down here only a couple of weeks ago. She and Uncle John were looking around for a small retirement place. I don't know how serious they are. Some people make a pastime of just looking, but she was brought up around here."

"I know," said Jeremy, pressing in another two ten pence pieces, "and this is why I was hoping to get an address so that we could write to her. I have a friend who's trying to set up a school class reunion. She was in your Aunt Linda's year, and she only had the name Adams, Linda and Raymond Adams."

"I can tell you the address. We used to go there to stay quite often.....36 Velwell Road, Exeter. It's sort of between the University and the prison. Not far from the main Station, if you don't mind hills. I think they'll like the idea of a re-union. The retirement offer was a bit of a shaker for the old boy..... liked his work he did, good pay off though, too good to refuse."

"And the surname is....?" Jeremy was careful to ask, even though knowing the answer.

"Taylor."

"That's brilliant. Now can I rely on you to make sure this comes as a surprise?"

"Of course," was the reply, and Jeremy returned to the library beaming his delight. As well as information he'd gained time. No longer did he need to trek into the Kingsway registry. He could linger awhile here, go back to the beginning and look a little more closely at the earlier parts of the story, as Francis Cairns would have done, might have done even.

This tale of the young Cornishman, the student at Manchester who rode all the way to Stoke to put his shoulder to an election campaign being fought by his neighbour's step daughter was hardly of national interest. It had to be provincial and though it reached the Plymouth press it must have emanated from the foremost of the five towns. He went to the index shelves, and then once again to the desk.

A likely daily was *The Stoke Sentinel*. And volume bound by the month's worth Jeremy would again be handling a specimen of what had actually been printed for real, and sold to the public and read. Here was a feel of those times.

The 1931 election had been held in the fourth week of October, on the 27th. Many would have been content with the one volume for that month, but his interest was wider, deeper. He wanted to assess Ida's victory in the context of the constituency's continuum. A quick discussion with the desk clerk confirmed the previous election to have been at the end of May 1929 with the following in mid November '35. Volumes of the *Sentinel* were duly ordered for these months.

While arriving together it was '35 volume that came initially to hand and Jeremy, curious as to the result rather than the campaign turned to Saturday 15th. And there it was.

Stoke on Trent

Ellis Smith	*(Labour)*	*20,992*
Mrs Ronald Copeland	*(Conservative)*	*18,867*

She'd lost, just as the Plymouth paper of fifteen years later had told, but the margin was barely decisive. She'd fought hard and maybe had indeed failed for want of that extra ounce of support that the likes of Edward Trembath had lent four years previously.

Closing this volume Jeremy moved to that of October 1931. Jeremy had always considered psephology as one of the more obscure branches of political science, but as ever he was up on his history. He knew that from their '31 nadir there'd only been meagre gains for Labour in '35 and accordingly he expected Ida to have been a marginal winner in that first poll. Again he went straight to the report of the declaration... Saturday 29th.

And he was stunned. What was he reading? It wasn't the figures, not yet. It was a name, one of the candidates. The result was immaterial. In the poll he was nowhere, but in the circumstances that had brought Jeremy to this dowdy, distant archive of populism here was a figure suddenly barging his way to the fore, demanding attention, and he wasn't to be denied. No longer could he be deemed an irrelevance, as nothing more than a caution rendered inert by passage of time. This character had actually, in some way, mattered. Jeremy's heart thumped. Giddied by adrenaline he struggled to take in the full result. He attempted to note it down. His hand quivered. He scanned the page again, scarcely believing what he read.

Stoke on Trent

Mrs Ronald Copeland	*(Conservative)*	*19,918*
Ellis Smith	*(Labour)*	*13,264*
Sir Oswald Mosley	*(New Party)*	*10,524*

Ida had won, and yes, with a slightly higher total, but her proportion of the total votes cast for all candidates was actually lower. The impressive majority over Mr Smith could be attributed to her opponents having this time split what four years later would be a unified and winning anti-coalition vote.

There was irony in this, thought Jeremy, for now, more than fifty years later, the Conservatives were again holding sway at Westminster by courtesy of a fractured working class vote. And the issue to the fore, then as now, was 'sound money'. In '31 the orthodox line favoured a balanced budget to hold the recently unpegged £ as closely as possible to its former 'gold standard', even where this meant cutting welfare provision, and the earnings of those paid from the public purse.

The radical alternative preached 'unhook and slide'. Borrow, spend, reflate. The cost, a devalued currency, was sustainable. Indeed it was to be welcomed for more competitively priced exports could mean jobs at home, much needed jobs.

Then came the second great war of the century. Soldiers had to be paid, they had to be armed, and when they'd done what soldiers do then nations had to be repaired, and people mended. Cities and ships had to be replaced, food had to be found. Pre war radicalism became post war orthodoxy. It was confirmed at Bretton Woods. A brave new Pax Americana would be underwritten by the Gospel according to Keynes.

And for a quarter of a century it had just about worked. But it could never provide the complete answer. If the gold men could be ignored, the oil men certainly could not. The drilling nations had tired of funny money, they'd blown the whistle. The ploy of print and spend was now looking played out.

And that epic fifty-year debate had opened in '31. In Government, as a Labour Cabinet minister, Mosley had said spend. When the bankers had said cut, his Premier had chosen to heed them. Mosley had resigned. He would make his point with his own party, a new party, The New Party. And here he was attempting to sell it to the constituents of Stoke on Trent.......but Sir Oswald had obviously reckoned without Ida and the likes of her young Cornish neighbour.

And yet Edward Trembath had been a student of economics. He was to graduate well from Manchester. Jeremy had seen the 'holding the scroll' portrait. What then would the young tyro have made of the gold standard issue? A good student would have stayed with the orthodoxy of the text books. An exceptional student would have perhaps been more open minded and listened to the debate. Whatever, he'd certainly been a good neighbour.

Campaign coverage began in earnest on Saturday 15th and it was in this day's issue that Jeremy found mention of a student who'd cycled from Manchester to present himself at the office of the Conservative Association as a neighbour of their candidate. It was just the few sentences in a larger piece compiled probably from bits and pieces forwarded by Ida's agent.

It was stated that the lad was from Cornwall, and also that his home was close to Trelissick, but no name was given......that detail would have been deduced and added when the story eventually reached Plymouth.

Jeremy glanced at his watch, wondering if there might be time to summon a *Western Morning News* volume.....for the moment though he decided to stay with the *Sentinel*. He turned on into the last full week before polling. Ida's campaign was as low key and as cautious as her message, yes, 'Safety First'. The real battle was for the vote of the working man and therefore between Mosley and Smith. The Labour candidate had an advantage. He could stay in the Potteries while Sir Oswald was having to travel the length of the country, as would befit of course a party leader.

But Sir Oswald was back at the constituency on Friday 21st, for in the next day's issue there were three impressive photographs. Two caught this renowned orator addressing a street gathering, and the third he was moving towards the camera through a group of back slapping supporters.

It was a familiar image, and it took a moment or two for Jeremy to realise just how familiar. It was larger in this paper than it was to appear some nineteen years later in *The Limerick Examiner,* and, better preserved, the ensemble was more sharply defined. Jeremy took out his smudged, shadowy equivalent.... how different, but unarguably the same moment in time, the same person.

The man of the left..... *'El hombre de la Izquierdas',*
 actually, for the pedantic, 'la' was superfluous.......unless it was *'El hombre a la izsquierda',* in which case........ He looked again at the *Sentinel.*

Within the minute Jeremy was outside, across the road, and once more on the phone. He was through to Lanmouth Farm.

"Steve?....This is Jeremy. Listen, thanks for the note you passed in, that was well spotted, very well spotted. Now I've been doing a bit of my own research and I need to speak to Alan about it as soon as possible. Can you tell me where he is at the moment?"

"We're meeting on Monday evening, at Jane's place.......you know that?"

"I know that, but I want to get to him this evening if at all possible."

"Are you in London? I spoke to Kate yesterday and she sai....."

"Alan Steve, if you can." Jeremy was struggling to stay calm. Steve confined himself.

"When she isn't on the Carrick Roads the *Speedwell* is down at St.Mawes. Try Percuil Yard. He might still be there. If not, then where else they'll know better than I."

"Thanks Steve, I'll see you at the Monday meet. It should be a good one."

"One little thing," added the boy. "In case Kate hasn't had the chance to say, Sir Edward is back at Carwinion House."

"I like it. See you soon." With that Jeremy hung up.

*

At Polkerris the *Rashleigh Inn* is a waterfront pub, but not so the *Rashleigh Arms* at Charlestown. Customers at the latter have no sea view, instead they look across the car park to the back of a long stone and slate shed in which pilchards were once smoked and packed by the thousand. The port had its own fleet then, a century back, at the time of the shoals, but the shoals are no more.

At one end, that which faced the Shipwreck Museum, curing has been re-established. A small firm offered a selection of inshore fish, vacuum packed of course, to the specialist market...... the restaurant and the delicatessen. With just the one refrigerated van waiting idly in the corner of the pub car park and no people or bustle about the place, only the lingering odour offered any tang of former times.

Passing the *Rashleigh* and the main entrance to its car park Gareth had turned along the back of the dock. On the seaward side of the cure he looked down on the full length of the harbour. There was a ship against the far quay. No more than six hundred tons it had been brought beneath a chute. It waited with hatches wide. Gareth rode on. He'd noted the Belgian flag blazing from the masthead. What he'd despaired of finding at Par and at Fowey was here, in a glimpse.

He was in business. He wanted to know more, but he would need to take care. Nothing was moving at the moment. He needn't rush.

Turning away from the sea between cure and Museum he found an access into the car park from that side. There was space for his bike between the wall and the fish van. There it would attract little notice.

He lifted his camera case from a pannier, but he wasn't to start snapping yet. It was 4pm. The Shipwreck Museum was still open. Where better to enquire. He entered and wandered amongst the exhibits for a good half an hour. It was an impressive collection. There was a gift shop of course, and from the selection of booklets he chose one that told the history of the port. He waited for a slack moment at the till. Up to date information he wanted too, and perhaps the assistant could help. The opportunity soon came.

"These ships that still come here for the clay, how many, how often?"

"They'll average out at about three in a fortnight." Answering, the young assistant slid the booklet into a thin plastic bag.

"And do they tend to be the same ones, so that you get to know them as they return?" Gareth took the bag and proffered the money.

"Most are regulars in the sense that each order will require them to collect a series of shipments, and that means you'll see them quite often until the order's completed."

"And the one out there now, is she a regular?"

"Four or five times over the past couple of months." The assistant held out the change, but there was no move from Gareth to take it.

"And she shuttles across to.......?"

"Belgium, I think they said....."

"....and she'd be able to use the canals, that one." Said Gareth. "She could get us a lot further than Antwerp. And these ships come in empty, fill up and leave.... nothing's ever brought in?"

"What could you unload here on this side of the dock? And look at the ships, the holds. Even when empty, all that powder, all that dust, what else are you going to carry around? This is why this port's so open.... that, and it being strictly EC trade. The boats are just oversized lorries. Freedom of movement, you see. You get bigger crews on fishing trawlers."

Gareth at last took his money. Thanking the assistant he climbed stiffly onto the steps to the 'Bosun's Diner'. He was ready to eat, and here on the balcony cafè he could read the booklet, and he could watch. He felt secure. He wasn't out in the open, and yet what came and what went he could see.

It was sound positioning. At about 5:30 a rental truck eased past the nearby weigh bridge, and swung seawards past the museum and the loading chute hoppers, and then carefully negotiated the steep hairpin that offered vehicular access to the clay quay. Gareth recognised the driver. It was Baz, the ferry hand. He was alone. Would he be followed? There was nothing yet, not on this side of the harbour, but there soon could be he sensed.

The Guardsman didn't know Prout, but he had been told of the kind of vehicle the man drove, and initially it was for this that he was watching, listening. But he was thinking too, and was such an entrance really likely?

If the man was following, and following at a distance, then he would be either watching, like himself, or watching for watchers such as himself. Either way, and especially if this was the third or fourth time, he was hardly going to come lumbering into the place with an ex British

Gas CF. In fact it was more likely that he would be heading for this restaurant and this same vantage on foot, having found somewhere discrete for the van.

Gareth shifted uneasily in his seat. He glanced back into the main dining area. What if the man suddenly arrived? There was no way of slipping out to avoid him. It was time to settle his bill. He gathered together his maps and the booklet, and the camera that so far hadn't been used. He hesitated. A shot of boat and van together could be useful, he thought, but it would be a risk for the truck was out of sight from this side, the dock having been cut so steeply beneath those chutes.

He would need to stand on the other side of the basin and he would be exposed. To leave himself less so, he could choose and fit the appropriate lens now.

Through the viewfinder he found and focussed the dock gate and the zigzagged piers of the outer harbour. There was another pub down there he noticed, *'The Pier House Hotel'* the sign read. He used the letters to sharpen his image. He steadied, he had the far edge of the building, and there was a person there. It was a man. The camera dwelt. It was because the face was looking directly into the lens, almost as if he were aware that it had settled on him. From that far the figure wouldn't know this, but he could rightly be thinking that the balcony offered a good vantage.

The eyes then moved around, down to the quay on his side and then across the lock and up to the chute tops. They were every where, save for on the coaster and the just arrived truck.

The fellow was keeping watch. Gareth could empathise, totally. He'd often done this for armed comrades. A set procedure was being followed, a drill. Nothing was going to move until all had been routinely checked. It was as well that he'd arrived earlier, and stowed the motorcycle where he did.

That had to be Prout. He was close to sure. And the man was working with the ferry hand. He was an accomplice, a minder. He was watching for watchers. And were he himself in that role, he would certainly be in the habit of checking out this cafe, set as it was in such a commanding position. He didn't need the camera now. The person was moving, climbing, making to come around the back of the dock, making towards where he sat.

This was enough. He had to make himself scarce. He was too

recognisable, and so was his bike. Within three minutes it was roaring up the broad wagon way towards Mount Charles. Only as he approached the roundabout with its main road traffic did the anxiety for distance abate. He needed petrol and although not in his intended direction he'd earlier spotted a filling station, no more than a hundred yards or so in the direction of Lostwithiel and Liskeard, right against where the road was bridged by the main railway line. He coasted down to the canopied forecourt. He dismounted. More relaxed now, he could take stock.

A westbound Intercity 125 whistled over the road, rattling the garage canopy. Had he looked down then one of the second class occupants might have caught a glimpse of Gareth and maybe recognised him even. Jeremy sat in the fourth carriage. He was on his way back, two days earlier than envisaged. He had to see Alan, to speak to him. It was a matter of urgency.

After phoning Steve he'd returned to the library. He'd considered requesting and waiting for a copy of that page from the *Sentinel* with the picture of Sir Oswald, but then decided against. There would be a voucher to fill out, and that would mean giving a name and a number for which they had an address. Cairns would have gone to London, summoned to the *Chronicle*, and maybe, in a spare hour or two, he'd come to this place, and perhaps found this....... and been fatally indiscreet. Jeremy was wary. Even now, after more than thirty years, an interest in this specific page might be noted.

Instead Jeremy had made a forty minute browse through the last year's worth of *Observers,* and it had been time well spent. The Sunday paper was excellent as a weekly digest of foreign news, and in keeping with its liberal tradition it maintained   detailed and   fearlessly informative coverage of the revolutionary and reactionary movements contesting that impoverished mosaic of central American states that lay between Mexico and Colombia.... Honduras, where Washington held sway, and El Salvador, Guatamala, Nicaragua, and Panama, where it wanted to......but couldn't quite. And amongst all this there'd been the Grenada take over.

He'd made a few notes and had been back in Kentish Town for a snatched lunch. The bemused friends learned that having gathered all he needed from the big city he was returning west. He would find adequate resources at the University in Exeter, they were informed. He was at Paddington by 3pm, and within the hour, without phoning Kate, he was on his way back to Redruth. Through Berkshire and Wiltshire he'd made more notes, and then slept through Somerset and Devon.

Now, as the train wormed its way deep into the Duchy he was re-reading those notes and that delight was growing to elation. Connections were happening, and though as yet vague the picture sought was beginning to shape. Some key pieces he'd found, others he'd already had but not, until now, recognised. They would impress, and none more so than that put before him by the boy, young Steve.

Sharpening his excitement was the fact that none knew of this return. There was this riddle. He was on his way to a solution, and so uniquely close that it brought him a sense of freedom, power. Arriving unannounced he was placed to progress as and when, and with whom he chose.

It was to Alan that he wanted to speak, man to man. OK, the guy was in charge and would remain so, but this time he would listen. He had to. Close scrutiny of the past was relevant, and it was to Exeter that the trail led. It had to be followed, but not actually to the University Library as he'd led his London friends to believe. He wanted a green light from Alan, his consent to go to Velwell Road, to number thirty six...... for there resided a first hand source.

Returning from the console Gareth now had a replenished machine. Remounting, he rocked the bike off its stand, just to let it roll clear of the pumps. He pulled the map from his jacket pocket.

Charlestown.....it was obvious now. There was even a side way into the small port, a quiet minor road that wound between Polgooth and Mevagissey. That's where they'd previously been sighted, when it had been assumed that the fishing harbour had been the destination.

And what of Prout?....for he was sure that was him. A soldier, whether tracking or discretely covering the rear, would be expected to close in on foot. The one leading vehicle was enough in such a tight place. He would have left the van.....but where?

Perhaps he'd come along the coast path, thought Gareth, sizing the map. That's probably how he'd have done it himself, because there looked to be access to the path through a small cliff top residential estate, just along the coast to the west.

It was might be worth a casual look, and the Porthpean road offered a way around to the estate without retracing through Charlestown. If he could find parked there a warm engined CF then his scrambled retreat would be looking all the wiser, and his theory all the more convincing. He refolded the map and headed back towards the summit roundabout.

Into the estate and the houses were large and well spaced, the trees mature, the hedges conveniently high. It suited him too that there was more crescent than there was close and maybe it suited Prout too..... for there was the van, the CF, ex Gas Board.

Gareth cruised slowly by. Before stopping he wanted to be sure that it was unattended...... and unattended it was. He turned and drew up by the driver's door. Straightening his back and stretching his neck he peered through the side window. A sturdy looking send and receive radio tuner was housed beneath the dashboard, a little to the left of the steering column. A handset was hooked between.

The former guardsman had seen its like before, but never before in any land civilian context, commercial or amateur. This kit was of military spec. In the back somewhere there would be an even weightier companion piece, the range-giving transmitter, securely bolted onto a purposely-strengthened corner of bodywork.

Gareth edged past a rear wheel to peer into the nearest of the two back door windows. Across the corner between the off side rear wheel arch and the driver's seat there rose a crumpled tarpaulin. The technology would be beneath, he decided.

Further towards him, on the floor, there lay an open metal toolbox. Within, amongst the tools, there lay a packet. Again he'd seen the type before. He was familiar with the content. He'd used these things himself, professionally. Detonators they were..... of the kind that were triggered by radio signal, in his experience from anything up to five miles.

Prout handled Semtex. Here was confirmation. On reflection maybe it wasn't so surprising, if he had indeed been a mercenary and mining and quarrying had come into his line of work. This was as maybe. The uncovering of such capability in these circumstances was nonetheless alarming. The driver of this motor, outwardly an unkempt Bedford CF, wielded a fearsome weapon. He could kill at range.

Gareth was promptly away, striking westward through the lanes for the Roseland. He decided this time to camp at Jane's. The field there was spacious. He chose a corner.....that furthest from the house and closest to the road, where the hedge offered both shelter and privacy. As the sun sagged onto the Philleigh skyline he swiftly positioned and pegged the tent. Shadow rendered the grass moist, and the scents of evening mellowed to those of dusk.

He'd been a late comer, but not though the last to arrive. Two very similar caravans, each hitched behind a Cavalier, followed him by about ten minutes. They parked together. Clearly it was how they'd travelled. These were companions. A further ten minutes and in clattered a rear-engine VW camper. Of good age, it circled the site giving Gareth a chance to note five occupants, three male, two female. Window stickers and sweatshirts proclaimed them, and probably the van too, to be Christian. These were mission people. Propriety required a tent and up it went next to the vehicle. The smooth erection was celebrated with a clutch of faith affirming choruses. Gareth's thoughts were moved towards the morning. He was expected at Penryn. He was still shaping his contribution. He would certainly be there. It was one he was determined now not to miss.

*

Jeremy stepped lightly from the train. He strode confidently to his waiting car. He could go where he wished. Home to Kate, or to Carwinion, or to Mylor, or he could even set off for Exeter now..... though at this hour it would mean spending the night either in the car or a road house.

The favoured option remained St. Mawes. He wanted so much to draw Alan's admiration. This was about pride.

He drove straight for Percuil Yard where, despite fast fading light, he was quick to identify the *Speedwell*. She was tied at the end of the more seaward of the two pontoon jetties. The cabin windows were lit. Alan was there. Gathering his papers Jeremy locked the car and walked purposefully out onto the slats. As he approached the vessel he slowed, he wanted to knock, but where he wasn't sure. Then he heard a voice from within.....and he froze.

"Don't worry Alan, he's miles away and he's doing what he likes to be doing. I'm here, and this is what I like..... what I've been waiting for, waiting too long."

Jeremy knew the voice, a woman's voice, his woman's, and he knew the inflexion and what it promised. He knew this too well.

"So you're free to join me in a bit of undercover?" smirked the other voice, male, Alan of course.

"I'm ready to come undercover with you Mr Grigson......whenever you like."

The suppressed chuckle that delayed that last phrase drove Jeremy into retreat. He was almost running. He had to get to his car. He wanted himself away, far away. He was shrinking, slinking. He feared being seen. He wanted it to be as if he'd never come.

He got to the car, climbed in, and he got it out of St. Mawes, but where it would then take him, he didn't know. He had to think. He had to find a place to think. He chose Pendower.

He'd understood that Kate and he were unlikely to be a forever thing. They'd talked about this. Both had outgrown relationships before, and they were agreed that should this happen between them then they could talk with frankness, with honesty, without pretence, deceit, betrayal. And it had come to this. He was hurt. He was angry, angry with the pair of them. And he clung to this anger, for beyond it lay devastation.

He could have raged, and maybe that would have been better. Instead he fumed, and breathed a more insidious and bitter poison, the measured catalyst. Fission was inevitable.

*

The Falmouth 'Working Boat'
Flushing Run 1985

BOOK 3

Sunday

Blessed is the man who finds wisdom, the man who gains understanding, for she is more profitable than silver and yields better returns than gold.

She is more precious than rubies; nothing you can desire can compare with her.

Long life is in her right hand; in her left hand are riches and honour.

Her ways are pleasant ways, and all her paths are peace.

She is the tree of life to those who embrace her; those who lay hold of her will be blessed.

By wisdom the Lord laid the earth's foundations, by understanding he set the heavens in place; by his knowledge the deeps were divided, and the clouds let drop the dew.........

Do not withhold good from those who deserve it, when it is in your power to act...........

Do not plot harm against your neighbour, who lives trustfully near you.

Do not accuse a man for no reason-when he has done you no harm.

Do not envy a violent man or choose any of his ways, for the Lord detests a perverse man but takes the upright into his confidence.

The Lord's curse is on the house of the wicked but he blesses the home of the righteous.

With an ever so slightly adjusted selection from the Old Testament Gareth Hughes completed his second contribution to the service. The first

274

had been the 23rd Psalm, that complete. To give each reading he'd stood at the foot of the pulpit stair and then returned to front row pew that he shared with Sir Edward. There followed now a Hymn.....'Fight the good fight' the congregation sang, then the younger Trembath would give his address.

Steve sat in a pew closer to the back. Beside him was young Jack Spargo, and next to young Jack, old Jack Butters. Steve had been surprised to see them, but also relieved. When he'd entered the grandson had made room. The boy hadn't hesitated. Hugh, Sir Edward, and Gareth were centre stage, and to that they were welcome. He was content with a place in the wings.

The themes of the address were predictable......courage, comradeship, sacrifice, reconciliation, and all developed and delivered quite well. Or at least Steve thought so.

Another hymn and that was the service done. Young Jack led his Grandfather out immediately, before Hugh had even had time to descend from pulpit to porch. Steve followed them. It seemed natural. *Flushing Run* was down at the wharf. They'd sailed around from Mylor and it would take some time to return. But they seemed in no hurry now to make their way back to the boat. Having been smartly out, they seemed loathed now to move away....why?

Steve saw. They were lingering by Gareth's motorcycle. Old Jack was angling for an introduction to the Welshman, but one preferably not made through the principals from Carwinion. This was tricky for Steve. Sir Edward had driven him here with Hugh, and it was understood that there would also be a lift back.

Gareth emerged. He was with Sir Edward. Young Jack whispered in his grandfather's ear and the pair turned to leave. Linked, they had to move across Steve and as they did so the old man gripped an arm and leant towards him.

"The Welsh boy...... tell 'n I'm wantin' to see 'n, an' see 'n today. Say I 'eard 'n. Say that I 'eard ev'ry word an' more besides. Tell 'n where I live, an' tell 'n I'm waitin'...... but I wan' e t' wait t' when they others i'nt lis'nin'."

*

Three hours of fitful sleep in the reclined front seat of his car had done little to assuage Jeremy's anger. If anything, under dawn's cold light, it was intensifying. He'd parked beneath the trees on Haldon Hill, no more than a stone's throw from the ridge top steeplechase venue. He pulled off the grass and rejoined the A38. Exeter was spread before him. He swept down and across the river, and as the motorway began he was off into the Grenada Services.

He was beyond hunger. It was only with an effort and the assistance of an extra coffee that he could swallow back so much as a service station baguette. It was the toilet he needed. He had to make himself presentable. He would be calling on a stranger.

Duly freshened he then drove into the city. Finding the road and the house was easy matter.

It was terraced but tall, being built to three floors. While close to the centre it was quietly positioned, and as it was a Sunday he could park in a kerb space.

He wouldn't yet, though, for he was wary of seeming desperately early. He could go around to the University, to the library, it was only two or three minutes away. He was known there and were he to be later challenged as to his weekend movements then what he'd said to his friends in London could be at least partially vouched.

But there was more in here than just an alibi. He came often and an invariably useful quick reference were the volumes of *Times* obituaries. Yes, they tended to eulogise, of course they did....... but allowances could be made to render them concise personal fact files.

Walter's entry, in the '60s volume and covering the best part of two triple column pages, didn't disappoint. Jeremy read it closely. He then took the volume to the copier. It wasn't so much for the interview here, in Exeter, he was arming himself as for an envisaged late in the day second, back in Cornwall.

Another entry caught his eye, that of Marilyn Monroe. She followed Walter. He copied hers too. Such are the ways of the inveterate conspiracy theorist....even whilst angered.

The copies joined the others in his folder. The volume was returned to its shelf. He looked at his watch, it was a reasonable hour, and he could leave his car here. There was footpath along the near side of the Cricket ground. He could take this and be in Velwell Road in less time than it would take to drive.

And it was wise to keep his car away from the vicinity of the prison. Jane's mother would often visit on a Sunday, and she'd been known to bring the girl. The risk of recognition was slight, but why leave things needlessly to chance?

Ten minutes and he was there, at number 36. He rang the bell. He waited. Would it be answered? Would it be a he? Would it be the she?

The she it was ....for certain. The hair had greyed, and the face had lined, but the eyes were unmistakably those that he'd encountered at Colindale, unmistakably so. The same resolution they had, the same hint of loss.

"Mrs Taylor?"

"Yes. Do I know you?"

"You don't, it's Jeremy Barnes..... I'm up from Cornwall. I live in Truro, and I teach in the college at Camborne." The woman merely nodded. The caller was being required to continue. "I obtained your address from a grand daughter of your brother. I spoke to her yesterday on the phone. I said I wanted your address so that you could be notified of a school reunion. That wasn't the truth. Now I've found you I want to be honest, and I'd like you to be."

"And your business?"

"I have a friend. She lives in Philleigh."

"I know Philleigh." The woman remained impassive.

"Her father is in the prison here, wrongly I believe. My business is what I see to be a connection between his plight and one Francis Cairns."

"Francis?......Francis died in......."

"........1951, in Korea," finished Jeremy.

"This sounds like McKinley. Did he put you on to me?" Jeremy looked puzzled. "He's an American."

"Jack Butters I've spoken with," said Jeremy. "He's a blind old riversider. He seems to have always lived at Mylor. Years ago he had a friend, a Liverpudlian, who went by the name of Rory Duggan. I've also spoken with one Ralph Bartlett, an early school friend of Francis. Both are Cornish through and through."

"Look, I'd rather you didn't come in, and I'm not happy with having to talk to you on the doorstep." Jeremy looked down, dismayed. "But if you go down to the station, the main station, to the buffet, I'll follow you. I've got an hour. You go on, give me 10 minutes. I'll straighten what I'm doing, find my shoes,.......and I'll leave a note for my husband, he'll wonder else. I'll see you down there."

*

"So you mus' unnerstan' son. I knaws summin' 'bout wad they in your parts calls the tease an' the doubt of shellin'. An' I knaws summin' 'bout being shipped out ready t' fight only t'be caught cold, an' then sent 'ome a wreck. I knaws 'bout courage too. I seed it at St Nazaire like you seed it at Bluff Cove. An' I reckons I knaws more than most 'bout you, jus' from your voice on the wireless an' in that chapel. It in't the words you chooses, 'tis the way you chooses t' say 'm."

"What then has this well tuned ear of yours gathered?" challenged Gareth.

"That t'day it were you down there doin' the preachin'. Most 'eard you read the lessons. I 'eard a proper sermon, one tailored fer some of they present.... 'do not withold good.....do not accuse'. You just 'eard me tell of Rory Duggan, 'bout 'ow some who knawed bedder 'llowed others t' think 'im treach'rous when truth t' tell 'e were one of the best. Now tell us you 'adn' 'eard it b'fore,'eard it from the boy, or p'rhaps from that teacher fellow 'e brought down 'ere t'other day."

Gareth smirked. The old man was so right about him preaching, and yet so wrong about on who's behalf. Until coming here he'd known next to nothing about this long buried Rory Duggan. As he'd read aloud in the chapel his thoughts were for two others, for a man wrongly jailed in Exeter prison, and for Hilda...poor dead Hilda. He studied the old man's face, and looking into those inscrutable eyes the smirk faded.

Was this a genuine misapprehension, or could it be an error feigned? How could he be sure? And did he deserve to be sure if he was himself holding back?

And if he couldn't open up to one such as Jack Butters, one who'd preceded him through hell and high water, then in whom could he ever confide? It was time to be straight.

Gareth reached into a jacket pocket. He drew out the spent bullet returned to him by Steve. He then took one of the old man's hands. He gently turned it and placed the item in the palm.

"You know what this is?" The hand clenched to a bony fist.

"That's a bullet you'm givin' me. A rifle bullet."

"But you don't know what sort." Gareth spoke quietly and carefully. "I'm going to tell you what sort, and how I came by it. Then I'm going to tell you why I'm wanting your help. I'm trusting that it'll be forthcoming."

*

Jeremy returned from the counter with two teas and two packets of biscuits. As she took hers the woman thought back to '57, to another man and another conversation. It was the same buffet room, and she knew it was about to be the same topic.

Then it was china, and metal spoons, and real leaves. Today it was polystyrene and plastic and a teabag apiece.

He'd had to queue, and while waiting she'd read the article he'd placed before her. She'd remembered it, only too well.

"This was the last piece he did for the *Independent*," she said. "How did you come by it?"

"It was given to me, by someone to whom it was given by someone else. My apologies if that makes it sound like a disease."

"So long as it's nothing fatal," said Linda Taylor, smiling thinly.

"I'll get on to the 'some one else' in a minute. If you can remember at all, I want you to tell me what Francis thought of the piece. His old school chum considered it below par."

"Francis was livid. What he actually submitted I was never sure, but it was certainly changed about. He had a blazing row with the editor. He said he'd never do anything for them again."

"And he never did," said Jeremy.

"But he would have," insisted the woman. "There was anger and there were threats, but that was him. It blew over and within a month he was pulling together a follow up piece. He was getting quite excited about it."

"Any idea what that was about?" asked Jeremy. He could have made a good guess.

"It was local stuff again, you know, Falmouth and around. There was this boat operator, up and down the river. The one you spoke of, from Liverpool. He'd actually contacted Francis after reading this, the Trembath piece. He had another story from the '30s. something to do with the war in Spain."

"Related in some way?"

"I've come to think that. I didn't at the time, and I'm not sure if even Francis did."

"And that was when the offer came to work for the *Chronicle.* Somewhere I've a copy of their obituary for him." The hand that moved towards the folder was checked by the woman's.

"So have I," she said, and as she spoke an arrival rumbled in, causing her to look to the window. It was announced to be from Paddington, and bound for Penzance. The stations were listed ....
Liskeard, Lostwithiel, Par, St Austell, Truro.... Again in her eyes there was that trace of grief.

"I also have a cutting from The *West Briton* reporting the inquest into Rory Duggan's death. It was of he that you spoke just now, when you mentioned a boat operator. The boat was the *Viceroy.* He fell from it just above Tolverne. He was mooring. He was on his own. It was almost dark. He'd been drinking, allegedly. 'Accidental,' the court said."

"I cut that out too. I sent it out to Francis. You'll know, he was in Korea by then."

"And how did he feel about the verdict?"

"It was puzzling ...at least it was at the time. This letter came back, and it just wasn't him. There was an indifference to Duggan, and his tone was almost arrogant. It was if he now considered himself above such local issues, and also local people. It angered me. I threw it away. Later I wished I hadn't."

"So with Duggan buried, and the Coroner's business done, he and the *Viceroy* faded from memory."

"Certainly from mine, and seemingly from Francis's," confirmed the woman. "And Francis himself was getting to be more remote. From where I sat the war work was changing him. Privately I had concerns over what was going to come back."

"But he never came back of course," prompted Jeremy.

"And in a way the concerns I'd had helped me get over his death, helped me to move on. It was as if I felt that the best part of him had been already lost. People didn't know this. They were surprised how quickly I met and married John. He's a good man."

"But not quite as special." Now Jeremy was probing.

"But that's not his fault. He's been a devoted husband and father." To Jeremy this rang of consolation. Something remained unfulfilled. "Getting away from Cornwall, staying away, the kids, the work, all was going fine, until one evening early in '57........and since then I've had a ghost to contend with. A phantom, raised in my mind by the one person who perhaps got closer to Francis than myself."

"The guy you mentioned on the doorstep. The American you thought I'd met."

"Ben McKinley...... He, too, was a front line journalist. I think with one of the Washington papers. He'd got to know Francis in Korea and what he'd remembered as unusual was Francis being assigned singly to a US Unit, and this of course had isolated him from the rest of the Fleet Street pack. He was busy, sending plenty of copy back for the paper, but he could never be sure how much of it was being used. According to Ben he'd attempted to get some kind of feed back by mentioning this in the letters that he was sending to me. But my letters seemed to ignore this anxiety, which he at first found puzzling, and then frustrating, and eventually, of course, annoying."

Jeremy understood.

"And this came as a revelation, because whatever he'd written there was nothing of this in the letters you read. With the help of Mr McKinley you had to conclude that the letters you received were in fact written by someone else."

"And if it was happening in one direction......"

".........then it was likely to have been happening in both," completed Jeremy.

"And this means that while I'd written and told him of Rory Duggan, and even sent what was in the *Briton* about the inquest, actually none of this reached him."

"So can we assume that Duggan's tale, and also his accidental death, in some way touched upon an extremely sensitive issue? And this issue, was it likewise bound up with what Francis had or hadn't written about Edward Trembath and his neighbour, Mrs Copeland? Was there any suggestion of this from the American? He and Francis would have been following the ebb and flow of battle. Did he say if your man was giving any thought to Cornwall?"

"Well according to McKinley the ebb and flow as it had been in the back half of '50 tended towards a stagnation as '51 wore on, and this gave the pair of them ample time to reflect on their differing perceptions of events. They learned from each other. From the American, Francis heard that however the US government might seek to cloak their intentions abroad, at home big business made no secret of what they saw to be the challenge of the brave new post war world. It was about cultivating an ever-wider market for their products. Since '35 rearmament and war had brought vast profits. They had to be maintained."

"So communism had to be resisted, and also third world colonies had to be encouraged towards independence from their beggared European masters....where possible into a dependence on Uncle Sam." The woman gave a nodded approval as she lifted her cup to take a sip of tea. "And what did the American learn from Francis?"

"He said he learned about wartime Cornwall, and just how comprehensive the GI occupation was during the year before D Day. He also learned about the British Conservative Party and what a thoroughly mixed up and crippled creature it had become during those dozen cataclysmic years since '38 and the trauma of Munich. My guess is that Francis pointed out the contrast between Ida Copeland and Edward Trembath."

"The first a champion of the gold standard, the imperialistic device by which the value of profits from abroad could be upheld... provided the products were in place and the market protected. The second, one ready to entertain a more flexible currency so as to facilitate reconstruction, welfare, and job creation at home." The woman just shrugged. Jeremy apologised. He was sounding too much the lecturer.

"What about Rory Duggan" he continued. "You've said your news of his death never reached Francis, but was there any indication that he spoke of the man anyway?"

"I know they'd discussed the Spanish Civil war generally, and the American attitude to the thing. And also the fact that Duggan was certainly looked after by the Americans when they were in Cornwall. As well as the boat they even let him have one of the Trembath's cottages. That was when they requisitioned the estate."

"But it would seem that it was not until 57 that McKinley at last learned of Duggan's death. Six years after, was he ready to draw any conclusions?"

"He was, but I made it clear to him that I didn't want to know about them. And he respected that. He saw how I was set up, husband, kids, house, job, and he didn't want me getting into any bother. But one thing he did say was this. He'd looked at some back issues of the *Chronicle,* those from'51 which carried reports attributed to Francis. He said he wasn't there."

"Who wasn't where?"

"Francis.....the despatches printed by the paper were about events at places which were miles away from where they were actually working." Jeremy sensed a chill rising from his lower back. It spread to his shoulders and then down to his hands and to his fingers. He gulped at his tea. Even that was suddenly cold.

She watched him, reading his thoughts, she could see he was groping for words. Eventually he spoke.

"Were he to have found this out he'd have been a lot more than livid." The woman nodded him on. "So much so, he'd have been a danger."

"Which means?" She prompted.

"That he was going to have to be silenced. That his death was predictable...... planned. Was this confirmed by McKinley? Was that his conclusion, that he'd befriended someone unknowingly under sentence of death, someone awaiting execution?"

Linda Taylor had maintained an impressive composure. Now it dissolved. Hands went to a bowed face. She was weeping. Others turned and Jeremy was up from his seat and around to her side. He crouched. She clung. He consoled.

"Do weep Linda," he whispered. "Share it. Let it out. You've waited long enough."

It was remorse that surfaced first, quaking from deep within in stilted, sob shredded sentences.

"I should have known, I should have known those letters to me weren't his, I should have seen that it was just his name in the paper and not his work. It was what happened before with the Plymouth paper."

"You weren't to know Linda, not until long afterwards and by then too late. You can't blame yourself. You know that. For your family's sake you can't. If he could speak to us now Francis would say the same. Wouldn't he?"

"But to have been so far away, on his own, in such danger......."

"He was there, out in Korea, because he wanted to be. Just as before him it had been Duggan's choice to come to Cornwall. For both there were safer places, but that was never the point, was it? Not for either of them. Be proud of Francis, be proud of yourself for having known him, for having encouraged him in his work. Many might have been bought off, not he. You saw that, they saw that. That's why they never tried."

"McKinley said the same," sniffed Linda, rallying a little now.

"Was *he* ready to be bought off do you think?" asked Jeremy, and for a second as she looked up there was a glint of suspicion in her eyes. But then she remembered the earnestness of the American. He'd loved Francis as much as she. The moment passed.

"I'd say not, if only because he risked quite a lot in coming to see me when he did. But having seen Francis blunder into a trap he was naturally wary. On Francis's death, he went with the official version of the jeep and the explosion...... but these things can be contrived, he knew that. Francis had been a marked man, and if Ben was minded to make anything of it then so would he be too."

"So it was just you he contacted?" asked Jeremy.

"Two others. One a friend of Duggan's called Jack Butters, near blind he was then. The other was a man called Arthur Stanaway, Francis's boss at *The Falmouth Packet*. McKinley found him at a nursing Home in Plymouth, close to death. Like me, Arthur felt that he hadn't done enough for Francis. I escaped to here, a new life. His solace was the bottle. It killed him. To the end I'd get a Christmas card. It was through Stanaway that McKinley traced me, and it was from Stanaway that the American obtained this."

The woman's shoulder bag sat on the floor, resting against her seat. She reached into it and drew out a book. The faded red hard cover carried no words. With her fingers around the spine both title and author were as yet obscure, and for the moment it was remaining in her hands. She was in no hurry to pass it across.

"He'd read it by the time he got here, or at least those parts that poor old Arthur had been sober enough to mark."

"And he left it for you?"

"For me to hand to the likes of yourself, actually. I was told that should anyone ever come to me with the kind of enquiry that you've just brought then even should I be reluctant to talk I should pass this on.....for Francis's sake, he said."

"But you're not so terribly reluctant, are you?" Jeremy observed.

"A lot less than I once was."

"And it's had a place on your shelves since '57?"

"Twice it's moved house with me. It's an autobiography, written in the early '50s when a lot of the recollections were then quite recent. It mainly covers the between the wars years and much of the backdrop would have been fairly fresh in the public memory. The author tells of his early career as an aircraft designer, and then of his time as a director of a small company that actually constructed and attempted to market the things. It was tough going, in both respects."

"Cash strapped times," remarked the historian. "Did this company make any sort of name for itself?"

"Airspeed," announced the woman casually, oblivious to any significance the word might carry for the listener.

"So you're going to read me that book are you? You'll find me hanging on every word." Jeremy somehow contrived to sound less eager and sincere than he actually was, and perhaps that was as well.

"Extracts for now, as underlined and numbered by Arthur Stanaway, and subsequently put to me by Ben McKinley....here in this very buffet. At one time I used to rehearse reading these, even got to know some of it by heart."

"Just read," urged Jeremy, almost rudely. "The long prepared for performance can begin."

"The full title of the book is *'Slide Rule-- The Autobiography of an Engineer.'* You'll hear the author's name as I read. In this opening piece he tells of his first job in the aircraft industry, working for Captain de Havilland, the co founder of the company that bore his name.

'The policy of the firm at the time (1921) was to make its living by designing and selling civil aeroplanes rather than military ones. The greater freedom from Air Ministry interference suited the genius of the directors for one thing, but to a great extent the policy arose from de Havilland's strong antipathy to war and anything to do with it.'

I think Stanaway chose this as a starting to underscore the fact that the good Captain's antipathy seemed not to have been shared by the then young author. Soon he was moving on;-

' In the autumn of 1924 I left de Havillands, with some regret. It was a delightful company to work for, but it was staffed by seniors who were all young men and all vastly more experienced than I was, so that no promotion could be rapid. In aviation at that time there were opportunities on every side for those with the wit to take them, and Mr B.N. Wallis, who was then a designer of rigid airships working for Vickers Ltd, was gathering together a staff for the design of a very large airship to be known as the R. 100. I joined this staff in the capacity of Chief Calculator...."

'Vickers'..... this Stanaway character had had something, Jeremy was convinced. 'Airspeed' on its own might have been coincidental, but the two names, the same as were paired in Duggan's log, they were going to have to be somehow related. Jeremy wanted that book, badly. He was careful though. He slipped back into his chair. This woman was happier now. Having owned to misreading her Francis, she was welcoming an opportunity to atone. He'd been half a world away and so, so vulnerable. She'd known in her heart that something was wrong, and she ought to have found some way....but how?

At last, she could now at least do this, and Jeremy was of course ready to encourage. He was attentiveness itself.

"Vickers, yes they made arms at that time," he commented. "One of the biggest they were, building tanks and cannon and machine guns. They built warships, and also military aircraft. That would be the Barnes Wallis who famously became a sky bombing specialist....the dam busters and all that."

"He built airships?"

"Looks like he did," said Jeremy. "This was the '20s remember. Back then planes were small. It was thought that only an airship could lift and carry anything big, bomb-wise......as the German Zeppelins had during the Great War. For the while, defence money and brainpower was still going into balloon technology."

"And a short while it must have been," continued Linda Taylor, "for within six years it was clear to the author that wings were the future. He left Vickers to start his own company."

"......Airspeed," nodded Jeremy.

"Yes, and it's said here in his book to have been for the construction of civil aircraft. And that may have been so at the time, but times do change. For the next extract I have to jump ahead a little, a further six years, the point being to show that as another war loomed the tuition received from Mr Wallis was starting to prove useful:-

'By the beginning of 1936 an order for seven Envoys had been received from the South African State Railways. It reflected the condition of the world at that time, that these were civil aeroplanes for use on an airline but they were to be readily convertible to military purposes. Bomb racks and release gear were to be provided, a mounting for a forward firing gun, and the roof of the lavatory was detachable and replaceable by another roof which carried a gun turret.' "

"Forgive me," pleaded a tactful Jeremy, "we do seem to have flown some way from Spain. Is there a relevance here to Duggan?"

"Stanaway thought so," asserted the reader, " as did McKinley. Just hear me through."

"Carry on. I'm sorry."

She did:-

"The product was being sold openly to South Africa, we are told that. We are told also that the model's development had been progressing rather less openly over the previous eighteen months or so, the thrust of the programme being the designing and the testing of an *Envoy* with an enhanced speed, power, and a range."

"..... an upgrade on its initial civilian use specification."

"Quite, and then, so as to impress potential purchasers with verified performance, it was the usual thing to enter modified aircraft into international races. There was a succession of such competitions during the '30s. These days intercontinental flying is commonplace....."

"Contrasting with then, when it was more a sport.... endurance being the test as much as speed."

"And that's counting the personal endurance of the pilots."

"They were celebrities."

"And exciting times they were," continued Linda Taylor," the more so because of the parlous financial state of many of the companies."

"Who were having to compete for capital as well as customers."

Jeremy was succinct. Eager he was to hear more.

"And *Airspeed* was no exception. The author is happy to admit as much. Listen as he chronicles the re-launch of his firm as *Airspeed (1934) Ltd*. I'm moving back to the start of chapter 9. The author writes:-

Two extracts from the minutes of Board meetings in the last weeks of the old company are of interest.

On 15/6/34;

The amendments of the prospectus were read and discussed, particularly the Directors' statements as regards the profits payable in the first year. Certain alterations were agreed upon, which Mr Norway *(he being the author)* undertook to see were made in the next proof.

And on 22/6/34;

Mr Norway reported that considerable delay had been caused in the progress of the (share) issue by the auditors taking very drastic action and views in regard to orders in hand, value of stock, and profits made, and he expressed the opinion that their action had been in no way helpful to the Company.

Writing on, Mr Norway straightway offers what looks to be a candid admission:-

'At the time I was acquiring a reputation with my co directors, and with my City associates for a reckless optimism that came close to dishonesty. I think this bad reputation was deserved, for having set my hand to Airspeed and brought it so far up the road to success I was intolerant of obstacles that seemed to me to be based upon an ultra conservative and pedantic view of business. ....Each year our competitors with their superior organisation lowered the cost of civil aeroplanes, and overall there was now the change from wood construction to metal becoming imminent, with all the vast incalculable capital expenditure that that change would involve..... All we knew in 1934 was that the capital requirements of a company in the aircraft business were rising very quickly, and the only safe course was to gather in as much as we could get hold of.'

Now what do you make of that?" the reader then asked, looking up.

"This Mr Norway, he appears to have attracted criticism for deliberately understating costs incurred, losses sustained. He was suspected of exaggerating the value to the company of unsold planes, both complete and incomplete, and perhaps also by entering 'maybees' in the order book as 'certs'. "

"You're listening Mr Barnes. That's good, for what we get from the man now is an attempt to persuade us that his optimism was more calculated than blind:-

I knew instinctively that if war should break out anywhere in the world every civil aeroplane of any size would sell immediately for military transportation or even as an improvised light bomber.... I was determined to resist any attempt on the part of the auditors or anybody else to write down their value in our accounts.'

On the following page we read of a number of repossessed aircraft.

'My hunch that this was the right course was justified. They all came back to us when the operating company suspended operations a year later, but shortly after that the Spanish Civil War broke out and the machines sold immediately to various intermediaries for better than the original prices, and all went by devious routes to Spain. I do not think that Airspeed ever failed to sell a speculative aeroplane that we had built for stock at the full price; wars came eventually to clean up the position for us.' "

" It's an ill wind..." remarked Jeremy, too gripped to think of anything more original.

"Indeed," said the reader, "but there's a question mark here, in the margin. Even when drunk Stanaway was adept at reading between the lines. McKinley saw this and he made sure I was under no illusions. These planes, he said, were almost certainly being recovered from operating companies who were hire purchase customers, small, desperately undercapitalised airlines......"

"......hoping to pay their way in time, but looking first to get things off the ground."

"And, under cash flow pressure, they were likely to default by a few days on their agreed weekly or monthly or quarterly repayments. This is where Mr Norway, himself under audit pressure, seems to have been very much on his toes. To have been patient would have risked giving first bite at the distressed cherry to the banks and the bailiffs. He has a queue of cash customers at the shop door and they're all ready to pay double for the same thing, no matter that it's been used."

"So he'll have his heavies there, in a matter of hours......."

".........to throw off cargoes or even passengers if necessary, to take summary possession. That's why Stanaway questions the phrase *'when the operating company suspended operations'*. And I know that this is what actually happened. I've spoken with one of these operators quite recently. You're the first I've told. Five years ago now, I was listening to the afternoon radio. 'Woman's Hour' the programme was. This lady was being interviewed. She was in her 80s then, and to start with she was speaking of early century motor rallying, the Brooklands events, and the Monte Carlo, things like that."

"She competed?" asked Jeremy.

"She won prizes, set records. And after that, in the early 1930s, she took up flying....with much the same success. In '37 she sets up a small airline, *'Air Dispatch Ltd'*, based at Croydon. The idea was to fly newspapers across to Paris for English speaking tourists."

"And she obtained her planes from *Airspeed*, on HP," ventured Jeremy.

"She did, and there, out of the blue I'm hearing the firm's name on this radio programme. And she's telling the nation how they moved in and almost put her out of business for being just two days late with a single installment."

"Was there mention of the war in Spain?"

"Not in the programme, but it did come up later, on the phone, after I'd written to her."

" Asking her...?."

"....more specifically about the type of aircraft *Airspeed* had supplied her with. She'd talked of her *Envoys*, and these, she explained later, were fetching good money in Spain. The author tells of 'various intermediaries'..."

"Sales agents," Jeremy put in, "of the confidential variety.

There's a whiff of Greene running strongly through all of this."

"But these were selling them to both sides in the conflict, the demand having been heightened by one particular model which had been especially modified for the October '34 'MacRobertson' race from England to Australia. We can read of this event in the book. Arthur Stanaway did, and he came to the view the fate of that machine came to have a bearing on the fate of Rory Duggan. Ben McKinley agreed, and after actually speaking with Mildred Bruce I'm fairly sure they were on the right track."

"So let's hear about this plane, the racing *Envoy*." Jeremy was all eagerness.

"As originally conceived the *Envoy* was a short haul passenger and light parcel carrier. On this one the seating and hold space was cut to accommodate a much larger fuel tank, the additional weight to be lifted by an up-rating of the two wing mounted engines. Along with its racing speed the plane looked to have power to spare, and also a lengthened reach."

Linda Taylor flicked on to the next marked page.

"The author further records:-

'It was so much modified from the Envoy that we gave it another type of name, and christened it the Viceroy.'

......a name you've heard before? "

"I have," Jeremy whispered.

"From her working up performances many saw the machine as the likely race winner. Amongst them was the pilot who, having secured the plane for a deposit, was confident that the prize money would meet the full price. There could be profit then from selling it on in Australia, or perhaps in acting as a middleman for the order and the delivery of more of the same....... to wherever along the route the machine might attract that kind of interest. Mr McKinley was ready to suggest that some people were so impressed that they were reluctant to see such a specimen disappear from the Northern Hemisphere. It seems that on starting the race the plane was afflicted by a series of minor faults and these caused it to get no further than Athens."

"The implication being that these faults derived from measured acts of minor sabotage, perpetrated by the makers even....."

"...who'd been tempted by the better money all of a sudden being waved at them from elsewhere."

"His speculation ruined, the pilot wouldn't have been a happy man. Did he suspect?"

"If he did, what could he prove? Nothing. He was obliged to return the plane and accept too that his deposit was lost. The plane comes back and surprise, surprise, we read that shortly afterwards of Airspeed being approached by an agent working on behalf of Emperor Haile Selassie of Abyssinia."

"Who was having to defend his nation against Mussolini, and do it virtually alone, despite a plea to the League of Nations." The historian was on familiar territory.

"According to the author, this agent brought an enquiry about the one and only *Viceroy:*-

' *"Tell me Mr Norway, could we fit bomb racks underneath the wings?..."*

I told (the agent) that I was fitting no bomb racks, that I was selling a civil aeroplane to be delivered on our aerodrome at Portsmouth to his company, a British concern. He then asked if I would provide certain lugs under the wings to which they could attach anything they liked, and I agreed to this.....

The army of Haile Selassie had no hope of standing up against the Italian invaders of their country unless modern arms and equipment could reach them. The job of the Viceroy was to bomb the Italian oil storage tanks at Masawa and so halt their mechanised advance......this mission was well within the capabilities of the machine. It was, however, vital to maintain complete secrecy, because if the Italians were to get to know about the Viceroy they would move a squadron of first class fighters from Italy to defend Masawa, with the result that the plane would almost certainly be shot down.' "

The reader paused so that her listener might comment. He did.

"Fascism, generally, took heart from the Italian action against Abyssinia. As it did from the Manchurian incident. The League might have made the right noises, but what did it do?"

Linda Taylor answered by pressing on.

"The author then explains how he assisted with training the

pilots who'd been engaged by the agent to deliver the plane and also take it into action:-

'.....by that time I had reason to believe that the Foreign Office knew all about the venture, and were friendly to it....'
But......

'It proved impossible to get the supplies of bombs and fuel to Abyssinia in time....and by the end of April the Emperor had been defeated..... The Viceroy never left our works. So far as I can remember, it was finished and paid for but resting in our works till it was time for it to fly to Abyssinia, for they did not want it to be seen on public aerodromes.'
Nevertheless.....

'It was sold again quite soon...' "

"One would hope the money going to the exiled Emperor," interjected Jeremy, again to be ignored by the woman.

" *'An air race (yet another) was announced from London to Johannesburg in October 1936, and two well known British pilots, Max Findlay and Ken Waller, secured finance to take part in this race and came to us and bought the Viceroy.'*
Now, Ben McKinley reckoned that this finance was provided by the South African government, the *Viceroy* being as close as made no difference to the convertible *Envoys* which had been ordered by the State Railway airline earlier in that same year. There was every indication that had it reached the finishing line then it would have been thrown in to make a job lot with that other seven. As it happened though, it was never even to make the start line."

"More chicanery?" Jeremy asked, faintly smiling.

"At this point Mr Norway's narrative becomes markedly ragged. McKinley suspected a selective memory. Mildred Bruce shared the suspicion. She commended Mr Norway to me as a writer of fiction."

Jeremy assumed her to be again referring to the sanguine business projections. Had he said this then Linda Taylor might have enlightened him. Instead she read on.

"They made a strong team (Findlay and Waller), for the machine was very fast and capable of carrying a crew of four including a radio operator. They were regarded as very likely winners of the race. In July 1936 however, the civil war in Spain broke out and an agent of some continental nationality came to them and wanted to buy the Viceroy.

They told him the machine was not for sale.

Between friends, he said, everything could be arranged.

They said they weren't interested in his friendship. They weren't selling.

He said that was no way to talk between friends. He knew how much they had paid Airspeed for it. They had paid £5,500.

They said that it was nothing to do with him. They were going to fly the Viceroy in the Johannesburg race and win the first prize. The machine was not for sale. Now would he please go away and stop wasting their time.

He said that the first prize in the race was £4000. £4000 and £5,500 made £9,500. So that they would not have to fly at all and could save the cost of the petrol, he would give them the cheque right away.

They took it, cashed it and saw that it was good, and handed over the Viceroy, which left for France without delay and was never seen again.'"

Linda Taylor looked up. An arched brow now begged a response.

"Sweeteners," responded Jeremy.

"McKinley thought that. As well as the cash mentioned there would have been other inducements and not just for the pilots. For *Airspeed* there could well have been the prospect of further orders, and perhaps diplomatic pressure was being brought to bear.....but that was beside the main point."

"Which was? " pressed the lecturer.

"That the prototype fighting *Envoy* had been diverted towards Spain, and that it was likely to have been followed by a number of civilian machines, some newly constructed, others repossessed from defaulting HP purchasers. While being sold and delivered these could be passed off as-non military equipment, on arrival though their warplane potential could be swiftly realised."

"As with those that went to South Africa."

Linda Taylor nodded concurrence.

"This is it," she said. "The international embargo that restricted the sale of weapons to Spain could be to an extent dodged. With the template there, in the shape of the *Viceroy,* it was a relatively simple matter to fashion or to ship in the appropriate attachments and then fit them as per the designer's instructions."

"So where lay the author's sympathies in the conflict?"

"There's no mention, and it's not strictly relevant. To whom the hardware went, and how, was a matter for the agents. Norway's concern was getting the best price. His loyalty was to his fellow directors and shareholders, and also to his workforce. It is known that *Envoys* found their way to both sides, but then there's the complication of one side capturing equipment sold to the other. Betrayal sometimes played a part in this. There were agents who weren't above selling arms to one side and then selling information as to transit arrangements to their enemy. It was open season for double dealing, and Stalin's mob were in there leading the way."

"I was only yesterday thinking of the *Mar Cantabrico* and her shipment of aircraft components. How she famously won her race against the US Congress to load and to sail from New York, but alas into a trap. One laid by Franco's people with the assistance of waterfront informants. It was something similar that Duggan was on to, don't you think? a variation on the same theme, smaller in scale, some five months later, and this time out of Falmouth. Duggan wasn't meant to be the fall guy, but that's how it worked out later, with the Russians coming into World War Two when the Battle of the Atlantic was at its height."

"Smaller in scale of incident maybe," said the woman, with care, "but larger in scale of cover up, much larger it seems. Some people were wary of Duggan, others had different grounds to be wary of Francis. Suddenly there was the prospect of the two getting together. That was alarming to all. Stanaway smelt a rat, I'm sure.... and McKinley, I think, was ready to identify the actual species. He needed to be careful though, very careful."

"Why was that do you think?"

"You tell me," the woman challenged him.

Jeremy opened his folder and out of all he'd copied and collected he drew out the most recently acquired. He held it in front of Linda Taylor. The page comfortably covered her book.

"This man," he said bluntly. "Has he been mentioned to you at all, perhaps by the American? When was it he came here?"

" '57, and that might have been significant. He didn't give the actual name. He was oblique. He suggested that I check out a few of the former Cabinet Ministers who'd served under the recently replaced Mr Eden, and who'd been raised to a peerage along with their old boss. He told me to look at the dates on which they'd first been elected to the Commons, and also where they'd worked before, and who they'd worked with. He left it at that, and so shall I. He saw I had my hands full with the youngsters. He didn't want me attracting trouble. His concern became to leave me well enough prepared for the time when someone such as yourself might eventually knock. Now you have, and you're showing me this, and I can see our conclusions..... yours , mine, and McKinley's, will closely match."

"And you never heard from McKinley again, he didn't leave a contact address or anything? "

"For the same reason," the woman replied. "He said that in the States he was a marked man, he was being watched, closely. And he expected things to get worse, for already he was questioning his country's attitude to Vietnam."

"He saw what was going to happen."

"He did I think, but before embarking on that crusade he wanted to leave a marker for anyone attempting to fathom Duggan's death. That done he was anxious to be clean away again, as I said, thinking of me, and John, and the kids."

"Your author, Mr Norway, the engineer, is he still alive?"

"Died back in 1960 I'm afraid. Inconsiderate that."

"What about his customer, the lady who phoned you? "

"Still going I think, to the best of my knowledge. But she'll now be very old. Mildred Bruce was born before Norway, and the way she's going she'll outlive him by a good thirty years. I can't give you a contact though. She'd told me all she could and she was saying it just the once. I wasn't to bother her again, nor on my encouragement was anyone else. She had my promise and I don't regret giving it. From what we read now in the press not even little old ladies can feel safe with their secrets."

The point, casually made, was general. But there was a specific victim here, a particular 'little old lady' of whom Jeremy knew. He'd read of the death, and of the investigations, and he'd read too some of the theories.......... and he'd listened to Gareth's.

He couldn't let this pass, not from a person who perhaps might share a professional's insight into one nagging aspect of the case.

"This is Hilda you're talking about, the rose grower from Shrewsbury. Talk to me about telephones. Hers had been interfered with, that's what they say. What's the buzz on this in the trade? Was there a tap? "

Linda Taylor was thoughtful. There was her husband's position to consider, or if not that then at least his pension. How might he have reacted to this? But then there'd been Francis too, and herself. Hadn't they trusted the Post Office, and hadn't that been a trust betrayed?

"Every indication suggests there was," she replied. "And some of the calls the police made both before and after the finding of the body......they wouldn't bear too close a scrutiny. But we're not going to get any further with that one, neither of us, not sitting here. You've had as much as you're going to get from me, apart from this book. You can take that, and also a final piece of advice given to me by Mildred. This wasn't the only thing that Mr Norway wrote. There were other things he did before the war, between the airship work for Vickers and the *Airspeed* venture. Have a look at some of that, she said."

"Technical journals I suppose," muttered Jeremy, but Linda Taylor was already on her feet. She thanked him for the tea, offered a curt farewell, and left. The book, Arthur Stanaway's book, lay open still on the table. Jeremy reached for it. He turned it, at the same time lifting slightly so as to peer beneath at the title on the spine and at the author's name written below.

*

" 'ilda ? 'ilda M'rrell ? Yes, I've 'eard mention of she. It' ve bin on the wireless 'ere two or three time, an' you knaw each 'ccaision it's brought Rory Duggan to mind. 't were the way things 's bin 'nvented. "

"By whom? " asked Gareth.

"By they that ought t' knaw bedder. They said Rory 'd bin drinkin, but not when I'd seen 'n 'e 'adn't. An' if that were a tide what took 'n where 'e were found then that were a funny bleddy tide. Jus' like it would 've bin a funny bleddy burglar who spent time fiddlin' with the old lady's phone set, an' then took 'er out t' where she were found dumped, on the way to 'n old airfield some 've said. One laid out by the 'mericans back in the war."

"Duggan, did he say anything to you about Americans? They helped him didn't they? Back in the war, they trusted him and gave him his boat, the *Viceroy*. Isn't this the tale? "

"This were 'ow I telled it to McKinley."

"McKinley? I've not heard that name yet. Sounds American," said Gareth.

" 'e were 'merican. 'e comed 'ere jus' the once, near thirty year 'go now. Me eyes was jus' 'bout cap'ble of makin' 'n out.... smart boy 'e were. 'e 'd knawd Cairns you see. They'd met t'gether out 'n Korea. Cairns must'v' said for'n t' come 'n see me, an' 'e did, jus' that once. I were never t' see or 'ear from 'n 'gain."

"And he was a journalist too?" asked the Welshman.

" 'e were, an' Cairns 'ad told 'n 'bout Rory an' also told 'n 'bout a piece 'e 'd already put in the Plymouth paper....Th' *Ind'pen'ent*. 'earin' this 'n seein' ow our boy were bein' 'eld in virtual quar'ntine, an' then 'ow 'e were killed this McKinley were sayin, that they 'ad to 'ave bin 'fraid of 'n, the top people."

"In London, at the paper, *The Chronicle*?"

" 'twad'n London 'e were thinkin' of, more Washington. When I says to 'n that Rory Duggan were useful to the 'mericans back in the war, e says t' me of that p'rhaps bein' a usefulness outlived....lit'rally. 'e'd bin a 'andy little lever fer gettin' people into place an' keepin' 'm firmly there, now they was wantin' this lever eased out..... lest others might use 'n t' loosen up what were be then bedded in good 'n firm."

" 'Others' meaning Francis Cairns, and his potential readership. The electors of Plym....."

" An' the rest. You can start with they if you want, but this were bigger. Wider, you 'as t' look, much wider, an' higher too, t' the very top."

Gareth looked perplexed. Butters continued.

"We'm into the new year now, 1951, an' within six weeks of me buryin' Rory they 'm havin' a by 'lection up t' Bristol.....Bristol West.

That's best place t' start. That's where 'e did, the 'merican, McKinley."
Gareth still looked perplexed.

" S'bversion, that were McKinley's word fer 't all. It were comin'
t' be the work of what 'e called their Central 'telligence Agen........"

".......CIA, " said Gareth, at last grasping a handle.

".....only then they was usin' tools 'oned by that Mr 'oover who
runned the....."

"FBI." The Welshman was starting to get the drift.

"Agent, informer, puppet...... whatever anybody were at top
level, in they days it 'ad to be on 'oover's 'pproval. 'e were the
manip'lator. 'The boss', that's what McKinley called 'n."

"And this was at top level, this subversion? "

"In this 'ere country, yes cert'nly, top table, an' likewise over
there, 'ad t' be. 'ere's why Cairns were tak'n well out of it, quar'ntined."

"And then liquidated," added Gareth. "As Duggan had been, for
knowing too much. And you've heard me say similar about my Mrs
Murrell."

" 'cept that I would n've thought 'er death so calc'lated. They
was asked over though was'n'm, these FBI. They experts they 'as was
s'pposed t' 'ssemble some sort of psychiatr'cal profile for 'elpin' our
p'lice with. That were what they put out on the wireless, last aut'mn time.
B'lieve that do 'e ?"

"It'll be part of what was going on. The part people heard about.
I can believe it, yes, but I believe there to be more. We're at a critical
time in the Cold War. The West must be together, strong. If London and
Washington bind the others won't flake, but suddenly from Washington
there's a seepage of sensitive information. It's perceived to carry a
corrosive potential. A wider spillage might be catastrophic. The leak
must be contained, and it is, but first off in a hasty, clumsy, crude
manner. The traces are going to need tidying up, covering up.......and
that's why they came, to make sure everything was tied down, no loose
ends."

" 'an all you 'as is spec'lation, spec'lation based on what've
already bin writ off as wartime propaganda...."

Gareth was used to this. He ignored it.

"But you know more about the *Kampala* than you've been
letting on. You told Steve she had a Spanish crew, but you've known
otherwise throughout. You sent the boy on a fool's errand."

"Oft'n it do take a fool. The inn'cent 'll sometimes get easiest to th 'eart of things. Take Carwinion. There's new stuff I'm learnin' 'bout the place even now, an' that comes from the boy goin' in there talkin'. An' you bin' usin'm the same. Didn' you tell me earlier 'bout that bullet? You says I knaws a bit 'bout that ship, an' maybe I 'as learned a thing or two since 'er bin up there, but that id'n t' say I knaws who her 'd bin carryin' 'round three year 'go. "

"But you've worked out Mr Alan Grigson, I don't doubt, and why we had our morning on the *Kampala*. "

" 'e were the one I 'oped would be pickin' up on what I gived to the boy. 'nstead it's been that other one , Jeremy. What to make of 'e I id'n so sure. But there 'tis now. 't were in my 'ands long 'nough.''

"And the ferry hand, this 'Baz', surprise me and tell me that you've not got an angle on his link with the *Kampala*."

"You'll knaw 'er was back 'ere fer a fortnight or so late in '83. Dry docked, jus' fer a buck up after a long 'n busy South 'lantic winter. At the time this 'ere Baz were down there in Falmouth too. 'e were with an RFA vessel...."

"........ the *Fort Belmont*."

" I 'eard 'n radio 'cross to the Kampala when she 'rrived. 'e were doin' the tellin' as t' what were t' be shut down, an' what were t' be locked away, an' who was t' be 'llowed into diff'rent parts of the ship. 't was clear 'e were more than RFA. Then this year young Jack takes me up through the passage on *Flush* an' I catches 'is voice...... an' I knaws then that that there Baz is a good deal more than a ferry'and."

*

Within twenty minutes Jeremy was in his car and leaving Exeter. A further hour and he was again in Cornwall, at *Jamaica Inn,* resting in the broad car park. For a tired man he'd driven more than far enough, but though the eyes were weary there was still no sleep.

In Exeter he'd found relief, it was in the talking of the past. He was returning to a harsh present, and all its pain. With each mile the revived anger was re-intensifying, and still there were more than thirty ahead. He would get back, and she would perform, put on an act, and yes, he would too.... the hurt, though, would be solely his.

And there was another one down there who was taking him for a mug. Wizened, withered Jack Butters was now revealed wily also. The American had travelled far, and at considerable risk. He'd reached Mylor, and he'd brought pivotal information. What had the old man said of this? He'd said nothing.

He'd had to find out for himself, which he'd done...... but was this in spite of the old man, or was it because of him? Had his lines of enquiry really been freely chosen, or had there been a subtle manipulation?

That errand given to Steve, getting those documents onto the *Kampala*, it had been a fool's errand. Jack Butters had had months, years even, to get the things to Spain. Instead he'd been sitting on them, almost as if in defiance of his original instructions, only to produce them ostensibly for a group of 'Spaniards'.....who were no such thing!

Would a man as careful as he wait this many years to bungle things so? Of course not..... it had to be calculated. But to what end?

To a fitting end...... for he was fashioning a finale. He'd fathomed the facts long ago. Invention wasn't required, nor trickery. He'd simply had to bide his time, and this he'd done, trusting, hoping that the moment would arrive, and at last it had. It had arrived with the *Kampala*.

There she was, an epitome of post Imperial Micawberism. Built for the Suez route she'd weathered the winds of change and adapted to the reduced means of her mother country. But to come to this.....accommodating a tawdry barter, guns for drugs!! What could better symbolise the gimcrack New Toryism hawked so cynically, so successfully, to the electorate back in '83.

And who was behind it? It was them again... who else. How sad, how Thatcherist.

And this blind old man was reading her, every inch of her. He was in this game big style, playing cannily from what was a strong and closely held hand. He was playing to win, and yesterday Jeremy would have been content to see him do so, together with Alan, and Gareth, and Jane. But not now, for overnight he'd drawn the wild card..... ANGER!

The past, as found in Exeter, offered some sanctuary. But returning to Cornwall was having to again face the present and here the rage was consuming him still, wave upon wave, obliterating rationality, each backwash scouring an ever deeper despair, and the fatigue, ever that fatigue. How could he let them win. He'd gone for them, to impress them, to help them, and it was to them that he'd been bringing back the insight won. And to meet what?.....Betrayal.

They didn't deserve, not if it left him the loser. What could they do anyway? What could he do? What they were against was too big, too powerful. It wasn't to be beaten, and neither was he. This left but one course.

If you can't beat them..........

*

"I'd given up on you," glowered Jane. There was no name. There was no smile. This girl was not happy.

"Well I'd told you where I'd be," pleaded Steve. "In fact I think I've done well to be here by now." And this was true. Hugh had again brought him most of the way. Having returned his father to Carwinion the man had had to make straight for his shift at Porthscatho. The girl pouted. Rinsed out crockery dinned onto the metal drainer.

"Is this about your mother?" Steve's voice carried concern. It was calming.

"Not this time," responded Jane, a shade less irritably.

"Your father?"

"In a way, but the actual person is Alan." Steve waited but Jane wasn't going to continue, not before at least a little encouragement. It came.

"He's upset you?"

"It's the way he's just upping and leaving. Just like that, without saying where he's going, or when he's coming back, or leaving anything that could tell anyone what he's been doing here. When he goes, what then? What'll be left with us that we can work with?"

"And you want...?"

"Something written down, and preferably sworn to be true. Something a lawyer could use."

302

"And you think a surveillance man is going to leave such a heavy footprint as that? He wouldn't be allowed to." Steve reached for her hand. It was given, but not unreservedly, her tongue loosing a 'tut' of frustration. "I know it's harder for you," he continued, "but we just have to trust the guy. You're thinking about all these boats, *Kampala, Speedwell,* the Russians', and you'll be worrying that they can all be here today, gone tomorrow." She squeezed his fingers, a reward for listening, and almost understanding.

"Remember," he went on, "he wouldn't have included us without clearance from above, and they've given this because we've been deemed a risk to ourselves...."

"......as well as to the outcome of their precious operation," countered the girl. "I reckon they're looking to reserve their position all the way up. At top level they'll be wanting to offer their political masters an option of letting it all go, of nodding things through in the name of some greater good."

Steve merely nodded. He'd heard something like this before. The Board of Trade came to mind. Take care, he thought. Paranoia was lurking. Jane was adamant.

"Well I'm not having it," she insisted. "We get my father out. That's what's paramount. Nothing matters more."

"We see Alan tomorrow evening," said Steve, "you can have this out with him then, and on your own ground. I'm waiting to see Jeremy again. I'm getting into his historical slant. Did you know he's in London for the weekend?"

*

"So what you'm sayin' of 'ere, Gareth, is that you'm thinkin' that tomorrow evenin's goin' t'be creddiggle." Old Jack spoke firmly.

"I am, because our Mr Grigson is letting people know that the following morning he'll be sailing back along the coast. Put with that tomorrow evening's get together at Philleigh and yes, I do see opportunity for mischief, dangerous mischief. I'll be at the meeting of course, and so will the others, but I want his boat watched. if I do nothing and injury or death happens, be it preventable or not, then I'll be struggling to forgive myself."

"This were Rory's thinkin' out in Biscay. When 'e wen' 'gainst they orders wad 'e 'ad."

"And I'm saying we honour his memory, and that of the lad you said went to Korea. And I've told you about Hilda, and I've mentioned Brian, and there's another one in jail for nothing. I'll not have that list getting any longer on my account."

"So you'm settin' up your own liddle piece 'v I spy, an fer 'elp you'm recruitin' a man who's bin blind now for near on thirdy year."

"Because you, more than any of us, know the full story...... and also the dangers. And you have resources, resources I can use."

"Such as?"

"Your grandson, and that boat of his. I'd like him to keep a watch on Grigson's boat, the *Speedwell,* whilst it lies unattended."

"You mean while 'e's chairin' this secret meetin' you'm all 'avin'..... but which you'm 'fraid's aliddle less secret than you an' 'es bin 'opin'." As attuned as Gareth was becoming to the Butters' accent he needed time to fully appreciate the perspicacity in this last remark. The Welshman's response was delayed, and it was thoughtful.

"Actually, I hadn't considered a leak from within. I envisage a network of casual watchers, strategically selected so as to appear to be doing no more than their normal daily business. People like the owner of the yard across there, around from St. Mawes. He'll be noting Alan's movements, I'll warrant that."

"So you bin assumin your own team t'be sound?" Again Gareth wasn't rushing to answer. The words were considered.

"Because, as individuals, that's how I've found them..... but now you say 'team' perhaps there are tensions. The odd hint of rivalry, of jealousy, resentment, but that's the way in any group. These things and a lot else, negative and positive, make up the nature of the beast."

"Not fergeddin' b'trayal," mumbled the sage.

"Anyway, your grandson, young Jack, what time will he be calling here tomorrow?" Gareth was rising from his chair, moving toward the door.

"Be 'ere at one an' you'll catch'n. Take care."

1949/50

Most reluctantly, the Chancellor (Cripps) agreed to a devaluation of one third of the pound's value against the dollar to $2.80 from $4.03, and a programme of swingeing public expenditure cuts duly resulted. A public statement was agreed to in Washington and the fact of devaluation revealed to the world by Cripps on 20th September. The Chancellor regarded this as a serious economic retreat and perhaps a lasting blow to his moral authority as well.

In fact, the devaluation gave Cripps' policies further momentum......The currency reserves began to turn the corner and to mount steadily. In 1950 the economy was once again very buoyant and the balance of payments firmly entered the black. Exports soared, including remarkably to the North American markets where British 'small cars' did very well. Indeed the energy and initiative displayed by car manufacturers and salesmen was remarkable at this time, boosted by the fact that rivalry from German Volkswagens, French Renaults, and Italian Fiats lay in the future. In June 1950, at the time of the outbreak of the Korean War, Britain's economy showed all the symptoms of steady growth without overheating. It was amongst the most thriving periods economically that the country as a whole had experienced since the late-Victorian era. Cripps himself, with a strict regime of budgetary management, and with high government taxation to make up the difference between public expenditure and the goods available for private consumption, had created the basis for a new affluence.

K.O. Morgan   'The People's Peace' p 74

1985 (still the same Sunday evening.)

"Who killed Harry Oakes?"

"Not that one again," Sir Edward released a hearty chuckle into his tumbler of whisky. "If I'd had a £5 note for each time I've been asked that then I'd be even richer than Sir Harry was himself. If you've called this evening just to ask that then I'm sorry, I just don't know. The killer was never found."

"And you know why, I think," Jeremy wasn't holding back. "Like you might also know why the Murrell case is unlikely to be solved."

"Murrell?" questioned the younger Trembath. "Is this another from back in the war?"

"More recent," sighed said the father, the jokiness evaporating.

"Far more recent," re iterated the caller, encouraged by Sir Edward's decided unease. "And should we be leaping forward a shade too quickly then we might consider as well the unfortunate passing of a Mr Rory Duggan, once a tenant of yours I believe, and also the disturbingly premature death of one Francis Cairns in far away Korea. Both died within the space of a year, the year in which you won your way to Westminster."

Sir Edward gulped at the last of his drink. He stood, moving to decant a second..... speaking as he was thinking, on his feet.

"You would have read of Oakes, and of the old lady......not of the other two though. You've been talking with someone."

"With several actually," Jeremy was growing in confidence. "But back to Oakes for a moment, you were there with that one I believe, out in the Bahamas, a minder attached to the illustrious Governor. Tell me about Melchen and Barker. Whose idea was it to put the investigation into their grubby little hands?"

"Whose do you think?" returned the older Trembath, visibly rattled at hearing the two names.

"The Governor called them in....... but I'd say this was because he'd been leant on."

"By someone in London, in the Colonial Office?" This was Hugh, following the exchange.

"By someone in Washington," said Jeremy firmly, and he sipped at his drink.

"But the pair weren't Federal investigators," returned Sir Edward, hoping to trip the lecturer. He failed.

"Precisely," said Jeremy calmly. "If the whole idea was to facilitate a foul up then who better to call in first than a couple of clowns out of an American city police department. Bringing Melchen and Barker in put the case beyond the remit of the Federal people. The pair could botch and take the resultant opprobrium while the string-pullers stayed clean."

"Sounds like our caller has read all the books on this one," scoffed Hugh, implying all this to be merely academic. He'd invited Jeremy into Carwinion after a seemingly chance encounter on the ferry road. Hugh had been in his Land Rover, returning from Porthscatho. Jeremy was crossing the road, ostensibly returning to his car that still stood in the car park across at Trelissick.

In fact Jeremy had engineered the encounter. He'd phoned the House earlier and been told by Sir Edward where Hugh was and when he was likely to be back. Thereafter it had been a simple matter of loitering above the ferry and watching for the coastguard's return.

"I think we can assume that FDR had the Duke under his thumb," said Jeremy. "Don't you agree Sir Edward?" Sir Edward, back in the chair now, fidgeted.

"And why such an assumption?" He was testing the rigour of Jeremy's line. He seemed to know that he was in for an uncomfortable listen.

"Because we know now about Hoover having the low down on David Windsor's Nazi contacts, and also his shady currency dealings." Jeremy was wading ever deeper into those treacherous Bahamian waters.

Sir Edward looked towards his son as if to question whether this 'guest' was house trained.

"I think we have ourselves a conspiracy theorist," said Hugh, his tone patronising.

"You have yourselves a very good one," continued Jeremy, unabashed. "FDR and J Edgar are only the beginning, so listen carefully because I'm sure that I can be of considerable help to you both........" he looked directly at the son, "and especially to you. I think it about time you learned what you were born into."

"Let's have it then," said the father, resignedly. Looming was a unique embarrassment. His integrity was to be questioned before his closest and dearest.

"The ship down on the river, the one you let us onto the other day," Jeremy was still addressing Hugh, "I know that there's cocaine on board, and I also know there's weaponry." Father and son looked to each other for an appropriate response. Jeremy took advantage of the joint hesitancy. "You needn't worry. I'll tell you what others know, and then tell you why I know a little bit more. And after that you'll hear how I think we, that's you and I, can draw profit from the difference."

The lecturer proceeded, and father and son heard first how master of the *Speedwell* was more than he seemed, and how the seemingly solitary Mr Grigson had recruited for himself a team of five, of which he, Jeremy, was a peripheral member. He then focussed on the dope. How it was known to be Colombian, how it was thought that there were at least two Colombians on the Kampala, how the City based mules used the ferry, on which the deck hand had a pivotal role.

It was through him that the cash returns became guns, he said confidently, the money being laundered with the connivance of a neighbour in Truro, one Mr Morrish, a solicitor who'd recently joined *Conway's*, there replacing Jane Byrne's father, he conveniently being in jail.

Sir Edward lamely commented that they knew the family. Hugh, heightening in colour, said nothing.

Jeremy moved on to the arms. The pair heard that it was thought that the same ferry hand was involved in trucking cases of shoulder weapons down to the waterside shed in Lanmouth Creek, and that from there they were collected at night by a boat lowered from the *Kampala*.

They were on to Hugh's domain. He reacted sharply.

"So you reason that because the shed is part of the estate, we at Carwinion House have complicity? All the lettings are handled by an agency. The boy could have told you that." He was dismissive, and the father took heart.

"Preposterous, the whole thing," blustered Sir Edward. "You do realise that my son is a coastguard?"

Both points were ignored. Jeremy continued.

"This is where you'll do well to listen closely. The prevailing analysis, so far not discouraged by myself, is that with the Colombians on the ship are two Cubans and that together they're receiving guns of Eastern bloc origin. Kalashnikovs are favourite, and it's thought that these things are finding their way off one of the Russian factory ships that we have sitting off Zone Point. The theory runs that there's a few trawler owners earning themselves a no questions asked bonus by landing the cases at Mevagissey. To check on this, our Mr Grigson is planning to sail over to there first thing on Tuesday."

"So you're trying to enlist our help?" ventured Sir Edward, hopeful now rather than indignant. Jeremy had to laugh. He'd ever been amused by the antics of cornered politicians, and here, in quick succession, he was hearing the gamut.

"Sir Edward, I am here because I feel that you might want to enlist mine. Don't think the view that I've listened to and encouraged is one I necessarily believe."

"OK, so we'll hear now what *you* believe," said Hugh.

"That wherever else in this world the Commie-Cuban-Kalashnikov scenario is being enacted, it's not what we have here.... not this year, and not with this ship. What I perceive is in the way of a mirror image, something soundly in the anti communist tradition."

"And you would quarrel with that sentiment?" asked Sir Edward. There was no denial.

"Depends on the means," answered Jeremy, promptly. "I don't hold with democratically granted authority being exceeded, or democratically enacted laws being held in contempt. I don't like seeing individual rights and liberties being abused. I don't like seeing whole nations being subverted..... especially when it's this one."

"So you don't hold with fighting fire with fire?" the question again from Sir Edward.

"Depends on who gets burned, and how badly," answered Jeremy.

"Very high minded," said Hugh, "but you've been hinting a readiness to nod this one through, if the price is right. That's why you're here, to extort, but first you've got to impress us, to convince us that what you say you know you actually do. Have you been talking with the people on that ship?"

"You were there. You heard me conversing in Spanish. You'll know I'm fluent, you'll learn I'm good on dialects. I identified the two Colombians, and I also placed the other two........ but not as Cubans as I told the others."

"So you have them as being from......."

"........Panama," volleyed Jeremy with a challenging confidence. "Which suggests to me that those guns are far more likely to be of a NATO species. I spent a part of yesterday reading recent press reports from Panama. It's '30s Spain revisited. Democracy struggles, largely in vain, to deliver a stable economy, so step forward the US approved military general, yet another tinpot. This one?....He's called Noriega. Washington fixes him up with equipment and advisers, and Washington gets itself an outpost from which to press all the harder against the Reds in Nicaragua and El Salvador. Also it gives them another check point by which to contain the narc mafia to the south. The barons won't be allowed to claim Panama...... anymore than they were Grenada."

"So you're saying the ship's being lined up to go through Panama?" said Hugh.

"She always was I think. She's already been sold for scrap, and that's going to be her route to the Taiwan breakers. Step in the CIA, ever the opportunists."

"And these guns you speak of, they're going to come off where?"

"Out in the Caribbean. On to a smaller boat they'll go, something provided by Uncle Sam, perhaps based in newly acquired Grenada. From there it's across to and up the Orinocco, back along the route by which the drug came out of Colombia. It's not Medelin or Cali stuff. It's not been a Medelin or Cali operation. The Medelin and Cali people are the enemy. It's because they've so undermined law and order in the western parts that people in the US have deemed it necessary to arm and train local militia groups for the rural east. The idea is to take containment into the country itself. "

"And you see no merit in such a strategy?" said Sir Edward. "One that at least gives the natives a fighting chance against a return to serfdom?"

"I see more merit in giving them a fair return for sugar and coffee and bananas. There's better ways of running the world than by fire fighting."

"Ah, an idealist, of course," countered the former MP. "For we practitioners of the art of the possible your sort are ever the awkward ones."

"But not quite father," corrected Hugh, missing the parental irony, "because from his tone this one's here to negotiate. You've not come to lecture us, have you Jeremy? You're wanting a slice for yourself."

"What I know is irrelevant to whether or not this game is stopped. That's out of my hands, and out of yours. Where it is relevant though, is to whether or not any complicity of Carwinion House is exposed.

310

There are cut-offs in place, I know that. Potential stooges, patsies, people who'll take the rap and not be believed should they attempt to finger anyone here. Using them successfully demands timing, and this in turn requires the best information. Then you stay ahead of the game, and that's what I'm here to help ensure. Can you afford to neglect such an offer? I think not."

"And if we do then it'll be your accusing finger, one that'll be believed. Is that what you say?" Sir Edward was starting to show respect. Due respect thought Jeremy.

"What I'm saying is that there's a continuing investigation, one which seems to me at this moment to be searching a blind alley. This won't be known until one of the investigators peeks inside one of the crates being taken onto the *Kanpala*. Left where they are this is going to happen, and fairly soon. When it does the net will be re cast, very conceivably in this direction. Thereafter my quietly held personal perspective could well become general. The old red mist will clear and what I see will be seen by all."

Sir Edward fidgeted. Sweat shone at his temple. As large as the room was, the atmosphere was oppressive.... so heavy was the innuendo. Of the two the more composed was now Hugh.

"Slow it a moment," he said. "You're wanting me to be leaping to my feet, ordering for this and that to be moved from one place to another, and that would amount to a confession, a confession you would have tricked from us. Who's to say you've not been sent by Grigson for this purpose, perhaps with a concealed tape recorder, or transmitter maybe?" Jeremy was quickly to his feet, his hands high.

"Search me," he invited. Hugh didn't move. Jeremy's hands lowered so as to implore at shoulder height . "Trust me. Grigson is clearing out for a few days. There's Mevagissey, as I said, and he's also wary lest the Foreign Office have their own spook on this case..... he being Home Office."

"MI5 and MI6 ?" queried Sir Edward wearily.

"Don't worry. I think he's wrong, but he won't be persuaded of that yet. He'll want to play safe. He'll want to take what he knows back for JIC deliberation. That's his job."

"Joint Intelligence Committee," mumbled Sir Edward, to himself, for himself. His son would know this as well as he. "The forum for MI6 to come and declare what they know....... "

"........and the CIA as well perhaps. How ironic!" Jeremy was smugness itself, so pleasing was it to slide this in. "As would any good surveillance man, Grigson's looking to give masters the fullest range of options, including that of doing nothing, of letting things be for fear of disturbing some far more consequential diplomatic delicacy. But don't bet on it being followed with this one."

"And you can be so sure?" challenged Hugh.

"For two reasons," countered Jeremy. "Firstly MI6 will have been warned off before this thing started."

"Warned off by who?" interrupted Hugh.

"I'll come to that in a minute.....Secondly, there's a girl I know who'll kick up one hell of a stink if she's told that her father's staying in jail. And he's a lawyer remember. On the drugs aspect their picture will have become relatively clear. With what they now know Byrne will have to come out and Morrish go in......Morrish and a few others. I'm here to ensure those won't include yourselves."

"There you go again," said Hugh, "that veiled all knowing threat. Let's hear exactly what you know."

"I know your father has had a remarkably successful Westminster career. And I know you've an impressive House here now, a lot to be proud of in fact. But I know that alongside the Trembath diligence, and the good fortune, there has been sustenance from a hidden hand. It has been, and it still is, a powerful hand, very powerful, and getting more so. When it feeds you take, you must, you certainly don't bite. Likewise, when occasionally it presses you to its purposes..... you comply. For what the hand can give, the hand might also take away."

Puzzlement crossed Hugh's face, to be supplanted by alarm with a realisation that his father was nodding.

"Is this the Mob or the Masons or something?" demanded the son.

"Warned off by Langley," muttered Sir Edward, still nodding.

"Langley?" Hugh was little the wiser "Is that a person or the place..... somewhere near Windsor?"

"In America is this one, in Virginia. 'The Farm' they call it, headquarters of the CIA."

Hugh's mouth dropped, and then turned crossly to his father.

"You just said it was friends, in the City, a firm called Peregrine, and a few on the fringe of the Party. When I heard the name 'Mar....' "

"Kantabrico," shot Sir Edward, thinking quickly, speaking sharply. The cut in by father on son was as timely as it was clever. "A caution against careless talk, that was meant as," he added, and Hugh had the message. He was to be more careful. And now Sir Edward was taking things on. He had a challenge for this 'visitor'. "I hope you're noting how ignorant my son is in all of this. Go ahead. Enlighten him further. Truly convince him you're not riding on flimsy speculation......and you can convince me too."

Jeremy wasn't unprepared. Next to his chair lay the folder, his weekend companion. To the hosts this hadn't warranted a second glance. Lecturers carry folders, much as market researchers do clip boards. They were now to learn the content, and of the full clout gathered in this 'guest'. He stretched for it, lifted the fold over flap and drew out *'Slide Rule'.* Marking a key page was the other document collected at Exeter. The page and the Monckton obituary would be a start. Jeremy spoke.

"Young Steve who came on to the ship with us, you've been talking with him about this place and its past....... and a very interesting past it is too. You've covered a range topics and events, so I'm told. How friendly, how sociable...... and how harmless, you wrongly thought."

The photocopy was passed to Hugh. He scanned it, and with barely a reaction passed it across to his father. Agitation flickered in the elder's eyes. The set jaw held muted anger. Anger at his son was it, or anger at himself....... for an error of judgement made long, long ago?

"So Hugh, you've been talking to the boy about Walter," grunted the father.

"Only through talking about your work with the Duchy," claimed Hugh. "You like to do that yourself. I've said to him how you so much enjoy relating that tale of the wedding presents. He's wanting to hear it now of course....."

"...... as I am too," interrupted Jeremy, "and all the more so since I was given this book to look at." It lay on the arm of the chair, still open. Their attention drawn, both eyed it with suspicion. What were they about to hear now?

"Hugh," continued the lecturer, "Steve has told me that it's only been within the past few months that you've properly learned how that shed of yours down on Lanmouth Creek came by its name.....the Viceroy shed. You told him that you'd recently had the story from a veteran GI, one who'd been quartered here during the war. Prior to hearing this account you'd shared the general assumption that the shed had taken the name of the ferryboat operated from that quay by the late

Mr Rory Duggan..... the very man whose untimely death I briefly mentioned earlier. In fact the boat took her title from the shed. The building having been so named by the Americans after they'd discovered therein a set of technical plans pertaining to a parts of a particular machine, some kind of craft, the name *Viceroy* being prominent in the legend. This is what you told Steve isn't it?"

"I did," conceded Hugh, "without really expecting it to go any further."

"And I believe that," Jeremy assured him. "You'd have no reason to attempt to mislead the boy, just as he'd have no reason to keep all you said to himself. You were but one of the almost all who'd made the erroneous assumption, I can see that. But you weren't though, were you Sir Edward?"

With the question came a fiercely accusing glare, and the former MP was lost for an immediate riposte. Jeremy took his opportunity. Lifting the book he read:-

" 'It was so much modified from the Envoy that we gave it another type of name, and christened it the Viceroy' "

"And this *'Envoy'*, she was a vessel?" asked Hugh.

"Sir Edward," prompted Jeremy, looking up and angling the opened book towards the father.

"I know the book. In it we learn that the *Envoy* was in fact a late 1930s commercial aircraft, the production model. The *Viceroy*, as we've just heard, was a modification. We can read of the enhanced performances offered and the hopes raised for the machine in the international air races of that time. It seems that the plane also acquired a military capability, and this attracted the interest of agents acting for both sides in the Spanish Civil War......"

"......which is a story in itself," continued Jeremy. "One that you might be better able to tell than the designer does, Mr N.S. Norway, who wrote this."

Sir Edward hauled himself imposingly to his feet.

Forty years slid away. Jeremy was momentarily taken aback. Before him was the directness and the push that reinvigorated flat and rubbled Plymouth. The challenge was there and he was meeting it full on.

"OK Mr Barnes, Mr Jeremy Barnes, you win..... impressive

research. This, and two nights work, can earn you £10,000. It buys the help you offered earlier and thereafter your silence."

This was no invitation to haggle. It was a straight offer, firmly tabled, a direct response to that brief sentence from the book plus those earlier mentions of Monckton, of Duggan, of Cairns.

"Conditions?" responded Jeremy.

"That you stay with us until the job's done. If done to plan the operation is called off, no one gets hurt, the lawyer is probably out of jail, and you're substantially the richer." Sir Edward was clearly falling back on to contingency arrangements, measures about which a puzzled looking son seemed no less obviously ignorant.

"Count me in," said Jeremy.

"Hugh, instructions now for you." Sir Edward was taking control. "The history lesson can wait. I've a quick call to make. When I've done that, use the phone, use the radio, use the Land Rover, the car, use whatever you have to. I want Jim to be found. Get him and his boat against the end of the ferry as soon as it's made the last crossing. I want him here tonight, preferably within the hour."

"And you're contacting who?" asked Hugh as his father turned to go to the phone.

"St.Mawgan. I just give them the word and they're there for us. Think of it as calling out a lifeboat."

St.Mawgan, USAAF St.Mawgan, thought Jeremy, an obvious resource. The airfield just to the north of Newquay was one of many built in Cornwall during the war. All save this and Culdrose had fallen to disuse. The RAF had continued to fly coastal reconnaissance planes from St Mawgan, and a corner had been adapted for very short haul commercial operations. Another corner accommodated an outpost of the US of A.

In the '50s there had been American planes here. Now, should they be needed, they could be brought over to what amounted to a ready equipped forward base. There were workshops, and there were weapons, and there were trained personnel. If not on alert then all was certainly primed, and this had to mean strict security......which in turn, for this band of shady south coast operators, could mean an available sanctuary. Should things start to founder then Uncle Sam wasn't so far away. He'd been at hand since the late '40s, the time of the Berlin airlift. The *Kampala,* she'd sprung a leak. And as Sir Edward had said, it was

. time to summon the lifeboat.

How big was it though? How many could it discretely carry to safety? Who would it pick up, and who would be abandoned to fend for themselves?

Two nights work, that's what Sir Edward had said, and in so short a time how many could even be made aware of the alarm? Prout was being mustered, and if he was coming by way of the ferry then 'Mr Grim' down there was also going to be apprised, as he would have to be....... for he was a pivotal figure and surely there would be a reserved seat for him in whatever transport was now being arranged.

Not Morrish though, certainly not Morrish.... he was just as certain to be on his own. Another knock on betrayal, reflected Jeremy. Trust was going out of fashion. Where would it end, he wondered.

Hugh set off as instructed. Sir Edward was now at the phone and the lecturer was left to ponder upon the beast at the very heart of this maze. Though professionally he'd long known its ways this was a first personal encounter. He was a lecturer of course, in politics, and he was fond of quoting from the Doolittle Report. He recalled the central tenet:-

'If the United States is to survive, longstanding concepts of fair play must be re-considered. We must develop effective espionage and counter espionage services and must learn to subvert, sabotage, and destroy our enemies by more clever, more sophisticated, and more effective methods than those used against us.'

It had long been official, legitimised. Two wrongs could make a right. On this rationale Washington had sought and gained the assistance of the Italian Mafia back in '43. Oakes had had to go. Set the one man's life against that of a thousand and more of Clark's fighting GIs then, as hard as it was, here was a good, good bargain...... and a precedent also. Goodbye Oakes?....soon it was goodbye Sikorsky, and to follow, a whole procession of pawns in the Cold War game. Include Duggan. Include Cairns, and Brian maybe, and Hilda.

And now there was this novel threat to American society, South American cocaine........ and to fight a dirty war, bring out the dirty tricks. And if you happen to be in the way, Mr Roger Byrne, then that's just tough.

But look now at himself, look inward Jeremy, at one who'd for so long professed such high minded distaste for it all. A chance had come to match words with action....... and see, he'd sold out. He was joining the payroll. With his ten thousand he could move to Exeter, say, or Bristol, or similar. To a place that offered better prospects career-wise and, if there was a no Kate new start to be made, then on the social front too. Practical considerations these, but were they simply masking a petty vindictive spite? Just the question was enough, and he was feeling a shudder of self-disgust.

But he'd shown his hand and once bought then these people would always have his number. Walter's obituary lay in front of him still offering its Faustian caution, but it was too late now. He was in the cavern. Wherever it might lead there was no turning back.

Sir Edward returned from the phone. If anything he looked even more composed, and resolute. It was better to keep the man talking.

"One question Sir Edward," said Jeremy, respectful, outwardly, "before Hugh gets back to hear more from me on your life and times."

"About what?"

"About David Windsor. We read so much about him, and his political sympathies. You were there, working with the man, before the war and during. How do you assess him?"

Sir Edward settled back into his chair.

"He was a fine man..... not perfect, but then who is?" The lecturer coloured. That last phrase he took personally. "He was intelligent, he was able. Given responsibility he would meet it with diligence. He was a good administrator, both here in the Duchy and out in the Bahamas. It was more than a figurehead job over there. Leave aside the Oakes thing and he did better than many a Colonial Office professional, before and since."

The Monckton obituary lay where Hugh had left it, on the arm of his now empty chair. Sir Edward stretched for it....and then continued.

"Just as this man initially was naive, and I was naive, so too in his own unique way was David Windsor. He had this one off blend of celebrity and majesty. For characters such as Bedaux he could bring profile, the precious commodity for those seeking the widest and fullest exposure for their projects...... but that's not treason. Treason involves a far subtler kind of game, one played at a deeper, less obvious level." Sir Edward paused, and looking down at the words he held he was appearing to be taking a far less kindly view of this man of Kent who rose ultimately to cabinet rank. "One played long term," he added softly.

"Can we be talking of '56, of Suez?" probed Jeremy, but in vain.

At that moment Hugh returned. He'd contacted Prout as instructed and he was anxious now to report.

"I got through. He'll be around in about an hour. The St.Mawgan people were helpful I trust?"

"All under control," said an assuring father. "There'll be a lorry coming over tomorrow night. A couple of Puertos are to be swapped in for the Colombians. They'll be spirited off with the guns and the dope. Our task is to have all ready for loading as soon as they're here. We can sort the finer details when Prout arrives."

"Right," said Hugh, "in the meantime, maybe we can listen to more of........," and he tilted his head towards Jeremy.

The lecturer took the cue. He looked straight at Sir Edward, and he began.

"1937, I think, towards the end of May. Five months I'd make that, after the voyage of the *Mar Cantabrico*......"

"It wasn't like that," protested Sir Edward, "certainly not at the start. Again I must stress my naivety. Your man there, the writer, the author of that book, if I'd been just a little more familiar with his line of work....."

"Lines of work," offered Jeremy, firmly stressing the plural.

"Of course," conceded Sir Edward, his mouth lifting into the faintest and briefest of smiles. "But I wasn't, not then, and what I was told I took of course at face value. Repeating it, I expected others to do likewise. That's innocence."

"And it was repeated in the wrong place, at the wrong time, in front of the wrong people," said Jeremy.

"What was it then, that you'd been told," asked Hugh, "and who by? "

"It was by old Roger Carne, " answered the father. "You wouldn't remember him. He was finished off by that cold winter, '47 I think it was. He had the top farm, Landurgan. It was all a bit of a struggle back in the '30s, but he just about paid the rent. Shipping had been just as depressed, but by '37 things there were starting to stir again. The iron on the river began to thin out, and space on the quays was once more in demand."

"And all the more so where a quay offered secluded and secure storage," Jeremy added.

"I was the landlord, Carne was a tenant. He had a concern about another tenant, the party who was at that time renting the Lanmouth shed. This was why he came to me and spoke as he did."

"An access problem was it?" ventured Hugh. "A damaged hedge? A left open gate?"

"Of that broad nature," confirmed Sir Edward. "Apparently he'd gone up to one of the top lane side fields to bring in his cows for the evening only to find the gate way blocked by a small lorry. It was stopped there, with the bonnet open and the radiator steaming. It seemed that for the driver this was nothing new. He was prepared. He had water with him, in an old kettle apparently. He'd been caught out more than once before. Too hasty with the top up and the slight hitch might become major. He had to wait, and so did the cows, and so did Carne. They got to talking, and Carne enquired as to what was so heavy in the back...... that was putting the motor to such strain. And the answer that he was given was 'vacuum cleaners and suchlike'."

"And Carne was ready to believe that?" asked Jeremy.

"These things were the hottest of hot cakes then, much as these video machines are now. To the casual observer, though, it was never quite clear how they got to the customers. People didn't shop for them. There weren't the cars then for carrying them home. A salesman would call and often HP terms would be agreed. That was new then, and because it carried quite a stigma the deal could often be clinched with a promise of doorstep delivery out of an unmarked van. This meant that district by district they tended to be covertly stockpiled."

"And you bought this, this idea of these appliances being stashed down on Lanmouth Creek." Hugh sounded sceptical.

"Because Carne did, and if he did then I was happy to leave it at that," said Sir Edward.

"And happy enough to repeat it else where," said Jeremy, "and by my calculations that would have been in France, something like a week later, in the vicinity of Tours.....where the Duke was married."

"On the road from Cherbourg to Paris actually," Sir Edward corrected.

"Which was where you were headed on that wedding present jaunt, the one you so like to recount," figured Hugh.

"This was Monckton," confirmed Sir Edward. "You know the tale Hugh. There was something of a panic at Cande. The world's press was about to turn up for the big day, and they would be wanting to view and write about and photograph the gifts."

"Which were conspicuous by their paucity," continued the son. Sir Edward was sullen.

"I was summoned by Walter, and I went over from Plymouth with a crate or three of what the faithful around the Duchy had thought to give....but of course it tended towards the homely rather than the regal, and while appreciated it was hardly centre spread material. I'd phoned ahead to tell them this, and it was decided that I should be met at Cherbourg by a man and van. We were to make a lengthy detour...."

".....to Paris, " said Hugh.

"Help was at hand. Some of the top stores had been approached, and they were delighted to lend a selection of their best wares. My task, with the driver, was to collect."

"And this driver....? " prompted Hugh

".........was Spanish. He was Randolph's minder."

"Randolph.......?" Jeremy wanted to hear it.

".......Churchill, Sir Winston's son. He was into journalism then, always was I suppose. At that time he was covering the war in Spain, I think for *The Mail*. He was in the Franco camp, openly championing the Generalissimo."

"*The Mail* doesn't change then, does it ?" spat Jeremy. Sir Edward, acid resistant, resumed.

"It was no easy matter, moving out of and back into Spain, and so that Randolph might be safely transported this fellow was attached. Like me he was there as a kind of lackey. That we should be jointly entrusted with this Paris jaunt says all about this commonality. He has the usual pidgin English and we attempt conversation. We talk about the number of households the happy couple were having to furnish and maintain and as an aside, a quip really, I say that I could have brought across three or four dozen vacuum cleaners. They were being stored by the stack on my estate at home, that's all I said. And he must have remembered this and told the others."

"The others? " enquired Jeremy.

"Randolph, and this other journalist fellow. He was American. Downes his name was, and he was with one of the big American papers. He headed their Paris team. I think he was setting things up with the big shops there."

"And Walter?" asked Hugh.

"Maybe, but for him, then, as for me, vacuum cleaners would have been vacuum cleaners."

"And not components for realising and arming a warplane," said Jeremy with gravity. "But Downes, Churchill and his batman suspected, and they got you to find out more. How did they do that?"

"They drew me into these card games. They might have been rigged, who knows? I was out of my league anyway. Soon I was owing them £500..... not much to them but plenty to me, to Carwinion here, where so much was getting threadbare. My own father was on his last legs, I was wanting to get married, and just when wanting to show myself to be responsible I'd gone and done the opposite."

"But there was a way out," suggested Jeremy, and he drew out his copy of the signals that Duggan had logged, the enigma letters and the latitudes and longitudes at which they'd been noted. "The first fix on Duggan's ship was made when she was barely out into Falmouth Bay!"

"Downes said he would settle all, and also enhance my expenses claim. All I had to do is come back here and find out if these vacuum cleaners were being loaded onto a ship.........."

".....and if so which one," added Hugh.

"He gave me a telephone number, a London number. It came under the US embassy, but definitely one of their shadier desks. By this time I'd cottoned on a bit. And yes, the *Cantabrico* was called to mind, and what Senator Nye had said about it all.... correctly enough I think. But of course I was hopelessly compromised, and by then everyone seemed to be swinging behind Franco. He was the future there, it was becoming clear."

"And you watched, and you saw these things were going onto a ship, and you noted its name, and you dialled the number. *'Usk Vale,'* you said, and you'd probably even found when she was leaving and passed that on too," Jeremy summarised confidently. Sir Edward contested nothing.

"That sort of thing went on at that time. A lot of people did a lot worse, and got away with it. If the war hadn't happened, World War II I mean, it could all easily have been forgotten... along with so much else. The war drew Downes into senior intelligence. He was made a top officer in the OSS, the nascent CIA. The war made Walter an influential political figure. The war ushered in the Churchill cronies from whom there had to be at least a show of respect for the incorrigible Randolph."

"And you Sir Edward, what did the war do for your prospects?" asked Jeremy.

"Everything, provided I did exactly what I was told. Mr Ken Downes became my controller. And thirty years later I was still having to follow his bidding.......although by the mid '70s at least Hoover was dead. J Edgar had been the spider at the heart of the web. Downes was reporting to Hoover from Cande. When the US Army came here in '43 and sniffed into every nook and cranny, and found those *Viceroy* plans down at Lanmouth......"

".......and worked out the connection with the story of the *Usk Vale*, as it had emerged the year before...by courtesy of the communist network...."

"....... and then began to reason that I might have had a part in it all," continued Sir Edward. "It could quite easily have been my ruin."

"Save for the fact that their Mr Downes was found to have the grubbiest hands of all in this matter and, being now one of The Boss's top men, his position had to of course be protected." Jeremy was into his stride. "You were lucky. They might have arranged a fatal accident."

"Instead they raised me above suspicion, sending me to the Bahamas...."

".......and giving the estate here a liberal smothering of whitewash," added Hugh.

"Because they had a use for me, and a use for Carwinion. Had anyone else seen those plans in the five years that they'd lain in the shed down at the creek? They couldn't be sure. Others had used the store, but nothing had been said...... not openly.....not yet. To the lay person, of course, those diagrams could have been of anything."

"So the only real difficulty lay in the person of Rory Duggan, one time radio operator of the *Usk Vale*," said Hugh.

"There could be no surprise at his return here, not for those of us in the know. And it was clear that any attempt to move him on would only fuel his suspicions. The Americans were looking closely at everyone. They would have been aware of what was passing between Duggan and the Board of Trade. There was no indication that the man was alive to the particular significance of the name '*Viceroy*'......"

".......but he was on to the company name, '*Airspeed*'," said Jeremy, "this suggesting that a linkage could only be a matter of time."

"Quite," confirmed Sir Edward. "So something had to be done, and it had to be done quickly and subtly. It was decided that as the particular local and historical significance of the term *'Viceroy'* had not yet been unearthed then the best course was to bury it a little more deeply, and where better than beneath a very different current significance.... one that the Americans were well placed to construct. The subtle part was in their giving Duggan an unknowing part in the actual construction process. They had him helping to bury the very answer that he sought."

"While at the same time they could keep him under close watch." Jeremy added, admiringly. " Find a boat to give to the man, call it the *Viceroy* and have it based in Lanmouth, and then let his skill, his enterprise and his doggedness establish this newer meaning as the only meaning"

"That was the idea," confirmed Sir Edward. "The longer he looked, the better protected Carwinion became.... provided of course that I did what I was told. Keeping the truth from Duggan whilst keeping him conveniently to hand was one of their levers against me. They wanted me in the Bahamas, and if I didn't co operate then Duggan might be fed sufficient to effect my ruin."

"So you knew about *Airspeed's Viceroy,*" said Hugh.

"No, not then. I was just told of something having been found down there in the creek side shed, something rooted out by a gang of doughboys who'd been set to tidy the place. With what they'd found out from elsewhere it was enough to connect my trip to Cande to a distressing incident a week or so later out on Biscay. Those soldiers had been sworn to secrecy and re-stationed. All I had to do was behave and when were any of them going to get back here and spill the beans?"

"I think your son can answer that," answered Jeremy sharply.

"Fifty years later," said Hugh. "One called here a couple of months back.....Leonard Hayes."

"Just when the very same shed is again being put to a very similar use," chuckled Jeremy, elated almost.

"But if it worked so well for so long then you must be adrift in your suggestion that for some reason Duggan had to be silenced," protested Hugh. " He can't have been both deceived and dangerous."

Jeremy turned to the father, grim once more.

"Sir Edward, can you comment?"

"He was killed all right. His boat had been searched, and his cottage, meticulously. They thought he had something. What it was, and whether or not they actually found it, these things were never made clear to me."

"This book," ventured Hugh, "had he read that do you think?..... And divined something from it, and maybe contacted the author?"

"Didn't come out until '54," answered Jeremy. " December '50 is when Duggan died."

Sir Edward nodded.

"To him, then, the one and only *Viceroy* was his *Viceroy*. I'm fairly sure of that."

"And I tend to agree, Sir Edward," said Jeremy. "We read this and we're told that the *Airspeed Viceroy* was a one off affair. But he did have a lead. He had the name of the company that built the thing, and also the name of an arms manufacturer with whom the designer had been closely associated. In the fullness of time, after this book came out, he might well have got quite close to the truth...... especially with the kind of help he seemed to be lining up."

"From?" quizzed Hugh.

"A young journalist, Francis Cairns. Worked on the *Packet* down in Falmouth, and occasionally for the *Plymouth Independent* ....isn't that right Sir Edward?"

"I remember Francis Cairns," sighed Sir Edward.

"Who was also to die unnaturally in the late summer of '51, just a couple of months before the election of that year.......... the year that Walter had entered Parliament, the year that both you and Randolph were seeking election in neighbouring Plymouth constituencies. It was a pivotal election that, both in national and in global terms. Weary though he was, Washington wanted Winston back. They needed a compliant ally, much as they have done again over these past three years. They knew it was going to be close, and that the hopes they nurtured were just one scandal away from being dashed." Jeremy was almost teasing now. Hugh leapt to his father's defence.

"But we're still three years from this book coming out!"

"Forget the book for a moment," said Jeremy. "All the book tells us is that the Americans knew exactly what had been shipped out of Lanmouth long before anyone else."

"Including me," Sir Edward reminded them. "If it wasn't vacuum cleaners then obviously it had to be military equipment. I'd worked that much out, but I was told no more."

"And from what he'd possibly heard on board the *Usk Vale,* Rory Duggan was only slightly better informed. For me this would suggest that his concern, during the war years and just after, was to identify people rather than 'equipment' as you put it. He was looking to identify people who lived in the area in '37, whose political sympathies were at that time pro-fascist, and whose movements and contacts might give those on the look out an opportunity to recruit them as informants. He was still on this tack in 1950, in the autumn of that year, when he came upon this, and this, and he put them together."

As Jeremy spoke two documents were slid from the folder. The first was a copy of the annotated cutting from *The Limerick Examiner;* the second, a copy of the Cairns' piece carried by the *Independent*...the underlined quote from Ida Copeland now florescent pen highlighted.

"Stoke on Trent, 1931," he continued, "and you, Sir Edward, you are pictured to the left of the main man... young then, still at College I believe. Manchester wasn't it?" The picture was passed to what was surely the only survivor amongst its subjects.

"That was when you helped old Mrs Copeland out," blundered Hugh as he waited.

"So legend has it," said Jeremy, wryly. "Maybe myth is the better word."

Hugh took the page. He weighed the image, then frowned powerfully across at his father. The look spoke less of censure, more of puzzlement and dismay. For the first time, from father to son, explanation was owed....... and if not offered it would be demanded.

But Sir Edward Trembath, ever the politician, wasn't to be so easily cornered. He fired back, eyes darting rapidly from son to guest, and back to son.

"When I campaigned for him it was for his New Party, not for his Blackshirt movement. He was part of the democratic process still. Since when has it been in any way dishonourable to work and vote for a losing party after a properly conducted campaign. He had some good ideas, a New Deal he was devising. He was ahead of his time."

"On his seeking a democratic mandate, perhaps you make a fair point," conceded Jeremy, "but it wouldn't have counted for much in the journalistic rough and tumble of another election year, one fully two decades later, and such eventful decades at that. After all that had happened between '31 and '51 people were going to look at this and immediately dismiss all pictured as ideologically suspect, if only by association. You can say now, Sir Edward, that you never so much as even dreamt of chasing Jewish people through London's East End, and I'd be happy to believe you......but that misses the point. Association is about taint. There can be no end to its virulence, particularly in politics, but more of that in a minute."

Already Hugh was looking at the second cutting.

"Mrs Copeland, the lady who won the poll in '31, she seems to have bought the myth. She couldn't have seen this picture. She says here;-

'Had it not been for busy campaigning by the likes of the then young Mr Trembath, and his fellow activists, then I have little doubt that my seat would have been retained by the Labour party.....' "

Jeremy interrupted Hugh with a forced cough.

"Sir Edward," requested the lecturer, with an affected, exaggerated politeness, "would you care to comment there, also?"

"She did say that, or something very like it," explained Sir Edward flatly, "but actually she didn't mean it like it sounds when you read it. She meant something very different and, to his credit, this different meaning was I believe faithfully reported by young Cairns. The editor in Plymouth wasn't having it though. He was being leant on by Central Office, just as Ida was."

"And as well as Conservative Central Office there was far mightier hand," prompted Jeremy. "And during those weeks, critical weeks in Korea and in Europe, it was acutely alert....on a hair trigger you might say."

"So Cairns's involvement preceded whatever contact occurred between him and Duggan," figured Hugh.

"He went to Trelissick at the suggestion of his boss at the *Packet*," said his father.

"Arthur Stanaway?" shot Jeremy.

"Spot on, " said Sir Edward. "The pair of us attended Duggan's funeral together. He told me then. He'd remembered the small piece in *The Western Morning News*, the Plymouth daily he'd been working on at the time of the '31 election. It had briefly featured the famous cycle ride from Manchester to Stoke, by the student who was a neighbour of

326

favoured candidate's family no less."

"And he'd swallowed it, old Stanaway," said Hugh.

"Whole," confirmed Sir Edward. "And though by reviving the tale he was to open a can of worms, this had been far, far from his intention. A feel-good story was what had been envisaged.....good neighbourliness reciprocated. But what Cairns came away with was, I suspect, very different. I don't think Stanaway actually saw it. It would have gone straight to Plymouth, Cairns was fearless like that."

"So what had Cairns actually heard over in Trelissick?" asked Hugh.

"Only that I'd changed sides. Where she says *young Mr Trembath and his fellow activists'* she's speaking of New Party supporters, supporters of Mosley."

"But she credits you with helping her to win," protested Hugh.

"Because they did," smirked Jeremy. "You only need look at the figures." He'd written them down whilst at the Colindale archive. The notebook was produced and opened. "Compare the '31 result with that of the previous election. From the later of the counts you see that Mosley's New Party vote was won largely from the Labour Party, for whom his wife had stood in '29. The Conservative turn out merely had to be repeated for Ida to secure her seat. You, Sir Edward, were pulling against your neighbour and she was entitled to be cross at that, but at the same time you were pulling much harder against her main rival..... to a critical degree. You and your fellow New Party enthusiasts truly did win it for her!"

"And Ida would have been happy enough to live with this," said Hugh, "until, that is, someone asks her to endorse Edward Trembath's credentials as a prospective parliamentary candidate for Plymouth North."

"They'd never thought much of us over here in Carwinion," muttered Sir Edward. "While 'trade' they were a sort of new aristocracy...... almost on par with the old, by virtue of the quality and the reputation of their product. What the Copelands had crafted had come to help define this nation. And what were we by comparison? We were carpetbaggers"

"Ill-gained wealth yours was," said Jeremy, "money made during the war, out of the war."

"And money that wasn't going to last long," continued Sir

Edward. "That's what they thought, because we were only playing at working the land. When you're a lad you're oblivious to this of course, you're protected. So this means that when you have to take it..... well then it hits all the harder, and it hurts."

"And for you that was in '31," said Jeremy.

"Yes, there was me breezing down from Manchester with my head primed to the follicles with Keynes, and just turning up at Ida's HQ thinking that a 'National' programme would incorporate the best and the brightest that all sides had to offer......... ideas, men, women. At last we were off gold, we were liberated!"

"They weren't impressed?"

"I thought I'd stepped in dog dirt. They didn't let me near Ida. They'd 'win by doing nothing,' that's what they said. Bright ideas were what had fragmented the Labour Party, so they were welcome to them. That was their key strategy. Allow the government to break up, then just step in..... nothing constructive, no one pro-active."

"So our man here naturally appealed," said Hugh. He leant and lightly touched the picture.

"And he put up a good show," said Sir Edward. "He had conviction and he had courage, and he had progressive ideas. The Copelands could afford to say safety first. With their precious Spode they had a world famous brand. A pound fixed to gold had kept their returns up and wage pressures down......"

".......by holding down the price of cheap imported food," joined Jeremy.

"Unpegged a month before the election, it had then slipped. Good, I thought, but they were worried..... less profits you see. They wanted it held, and a balanced budget was essential. Sir Oswald said no, let it slide, and slide as far as was needed for people abroad to be able to afford and want our more run of the mill type of factory product. What we were making would sell then, its price reflecting value rather than national vanity. Add to this a programme of much needed public works and people would be earning again, and spending. That was the theory, and with dearer foreign food there was even something in it for our farmers."

"Enlightened policies," said Jeremy, "but he was far from enlightened in how they were to be pushed through. 'Streamline the executive' is the company speak. If he couldn't persuade, he was ready to coerce."

"But you don't know how feeble democracy seemed back then," protested Sir Edward. He wasn't going to be lectured, not even by a professional. "You only had to compare the mess that was Spain with what was being achieved in Italy. And here we had the Fleet in mutiny at Invergordon, and there was even rumour of a communist cell amongst the Devonport yardies. When you're young and you're patriotic you want someone to take a grip. I wasn't alone, far from it. Better men than me shared a platform with the chap.... Nye Bevan for example."

"Fair point," conceded Jeremy. "You were there, I wasn't. It was how you saw it then, it's how you see it now. But remember how things were poised in 1950, particularly in the last three months of that year, internationally and locally. With all that was running for you, and your sponsors, it would have been extremely impolitic to air such sentiments then. For anyone to have even hinted that you had at any time championed bad old Sir Oswald could have set to a wobble a rather precariously loaded apple cart...... and Ida Copeland certainly wasn't just 'anyone'."

"That's so," admitted Sir Edward. "And paranoia was rife. This, more than anything, was probably what did for poor old Duggan."

"Because a few very powerful people feared that he knew more than he actually did," muttered Hugh. "All he had was this photo, out of an Irish paper. Hardly a sharp likeness is it?"

"But he was reading something into it, and this something had been compounded by what had appeared in the *Independent*, " said Jeremy. "Someone was taking the trouble to distort the truth. This was the give-away."

"That could have been Ida, or even Cairns himself," argued Hugh, but without conviction.

"Except there are people around here even now who saw through that article, saw it to be far short of Cairns' normal standards......I was only speaking with one the other day. We can imagine that at the time Duggan would have assessed it likewise, and that he would have guessed also at Cairns' dismay....."

"So to Cairns he went," said Hugh.

"He did," nodded his father, "but not before going to Trelissick to discretely make a few enquiries of his own. I only caught wind of this later, much, much later. He didn't go to the lady of the house, you wouldn't expect him to. They had this gardener who was just going into what was his fourth decade of continuous service. Taciturn, watchful, he had the whole area weighed up. He had me weighed up. I would only listen to the likes of Carne when I had time. This character always had time. His employers of course were for Baldwin through and through, and the rest of the household was too....."

"...and by '35 that made anything to do with David Windsor deeply suspect, and that included his Royal Duchy, and even those employed therein," continued Jeremy, "particularly where it was whispered of one that back in his youth he'd shown a taste for political extremism."

"Duggan, from talking casually with Ida's gardener, managed to glean something on my movements of the early summer in '37. There was no secret about my going to Cande, it was regarded as an honour. But there were also movements on the river he learned of, movements between the quays and the ships, men and materials. What could be recalled and recounted, he very carefully noted, keeping all closely to himself. And then he made his move, contacting Cairns just after the Copeland interview and that article in the *Independent*. Now it looks as if the only definite thing he had was this picture from the Irish paper. If we'd only known this then maybe the response needn't have been so severe. It was said that there'd been this uncharacteristic, unnerving excitability in his voice when he'd phoned the *Packet*...... wanting to speak with Cairns, privately."

"He was overheard?" queried Jeremy.

"With his piece for the *Independent* Cairns had made himself a marked man. Phone wires both to his home and to his desk at the *Packet* were tapped. By his call Rory Duggan sealed his own fate...."

"......also that of Francis Cairns, " added Jeremy.

"They came out of St. Mawgan," continued Sir Edward grimly. "Just as they will tomorrow night. Desperate times, desperate measures....they were ready to murder."

"As they were in Shrewsbury, only last year? " Jeremy put in.

"This was no bungle." responded Sir Edward, carelessly.

"And neither was Chadwick's," stabbed Jeremy. Trembath was taken aback. He was on difficult ground. Hilda was famous, but not so Chadwick. He steadied himself. This caller was alluding to recent far away deaths. They had nothing to do with Carwinion. He wasn't going to bite, he was staying back in 1950.

"Into the river went Duggan, and around Trelissick the whisper was heard; from top to bottom, in every room, and in every corner of that lovingly manicured garden.... 'careless talk can indeed cost lives. Best to keep quiet lest any more be taken by the water.' "

"And all this just to get Edward Trembath into Parliament as the representative of the people of Plymouth North?" scoffed Hugh. "I don't want to belittle your career father, much respected father, but why couldn't they have just dropped you, found someone else with less complicated antecedents?"

Sir Edward sighed.

"You haven't really been listening, have you son?" The Monckton obituary lay on the floor. Sir Edward grunted as he reached again, now lifting it towards his heir. "Second page."

"Marilyn Monroe? I know he was partial to the occasional actress...."

"Top of the second page," prompted Jeremy. It was at the very top, the first full sentence. Hugh read.

"'In February 1951 he was returned as the Conservative member for Bristol West.'

.....but the '51 election wasn't until October. I remember that one."

"You would of course," remarked Jeremy. "It was your father's first victory, but not Walter Monckton's. Walter fought the '51 general election as a sitting candidate. He'd won his seat earlier in the year, in a by election."

"But Walter would have kept himself well clear of the likes of Mosley," declared Hugh.

"But not well clear of the likes of your father," Jeremy went on, "nor of the likes of the lovely Leonora." Out came the passage taken from Birkenhead's book. It went across to Sir Edward. He scanned Steve's photostat and then turned it, glancing at the boy's note.

"I can take it on from here," said Sir Edward. "From this point Mosley isn't a key figure. He never was really, beyond the fact that the picture said one thing about me while Ida was apparently saying another. The main man now is Sir Walter Monckton. As the biographer teasingly hints, it was in '41 that Walter slipped under FBI control, his letters to

Leonora gifting to them the opportunity......a valuable opportunity, one to cherish. He was with the Ministry of Information then, the Director, immediately below the Minister himself, one Duff Cooper. And not counting David Windsor, poor old Duff soon becomes the first of many. The Americans want him out, and their man, Bracken, in his place. They have him undermined....."

".......by the man immediately beneath," finished Jeremy. "Then there were the Poles I believe, their Government in London exile, they had to be sold out. '43 was that?"

"But you forget '42 and Walter's time in Egypt," said Sir Edward. "There's been many a book and film even in which much has been made of Rommel having a spy in Cairo, giving him the British and Commonwealth troop dispositions. In fact the spy belonged to Washington, and it was they who were leaking on to the Germans. Why? To give their own troops a better chance with the Torch landings and their drive through Morocco to Tunisia. Tobruk could be sacrificed. It was a lure."

"You're saying that British lives were traded? I'm not sure I can believe this!" gasped Hugh. His father wasn't to be deterred.

"Let's say certain investments were, sacrifices if you like, considered wise.... and that in overall terms they paid off. Were he here, Walter might strongly argue that in the long run allied lives were saved, a consequence of Rommel's over-stretching."

"So during the war we have Walter also being used as a tactical device.... as the Duke was." Hugh was starting to come around.

"Used by Hoover and a favoured clique of top generals," said Jeremy. "Few were the politicians who could have been trusted with such a resource, certainly while a pink tinged State Department carried so many 'New Dealers'. But times change. By 1950 the bear has become the large looming enemy. Capitol Hill is being cleansed and the Dulles boys are set to tangle with the Reds. They have a strategy. Defeated Germany, defeated Italy, defeated Japan, reclaimed France.....they can't be left to fall to Moscow by default. Their economies must be regenerated, and only the dollar can do this. On a promise of profits Wall Street will be persuaded. There will be investment, investment into research and development, into assembly lines. But whither the product? That's the question. Will there be the buyers out there, the markets?"

"There were," said Hugh. "Tell me where in the free world you can't now find a Honda! The strategy was a success."

"But not an automatic success," remarked Jeremy.

"Indeed," joined Sir Edward. "Threats were perceived, this country being one of the bigger. Industry here had more than a head start, an advantage further boosted by the US forced devaluation in the Autumn of '49."

"An own goal, that," chuckled the lecturer. The metaphor was so everyday, and yet so inviting. Sir Edward took it up.

"So measures had to be taken, not so much to ensure a level playing field as to fix it so that UK Ltd would have a long spell playing against slope and wind....."

"....and foremost among those measures was the installation of Sir Walter at the Ministry of Labour." Jeremy was now telling it straight. "And this brings us to the start of your time at Westminster."

"It does," confirmed Sir Edward. "And at the time there were some who argued that what was needed was what we've been at last getting over these past five years........ wage restraint, laws against restrictive working practices, and laws against the abuse of union power. Our task was then to marginalise those voices. Too greedy they were for those prized foreign markets. See what sad figures old Thorneycroft and Powell now cut. The country needed their prime of life vigour. Instead old Churchill was required to take on a Washington sponsored wrecker, one so well placed that by weak stand wage bargaining he could here put a drag on the kind of commercial recovery that so many of the other trading nations were starting to enjoy. How often have we read of damage done by Moscow trained leftists? None were so well placed as Walter. He worked fifty times their mischief."

"So this had to have been Churchill's responsibility," claimed Hugh.

"And the rest! The bulldog of '26 and '40 was by now a feeble poodle, picking at the economic scraps, helplessly haplessly enduring the dismantling of Empire, formerly the captive market. Whatever, where ever, if it in anyway rendered up for this country a competitive advantage then for the Americans it was fair game. Iranian oil wasn't to be cheap anymore, neither was African metal, nor Indian rubber. And where the people of those lands once thought to buy only British, now, for each newly independent populace there would be wider, freer choice.....the dollar backed multinationals were on the march. A tendency became the trend, and that in turn became the way of the world. Those who considered Suez sacrosanct became oddities, likewise those who championed the Rhodesias and their Federation. I saw this happen......"

"If you were in there to buttress Walter then you helped it happen," said Jeremy, "helped open things for Macmillan and Macleod, so that their way, the Washington way, could become the mainstream. And as Kenyatta, and Banda, and Kaunda played their get out of jail free cards and queued at Lancaster House, how they were feted in America..........no matter that the coloured man there was being held down still, being held back. Money talks..... that's the American way."

"Like it's looking to have the last word tonight," reminded Hugh. It was a timely thrust, but one Jeremy could dodge. He had the knowledge. Sideways he moved and back........ turning to Sir Edward, and once again to the past.

"So what about Monckton and Eden? Tell me about Suez. Birkenhead steps rather daintily around that one, but you were there. How did you see it? What thought you of our Minister of Defence......*dove or carrier pigeon?"*

Sir Edward considered, and yes he would respond. Here was an opportunity to spin out time.

"From where I sat, Suez was the climax to a protracted coup. Eden wasn't to the taste of Hoover and his ilk. This went back to '30s Spain. Anthony knew too well what the Americans could be like, and they were likewise unsure of Churchill's heir apparent. Was there an alternative? Not in '51..... so Winston, the poor devil, had to be flogged along for those few extra miles....spent as he was. In he came, and that gave time to we who were in thrall to Washington time to consolidate our position and nurture leadership material from amongst our own, in Cabinet and on the benches."

"And Macmillan was perceived to have the credentials," ventured Jeremy.

"Much more so than, for instance, Butler. Rab enjoyed the fuller respect within the Party, but he didn't have the kidology, the ruthlessness. Your average Briton still had to feel they were in some way superior. Mac had this elan. He could pull it off. All Butler had was honesty....... a dangerously impolitic honesty."

"......For who was going to buy 'the orderly management of decline'," said Hugh

"And Walter?" asked Jeremy.

"The executioner's assistant," said Sir Edward. "Anthony was no top table bully, not like Margaret. He was goaded into a bullying reaction, one that he didn't have the nerve to see through."

"A situation that the Washington men had been happy to foster," added Jeremy.

"Coming to the top job and finding things slipping away so, he felt he had to demonstrate that he could be as resolute as his predecessor had so famously been sixteen years before. But when in his career had Winston attempted a Suez scale operation without Washington's positively voiced prior approval?" Politicians rhetoric, this was, from Sir Edward.... suggesting infallibility. Jeremy wasn't letting it pass.

"Norway in '40, a bungle, and before that Gallipolli, back in the Great War..... a disaster. But Eden could have won the canal. Victory was within his grasp."

"The prize though," countered Sir Edward calmly, "even if claimed, could it ever be anything but a diplomatic headache? Washington didn't need that, not then. Ergo, Washington didn't need Anthony. The warrant was signed in America, where Harold was tipped off quietly that given a clean break the succession might still be his.... But he had to do the deed. Would he carry it through we wondered?"

"Did he have any choice?" Jeremy speculated.

"Buoyed by a successful party conference, and dazzled by the prospect of a victory in the field Anthony was slow to sense danger... the platform he strutted hid a trap door. What he attempted to stitch together with France and Israel became the noose. When it's a one man foray then one man takes prize or punishment."

"And punishment it had to be," added Hugh, "in capital measure, swiftly administered."

"Timing being everything," explained Sir Edward. "If the one could be quickly and efficiently dispatched then the others might be viable still, indeed all the better equipped for the future."

"Better cautioned as to what constituted a capital crime," said Hugh.

"And look who watches the proud Premier on to the trap, and who signals the moment for the lever to be thrown." Sir Edward lifted the obituary.

"His Minister of Defence," said Jeremy. "On the very eve of battle, with all cranked to full momentum, Walter wants out. Harold performs his *volte face*, the trap opens and there dangles Antony. Measure him up please for the ermine! Maybe his choice of Harold as Chancellor was unfortunate. Climb a greasy pole and there's slippery people all around. But to place Walter Monckton at Defence...... that sounds like carelessness." Neither son nor father were disputing.

"Pure theatre," reflected Jeremy, "such as could only be staged by the Westminster Palace of Varieties..... so clinical, but at least Anthony was granted a comfortable retirement. For Duggan, six years before, it had been the river.... and for young Cairns, the distant dirt of Korea. But back to earlier, I heard you say 'not counting David Windsor.' What did you mean? That the Duke was equally remiss in his choice of mediator back in '36?"

Sir Edward was thoughtful. His words were to be carefully chosen.

"In Duchy circles it was noted that Walter emerged from the abdication crisis with greatly enhanced career prospects.

"Unlike his boss," quipped Hugh.

"Quite," continued the father, "and it's been suggested this might have followed from the requirement placed on the former King that he should make his home, or homes, abroad."

"The issue of exile you mean," said Jeremy.

"Not strictly," Sir Edward answered. "For as a subject of his successor the former Monarch would have had every right to stay in this country. No one within the realm, King or Commoner, is statute empowered to banish another national."

"But you mention a requirement father," Hugh said.

"Which was made part of the financial settlement reached between Walter, acting on behalf of the Duke, and the Baldwin Government. This was akin to a contract. Were the Duke to repudiate part of this he stood to lose all promised to him by the whole."

"So this was where the Government imposed their condition," reasoned the lecturer.

"So far as I can work out, they didn't dare. The concession originated from Walter, totally unbidden apparently. He didn't so much as sell the pass as hand it over..... gift wrapped!"

Hugh gasped.

"With friends like that....!"

"Little was said about this at the time," acknowledged Sir Edward softly, indicating with raised palm that no more need be said now.....the more personal the betrayal, the more distasteful.

"But a grateful establishment would always remember," persisted Jeremy. "And remember in particular this talent for facilitating a tidy demolition. That knack of keeping things propped up until almost the last. Remember it at the expense of the exiled Poles, the Nizam, Eden, and, finally of course, poor old Welensky. He had to have known what was coming, he of Polish descent, and Prime Minister of a political anachronism, the Nizam of Broken Hill, uncrowned King of Kariba...... "

"....and maybe he did," continued Sir Edward. "Easy meat he, after all who'd been snared before, and if you're saying 'suspiciously easy', I can agree." He looked across to the wall clock. "But back to '50.... you're right. Washington had a strategy and they were looking to develop Walter as a key figure."

"And Randolph?" asked Hugh.

"Too high a profile," said the father. "Too much of an accident waiting to happen, a likely loose cannon. Journalism was where he belonged, the sniping columnist. How he would rile Anthony!"

"But in those two elections, '50 and '51, he was hammering against a lively young Mr Foot in Devonport," reflected Hugh.

"And that was bringing the media down in force, and it was feared that with my selection for Plymouth North, and Walter's by election so imminent at Bristol West then the whole project might unravel should those events of '37 some how come to light. Randolph had been there as well, you see. As I've said, they knew Duggan was seeking to contact Cairns but they didn't know exactly what he had...."

".........and naturally they feared the worst," Hugh put in.

"They thought he might have got right to the heart of things, as some one seems to have done with the *Kampala*," ventured Jeremy, angling, but the bait was seemingly being ignored, for the moment at least.

"So Duggan meets with his accident," reasoned Hugh. "His cottage is searched and also his boat, but what they seek is never actually found for the man has smelt a rat. And what he had he's concealed, and it stays concealed until now."

"But the full import, how it pertains to what's going on now off Lanmouth Quay, that can stay under the carpet," claimed Jeremy. "It's only me that's lifted a corner. Grigson is still checking out Russian factory ships, he's way back in third, easily a week behind I'd say."

"But there's a second, you're saying?" recalled Sir Edward.

"Quite a close second, clever undoubtedly, but he's old and he's infirm. If we move quickly we can be way out of reach." The former MP was looking puzzled..... who might this be?

"Think back to Duggan's funeral, " prompted Jeremy. "Who else was there?"

"It was me and Stanaway, Arthur Stanaway, Cairns' boss at the *Packet*. He was covering for Cairns, the youngster having gone for the job that took him to Korea. And I was wary about Stanaway. That was why I collected him and we went to Mylor in my car. I couldn't be sure Duggan hadn't confided in him, but when we got talking I concluded he hadn't.....I was fairly sure. But that's not to say he thought all to be what it seemed. He wasn't overly impressed with what had come out of his protege's interview with Ida, and I think there were misgivings too about the job offer....the way it had come out of the blue."

"He encouraged the lad to go for it though." Hugh was half enquiring.

"He did," confirmed Sir Edward, "because he took pride in his boys hitting the big time. A streak of vanity it was, one that would tarnish to a streak of regret. It came to poison his whole being. I suspect he'd thought to warn Cairns, but then thought better. It was Stanaway who sent the note and the Whisky down to *The Globe,* this at the purported request of Cairns. A telegram came down from London apparently. Stanaway obliged, but it wasn't long before he was doubting its veracity."

"And thereafter blaming himself," said Jeremy, "and finding solace in that same bad medicine. I've been told that this was what killed him."

"Told by who?" demanded Hugh Trembath.

"By the person who today gave me this book," replied Jeremy. His fingers double tapped on the hard cover.

"There was the curate who officiated the funeral," remembered Sir Edward hazily, knowing the fellow to be an obvious candidate for elimination.

"Getting colder," confirmed Jeremy. " *'Slide Rule'* was given to me this morning, by someone who'd been holding it since '57."

"And that person had obtained it from Stanaway," said Hugh.

"There was a go between," said Jeremy, "his name.......Ben McKinley. Heard that one Sir Edward?"

"McKinley, yes, one I've waited a long time for, almost given up on in fact. I've seen his work, briefly. It was shown to me once. That was in London, by St Paul's, another funeral, in '65. I was told to look out for him. He was a journalist, of Cairns' generation, but American. I did look out, but nothing, nothing at all in twenty years and six months........ until now."

"He'd befriended Cairns in Korea," explained Jeremy. "And were Francis to die, as we know he did, there'd been a promise between them that he would come to England, come to Cornwall, to check on Duggan... to see how he was faring. The promise was kept, but not until '57. This I'm told was significant. He wasn't stirring things while Walter remained at the top table, the circumstances surrounding Cairns' death suggesting to him that further lives might be at risk"

"And Duggan he found in Mylor Churchyard," said Hugh.

"But he traced Stanaway to some drying out place in Plymouth," continued Jeremy. "And, though he's not told me this, I'm led to believe old Jack Butters received a visit too. Old Jack, who's blind now and was almost blind then. We can picture McKinley asking quietly around Churchtown after Duggan and being told of the one special friend who still lived in Mylor."

"So it's old Jack who's been filling you in on all this," said Sir Edward gravely.

"Old Jack was at Duggan's funeral......remember?"

Edward Trembath thought for a moment, and then the words came slowly.

"He was. He'd given the plot, he'd dug the grave, and he was there to inter."

"And to watch I think," added Jeremy. "For though Duggan died before he could meet Cairns, or talk about him with Stanaway, he did confide in Jack Butters. On the day that Duggan died Cairns had agreed to meet him. Because of the unexpected job offer the appointment was broken. Duggan was never to know the reason, but he must have felt things to be awry. Jack was working on the ferry and Duggan pulled over and they talked. That's when what Duggan had hoped to give to Cairns changed hands, and this is why it was never found by those who so feared what it might be.....your associates from across the pond."

"And Butters was very careful," figured Hugh.

"He was instructed to be. For Duggan was as perturbed as he was disappointed. He hoped that Cairns would return but suspected he might not himself see that day...."

"....or even so much as another morning," said Sir Edward, hinting at his having endured similar misgivings.

"So Butters was told to save these things for Cairns," said Jeremy, "and should he also die then it was to be saved for when democracy returned to Spain. That would bring a free press, and amongst those who'd borne the consequences of the *Usk Vale* incident Duggan's name would at last be cleared. There were other things with these newspaper clippings. I'll show you."

All that was left to come out of the folder slid to the floor, every last scrap. Moving forward, and bending, Hugh lifted the copy of Rory Duggan's personal Falmouth-Biscay log. This and the two letters from the Board of Trade were quietly perused.

"Makes a good story," commented the son," and it might clear Duggan's name, but what else is there to suggest his death to have been anything but accidental? That's how it was recorded at the inquest, see here." Hugh had found the relevant cutting. He passed it to his father, and then produced the Cairns obituary. "And we learn from this that Cairns died on the battlefield. Dangerous places they are. Randolph himself took a wound in Korea. No one's saying that was conspired. Other journalists died out there, it was part of the chaos that war normally is. OK, so Stanaway felt guilty. That doesn't prove that Cairns was done away with."

"Fair enough as far as it goes," countered Jeremy, "and that's really no further than '57 when McKinley comes over. He visits Cairns' former fiance, as promised, and he finds out that what each had written and sent to the other was at stark variance to what had been delivered and read. He visits Mylor and he reads Jack Butters' long saved back issues of the *Chronicle*. He reads Cairns despatches, which aren't Cairns despatches. They can't be, for they report him to be scores of miles from where they actually were. And this can only point to him having been dead meat from the moment he left Cornwall, or at least from the moment it was realised that this story of Duggan's was still somewhere at large."

"And now, starting to see the fuller picture, this McKinley character needs also to be a bit careful," said Hugh.

"And I think he was," said Jeremy with confidence. "It would have been the suspicion that he could be a marked man that led him to delay coming across until '57. And by then I'd say that his discharge of this 'made in Korea' promise was part of a need to draw a line under his experiences on that God forsaken peninsula. Another conflict was brewing, in Vietnam, and we can bet he'd have had firmly decided views. There was much persuading to do, organising and campaigning. Nothing was going to bring Cairns back, or Duggan, and nothing was going to undo Monckton's work. Eden was yesterday's man and, the British economy had ailed to what looked an incurable condition."

"So this McKinley drifts out of it at this point," said Hugh.

"I thought so, until your father spoke just now of twenty years ago. That was the mid '60s?"

"1965, January 1965. I attended two funerals that month, the first a quiet Kent village affair. The second was an immense occasion, Winston's funeral, a State funeral, and it was after this that the name was put to me."

"I was in the guard for that one," said Hugh.

"Attending were world and Commonwealth leaders, each with their entourage of security people," explained Sir Edward. "And you know what any funeral is like, you get your mourning and behind the veil you get your politicking.....the bigger the funeral, the bigger the people there, the bigger the issues. And this was the biggest of all of course. Long planned it had been, and hosting what became a summit like gathering of world leaders was Harold Wilson, new to government.....in fact I think still in his first one hundred days. Schedules were adjusted to accommodate 'informal talks', and at the head of the queue was Lyndon Johnson. From time to time the Americans will seek to test just how special the 'special relationship' remains, and this was such a moment."

"He was wanting then to escalate the bombing of North Vietnam," said Jeremy. "He needed Wilson squarely behind him and he wanted the British people to be comfortable about the backing given."

"So what was being nurtured was a spirit of Anglo American

accord," said Sir Edward. "It wouldn't have done, for instance, for the press to have been harking back to the events of ten years before, to the Geneva summit of '54, to the elections in Vietnam that followed two years later.......nor to the fracture between Washington and London of that same autumn, over Suez. And they certainly didn't want an in depth analysis of the political career of Sir Walter Monckton."

"But what danger was there of that?" asked Hugh. "The man had quit Cabinet and the commons in '57. This was '65, eight years on for goodness sake."

"But the name had come back into the news," explained the father quietly. "Walter had just died. He'd passed away a little less than a fortnight before Winston. His was the other funeral I'd attended, in the quiet Kent village. We'd heard the predictable eulogising, but there seemed a strong chance of more besides..... for second in the queue for Wilson, behind LBJ, was a Mr Ian Smith..."

".....leader of the white tribe of Rhodesia, amongst whom the name Monckton would ever be notorious." Jeremy smirked. "Cause for Hoover to get jumpy."

"It was," confirmed Sir Edward. "McKinley had been identified as a potential trouble maker. That he'd met and befriended Cairns whilst in Korea was sure to have been noted, and now he was openly opposing the Vietnam project. They didn't want him snooping and stirring..... "

"...... snooping in Cornwall and stirring in London," said Jeremy.

"So if he happened to turn up, I was to tell them," Sir Edward continued. "They could then head him off. Downes it was who collared me, right outside St Paul's. I hadn't seen him for years."

"A surprise for you," said Hugh.

"It was, but I recognised him immediately. He congratulates me on the success of my career, and he thanks me for all that I'd done, and was doing...."

"....as if you had any choice," scoffed Jeremy.

".....And then he produces this American newspaper. It was an edition of *The Washington Tribune,* about four days old. It was folded so as to reveal an inside article, I've still got it. I saved the page. It's up in London, in the flat with the books. The article speculates on the after funeral discussions between Wilson and Smith, anticipating that they'll be fruitless. The author is McKinley, and he identifies a fundamental lack of trust between the parties. It stems he says from Monckton's attitude to the Federation almost five years before. He mentions Monckton's death and adds the aside that he'd been one of the mystery figures of international politics for some time. At turning point moments he'd often been pivotally placed.....and not so much for lending weight to the shove as for oiling the levers and the hinges. More was going to come out about all this, McKinley was sure. It went back a long way, to the darkest hours of the last war and before."

"And you're saying that whilst writing on Monckton for his American readership this McKinley would have been mulling on Jack Butters," remarked Hugh, now lifting and reading the Cairns obituary. The lecturer offered a 'why not' shrug and looked down again at the book, Stanaway's legacy.

McKinley had played this well, he thought. He'd planted this and then kept a safe distance. It was to be a struggle, dragging Washington from the mire of Vietnam, a firm footing would be required and finding that needed to be his priority. Others, though, were to join the legion of the less lucky. Who was to be allowed to know what? Who had to be silenced? The old questions that did for Duggan and Cairns were more recently to claim Chadwick and Murrell. South Georgia was hardly the point, nor were the Falklands and their put upon islanders. At stake was the credibility of the Iron Lady. This was a cold war issue. The east-west arms race was almost won. It just needed unity, and resolve, and as many Cruise missiles as could be mustered, and the lead would then be unassailable.

But Reagan and Thatcher had to be shoulder to shoulder. They had to look in earnest, look irreplaceable. She had to be victorious. The alternative might have been Michael Foot, he who had figured in '50/'51, the disarmer........ not a happy prospect!

If the task force had to be sent, and the *Belgrano* had to be sunk, then all had to be seen to be Washington sanctioned. Were it not, then the butcher-bird would have been out on a limb. She would have fallen, as surely as Eden had.

"And you're saying that old Jack Butters is the one we've got to watch," said Sir Edward, snapping Jeremy from the reverie.

"He's long had his ear to this place," replied Jeremy.

"But you maintain you're ahead of him, by virtue of having caught up with that book..... the link between Stanaway, McKinley, and the fiance who'd corresponded with Cairns whilst he worked in Korea."

"She thought she had, but was deceived in this"

"So I suppose she's been in the hunt too," said Hugh.

"Not actively. She's kept her nose clean. By taking this book from McKinley she allowed him to erect a signpost, but that was it. It points and I follow, and by a slightly different route I come to a closer understanding of Butters and what he already knows."

"So how can you claim to be ahead of him?" Hugh Trembath's wariness of a trap resurfaced.

"Treachery." Jeremy was blunt. "He's been feeding us clues, through the boy mainly, thinking that we'll stand together under Grigson. Thinking that what I hunt down I'll straightway bring back to the *Speedwell*......and yes, that was my initial intention I'll grant."

"There's been a fall out," said Hugh. "You've been let down." The assertion was correct. Confirmation from Jeremy was curt.

"If Butters has misread me it's because I've misread Grigson, trusted him too much."

"You sound vengeful," said Sir Edward. "You've sustained deep personal offence, deep beyond the blind man's imagination and measure. Sweet is it, this getting back at him.....or her....or both?" In fact it wasn't at all sweet. The pain remained. The hoped for balm was instead rendering a sourness that served only to further embitter. His course was set though. Too far in he was to disengage. He would have to see it through. There was the cash to come. That might console. In the meantime he had the past, always a sanctuary.

"This other American, Sir Edward, the one from the wedding who was on McKinley's tail.... was that the last you ever saw of him, at Churchill's funeral?"

"I spoke with Downes just once more, and again the encounter was seemingly casual rather than arranged..... but this time less of a surprise. Another funeral it was, in '72, at Windsor, or rather a 'lying in state' for I didn't go over to Frogmore for the actual committal."

"David Windsor's," said Jeremy.

"His death coming a matter of weeks after that of Mr J. Edgar Hoover. A good moment for them to sign me off, I thought to myself..... a little too hopefully. They were reviewing the old relationship again and there was a little packing and filling required."

"Was there a particular problem?" asked Hugh.

"Ted Heath, the Tory PM who'd been chief whip at the time of

Suez. He'd long been unsure of the US State Department, and at the Pentagon there was this increasing tendency to view British soil as its own. He wasn't for that. It was partly why he was so keen on the closer Europe."

"I remember, the Americans wanted to counter the Soviet backed Arab threat to Israel with British based squadrons," said Hugh, "and Ted was full against that."

"Precisely, and my brief was to identify those who were amenable to his being replaced and subtly guide them in their choice of an alternative."

"Towards one appreciated by the White House," said the son. "And you found the girl all right. She's there to stay, much to Ted's chagrin."

"But back to Carwinion," said Jeremy. "We hear of this high level intrigue, and then we get this low life barter of guns for drugs. How have we managed to stoop so?"

"Nothing new about our ruling party dabbling in arms transactions," said Sir Edward, "shady or otherwise. If Maggie's son is out there lining his pockets then why should I apologise for seeking to make this place a little more secure for my heirs. Back in '37 it only took a hand of cards to leave me financially embarrassed. I've come a long way, but there's still the occasional banking crisis to ride out, and the odd unexpected share collapse. No worries though, for reassuringly to hand there's the same trusty antidote for burnt fingers ..... the old green backed salve that you yourself now look to dip into. Be careful though. Scoop too deeply and you're trapped. When I'm long gone they'll be calling on Hugh here, and maybe on Helen. You want to talk to Rosa, and Nigel's boy."

The younger Trembath winced. It was a bleak future. He wasn't wishing to dwell.

"Tell me more about old Jack, Mr Barnes. He knows a bit about the *Kampala* you say, that'll be more than me, but how much and what? Last year my father here says she's coming back and I wonder why, like many others. He says there's to be an extension to her military role, and that this is an undercover thing. In other words, I must ask no further. He's been told because our creek side shed is wanted, the Viceroy shed, and also, just for a while, a particular person needs to be fitted into a particular job on our local ferry. The whys and the wherefores are not my business. I'm to keep to my usual general look out, and anything at all irregular that might pertain to the ship I'm to mention........ but only to that one person, the ferry hand."

"So having heard the term 'military role', you can't really be surprised at the mention of guns," said Jeremy.

"I've had clues, I've been brought clues even," said Hugh. "I'm not stupid. Where I can I cover them."

"But where you can't.....? And think of the number you might have missed," countered the lecturer. "Think too on how carefully that old man listens."

"So about the *Kampala* specifically," said Sir Edward, leaning back in his chair, "this is what Hugh's asking. What does Jack Butters know about that ship? What could he know?"

"I've heard that these last two years of troop ship service have not been continuous," began Jeremy, obliquely. "That she was brought back here, to Falmouth, at the end of '83, and treated to a fortnight's worth of dry dock work, engine and prop shaft jobs mainly. To the fitters, the bridge and the communications suite were strictly out of bounds. Media interest was discouraged. Security was tight. But naturally there was local speculation. Why had the *Kampala* been chosen to be a hospital ship in the first place? And why, when the job was done and at vast expense she'd been restored to her former school cruise specification, was she suddenly then re chartered by the MOD and expensively reconverted again, with all the business of refitting the landing deck? They'd had another ship lined up for all this, from the Cunard people. What was wrong with that? Answers would have been various...... official and unofficial. Some were best ignored, others warranted consideration. Jack Butters' antennae would have missed little......."

"........ leaving him to conclude?" said Hugh.

"......that the *Kampala* had been more than a hospital ship, because previously she'd been more than a floating classroom. From '68 to '82 she'd criss-crossed the Med in this role, taking the kids to Malta, Greece, Cyprus, Turkey, Israel, Egypt, and those were turbulent times for these parts, still are. She made an ideal listening station, that's what Jack Butters thinks. Appropriately equipped and manned, she was assigned to monitor and relay signals traffic."

"A spy ship no less," affirmed Sir Edward.

"A sideline that could only enhance the vessel's credentials when the call went out for a task force hospital ship" continued Jeremy. "And down there it would be about more than simple surveillance. There were operational commands to relay, and crucial commands..... relating to the deployment of armed units."

"Armed units?" queried Hugh, the Naval man.

"Such as your nuclear sub, *HMS Conqueror,*" replied Jeremy. "You'll be aware of her notoriety." Son glanced uncomfortably towards father. He wanted to see surprise or indignation, to perhaps hear outrage.....but there was no reaction. Jeremy sensed a hit, and in ascribing it to Butters rather than to Gareth he'd lent to the thrust an extra potency. Close combat this was..... stab and stab again.

"Brian Chadwick and Hilda Murrell, I spoke of them earlier, the cruise ship Captain and an Aunt to the Commander at signals HQ. Each could have learned of the *Kampala's* part in the attack on the *Belgrano*. Neither would have been happy, and each would have been feared capable of igniting, certainly fanning, a politically destructive scandal....as was Duggan all those years ago..... as was Cairns. Rumours emanating from Latin America might be rubbished as loopy propaganda, but home produced whispers are not so easily dismissed."

"Which is why the ship couldn't be allowed back to the Med and her former tasks," deduced Hugh. "Propaganda wise she was a bad risk...."

".... and the Americans, they now wanted her on a short rein." Jeremy explained. "They'd been bounced into taking Britain's side in an all out armed conflict. They'd been caught out. The ship had been instrumental. They now seek redress."

"And you're saying that the old man has worked out all this *Kampala* business, unaided, in that creek side cottage?" Hugh could believe only so much.

"He had these things taken from Duggan all those years ago, and, with this, whatever McKinley had told of in '57. He'd worked out that US Intelligence had never fully relinquished its wartime hold over this place. It becomes then a matter of merely identifying the next visitation. When it comes, *Kampala* shaped, he's tuned in....... quite literally. Up until '57 Jack Butters would have been pleased to do no more than his friend had asked, that's simply to wait for Franco's inevitable demise and then get the tale once intended for Cairns fed instead to the new Spanish media...... for them to make of it what they wanted. Big story, little story, or no story, it didn't matter. What had been asked would have been done."

"But after McKinley........" Sir Edward sighed as he spoke, he knew what he was about to hear.

"The blind man sees things rather differently. From then on he has it in for this place. Franco lingers, but he goes, as we all must eventually, and with the predicted lifting of Spanish press controls what does our man do? He does nothing. He sits tight, and he listens closely. He hears of difficulties afflicting the likes of your friend Mr Du Cann, and he senses that as prosperous as this estate might appear it could well be a good deal less secure than widely thought. It had happened before, and it's as if he knows that it's about to happen again. It's a simple matter of time, that's all....... and he's not disappointed. The burnt fool's bandaged finger goes wabbling back to the fire."

Sir Edward, downcast and lost for any reply shifted uncomfortably in his chair. There was more to endure.

"And you couldn't have given him fuller notice of course," continued Jeremy. "It was a clever idea, shifting young Spargo from the ferry with that unrefusable working boat, too clever, 'too clever by half' as old Bobbity might have said. Everyone's happy, everyone's sweet......," the lecturer broke into a chuckle, "but for the grandfather with the long memory you make it so, so simple. He senses something's afoot, and look what you do! You give him a patrolman, and to his patrolman you give a patrol vessel."

"So you're now saying young Spargo's in on this," Hugh was nervously to his feet.

"Not consciously, at least as far as I know, but this is the way the old man's been working it with all of us. You want to think back, the pair of you. Whatever you've said to the man, however innocuous, however far back, he'll have sieved every nuance."

And they were thinking when moments later a van was heard to swing in onto the outside gravel. A lighter vehicle than Prout's, it had to be the ferry-hand's. They'd driven up from the slip. Hugh rose. He went to the door. Sir Edward remained with Jeremy. Neither spoke. The expected two were admitted and all filed into the room..... a procession, ordered so as to declare a set rank as well as the root and means of its authority.

Hugh led, cowed and glancing nervously towards his father. Prout followed. More erect, he glared across to the lecturer, the dark eyes blending contempt with suspicion. The ferry hand was last, shepherding the other two, and now he had all corralled. Hanging casually in his grip was a sawn off shotgun. The message was chilling......I say, you do.

Here was a second requisition, a return after forty years. Then it had been Shermans on the lawn, now it was a twelve bore and it was indoors. Sir Edward offered no resistance, only a frown of distaste as the gunman, Baz, moved to a position behind his chair. He sneered down at Jeremy's papers, some on the table, most on the floor. He waved at them with the weapon.

"What does he know?" The demand was brusque.

"As much as we do..... and more besides," answered Sir Edward.

"And no one knows he's here?"

"They would work it out if I didn't show," said Jeremy nervously. The ferry hand ignored him. They all did.

"I've told them at the base," said Sir Edward. "You know the arrangements. You will disappear. Tonight, Baz, is your last night in Truro. Tomorrow's to be your last day on the ferry. They'll be sending a truck down to Tolverne tomorrow night. Our task is to have all ready. It'll take all the guns, and all the dope, your self, and the four on the ship. Suitable replacements will have been found, Puertos, suitably dumb. Carwinion will be clean, so too the *Kampala*. I'm getting back to London."

"Which leaves your son, and Jim, and this learned gentleman to carry their lives on as normal," said the ferry-hand, his cold eyes moving to each in turn. Jeremy remained outwardly composed. This was a test of nerve, a severe test.

"I'm looking to move up the line before September, time for a change, a fresh start," the lecturer announced shakily.

"And for this I've promised a little financial assistance," said Sir Edward. The gunman's gaze stayed with Jeremy, weighing the person, weighing the situation.

"But it's not all been about money," said Hugh, and Jeremy's face fell. "You never answered earlier. You were with the party that went onto the *Kampala* the other morning. Was it that woman, the nurse who went to war? Has she let you down? You've garnered all this and it warrants a lot more from them than you've been handed. You go away, you come back, and you find that she and the lawman are cutting you out. You had this, and you had it all ready to share...... but no longer is it going to them. Instead you bring it here." Jeremy's continued silence was confirmation, and Hugh wasn't about to relent. "The word from Percuil yesterday evening was that Grigson had a woman with him."

"Grigson?" Prout wasn't familiar with the name. Hugh obliged.

"He sails the timber cabin cruiser, blue hull, red sails, the *Speedwell*. Holds himself out as a writer, another journalist....."

"........when in fact he's with the law," added the father.

"Branch?" demanded the gunman.

"A Home Office department, one concerned with the movement of drugs through ports and harbours. "

"And what does he know?" demanded the ferry hand.

"Quite a bit," said Jeremy. "But not as much as me, not yet, and this is why I'm here. He knows you're at the heart of this, but for the moment he's looking the other way. Sir Edward's right. You can cut loose without having to write too much off."

"And me?" asked Prout.

"He's not sure. He realises that guns are being moved, but takes them to be of Eastern bloc origin, and probably coming off the factory ships. He knows you're close to the action, but doesn't count it out that you could yourself be a watcher..... like him but for the Foreign Office, their concern being with the weapons rather than drugs."

Prout was almost amused.

"Long time since I've taken cash from MI6," he murmured. He then became grave. "But if he's corrected, where do I stand then?"

"You carry on as normal," said the gun holder. "Get stuck into that odd job work. Don't panic. I'll be gone and so will the guns. You just stonewall. Hugh does the same. He can say he's aware of his Viceroy shed having been let out, and of the rent coming in for his agent ..... but as to the identity of the user and that person's actual business, why should he know that? OK, you're on your own the pair of you, but that was always possible. You knew that."

"Did I?" protested Hugh.

"Well you know now," said the gunman, sharply. "Be advised. What you don't do is run. At best that leaves you friendless; at worst, hunted by both sides. Stay put. The cover will hold, provided you don't bolt."

Neither looked particularly convinced.

"Might burglary or bonfire be options?" suggested Jeremy, tentatively. The others were listening. Encouraged, he continued. "Tomorrow evening the Speedwell and her contents are to be left unattended. The team will be gathering over in Philleigh."

"We sit tight," said Sir Edward. "Undisturbed, Grigson will be happy to set off on his Tuesday morning sail...... and, if he's away then for the best part of a week, we can be comfortably tidied up."

"And Morrish?" said Prout.

"There's nothing to connect him with any of you," answered Baz. " When he gets hauled in yes, he'll talk about me. But what will they hear that's not already known? And where are they going to find me anyway? I'll have left next door days before. And then there'll be the matching kilo of coke that'll be unearthed in his garden. With that he'll know he's going down, squeal and squeal as he might."

"The fall guy," said Jeremy.

"Save the sympathy," sneered the gunman. "He knew the risks."

Prout was far from reassured.

"If he's going in then the guy whose job he took will be coming out," he reasoned. "There'll be questions. For starters they'll be asking how the shit got onto his boat. Hugh, your man down at Percuil, is he going to stand the heat?"

The ferry-hand intervened, forestalling any reply.

"There'll be time to sort that out between you," he said gruffly. "In fact it's something you might ponder whilst taking this man's car over to the mine." He turned to Jeremy. "If we could have your keys?"

The scent of gun oil brooked no dissent. The lecturer's hand went swiftly to his pocket. "Jim can drive it. Hugh, you can follow in yours and bring him back when all's tucked away. It'll be time then to start thinking about emptying the shed."

Prout took the keys. He led, the younger Trembath followed. Baz took Hugh's chair. The gun was placed on the floor. Jeremy felt less oppressed. Where there'd been four there were now just two, the two who really mattered. He turned squarely towards Baz.

"You've been recognised, you know that?" Silence followed. Was this too provocative?

"Always a risk," responded the ferry-hand, coolly. "Tell me

then......who by?"

"By the nurse," replied Jeremy, emboldened, "and I think you know where from.... your recall being the more precise. You were looking to avoid her the other morning and maybe you thought you had, but not to sufficient degree. She had your face and the place will come....or places should I say?"

"And you've worked it out I suppose."

"Because I've worked out what you are,"

"So tell us, where do you think our paths might have crossed, hers and mine?"

The man needed to know, he was the anxious one now and the lecturer didn't need to be too immediate with his answer. It was the moment to angle.

"You take your orders from the top. You're permanent staff, unlike Prout. You take him on only when needed....like now, and when there's low life to be recruited, and instructed, and paid or punished. You've been associated with that ship for a good five, six years, possibly more. When she worked the Med she was one of your spy ships. The Captain, poor old Chadwick, he didn't mind that so much did he?" Jeremy paused. Would the gunman bite? He did.

"Not a fighting man, Chadwick, and he was adamant that his shouldn't be a fighting ship. With the over side Red Cross he'd have preferred her to be without the listening work even."

"But she was given a deal more than that," said Jeremy. "And you were there in Gibraltar to see that she was appropriately fitted out. You didn't sail with her, but you did fly down to Freetown when Chadwick had to be taken off. If it was medical alarm, then it was security alarm too, and you had to be there to oversee the appropriate treatment. Kate caught glimpses of you at both bases. At the time she thought little of it, that's why she can't quite pin you. It'll come though and then she'll tell Grigson, and whatever interest he's retained in those floating fish factories will suddenly wither. He'll be looking this way again, of that you can be sure."

"And he'll report upwards," countered Baz, "because that's his job, and do you really think his superiors to be above mine?"

" I don't, but you and they, you're still about to act on what I say. You're getting out, quickly and quietly. And that means it's now about fire proofing. Anything incriminating you either tidy away or you torch,

352

and that includes people. Morrish you mentioned. Others will be coming to mind. No warning they'll have. It'll be hitting them that they're on their own........ and you'll be wanting them to stay hit. Lest this place be threatened, and other bigger reputations."

"Not bad," answered Baz, cagily. "Not entirely accurate, but you've grasped the main essential....... why, for a couple of nights, we can't let you out of our sight. We wouldn't want you visited by the kind of misfortune that claimed Captain Chadwick and Miss Murrell."

"Misfortune?" Jeremy had more precise words.

"No one was intending to murder the old lady, even Dalyell can accept that. She shouldn't have struggled so. As for the Captain, you've said yourself that he hadn't been above a degree of subterfuge...."

".....a relatively minor degree, beyond which he wasn't ready to venture," argued Jeremy.

"Unfortunate in the sense of unforseen," joined Sir Edward, pleading almost. "Few had anticipated the Argentine invasion. Our response had to be a hasty affair. Things were eventually stitched after a fashion, but don't look too closely at the seams. The rough edges were very rough..... they still are. Who would have guessed that so many on the *Belgrano* would be lost? This was when Chadwick truly became a problem, but remember, he was seriously ill. None of it can be said to have been calculated"

But it was a mention of Hilda that intrigued Jeremy, from one who hadn't been there to hear him earlier. It was careless of the man, and this made him all the more threatening. The lecturer chose not to challenge. He could raise this later, perhaps, with Prout. They were going to be working together, that would be the time. He must take care, with his choice of moment and choice of words.

Sir Edward stood. He moved to leave the room, beckoning Jeremy to follow. "I'll show you to a bed. It'll be three or four hours before you can start. You need sleep, I can see."

The ferry-hand lifted and 'broke' the shotgun. That was his assent..... no argument. Jeremy scooped together his papers, the book, and the folder. Clutching all he was led through to the staircase and up. Baz remained seated, the gun to hand. The others would soon be back. He had firm control.

*

"........so if we're gathering at Philleigh for eight o clock I want you Jack out on the water from seven until......."

".....the light starts to fade. I'll need to be back 'ere before ten, else I'll not be seeing my way back in."

"That'll have to do then," said Gareth. " Any one intent on mischief will have the same problem. The critical time, when he'll be at his most vulnerable, I think we've got covered."

"Any partic'lar boat you'm spectin'?" asked the old man from his chair. The Welshman again turned to the grandson.

"Seen anything of the *Spartan* these past few days?"

"Prout?......Seen 'im only this mornin', before nine" declared young Jack. "In 'is boat, 'e crossed in front of me where the rivers come together just above Tolverne. I were comin' down...."

".....past Tregothnan," said Gareth

"And 'e were movin' up river, as if crossin' from Roundwood to Tolverne, but going past the slip...... not pullin' in."

"Following the Fal," said Gareth.

"Okkerd thing t'attempt 'round low tide," remarked Old Jack.

"An' bein' so low in the water," added his grandson.

"You mean weighed down?" Gareth was alert. "What with? Did you see anything of his load?"

"Only tarpaulin."

"So why up there do you think........ at low tide, so early in the day? Where could he have been headed?"

"Did'n 'ave t'be goin' no where," offered old Jack Butters. "P'raps 'twere only quiet anch'rage he were seekin', that so's he can unload later on.......when 'tis dark 'gain."

"You want to look along there before you go off to this meetin' you'm havin'," suggested the youngster. "If the *Spartan's* still sat up there 'mongst the mud then that's where 'er'll stay fer the rest of the evenin'."

"Do that," urged the old man. "They'm givin' cossle mist fer lader. Boy 'ere idn go'n'be seein' much if that come in. 'E 'll be longer gettin' back too."

"Whatever you do or don't see this end, I want you to phone this number as soon as possible after ten." Gareth passed a note to young Jack. " You might need to wait for the girl to call me in from the field, bear that in mind if you're having to use a pay phone. If, for any reason, I don't hear from you then I'll try you in the morning. I'll phone to here, Mylor, hopefully before nine, certainly no later than ten."

*

Kate was awake by mid afternoon. She was concerned. Why hadn't she heard from Jeremy? They were due to be at Jane's at eight, and she had another shift beginning at ten. She phoned the college and learned that he hadn't appeared for his afternoon class. This was unusual. The car park was checked, and there was no vehicle. This was odd.

He must have returned and then gone again, but when and to where, and why no word? Had she been found out she wondered. No........ for he would surely have confronted her.

The getting to Philleigh posed no problem. She had a colleague who lived that way and she'd be leaving work at seven. A message to the hospital and she could call by. As for the return, Alan would have to stand a taxi......for the second time in two days, unless of course Jeremy was planning to appear there. What was his game? she wondered.

*

Fog set in on schedule. With a quiet stealth it over rode the late afternoon ebb, choking the estuary with chilling ease. The Carrick Roads felt no sun. At Lamorran, though, light and warmth still filtered, and sufficiently to render from the drifting mist a steam like quality as it crept off the ebbing river onto the faintly glowing estuarine mud.

Gareth was once again on Tregothnan land. He'd propped his machine close to where he'd first been surprised by Alan. Now he was edging his way down river. He stayed beneath the oak. The footing was difficult, but the more sturdy of the dipping branches offered hand-holds as well as cover. He knew what he sought, and there it was, just as young Spargo had predicted.

The craft was anchored, and more towards the far side, at the very edge of the channel. The mystery cargo looked to be undisturbed. The boat had settled beneath its weight. This would be a deliberate grounding, a stranding until the next tide. There was an hour yet of ebb. Nothing was going to move before nightfall. Prout was at the forward, wheelhouse, end. Gareth could hear the rasp of a file, and then there was the glow of a welding torch and a crackle of sparks. The man was at his trade.

But why this wait, and in this place? The size of the boat, the height of the tarpaulin...... it had to be just the one consignment of crates, and the most recent surely. If these had been collected from Charlestown on Saturday and taken to the shed, then they would have rested but one night therein. They'd been smartly moved out, as a precaution maybe, but why not simply across to the *Kampala*? Why should they need to be held here? Maybe later they would go back. They would have to go somewhere. Prout would have to come in at some time......where though?

As he watched there grew the strengthening purr of an approaching boat, something smaller........ necessarily, given the restrictions of tide and visibility. It was moving up river, and as the sound became an indistinct form so it slowed. And Prout had stopped working. There were voices, but the words were no clearer than the shapes.

Gareth moved closer and for a moment the mist thinned sufficiently to allow him to identify the boat, and yes..... at the tiller it was the deck hand. The pair he'd seen at Charlestown were again together. Those were guns out there, beneath that cover. And if they weren't being moved they were being looked after. In the shed they would have been unattended. Was this arrangement, now, felt to be less of a risk? And was this food that was being brought? wondered Gareth. No, for they were both in the open boat now and it was the other who was climbing back on to the *Spartan*, Baz. This was a guard change. The ferry hand was staying. Prout was being relieved. He was taking the smaller boat back to the ferry, its customary place, or perhaps beyond.

*

"We wouldn't have happened to have upset the guy....I suppose?" Jane's sarcasm was not lost on the gathering. The girl was troubled and before they went she was meaning to let them know why. The enquiry was directed at Alan, and for a moment he had no answer.

"If we had then I think we'd know about it." Kate intervention lacked conviction.

"So why hasn't he phoned even?" persisted the girl. "It's the least he could have done."

"He might yet," managed Alan. "And in the meantime we're best to continue as if he were here. If we don't we're wasting time. Kate has to be back at the hospital for ten, and your mother, Jane, she'll be not long after. Gareth, have you had anything more on the ship from your Argentine oppo?.....Gareth?"

The Welshman had slipped out of the conversation. It had been the mention of the missing car....... that was the distraction. If a local map had been produced and he'd been asked to point to where he thought the vehicle might be then a speculative finger would have gone to Lanmouth Creek.......to the Viceroy shed. The loading and the positioning of the *Spartan* had had to be a response. If Jeremy had been blundering about across there, chasing a hunch of his own then Young Jack and he might have witnessed a direct consequence, except that those crates......they hadn't been hoisted onto the *Kampala*. Why not? "Gareth?"

"What took him to London anyway?" Jerked from his reverie, Gareth stumbled back into the conversation. Puzzled silence ensued.

"We've had enough about Jeremy, Gareth," said Alan. "I'm asking about your trip back to Welshpool. Do you have anything new on the ship, from the Argentine." Gareth apologised. Producing from his jacket Alberto's most recent letter, he read the relevant parts. The others heard of the *Kampala's* reported movements and of a possible change of ownership, but were these things really news to Alan? And were they really to the point? One of their number had disappeared. Shouldn't this be the immediate concern?

Jeremy had been peripheral, but no longer, not to Gareth, not since that after Chapel chat with old Jack back at Mylor. There he'd produced that bullet, and as a consequence learned that there were even richer clues to be gathered from the past, and that was Jeremy's element....... one through which he will have trawled at depth. So where had he gone? What had he been doing? Gareth wanted to know, badly. The others seemed indifferent. This vexed.

"Steve, what from you?" asked Alan. "Anything new from Carwinion?"

"Sir Edward's back for a few days. Gareth would have seen him at the Service yesterday."

"Does Jeremy know that he's about?" asked Kate. "We can all recall his interest in the guy when we first met here."

"He knows," confirmed the boy. I phoned your place to tell him last week, Thursday I think. He was grateful. And he was looking forward to coming here tonight, I was looking forward to seeing him."

"Because you hoped that by now he might have perhaps called on the illustrious father and son?" suggested Gareth.

"Yes, and there was something else, separate but in a way related. Again it goes back to our first gathering. When we talked of the Trembaths I mentioned one Walter Monckton. Before the war he was legal adviser to the Duchy, that made him an associate of the young Edward Trembath. Then he got mixed up in the haggling which surrounded the Duke's abdication. He must have impressed the establishment because during the war there were series of top admin jobs and then later, in the 50s, a safe seat at Westminster with front bench positions under Churchill and Eden."

"And this is related?" Jane's bluntness measured impatience.

"Go on, " said Gareth, now he was listening intently to Steve's every word.

"The pre-war association between Trembath and Monckton was to an extent revived when they both became MPs, although of course Sir Edward was never anything but a back bench man. Holding particular fascination for Jeremy is the role Monckton played during the Suez crisis, the fiasco that saw the end of Eden as PM. Washington wanted him out, that's what Jeremy reckons. And they wanted Macmillan to succeed."

"Which he did," said Gareth.

"Well Jeremy's suggestion is that there was more to this than the Premier's hot headedness, that there were external forces at work...... Washington levered, some of them. He would argue that Eden was encouraged to overreach, and then undermined in what amounted to a sophisticated coup, one that required precisely timed communication. At the heart of this he detects Walter..... the fulcrum. At the time the guy

358

was Minister of Defence."

"So he's saying Eden fell victim to a Washington orchestrated conspiracy," said Gareth.

"What else?" sighed Kate. "That's what's going to do for us all, according to Jeremy."

"But I find him a welcome change," countered Steve. "We get so many who lean the other way, who'll put everything down to the Red Menace."

"You listen and he'll talk," quipped the nurse, but Steve was standing firm.

"Well I was interested, and he referred me to a biography of the man. He ordered it for me at the library in Truro. I collected it last week. Before I even left the building I was scanning the book for two or three of the names I'd heard from Hugh, and that's when I stumbled upon what Jeremy might have viewed as a vital indiscretion."

"On whose part?" asked Gareth.

"Monckton's. There was this actress that he was besotted with and she was working in the US during the early years of the war when he was at the Ministry of Information. It seems he was writing to her telling of everything and anything."

"Which for the FBI would have been like saying 'come and get me I'm yours'," remarked Gareth.

"Exactly, so I copied the page and Kate, I slipped it through your door for Jeremy. I was on my way home."

"And I'm sure he was fascinated Steve, and no doubt eternally grateful, but please, please tell me how all this relates to a ship load of Russian guns and Colombian cocaine, and my father's extended tenure of an Exeter prison cell." Jane was becoming animated. It was Gareth who intervened.

"I think what's being said is that maybe Jeremy's no longer so convinced as we are that these guns are of communist origin. Indeed, if he's allowing the factory ships to be just factory ships then he could be seeing the whole transaction as something anti Red in inspiration, anti NARC-FARC anyway. This would fit in with Alberto's account of the ship's return."

"And that means Washington again I suppose," said Kate wearily..

"The CIA at least," said Gareth, "an arm of the White House that where possible strives to keep itself independent of Congress funding, if only in the interests of secrecy. As Grenada is an island in the Caribbean Sea, so there are islands within mainland Colombia, islands of resistance, communities under siege. The nation is slipping back to feudalism. Having carved up the western provinces the coke barons must expand eastwards, expand or wither, it's either one or the other. And who's to stop them? Not central government, not now. It's being left to provincial militias...."

"And they need to be appropriately equipped and trained," said Steve.

"Which they can be," continued Gareth. "But they've got to put up their own money, and that has to come from that same cash crop that's driving on their assailants."

"Fire with fire," said Jane. "So you're saying that the marketing of the drug and the purchase of guns could be a CIA arrangement."

"Why not?" said Gareth. "Think back. We've heard that a little over forty years ago the Carwinion Estate was tightly in the talons of the American eagle. The owner was then brought back, and the place refurbished for him and his heirs to again enjoy, as they do now, but there would have been strings.......surely."

".......and if attached still, that they're not capable of being tugged from time to time?" Said Steve. "Just from talking to Hugh I get a clear parallel between his father's career and that of Monckton. Trembath was ever the underling, but at his more modest level his speed of ascent was no less impressive. There was the Duchy......"

".......the wedding," said Kate, beginning to listen now.

"The good wars for each, " continued Steve, "the reshaping of Plymouth for one and India for the other, then on to Westminster and the impact made there. From this range they do at times look to have been a double act."

" 'And no wonder' is what Jeremy might say," continued Kate, "with each being sustained by the same power."

"And one still is perhaps," suggested Gareth. " Perhaps at this very moment he's being asked to earn his corn."

"Do you buy it Alan?" asked Kate. Grigson was diplomatic.

"Jeremy is obviously an able and enthusiastic historian," he acknowledged, "but to me, in my line, the past is more a source of theory than of hard observable evidence. Yes, it's an intriguing line of enquiry, but that's never the same as fruitful. Shame he's not here to tell us what he has."

Jane eyed him suspiciously. She'd remembered Polgooth, and the camera.

"Are you sure your people haven't apprehended him?" she asked sternly.

Gareth straightened in his seat. He hadn't thought of that. Alan remained calm.

"I'm sure," he said , "and look, so far he's only half a day late. Let's not get paranoid."

"So will you wait around for a day or so until he does turn up?" The girl was almost pleading. She wanted clear progress towards her father's release, more of a commitment.

Alan was, for once, without a ready reply. Kate sensed his difficulty. She could win him a little time.

"At last week's meeting," she began, "the one I didn't come to....did Jeremy mention what I told him about the ferry-hand? I asked him to. Could interest you this, Gareth."

"I don't recall," said Gareth. "It was to do with what?"

"When on the *Kampala* as a nurse I saw him, I'm sure I did, but I'm less sure as to where."

"Actually on the ship? Surely you could have said last week." Jane was almost critical.

"There's nothing 'surely' about this, except that he wasn't on the ship. He was part of a dockside melee. It could have been at Gibraltar, or at Freetown, or perhaps even Montevideo where your pal was disembarked Gareth. I'm certain about the person, I'm uncertain about the place. But he didn't sail, I know that."

"The *Kampala* was part of the task force....... and the floating element, remember, was sustained by the RFA fleet," reasoned Steve. The ferry-hand had been with that service, that was his train, and the others were with him........ but none were inclined to make any more of it now, not at this moment. Jeremy was likely to have worked this much out, but surely not acted upon it. Confrontation was unthinkable. All was too vague and shadowy, and also there'd been Alan's 'keep clear' strictures.

The suspicion remained, though, that Jeremy might be cooking something of his own. There was that singular appetite for history, and there were the fresher, local, ingredients. Gareth needed only to be partly accurate with what he'd earlier said, and there would be a feast here for the lecturer's prejudices.

"But now you're telling us this," chided Alan. "It's been nearly a week since you were on the *Kampala*." The words were neutral, but not so the voice. With the rebuke there was hurt. Here was a fractured harmony. Jane heard, and she knew..... intuitively. A closeness had developed between this pair. It should have excluded Jeremy, but hadn't........ hence a pain that wasn't to be concealed. The girl looked hard at the nurse, and she felt this scrutiny...... a blush rising into her cheeks.

She had no reply. She wanted someone else to speak, and it was Gareth who obliged.

"This is to do with Chadwick," he announced. "It fits with all I've said so far. That Baz character is with Intelligence. We can call him a technician. His association with the *Kampala* will stretch back to well before '82. Originally it will have been an Anglo-American project, as most of what goes through GCHQ is. Then we have the Falklands, and his terms of employment are adjusted. As a contingency we Anglos want to reserve for ourselves a course of unfettered unilateral action, an option that he's required to help provide. The option is then utilised, and the consequences are grave. The Americans are bounced into lending a reluctant blessing, North Atlantic unity being paramount. This rankles, and all the more so as Galtieri is out....... this jeopardising Washington's anti Red crusade in Central America. Redress is due. The *Kampala* and those running her need to be brought demonstrably to heel, and how better to exact the amends than in Colombian fire fighting."

".......using the same vehicle, and perhaps even some of the same personnel," joined Steve.

"For the imperative now must be to smooth things over," said Kate, and from her this was a radical change of stance. No longer was she dismissive, and Gareth was taking encouragement.

"That 'Baz' is our man. He'll know what really happened with the Captain, and he'll know too how the old lady back in Salop came to be botched to death." He turned challengingly to Alan. "And how about it? If he and the *Kampala* are now being loaned out to the CIA, can your people move to net him? Could you really take so big and slippery a fish?"

"It's not my decision," replied Alan, "I've said that before. It's the way the game's played. Yes he'll have access to people who are above me, but they have to have my report all the same. That's my job. They'll read it. That's theirs. They then decide, to act or not. It's not for me to narrow any option, even the do nothing ones."

"So as an unrestrained amateur it's conceivable that Jeremy might be getting closer to this guy than you ever could," reasoned Gareth. "You're still waiting on permission."

"Conceivable," agreed Alan, "but unknowingly he might be exposing himself and others to much greater risks. Jane's father for instance, who shares an exercise yard with some dangerous and ruthless people....the kind that maybe saw to little old Hilda."

"But I don't think he's trying to detach himself, " protested Steve. "He just has his own angle that we've tended to belittle. If he gets on to something he'll want to share it, I'm sure of that, indeed if he came back early on Saturday it was perhaps because he was wanting to do just that. Were you working that night Kate?" The question was innocent.

"No, but I was .....out." The unease was transparent.

"Not another evening out with that Morrish guy." Steve was trying to lighten the exchange...... without success.

"What Kate does on an evening off is her own business," rapped Alan. "She's not answerable to any of us." This was too strong, and it was too immediate. Perhaps in his tone there was a hint of conspiracy, or maybe it lay in the glance shot to him by Kate. Jane noticed, and what she'd intuitively guessed became boldly stated fact. She pounced.

"You were together," she glared, "you and Kate on Saturday night." The pair were speechless, neither could summon so much as a gesture of denial.

"I think he did return," she continued. "He had something for you Alan, and he came to find you. He came to the boat, but on seeing you two together, or hearing you........ then that was it. That's why we've not heard from him. What ever he might have been bringing you've lost. Where is he? He could be anywhere, thinking anything."

Still there was no denial. Gareth and Steve, embarrassed, dumbstruck, glanced to each other. "You've lost respect, you've lost control," the girl was raising her voice "And now you're all the more determined to slide off of course. For now you're seeing that ship for what she is, a can of worms, Washington incubated. You're fearful now, that Jeremy will be prising at the top. You want to hand it up to your boss people while the lid's still on. They might yet be able to screw it down, but only if you move smartly. Meanwhile, what are we left with? A fortnight ago I thought my father as good as out. Can't be so certain now, can I ?"

Here was the root of her anxiety. This was what fuelled the outburst, and nothing Alan could now do or say could mollify. It was a rolling surge of anger, and he had to ride it, use it. His team was disintegrating. Of the initial five in hand one had bolted and a second was kicking wildly over the traces. The third and the fourth were here, and calm enough for the moment, but quietly they would be questioning the propriety of his conduct with the fifth. The girl was right. Control and respect were forfeit. The group was unmanageable, together they were a liability. It was the moment to shatter and to scatter.

"Your precious father," he countered. "If there's nothing else you ever think of then consider this. He's in prison, right? Why? Cannabis was planted on your yacht. He was set up you say. But was he? Maybe it's part of the plan, something he's in on. He loses a while of liberty, but at the end there's a nice lump sum. He's had enough of being a lawyer anyway, especially in sleepy old Truro. Might even have had enough of his family......." It was preposterous bait, but in her rage the girl took it whole, hook line and sinker.

"You will get out of this house! All of you! Now! All of it I'm taking up to my father, tomorrow. You think I'm going to see him shafted for a second time....... by your people? There's a want of trust in your world, and betrayal comes so easily. Get out of the door. Move!"

And they had to comply, Alan leading and then an embarrassed Kate. Gareth followed. At least he'd paid for his pitch in the field. Lastly it was Steve, and with him Jane was no less adamant. He wasn't to phone or attempt to call on her, not here, and not even at the cafe. He was to wait until she chose to contact him. She would know when. It depended on what was happening with her father and what he had to say..... if anything. Stepping through the kitchen he stole a glance at the oven clock. It was barely eight thirty.

*

It was an hour since they'd brought her into the mouth of the Percuil, since slipping in behind the last ferry across from Falmouth and dropping anchor before St.Mawes.......about 100 metres off Tavern beach. The fog had thickened. They could see nothing. Nothing was likely to see them. Old Jack was still at the helm. His grandson stood by the mast, the mainsail downed. The slow mist saturated air wiped against his searching eyes. No canvas remained aloft, no hindrance for scent or sound. In these conditions it would be an imprecise business, but they'd made it across and now they would stay. A qualified report had to be better than none, if only to confirm the fullness of their endeavor.

Sound, near and far, was what shaped their arena, little else. The nearby shore was the whispered lapping of tide on rock; St.Mawes, a thin murmur of sparse creeping traffic; the elevated slopes beyond, the distant toil of a farm tractor.

Seaward, the repeated moan of a foghorn proclaimed Roseland's furthest headland, and from just a shade on to the west that persistent hum. It could have been slackening bustle of Falmouth. It could have been ship-board processing, the business of the factory ships. Probably it was both.

No one had followed them in, nor had anything attempted to leave the river on this side.......not yet anyway, for the ferry did have a return crossing to make. So far all other movement had been closer to the far bank, and without exception it was inward.

Three inshore trawlers had rumbled up from the bay, each trailing its distinctive bouquet of diesel and fish offal, and the inevitable scavenge of gulls. The first piloted two yachts, the second had one and the third another two. The sameness of the yacht motors and the chattering and the calling of the crews suggested they were all of the same class and that a decision to find anchorage in the Percuil, rather than take on the Lizard perhaps, had been reached as a fleet.

There was nothing though to indicate the *Spartan* to be amongst the procession.

"What about us movin' 'cross a bit more?" Asked Young Jack.

"We'm stayin' 'ere. Startin' and the stoppin' again idn' list'nin'." The point was amplified by the muted growl coming out of St.Mawes. It was the ferry. Taking on both tide and fog it was making for Falmouth while at least some light remained. Closer it came and louder, blocking all other sound, even at reduced throttle. They heard the surge of the bow wave, and the grumble of the diesel, and the splutter of the exhaust, and then......

"Anchor up, and mainsail!" Urged Old Jack, sharply "We'm foll'win'. We wants t'be out 'n 'round while they'm still in earshot." Jack Spargo moved. His grandfather had detected something more, something he hadn't. The boy wasn't going to question, not until they were under way, and then it would just be the whisper.

"You said they. More than jus' the ferry were it?"

"Keep list'nin'. You'm 'earin' one boat now. Dreckly you'll be 'earin' two.... an' like me thinkin' we knows 'm both."

They didn't catch up. They didn't even keep pace, but they did stay close enough for long enough. The ferry powered throatily away and yes there was something astern, a sound being left in its wake. It wasn't the *Spartan,* young Jack wouldn't have missed that. It was something smaller and much, much lighter. He knew it now, that petrol driven motor, he knew it well. As they cleared the castle they could just hear it veering away to the north...... where else?

It had been a good attempt, but never good enough to get past Jack Butters.

*

"Where now?" Steve asked Gareth. It was just the pair of them. Alan and Kate had smartly departed on foot, making for Philleigh and the payphone in *The Roseland Inn.* There they hoped to summon a taxi.

"You get back to the farm. If that's where she'll perhaps think to contact you then that's where you're best to wait. Leave your bike here. I'll get you down to the ferry." Gareth was calmness and authority. He'd been placed to make a relatively dispassionate assessment of the evening's events. He'd seen a bust up, that was for certain, but the outcome was fragmentation rather than dissolution, and to him this might yet bring advantage. Unexpectedly the boy, ever useful, was at his sole disposal.

"And you'll contact me tomorrow, early?" checked Steve.

"I'll want to," replied the ex soldier, "and that's because I've another finding-out task for you, one to be done tonight. It's off limits I know but I want that shed looked at, the Viceroy shed. If you can get down there unnoticed I need you to see for me what's inside, as you did before. Two nights ago more crates went in. Last night I suspect they came out..."

".......to be floated out and lifted aboard the *Kampala*."

"Not this time, unless it's tonight or later in the week. My suspicion is that the shed's been cleared, and at very short notice. It could be that it now holds Jeremy's car. That's what I want you to check, if you can. If not then tyre tracks on the quay, or in the lane, they might tell us enough."

Gareth knelt and burrowed into his tent. He emerged with a spare helmet. He tossed it for Steve, and it was caught and quickly donned. They mounted and they were away, comfortably in time for the ferry. From the slip-way the methane ships were vague shapes. The *Kampala,* slightly more distant, was invisible.

Steve dismounted, leaving the helmet he boarded as a pedestrian. Gareth watched. Of Baz, whom he'd earlier seen relieving Prout, there was no sign. The Welshman took quiet encouragement. The *Spartan* had to be still there, where he'd seen it tucked away, above Tolverne.

He would return now to his tent. It made sense to stay clear of the house, but he had to be available all the same. She might have simmered off a little by now, he thought, and perhaps, in another hour, sufficiently to bear fetching him in to the phone.

But wishful thinking this was. The girl was seething, her anger intensifying as her mind re-ran Grigson's words. She was going to Exeter, first thing. She had the train times out already, and her money. How dare he! And to have said these things in this house, where he was a guest.

She heard a rap at the door. She hesitated. Maybe it was Steve. If so, she would send him away. She went to answer.

No more than a touch on the handle, she managed, and the door swung suddenly inwards. It was expertly done, the three figures were in and onto her with what had to be a choreographed precision. Noise was minimal. They were strong. Nothing was disturbed, and nothing broken. She was lifted, gagged, bound, carried, and flung on to her parents' bed, all in less than twenty seconds.

The telephone was disconnected with matching dexterity. In half an hour, when he tried, the caller from Mylor would hear the ringing tone, but only as played at the exchange. In the house, no sound......... and in the field Gareth waited in vain, with some disappointment, but no surprise.

He looked across. The place was quiet. All appeared to be in order, more so in fact than the previous two nights. Even those evangelists had been less noisy, with hardly a glimmer from their curtained van.

He heard clearly the on time return of Jane's mother.

"I'm ho-oome," rang the voice as she opened her door. Maybe she was thinking that the young man was still there. She stepped through, pulling the door shut behind her.

The house was as quiet and as tidy as any teenager's parent could have hoped. Nothing had been used in the kitchen, nothing misused, no crumbs, no dirty mugs. She checked the downstairs rooms, no guests, no Jane even, and yet the lights were on and the door hadn't been locked so she had to be in the place somewhere. Why hadn't she appeared? Why no answer to her shout?

"Jane," she called again, this time as she climbed the stairs. Still there was no reply..... why could that be? Slipping the coat from her shoulders she went to her own bedroom first, and that's where they were waiting. They pounced, it was too easy and they were professionals.

From where Gareth sat nothing was amiss, save for the hoped for call from Mylor that hadn't so far happened. It wasn't to be, not tonight. He'd set the picket, and whatever its performance and its message he was having to wait, wait until morning. He was tired now. He needed to be fresh for the new day. Sleep was essential.

*

Tuesday

A bright dawn, and what remained of the mist quickly thinned to nothing under the warming sun. Perceiving no movement at the house Gareth made for Philleigh and its call box. He found it out of order. The pub wouldn't be open for hours. He had to decide.

He could ride down to St.Just, or St.Mawes even, and phone from there. If things were emerging that Alan should be told, he would be at hand. Alternatively there was the ferry. It could get him across to Lanmouth almost as quickly, and there, at the farm, would be a guaranteed to be working phone.

And there would be Steve, hopefully with information on that shed, critical information perhaps. It would be best heard from the lad in person. Given the conditions of the previous evening he was likely to have more to say than the pair who'd been bobbing around out in the estuary.

The batch of five cars headed eastward persuaded him. There was a ferry waiting. Lanmouth it had to be. At the crossroads he had to give way as the last vehicle up turned southwards. It was Hugh Trembath. On his way to Portscatho, thought Gareth. And he was right. Each acknowledged the other with a lift of a palm, and that was enough. Both were pressed for time.

On Gareth rode, with a rising confidence in his choice...... until he was actually on the ferry and it was pulling out into the river, away from the Roseland slip. There was no sign of the deckhand. It was the engineer who'd positioned the vehicles and the same man was staying to take the fares. It looked a stop gap arrangement, an unexpected absence, hastily covered......a pull out even. Baz, where could he be?

'Well clear,' that's what Jane would say. Jeremy, spite charged, had cut loose with a night, a day, and another night...... thirty six hours in which to do his worst. With so much time, insight, and venom what couldn't he do? The chances were that the *Speedwell* was compromised, and Alan truly in danger........ and here he was, the one with the fastest wheels, heading for the wrong bank.

The self-recrimination was momentary, for Prout had appeared. He was on the far bank, Roseland bound, queuing in his van, third back, just above the slip. Less mysterious than the ferry-hand, this was a character no less lethal. More so probably, if it was shut down time..... for he was likely to be left on the more vulnerable side of a smartly executed cut off, feeling threatened, thinking dangerous thoughts.

Jack Butters, the puppeteer, he might appreciate this. But would Alan? Gareth was all the more torn. He was committed to contacting the old man. He was anxious to share with him his fears. But with the cast assembling on the Roseland, it was on that side that he needed to be.

He had to come off the ferry. Prout would have spotted him, and he'd be watching to see that he did. It was only minutes to the farm. If he was quick he might be there and back before it left. The bank was reached. The ramp went down, and away he went.

He had to slow for the hairpin. The sharp steeply climbing twist through which slip way became a road offered a double glimpse of Prout's CF. With the second he was looking down from behind and, through the rear windows snatching a brief sight of an untidy van floor. Discernible through an untidy coil of rope was a crescent of moulded rubber. The spare wheel it was perhaps, or maybe just an old tyre. It could have been either, it was difficult to say which.

Whatever, it wasn't what had caught his eye at Porthpean. It was nothing so menacing. The bend took him up and away from the water. Getting to the farm was the priority.

Steve was there, tidying the yard, his ear bent for the phone. But he'd heard the bike approach, a sound he well knew. He was relieved. Eager to speak to the rider, his voice was anxious, breathless.

"People have been phoning here. Two calls I've had. The first from Alan, he's all right. The second was from Mylor, old Jack was wanting to know if Jane had gone away somewhere. He'd been trying to contact you at hers, last night, this morning, but no answer."

"He'll be waiting to hear from me now. I have to use your phone."

"This way," said Steve, alive to Gareth's urgency.

"And the shed, last night.......?"

"...........was empty. It was about one when I was down there. There was action of some sort, but it was happening across the water. I went along to Roundwood but it was still too misty. It was just noise I caught...... two or three boats, winch motors..... off the *Kampala* I'd say, and quite a heavy lorry. It sounded almost as near as the boats. That would mean Tolverne."

"When he called, did Butters make any mention of a visit from Jeremy over the weekend?"

"Nothing about Jeremy," confirmed the boy as he ushered Gareth into the house and to the hallway phone. "No help on that one."

"That doesn't surprise," said Gareth, lifting the receiver and jabbing at the numbers. "There's another place we can go looking for Jeremy, if we have the time, whether we will though........Hello, that's

370

Jack, Jack Butters? .....Sorry about last night, not my fault...... acrimony between Grigson and the girl."

The Welshman fell silent. He was listening. Steve watched his face, he saw the eyes glance down for the wrist watch. Then up they came to meet his and he was talking again, summarising.

"You say there was no *Spartan*......but that there was the boat which belongs this end, with the car ferry..... and you say you only heard it, young Jack wasn't able to see to recognise....That's fine, it fits with what I saw in the afternoon. I can't stop now. I'll speak to you later."

The receiver went down. Gareth's eyes hadn't left the youngster's. "There's mischief afoot, dangerous mischief," he said, his expression intense. "Tell me about Alan. Why did he ring? how long ago? where from?"

"From the yard, just under an hour ago, he said he was about to leave. He just told me not to alarm..... whatever I might hear. I thought he was alluding to last night at Jane's."

"Maybe," responded Gareth. He became pensive. He was contemplating Prout's van, and what he'd seen in the back, on the slip and at Porthpean. He remembered what Jane had said, when explaining how her father had been fitted up. The gas cylinders had to have been switched, she claimed, and now he could buy that. The possibilities were fearsome. It could be that this ploy had been worked again on an unattended *Speedwell*, but now with a deadly intent.

"Helmet on again!" snapped the motorcyclist. "I saw Prout waiting for the ferry. I have to know where he's bound. We could get on the same crossing. Move!"

But for the cattle truck moving towards them in the lane they might have made it. They were just too late, by seconds rather than minutes. The ferry, with Prout, was on its way. Gareth swung his machine around. He wasn't going to wait for the next.

"The Dodman," he shouted into his shoulder "That's where I'd be headed. That's where we're going. Hold tight!"

They roared up past Trelissick, easing for a moment as they went by the entrance to Carwinion. The Land Rover was on the Roseland, the Guardsman knew that, he just needed to check for signs of Sir Edward.... but there was none. The place appeared to be deserted. Even more now, he was sure he had it right.

He powered the Voyager on, quickly coming to the main road.

He turned northwards for Truro and held nothing back. The race was on. Corners were cut. Continuous lines were crossed. Approaching traffic was outfaced. Horning a way through the Arch Hill junction Gareth then swept down to the two edge of city roundabouts. The width and the alignment of the road into the first made it no more than a fast right hander. It was taken Manx style, and over the bridge they swooped and into the more severe second, the Trafalgar. Gareth swayed, the bike swung, Steve clung. The lights were with them and they were through, climbing now, hammering eastwards. At the Newquay junction the lights were against...... but no matter. There was a gap. They were into it, out of it, and tilting on their way.

*

Hugh Trembath took a casual sip at his coffee. He contemplated a tranquil sea. The pull out had been smoothly effected, he thought. The weapons, the drugs, their locally based porters and pedlars, all had been spirited away in the early hours. His father would now be well on his way to London. Alone now, he at last had scope to reflect.

He'd known that the shed held guns, and he'd known they were being put on board the *Kampala*. This much he'd been told, by his father. Where to though, and where from?...... he'd wondered, but known better than to enquire. Them that asks no questions, isn't told a lie. So they sits and they just imagines.

It was obvious that the ship's next voyage was to be a one way trip to the breaker's, and it was his guess that for delivery she would have been placed with a purposely created off the shelf company. He figured that an unlicensed consignment of guns for somewhere along the way was helping to boost the projected one off dividend.....

And the prime movers?....a cobbled together City consortium, no less temporary, drawn from those who were ever gathering at the fringes of the Tory party. They were always ready to help fund the movement, and they were never slow to gather reciprocal favour. He'd been aware of the potential embarrassment for Carwinion in the not so long ago secondary banking crisis, and he knew that the position had been shored up on the strength of a series of hastily mustered low rate bridging loans. The money had since been returned, plus interest, but favours were still owed and here, he imagined, one was being called in. It was a murky business, but like the fog of the previous evening it would be a localised and transient affair. That's what he'd thought. But he'd been mistaken.

A very different truth had emerged, an awesome truth. This game was global. It spanned a generation, and more.

His father was revealed as more a victim than villain. Though dubbed a knight he'd stood throughout as a vulnerable pawn, backward, isolated, under constant threat of liquidation......and yet despite all, the intimidation, and the duress, Sir Edward had survived and so also had Carwinion.

Hugh looked back over his Naval career. He'd won regular promotion, yes, but he'd had talent. His success had been merited..... in fact he might have done better, and maybe all that had emerged held an explanation as to why not. But that was the past. There was a better future.

For they'd come, and they'd come armed, but still they'd had to flee. Their game was up. The *Kampala* had seemed a different vessel this morning, as had the ferry. Even Carwinion had a changed feel. By taking his fee in tainted money that lecturer had, in his way, effected an exorcism. A new future beckoned and it would be all his, for what was going to bring his father back to Cornwall after this?

Locally there were a few things to smooth, but he had the resources. He had influence, he knew the right people. The girl's father could be quickly rehabilitated, and that would placate her. As for the old man down at Mylor, it was a matter of promoting just the right amount of media interest of just the right sort. If the girl's concern was her father, then Jack Butters' was the friend he'd buried all those years ago.

Accordingly there would be space for Rory Duggan in the local press, and time for him on the local airwaves. He, Hugh Trembath, could see to that, and see to it too that the story would be one of the *Usk Vale* and 'Enigma', and of the *Lancastria* and Corporal Jack Butters.

Cairns, Korea, and the Cold War needn't figure, not this time around, not in Cornwall, not in Liverpool, and not in Spain. Those high priests tasked to uphold the sanctity of the 'special relationship' will have been forewarned, their subtle means of suppression mobilised. Old Jack had played a crafty game, and he'd come close, but in the end there'd been too much reliance on that lecturer. He might well have been a diligent historian, Jeremy, but he was also corrupt. The pull out, quietly done and deniably so, was now complete.

Carwinion was fireproof. Morrish would have to take the heat. He might squeal about the shed, but the letting of that had been an arm's length arrangement, as with every tenant.

Hugh could see himself slipping back into his accustomed routine, attending to the usual jobs with his usual efficiency. No one was going to be any the wiser.

Visibility was good, the sea smooth. It was a day for lining and lifting crabs, and a group of small boats had ventured out from Portscatho to forage over the rocks away to his right. Amongst them drifted a bare masted working boat. This wasn't unusual in summer. Out further, also venturing from the estuary, there were the sailing yachts and way beyond them, creeping along the horizon towards the Lizard, a sizeable container ship.

One vessel held Hugh's attention. Trained towards the south east his binoculars had settled on the *Speedwell*. She was about four miles out and making perhaps five knots before the steady south westerly. Running on a north easterly course Grigson would be comfortably around the Dodman on the flowing tide.

This fellow was good at his job, thought the coastguard. Though futile now, the attempt was admirable none the less. Whatever he knew, whoever he was off to tell, and however they might then move, it would be all too late. For it was already too late. Their net would close on nothing.

The one worry was Prout. He'd seemed fidgety, preoccupied. There was no heat, not yet, but his bearing and his mood was that of one feeling it.

What was his concern? That he might share Morrish's fate? He needn't. He just had to stay cool and ride things out. Could he though? If he wanted his payoff then he would have to.

*

374

Bound, blindfolded, and gagged, Jane and her mother were still being confined to the one bedroom. Each had been granted just the one escorted visit to the bathroom, and from this and those muffled voices on the stairs the girl had calculated a guard of three, one female. Her mother was at last sleeping, she could listen more closely. She'd heard Gareth leave the field, and also the two eastbound 'off the ferry' convoys. The first she rightly estimated to have passed Gareth near Philleigh. The second, she would later learn, included Prout's van.

It triggered a flurry of activity. From the field came the distinctive air cooled clatter of the VW. It was lurching over the grass, coming towards the house. It paused close by. There were raised voices and doors being slammed and slid. They were moving out, all of them, and hurriedly. The transport ground away onto gravelled drive, low gear to the entrance but which way then.... to the left or to the right? Jane held her breath.

It was to the right. They too were headed eastward, steadily gathering speed, climbing through the gears, that clatter thinning and fading. The site was again silent. What now? Gareth was their best hope, but how long would he be? If only Steve had stayed thought Jane. If only she hadn't been so tactless. Ten, fifteen, twenty minutes passed..... and with the minutes the occasional car. And then one slowed and it halted. It stood briefly in the entrance, the motor idling. A door was opened, and with a hollow clunk, the boot too. A thud, another thud and the car was moving away...... to leave a footfall that ought to have been familiar. The walk was becoming a jog, the steps louder. There was no knock, no call, this one who knew what to expect.

Jane did not. Those feet were on the stairs now. Maybe if she could feign sleep......

The door opened gently, and a hand likewise eased the blindfold from her eyes... wide eyes now, for this she never would have imagined, not in her remotest, wildest, sweetest of dreams.

*

From Penair it was down again to Tresillian, the road winding, burrowing beneath the Pencalenick trees to again meet with the estuary now at its furthest reach. The water's edge highway was straight and wide and flat. It was fast. Sharp braking it had to be for the chicane like bridge, then again it was throttle wide as they thundered up to the Tregony turn off.

This was their road, an 'A' road, but narrow and winding. The rises and the dips were fierce, the hedges high. They had to cross the Fal and Tregony had to be the place, but where then? Behind Veryan Bay the Roseland lanes were a maze. Portloe looked across to the Dodman, but a straightforward coastal route didn't exist. A dilemma loomed. Were they to strike directly for the Dodman, or should they first check on the Nare?....Just in case.

They hurried on, flirting with the hedgerows. The way was narrow now, the clearances tight. Steve recalled his very first encounter with this machine. Now he was astride the thing.

Over the Fal and rising again, two more southward miles were consumed in less than three minutes, easily so. At Bessybeneath, no choice, it had to be left......but then, within half a mile, decide Gareth, decide. If it was the Dodman it had to be left again, but no. He wasn't braking, not until they were past and Steve was pounding at his back and screaming at his ear.

"In that lane......Prout's van, backing, he's met a combine." Gareth braked and half turned into a stop that gave an angle across the hedges. The high combine he could see, and ahead of it, reversing, there was a glimpse of van roof.

"Well seen," said Gareth turning the machine again. "It's not the Nare, it'll be the Dodman. He's headed for Portholland, or Porthluney, or Hemmick...the last probably. It gives us some time. I can put you down at Portloe."

"Why?"

" I'll explain there. We mustn't be seen here." They took off again, continuing southward.

Steve was dropped at the edge of the fishing village. Above cliff top height they had a clear view to Gull Rock, a craggy berg of a stack that looked to have snapped and drifted from the Nare. The *Speedwell* was there, a miniature, perhaps a mile further out. Gareth cut the engine and he lifted his helmet. He wanted to be clear.

"You see Alan... I fear he's in danger, grave danger. That Prout, he's a killer. I believe he's planted an explosive device on the *Speedwell*."

"The gas cylinder switch again...... but this time a bomb?"

"I think he's switched one of the fenders, one of the tyres that hang along the beams, probably at the cockpit end. He'd have done it last night in the St Mawes fog."

"When Alan was with us at Jane's. And you think an old tyre could hold enough?"

"Enough to blow the gas cylinder, and then there's the petrol she's carrying for her motor."

"And if it all goes up...."

".........it'll be matchwood and mackerel bait," said Gareth grimly.

"And he has it timed?"

"No. It'll be detonated by radio signal. That's why Prout's over here, why we are following. He has a transmitter in his van. He'll wait until she's right where he wants."

"Off the Dodman?"

"She's still intact and Prout's not here, where we are, nor any where to the south. Off the Dodman must be favorite."

"So what do we do?" implored the boy.

"Work out where he's likely to be." Hauling down a zip Gareth pulled a map from his jacket. Holding it with a hand each they studied Veryan Bay. "What do you think?" The Guardsman seemed uncertain. "You know the bay better than me."

"There's a lane that goes down to Hemmick, but the car park there is small and the cove looks this way. Though closest to the Dodman you can't actually see the headland, and it's the same at Porthluney where the car park is much bigger and the access a lot, lot easier." A finger went to the map. "There's a better view from the lay-by here, where the road climbs towards us, around the Caerhays estate. The problem there is getting a space. People park all day whilst walking the coast path."

"And down here?" Gareth was pointing now to East Portholland.

"Better, and better again just a short way along this lane towards West Portholland. It's quiet, you have a bit of height, and there's room to park, and there are no blinkering cliffs. Anything moving from Gull

Rock to the Dodman you'll see all the way across." Gareth studied the map, tracing a gloved finger along the lanes back to where they now stood.

"The ideal place," he said.

"So now....?"

"....I'm going down there." Gareth once again looked out towards the *Speedwell*. "There's a chance I can disable his transmitter. So long as he's in no hurry, and that's why I'll not have you alerting the Police or the Coastguards. He'll be listening to their channels, switching between them. I want you to stay here."

"To do what?"

"To watch that boat sail serenely around the Dodman, or should it not then to get out there as quickly as possible to pick up any pieces that might remain. Your friend down there with the sailboards, he should have a fast outboard inflatable. Make sure he's at the ready, just in case I fail." Gareth remounted. There was another glance towards *Speedwell*. She was cruising well, too well. Steve wished him luck. He rode off, making inland for Treviskey and the less than two miles of narrow lane which threaded down to West Portholland.

Steve strode down to the harbour. He wanted to do more. He remembered Alan's last words. 'Don't alarm,' he'd said and it was these words rather than any words of Gareth that kept him away from the call box. But he had to be able to do better than this merely waiting to gather pieces. Jo Bartlett was there, and so was the inflatable, just as Gareth had anticipated. Steve crossed the slipway, stepping over the winch cables to join the path that climbed onto the natural promontory beyond. He stopped at a bench, but he couldn't sit. How could he be expected to?

The *Speedwell* was by now well into Veryan Bay. The imposing Dodman stood like a wall, unmoving. From here the Caerhays beaches were hidden.... but not Hemmick. In the clear air the neat cusp of sand with its delicate frill of breaking wave looked close, reachable even.

*

The telephone rang. A hand reached across to lift the receiver.

"Porthscatho lookout, Trembath speaking."

"Mike here Hugh, Falmouth HQ, Call timed at 11: 20. There's an order that's just come through from well up, one for you. You're to leave the hut there and walk back to your vehicle. There'll be a senior officer waiting. He'll be needing your assistance. He's been told you're available. He'll have further instructions. Speak to you later." Trembath sighed. After a quick tidy around he picked up his keys, stepped outside, and locked up. He strode briskly along the cliff path. The Land Rover was soon in view, and yes there was a figure standing there, waiting, searching in his direction. The person was clad in black from head to toe. From this range it could be anyone, but there was something in that build which.........but that couldn't be because.....

*

Gareth had found Prout. Just beyond West Portholland the lane reached a low cliff, the seaward verge offering sufficient room for maybe a dozen side by side vehicles. It was early. For the moment the CF was one of no more than five. Gareth cruised by, and turned. He would dismount closer to cottages. To size the situation he needed space, and he needed a good view. Taking the coast path he climbed southwards, his movement matching Steve's at Portloe. Soon he had the bay before him, and below, the cab end of that van.

He could see Prout's head, binoculars to his eyes. They scanned, and then they steadied. He'd fixed his target. Gareth followed their direction and yes..... there was the *Speedwell*, on time, on course.

He knew what he had to do. He had the right tool, it was on the bike and he would need to fetch it, fetch it smartly. It was a short descent, tricky though to one with his disability. It was taking his full attention. He didn't notice the sailboard sweep out from under the cliffs behind him. It was close to the shore and coming closer, slanting towards the Caerhays coves.

For Prout, focussed way, way out, the rig was but a brief blur of blue and yellow, and the rider no more than a flash of buoyancy jacket dayglo. Had he dropped the binoculars, just for a few seconds, then he might have been alerted by the road-use style of helmet, and also by the legs. Wetsuited they were not. That was denim, farm soiled!

*

The wind was with Steve. These things could be fast, much faster than the *Speedwell,* which already he was out stripping. Too fast, hopefully, for anyone on the shore to discern either his identity or intention. Attire apart, he was making what wasn't an infrequent sight out in the bay, and this was his cover. Moreover, to a person looking out from Portholland and Porthluney his own course and Alan's would appear to diverge.

Steve was confident of reaching Porthluney. He'd done so before, during the previous summer, on a softer and more southerly breeze. Then he'd had to work out into the bay to make the angle to reach back to Portloe. This time he could run past Porthluney and beneath the cliffs veer away towards Hemmick. Off Hemmick, hidden from Portholland, a ninety degree turn would allow him to reach towards the Dodman ...... the natural marker for turning into the wind and working back into Portloe on a long starboard tack. Simple, except the Dodman had that tidal race, reputedly treacherous. To go so far was making a voyage onto the unknown.

But danger was integral to his attempt. He was out to contrive distress. As he closed on the headland he would hit the race and on this, still unseen by the assassin, he could ditch and let the current take him, with the board, out to and around the Point. He would be ahead of the *Speedwell* and Alan had to see him, he just had to. He would move to help, and then it would just be about shouting loud enough, and clearly enough. And after the warning.....?

The best case had Alan cutting free the lethal tyre to save both himself and the *Speedwell.* He could then become the rescuer and recover boy and board. At second best he might jump clear and share the buoyancy of the board, and share too the spectacle of his boat being blown to pieces. The worst case had Steve watching both man and boat explode, but he would at least know that he'd done his best, and know too that the rescue services would be on their way......if only to pull himself to safety.

He was off Porthluney now and beginning the gradual swerve towards Hemmick. The *Speedwell* was still out there, still intact. It had survived his passing Portholland. The riskiest part had been negotiated. Steve was confident now, exhilarated almost. He was going to be a hero. What could stop him?

*

Gareth, the professional, was doing his groundwork. Staying at careful distance he was studying closely the lie of the land, working out how he was going to move, where precisely, and when. He fingered the blade of his knife. It was keen enough. He was trained in its use, the thrust for the bone and the levered slice through the artery. The five inches of blade ought to suffice.

*

Steve had made Hemmick, he'd turned, and dagger down he was starting to feel the suck of the tide. The Dodman loomed, tall, imposing. The sea chopped against unmoving shadow darkened cliff. He could smell the bare rock, a jagged wall, topped with soulless, gale bent thicket.

Steve felt alone, exposed. A plan that had seemed so simple was no longer straightforward. He was wanting to check over his right shoulder for the position of the *Speedwell,* and likewise over his left so as to gauge when he might outreach the screening cliff at Portholland. But he could manage neither. Nerve and sinew were too stretched. White

381

knuckled, it was as much as he could do to hold a steady course and maintain balance. He would have to ditch though, and by now he would have been seen by Alan, surely.....so why not here?

He dropped to the rig. The sail fell. Into the current he rolled, clinging still to the mast. He could turn now. Up came his head, and there was the Speedwell less than half a mile away ploughing towards him, and yes he was drifting out with the current. Shortly he would be dead ahead of her.

On she came. Steve could hear her, the flap of canvas, the hiss of the bow wave. He was going to have to shout against the wind, but Alan must have seen him, he must have.

So why wasn't she slowing? The helm, sail hidden, should be reacting, but no. It was time to shout. He'd been told it was a floating bomb. He didn't want it on top of him. He drew a deep breath,

"AAAHL...AAHN !!" He screamed, but still no response. "THERE'S A BOMB......JUUUMMP!!"

*

Gareth stole forward. He crouched behind the neighbouring car. He paused for a moment and then ducked beneath the scope of Prout's driver's side wing mirror to slide head first, face up, beneath the back of the CF. With the knife in one hand it had to be a one arm, one leg wriggle...... it was awkward, it was painful, but he was getting there, inching closer. He could see the battery cradle, and by reaching he was feeling the cable that fed out and up into the floor port, through to the transmitter above. The cable, this was the jugular he sought to sever. He couldn't afford to fumble. He would have just the one stab. He was almost there, almost close enough.

Prout lowered his binoculars. He had that boat just where he wanted. It was just a matter of seconds now, but first he needed every watt of power that he could muster. He wanted the motor running, the alternator charging, and then he wanted to be away. So it was to the starter first, and then the accelerator, and then the switch on the tuner, his trigger. The key turned, and the two litres of reliability rumbled into life...... a critical moment.

Gareth was stretching beneath the exhaust. Alarmed, he dropped the knife. As he vainly groped the vital pulse was sent, and in the next instant received.

*

It was as well that Steve was in the sea, and fortuitous that the board was towards him at a slight tilt. He caught a brief vivid snapshot of flame and fragment before the blast hit wedge like against the underside of the board. Over it came and down Steve went, one hand gripping the mast, the other, one of the foot straps. Clinging with limpet tenacity he heard the splash and the clatter of the debris shower, the fragments of wood, plastic, and engine metal.

Up he came, gasping for air. It was acrid. The *Speedwell* was flotsam, the largest remnant being a section of bow. The sprit pointed skywards, a single stay trailing down to a lengthy, canvas flagged timber spar, all that remained of her rigging. Of Alan there was nothing. Aft of the mast all else had been shredded, splintered. Steve shouted again though, and again, as if by doing so he might will the man to somehow appear intact. But there was nothing. He was alone. He'd failed.

*

Gareth heard the crack, even from beneath a clattering motor. It gathered to a rumble as the blast reverberated along the arc of the bay. For dismay there was neither time nor space. He saw the clutch linkage move and he heard the gear selector snap into reverse. He had to get clear. Gambling that Prout would swing back and out on a full right hand lock he slid out under the driver's side sill. He rolled against the alongside car and lay stock still, a magnet against steel. He'd chosen correctly. Prout glanced across the roof of the car, not down. He then backed and turned, attending solely to his far side clearance.

The van whined and squeaked across the rutted, grit strewn apron before bouncing off onto the made up lane. There was the drag of fully locked front tyre, another grate of gears, and then the van was jerking its way eastwards. The lane was narrow. Prout couldn't afford a collision. It was murder, and this was a getaway going to plan. He needn't be careless.

Scrambling to his feet Gareth was smartly back to his bike. Steve was at Portloe, that's what he thought, and he would be doing as instructed. He could be left. Prout had to be followed.

He knew East Portholland to be served by a lane larger than that which had brought him. This was the valley access, and it could quickly take the van inland to Grampound and onto the busy Truro highway. This would be Prout's way back to Baldhu, the bolt hole.

But as he crept into the blind corner just above East Portholland and prepared cautiously to drop to the tortuous junction, the driver was suddenly confronted. Beak to beak he was with another van, a VW camper. It was being driven with no less care. It stopped and Prout naturally expected his counterpart to drop back, for they had the wider road, and it was straighter, with a better visibility. They had the more comfortable reverse, no more than fifty metres.

Prout brought the Bedford to a stand. He waited, but the camper wasn't reversing. The front passenger door opened. A figure, male, squirmed out and ducked beneath the window of the opened door. It became a shield. The man was crouching and peering, risking only the top of his head....... until a hand came up. It held a gun, a pistol.

Prout was a soldier of fortune. His career had been long and lucrative. The situation wasn't new to him, but it was unexpected...... this was mid Cornwall, not central Africa, not even central America. His response was instinctive. Finding reverse he backed at pace, deliberately swerving from side to side. With foot hard down the engine howled, but that was a steady gun. Five bullets were loosed. Two missed. Two hit the offside front tyre and one the near. Each strike jarred through the steering. Prout was driving on rims. They were still giving distance, but he was losing control. There was cover to be had from the bend. He was almost on to it.

Gareth, pressing in pursuit, was given no chance. But fortune rode with him. As he went for the near side bank a swerve of the van spared him a full on impact with the rear doors. Gouging into his false leg the wrap around tail bumper then hooked the pannier. The bike lifted with a jerk. He was thrown against the bank. The machine bounced down to grate and clatter along the side of the van. Prout braked, stopped, and thinking quickly pulled forward at an angle and then back and across, shunting into a blocking position. Snatching his keys he slid back his door and leapt out.

He crossed to Gareth and delivered him a hefty kick to the midriff. He lifted the bike. It was usable. He mounted, found the button start and swung away westwards. Gareth, pulling himself up against the bank, could only watch.

*

He was taken to the City Hospital, as was Steve....the boy arriving the later by some forty minutes. Neither had been seriously hurt. Gareth had sustained heavy bruising; Steve, mild exposure. They were kept apart, on different floors, each in a single room. It wasn't until early evening that they were to know of the other's admission....... when Kate came on shift.

The boy had been cleared for discharge, he was waiting for his Aunt to bring car and clothes. Hardly the stuff of hospital drama this, but for Nurse Rogers, the sight was as startling as any she'd ever known, in any treatment centre.

Of the circumstances of his admission she knew nothing, and Steve was uncertain as to how he might even begin to explain.

The manner of the *Speedwell's* destruction gave little hope for her master, so he made no mention of Alan, and none of Jeremy. In fact he said little, but he did listen. He heard from Kate how Gareth too had been hospitalised, that he'd taken a tumble from his bike and been immobilised without being too seriously hurt.

And yes, this did figure. The man would have been hurrying. He'd not prevented the explosion and this might be why. For the moment he was laid up, Kate said. There'd been damage to his artificial leg and his arms were too sore for handling crutches. He would be detained for one night at least, and there after would need supervision. He'd been given a private ward. Steve wanted to know where. He was told. The directions given and the permission, Kate bustled on with her duties.

Steve found Gareth awake, but he was barely responsive. Neck movement was painful, that was obvious. All movement was, but he did manage to raise an acknowledging arm as he recognised the voice.

"Gareth?" The boy leant towards a pair of sedated eyes. It didn't register that this was a fellow patient. "Can you confirm to me that he was killed?"

"Instantaneous boy, from what I saw and heard." The answer was a slow, slurred mutter. "Made a mess of the case, lost my bike too."

Steve was shocked. Even allowing for the man's condition this remark was callous. He'd heard that between soldiers there was disdain for death, and maybe there needed to be. But he wasn't himself a soldier, and neither was Gareth now, not any more, and nor had Alan been.

"You've not spoken like that to Kate?" chided the boy.

"You saw what he was trying to do," said Gareth wearily, his lips barely moving. "The guy was a killer."

He's confused, thought Steve....or maybe it was himself. The boy probed again.

"The *Speedwell* you mean?"

"You'd have seen her go up. I'm surprised you're not out there still, scooping up the pieces."

"You mean pieces of our friend?" Anger spilled from Steve's voice. "And very nearly pieces of me. I was out there too you know."

"You were?" This was new to Gareth, something to shake him from his torpor.

"I took a sailboard out of Portloe. With the wind and the tide as they were I was off the Dodman before Alan. I shouted, I thought he would see me, hear me, something....... and somehow get clear." Taking and holding a deep breath Gareth continued to stare ahead. Eventually he spoke.

"You fool. You plucky fool......dammed lucky too."

"I had to do something," pleaded Steve.

"You didn't actually," said Gareth. "What we weren't to know was that Alan got himself clear before he'd even sailed past Porthscatho.

He was over the side off Killgerran. Thereafter the Speedwell was helmed across Gerrans Bay and Veryan Bay by self steer rig. You didn't actually see him off the Dodman. I know that. I saw him near Portholland, later, when the ambulance arrived to bring me here."

"And you saw him alive? Just now you let me talk about his being killed! 'Instantaneous' you said."

"I thought you meant Prout. He died. They had him almost, and then he tried to escape on my bike. He rode into Hugh Trembath's Land Rover just outside West Portholland, on the lane that climbs to Portloe...... where I thought you were."

"When you say 'we', who else do you mean?"

"Those people in the camper van, the one's who'd have us all believe they're on a Christian crusade. They've been working with Alan...."

".....Polgooth," muttered Steve. He was beginning to understand.

".....and I think that there was also an arrangement with the blind man's grandson. He was out with his boat to pick Alan up when he jumped ship. Brought him in to Porthscatho apparently."

"Where he would have gone over to the Coastguard Lookout for our Mr Trembath. I suppose you'll be telling me now that this arrangement included him as well."

"He'd be wrong if he did!" Steve straightened. The words were from behind him. He knew the voice. He sort of half turned and half smiled, at the same time looking upwards at the ceiling.

"Alan," gasped the boy. "How wonderful that you should show yourself! How biblical!"

"Like you, Trembath thought me aboard my boat," explained Alan. "He discovered otherwise when ordered from the lookout by the Falmouth Command. By then I'd reached his Land Rover."

Steve shook his head.

"Clearly I'm missing something here," said the boy. "Forgive me do. I was enjoying my customary lunchtime dip.......off the Dodman."

Alan rode the sarcasm, he countered with sincerity.

"Young man, you were brave. It won't be publicly acknowledged......it can't be. But I'll not forget. You have my gratitude. You have my admiration." Steve coloured. The man was genuine.

"You were saying about Mr Hugh Trembath?" The boy continued.

"We suspected the Trembaths of having a hand in this thing. We knew there'd be cut-offs though, and difficulties in proving either father or son to be any closer than at arms length......not unless we could identify someone enough in the know, someone with enough to lose to attempt something reckless......someone sufficiently fraught, sufficiently resourced, and sufficiently desperate. Prout was our best bet......."

"....and he didn't let you down," said Steve.

"The idea was to let him attempt what he was planning, and to let him think for a moment that he'd succeeded and was getting away. The snare would then bite all the deeper........"

"....... and the squeal would be louder, and perhaps more revealing. The trap would then feel all the more fearsome."

"Our tactic then was to rattle and hopefully rile," explained Alan. "The shots were to rattle him and the rile part was to make it appear that Hugh Trembath was assisting with the arrest. Prout would infer Carwinion collusion, Carwinion betrayal, and then he'd spill the beans.... out of anger."

"Neat," acknowledged Steve, admiringly.

"Except that between us we manage to kill the guy," sighed Gareth. "You have him trapped, and I have to go and leave my bike lying around."

"Not your fault," reassured Alan. "We got the firearms out. That's always risky. When the bullets start flying anything can happen. And then there was Trembath. I was his passenger remember, sitting next to him. He had a good three seconds when Prout appeared, long enough to size up the situation, his situation, long enough to identify the rider who was fast filling the windscreen. Another driver might have avoided him."

"You're suggesting that the crash, with the death was intended, that it was a grasped opportunity?" Asked Steve.

"The *Belgrano* option," stated Gareth bluntly. "When the choice is either to hit or to lose face, and you decide hit........ you don't hang back. You hit hard. Especially if you're well placed to take the benefit of any doubt. Quick thinking. Good serviceman in his day, obviously. Any one searched Carwinion?"

"A team went in this morning after he left for Porthscatho," answered Alan. "Likewise we've given his father's place in London a good combing, but nothing...... either down here or up there."

"No luck at all?" asked Steve.

"Only at Morrish's place, and at his office. He'll go down, as will a few of his City associates. We took a useful trawl at the business end of things."

"So Jane's father, at least he'll be in the clear," said Steve, finding a positive at last. "Can I tell her he's coming out?"

"They let him out this morning, first thing." Alan's voice was flat. Victory for Jane and the boy was, for the professional, mere consolation. "Byrne was dropped at home with instructions to lie very low for the day....... and also to keep that daughter of his under control. She was the one we feared might do something crazy."

"Like?"

"Like taking on the Dodman with a sailboard, Steve." The youngster wanted to hear Alan's voice lighten. It didn't. He was unsure now. How should he respond to this? Gareth broke an awkward silence.

"Jeremy, where's Jeremy? Do we know yet?.... He could yet be a useful card."

"We had to cut deep," said Alan. "Prout had put him in the mine, Wheal Jane, bound hand and foot on the lowest of the dry levels. We retrieved him late this afternoon. His car was up there in the workshop, Prout's workshop."

"In the mood for talking was he?" enquired Steve.

"For straight talking?......No," said Alan. "At least that's my view. Said he'd spent two nights down there. He claims to have taken it upon himself to make a late Sunday evening inspection of the Viceroy shed. He tells us that he was assailed by Prout and the ferry hand, that they bound him at gunpoint and bundled him into the CF. They took his keys, and finding his car on the Cowlands side of Roundwood they took that up to the mine also."

"And you're not impressed by this tale?" asked Gareth.

"He's expecting us to believe he was down there for almost forty hours!" said Alan. "Looking at him I'd say no more than twenty. He's hiding something. He might have been threatened, he might have been bought, maybe it's both. Any way, he's been told about Prout and of the sudden departure of our man on the ferry............"

"......and still he won't change the story," added Gareth. "It'll be fear. To talk of a hidden hand is one thing, to encounter it..... that's something else."

"And he'll hold to his version in Kate's company, whilst living with her still?" This was clumsy from Steve. He was realising now. "Things won't be right between them," he stammered. "They can't be....."

"That's a question you can save for them, and I don't want to be around when you're asking it," answered Alan, cutting in.

"The ferry-hand," said Gareth tactfully. "What do you mean when you say 'departure'?"

"That he's cleared out completely from that house he was renting next to Morrish's, and that he didn't turn up for work this morning."

"Might he be on the *Kampala*," ventured Steve.

"We've gone in on the ship with a helicopter, with launches, with the dogs. They've sniffed the whole length of the thing....."

".......and no drugs , and no guns," said Gareth knowingly.

"And not even any Colombians," added Alan, "instead just a handful of Puertos."

"And in the shed?" asked Steve.

"Nothing again," confirmed Alan. "It's been a smooth pull out. I'd say there were arrangements for every contingency, well planned, well resourced. It was just that Prout lost his nerve, but he pays the price of this himself, we lose the smoking gun, the fireproofing holds."

'Smoking gun,' thought Gareth. Even if this were lost he did have something else..... the next best thing. But now, strangely, because of that loss it might be a disclosure too far. Yes, he could make trouble for Mr Hugh Trembath, but was there really advantage in this now? Others would suffer, undeservedly. There was another innocent daughter to consider, and also two sets of honest tenant farmers.

It wasn't that he could ever forget his friend in Argentina, grieving for a brother, or Hilda, or Brian, or what old Jack had told him of his friend Rory, and the equally fearless Francis. That one broken lifeless body was sufficient, it was retribution enough. The big fish had darted for cover. They wouldn't be back. He might thrash and splash amongst the small fry....... but to what advantage?

His weary eyes closed. For how long he couldn't be sure. When they opened Steve was there still, but not Alan. He'd gone... and to where, now the *Speedwell* was no more? The boy hadn't thought to ask. They never saw him again. His voice was heard. It came on the radio some weeks later, relating those impressions of the Fal, June gathered and June taped.

The next day's *Western Morning News* reported three local incidents, apparently unconnected. One concerned a small yacht that had caught fire and exploded off the Dodman. It was being sailed single-handedly and the one person involved, a teenager, had been brought into Mevagissey.... escaping with just shock and mild exposure.

The second report told of a road fatality. A speeding motorcyclist, said to have been not wearing a helmet, had collided head on with a Land Rover just a short way inland from West Portholland. He'd been pronounced dead at the scene

The third story was about an arrest. Police and custom officers had visited the premises of *Conways*, the Truro solicitors. They'd taken into custody one of their employees and seized a number of documents pertaining to the laundering of proceeds made from the illegal import and distribution of drugs. As the man was being questioned at the City's police station there'd been a search at his home. Evidence had been removed.

The paper was taken at Chapel Meadow. Though the details might have been sketchy, all there knew the incidents to be linked. Jane feared that it was Gareth who'd been killed. And if that exploding yacht had been the Speedwell, what then of Alan?

She phoned Lanmouth where Steve, as drowsy as he was, managed to allay those worst fears. It was arranged that the girl and her father would in the afternoon cross to Trelissick. They would meet up over a National Trust tea, and perhaps piece in a tighter picture from this final jumble of events.

It worked well. As lawyers do, Jane's father wanted facts, but he knew better than to attempt an interrogation. He brimmed with gratitude, and this was what Steve best needed to hear. For he was flat, indeed both youngsters were. They might have won through, but they'd gained no real sense of triumph.

There'd been the physical knocks, for both, but that wasn't what weighed. It was death that had caught up with them, grim death. Until now it had been distant, stalking through other times, and other places, claiming people merely heard of rather than people known.

Prout had been real to them. Deserved or not, intended or not, his death had to be absorbed. Time was required, time to grow. The cleansing hadn't been without cost. A fee was being exacted, Hamelinwise. Youth was forfeit.

And likewise the vindication, so eagerly sought and now secure, would take a toll. So cause driven a relationship could now only wane in intensity. The prize had been won, and to Steve, Jane was already changed. Where she'd been so forthright there was now a near apologetic coyness. On offer to all, it was by comparison impersonal. She was grateful of course, but so was her father. Her thanks were but an echo of his. Steve had known better. He'd known passion.

But this was bearable loss, for there had been a shift in his own perspective. The Roseland, hitherto like a land of dreams -so various, so beautiful, so new- was to him now a cankered bloom. The aptly named Dodman stood monument to irrecoverable innocence. It would remind him now of death, its inevitability...... *Et in Arcadia Ego.*

So between Steve and Jane there had to be adjustment, re-negotiation. The initial deal had been squared. There were new challenges. It did happen, but only with time, with agreement as to what to forget, as to what memories to preserve...... of special things, of special times, of special people.

Roger Byrne was free. He could take control. He best knew the terms of his own release, and he could address his future accordingly.

He was quick to disclose that he'd been told of the *Kampala* and of a hastily severed Washington connection. That this connection might reach through Carwinion he was content to leave as conjecture. Little was going to be proved against the Trembaths and maybe this was as well, for what were they but sad puppets? The strings should slacken now and from Hugh, there was prospect of a discrete yet worthwhile penance.

For himself, the lawyer could reclaim his position and also the respect of colleagues and community. He would be well placed to watch Carwinion, and to quietly scrutinise.

*

Within the week Jeremy had found temporary single room accommodation in Camborne. By October he was in a new job and a new flat, both in Bath. Though within easy reach of Bristol, Steve hadn't the slightest inclination to seek him out. Jane felt much the same about Kate who remained in Truro, continuing at the City Hospital.

Gareth was driven back to Welshpool to await a new bike and a new leg. Steve returned to Bristol for his new term.

In October the story of Rory Duggan broke in Spain. By the end of the month the tale was featuring in the Kernow media.

During the week prior to Remembrance Day the *Lancastria* made a moving tale, and to that hero of St.Nazaire who lay in the Churchtown yard there was at last due recognition. The grave, largely forgotten for so long, became, for a few days, a few days a poppy strewn shrine. But communal tributes fade. Another month and it was as it had been in the summer, just Jack Butters and a couple of companions.......
this time marking the anniversary of the man's death.

*

A little before 8pm Hugh Trembath heard the anticipated thud of his heavy knocker. He went to the door. They'd come as they said they would, and they were on time. He'd readied some mulled wine and a dish of warmed mince pies, appropriate fare for a dark solstice evening.

"Mr Butters, do come in. And Gareth, it's good to see you again. I understand you're stopping a night or two with Nurse Kate." The Welshman assisted the well wrapped octogenarian across the Carwinion threshold, and then before Hugh had even moved to close the door a third loomed out of the gusty December darkness, this figure unrecognised.

"We 'opes you i'dn goin' t' mind," said old Jack, "but I brod 'long 'nother 'quaintance of me own. Come a long way 'e 'as. Mr McKinley, this 'ere's Mr Hugh Trembath, son of Sir Edward Trembath........form'ly MP fer Plym'th North, now retired 'n' livin' in London. Never see 'im 'ere these days is, do us? "

"Not so much now," replied Hugh hesitantly. "How do you do Mr McKinley. Staying at Mylor are you?"

"In Falmouth, just for tonight. Last night it was Exeter and that's the length of my stay. Tomorrow I'm off back to the States. The family expects me back for Christmas. I trust all of yours is well?"

For the host, a jolt of trepidation......it came with the drawled 'Exeter.' That Jeremy character, the lecturer, he that they'd bought off and who'd then cleared out. When he'd turned up back in the summer, just to meddle, Exeter had been his previous call. He'd lifted the lid, but only briefly. It had been resealed, securely he thought, but now here was another. Things could yet spill. He needed to be careful, very careful.

"They're not here at the moment," answered Hugh, showing courtesy. "The wife and my daughter are in London. They do the big horse show and then the shops. It's an annual thing. My father likes seeing them of course. You'll be another of these media people that we've got interested in our Jack and the valiant Rory Duggan?"

"I used to be with the newspapers," drawled the American, "and I never fully retired. When you get so involved you don't want to."

"Involved?" queried Hugh.

"Mr Trembath, thiry five years ago I was in Korea. I was with the American press. I had the pleasure of meeting and working with a young English reporter. He was said to be with a Fleet Street paper. He told me he came from these parts, and you know he got me really interested in this house of yours, Carwinion. He spoke of it being requisitioned by the US Army prior to the Overlord operation back in '44. I heard that after the troops had gone the place fell into disrepair......," Ben McKinley paused, and a pair of venerable eyes scanned walls, ceiling, then floor. " ......straight enough now though. Must have taken a lot of time and money."

Hugh hung a dead bat.

"So you've been visiting this acquaintance of yours, he that you met in Korea. Lives in Exeter, does he? Must be nearing retirement I guess." The affected bonhomie irked Gareth, so brazen was it, so shameless. He held his tongue.

"He didn't survive Korea," said the American, content for the moment to play along, "and in a way that made this place all the more interesting, and likewise your father. There's some fascinating people he's worked with over the years."

"For instance?" questioned Hugh.

"For instance Sir Walter Turner Monckton, KCMG, KCVO,

MC, QC.....very fascinating."

"Then it's a pity my father's not here," continued Hugh. "I wasn't even a teenager when the Korean thing was on. And when did Walter die? Mid-sixties? I still wasn't thirty."

"I'll make my point." McKinley was suddenly abrupt. "My view is that while impressive, Monckton's career was also blighted. So much so that the odour lingers to this day......and not merely around his own family."

"Explain what you mean by 'blighted'," demanded Hugh, giving nothing still.

"I speak of a contagion, one at its most virulent thirty, forty years ago. Now people tend to be born with it, or they contract it seemingly from the air. Back then there were many who were inoculated with the thing, often under duress."

"And the condition...?"

"........was, and is, marked by a readiness to embrace our *Pax Americana,* and a willingness to indulge her venal appetite, a susceptibility to *Pox Americana* if you like. Often it comes with a slice of the action, if not then there's good, old fashioned fear. For your father it's been a mix."

"But you could have found him in London, " objected the son. "You're down here. You seem to want to point a finger at me. I don't see why."

"Goodwill's what we'm bringin'," said Old Jack. The two companions nodded. "Errlyer on when 'twere light these party bin down wi'me to Mylor Churchyard. We stood silent fer a mennad or two at Duggan's grave. Thirdy five year 'go t'day 'e were killed. Best part of a year later and this boy Cairns, Francis Cairns, 'e were killed in Korea. Now, in this year, 1985, we 'as 'nother........that Prout feller. Now I sees Rory jus' b'fore 'e dies. Ben 'ere likewise sees Cairns, an' with Gareth 'tis jus' the same with Prout."

"So?" challenged Hugh.

"So none of us 'ere thinks these is accid'nts. 'N fact we knows 'tis all linked in someway, an' linked t'gether with this 'ere place."

"You know nothing," asserted Hugh smugly. A faint smile flickered from his eyes.

"But we do have this Mr Trembath," said Gareth bluntly. He unzipped a jacket pocket and produced a bulkily folded handkerchief.

Holding it in one palm the fingers lifted a corner of the linen... a loosening shake, and the bullet within slipped free. "I believe you've seen this one before. It is yours. Thanks to you I know it's a .30, fired from a Garand M1 rifle. You told Steve, Steve told me. I've not told anyone else. I could do. I might yet."

"Tell who you like," scoffed Trembath.

"When I do then they'll hear that this isn't what I gave the boy to show you. You kept what was mine and gave him back something of yours, something very similar. My bullet, that which you hold still, I was given by an Argentine soldier. It was removed from him aboard the *Kampala*, in the South Atlantic. We're still in touch. It's a cherished keepsake. He's a cherished friend. I'd like it back. You can have this again."

Hugh coloured. He said nothing. Gareth continued. "Steve brought you a 7.6 fired from a British Army automatic assault rifle, our Fabrique Nationale FAL. It's a good tool. Of Belgian origin they go all over the world, and more often than not to areas where it's perceived that what we like to term as 'western interests' are under threat."

"You mean the Argentinians use them," scoffed Hugh. "So what?"

"He means they could also be useful in a place such as Colombia," McKinley broke in, "where the gathering might of dollar rich cocaine barons is attracting the understandable concern of Washington. A concern which our top men there would appear to prefer to address through covert means....... which is to say illegally financed, apparently by dabbling in the trade that's bringing in the money."

Jack spelt it out.

"They was FN rifles that were bein' stored in th' Viceroy shed, an' you knowed 'bout it all 'long. You knowed too 'ow they was bein' put 'board that ship, 'n you knows where they was put when they 'ad t'be tak'n off an' 'idden 'gain."

"And you might have thought that you'd got away with it all," said McKinley, "and in a way you have, but that's not because you haven't yourself been rumbled. We won't be bought off, or silenced, not like others.....so listen, if only for the sake of your daughter."

"If Gareth wants his bullet, he can have it. Of course he can." Hugh was suddenly in retreat, flustered retreat.

"Mr Trembath....," the Amercan was stern. "There's been a series of squalid transactions between Carwinion and those charged with promoting the shadier aspects of my government's foreign policy. It's time to draw a line. It's been going on for far too long. The cover's worn thin. The game's up, certainly as far as this place is concerned. One Rory Duggan is enough. One Francis Cairns is enough."

"And one Prout," added Gareth. "That's evened things in my book. Time to close the ledger."

"Would that it were all that easy," sighed Hugh.

"Think of the mire that enveloped your father," said the American. "Think of the way things were set in 1950. That's when things weren't so easy. When the likes of Joe Stalin and J Edgar Hoover were peaking, peaking in power, peaking in paranoia. Those days have gone. Think. You have choices where your father had none. Choose carefully. Choose wisely."

"Lest, 'n time, people come to judge 'e all th' more 'arshly, " cautioned old Jack sharply, and that was as much as he had left to say to Hugh Trembath.

*

MAY 1986

Another two weeks and a year's worth would have elapsed since Steve and Jane's first meeting. Ralph's cafe had been dismantled, and now it was the turn of the *Kampala*. Dishevelled, disfigured almost, she was tugged astern from the passage and, below Trelissick, turned and pointed for Taiwan. For delivery she'd been placed with yet another company, again purposely created, and as a final indignity her true name had been obliterated. *Neptune Eighty Six* she was now, the company name.

They'd found her some flags though, and the Falmouth tugs hosed high to salute her passing. With her full ahead run along the length of the Roads she raised a last, black fuming, blaring, vainglorious gesture of defiance.

Jack Butters, out on the water with his grandson, heard and smelt and felt her pass. Jane, with her father and his camera had an elevated vantage from the footpath between St.Just and St.Mawes. The best shots, those that took in both liner and *Flushing Run,* were next day developed and two mornings later reprints arrived in Bristol.

But they were not to be Steve's final image of the ship. Two months later the former *Kampala* was pictured in *The Times.* She was on her side. Typhoon 'Vince', sweeping into Kaishong, had swept her from a supposedly sheltered anchorage to leave her toppled in the shallows. It was a proud demise. She'd succumbed to the elements. The breakers had only a wreck to dissect.

The boy phoned Gareth. He wanted the Welshman's thoughts, and there might be an Argentinian angle besides.

"I'd always thought her unsinkable," the Welshman said. "When she left she looked as sturdy as ever. She could have taken on the Horn."

"And saved them the toll through Panama."

"Had that been the charted route," continued Gareth.

"You'll have to explain that," said Steve.

"I did alert Alberto to the *Kampala's* departure. In his country there were still people following her every nautical mile. Through him there later came confirmation of a last call into Gibraltar."

"For fuel?"

"That, and perhaps more."

"Are you hinting at a payload?........the Noriega connection and all that? He's firmly in place now, by all accounts."

"Forget Panama, Steve. They hear she's left 'Gib' but then they lose her, for the best part of a week. And then it emerges from Washington, and that's no surprise, that the Kampala is in the Red Sea."

"So she's gone the other way, along the Med, and quietly slipped through Suez."

"On her old route," Gareth confirmed." And then it seems there was something of a stir. In former days she would often call at Jeddah to top up with fuel and water, but this time no dice. It was remembered who she really was and the old *fatwa* was again invoked."

"So she had to go thirsty...."

"Only as far as Aden, but for her watchers she was now firmly back on the map....."

".....and half a world away from Panama," Steve observed. "And heading for where next? Colombo? Singapore?"

"Yes, but not before an interesting little detour across to Pasni. Know where that is, do you?"

"Tell me."

"Pakistan, the Iranian end, and not far from Afghanistan, about as close as the sea gets. A bit of a wild-west town this is, by all accounts, and apparently on one of her two nights there she was plundered by thieves."

"Who took what?" asked Steve. "She was bound for the breakers."

"'Stores and equipment,' that's about as much as anyone's been told," answered Gareth. There was scepticism there, just a trace, but Steve made nothing of it. To him it came with the accent.

*

For this year it was just the week in Cornwall, taken early in September. Any longer he couldn't afford. There was the University place waiting, and what he was earning from his long hours at the burger joint he'd need to save. Yes, there were dearer places than Swansea, but he was hoping soon to be able to buy and run a motorcycle of his own. With all the distractions and dislocations of his freshman start it wasn't until Christmas, and an exchange of cards, that any word either went to or came from Welshpool.

Gareth's to Steve proclaimed peace on earth. As it was opened a newspaper cutting fluttered to the floor.....a short article, and the actual thing, not a photocopy. It had been snipped from a broadsheet. By the type it looked to be the *Guardian*.

It was headed:

' Soviet withdrawal gathers pace.'
It went on:
'Senior Soviet military commanders seem, at last, to be falling into line behind the Gorbachev initiated pull out of Afghanistan. The

Premier would no doubt prefer it broadcast that it has been the strictures of Glasnost that have persuaded the 'die hards' away from their former reluctance. In fact the more telling argument is being advanced by the Mujahidin, the rebel force whose sworn aim it is to overthrow the hitherto Moscow backed Kabul government.

Of critical significance over these past six months has been the rebels' acquisition and trained use of American made 'Stinger' missiles. The hand held devices have been particularly effective against the Russian helicopter 'transports' and 'gunships'. For the Russians, to be denied ground force flexibility is to be denied a winning strategy. Morale is poor amongst the troops. Where they remain it will be as an increasingly vulnerable target.

It is widely thought that the CIA have been instrumental in supplying the Mujahidin with missile launchers and ammunition. Most observers agree that the hardware is shipped into Pakistan and then hauled overland to the Afghan border.'

There wasn't a deal of margin space, but enough for Gareth.

'Stores and equipment?' he'd written, beneath that 'Plus ca change!'

*

Deep and wide flows the tidal Fal. Quiet are its waters, and closely held are the secrets that repose therein. By 1994, Jack Butters was no more. His ashes were settled in the silt. Duggan's grave lay neglected, overgrown.

Judith Cook's first book on the Murrell case had appeared in 1985. Her second, with what will probably be her last words on the matter, was published nine years later to a very different world. The wall was down, the Cold War as good as over. To the questions raised by her first effort there were few clear answers..... and new scandal will always drive out old. But in Cornwall, a pocket of interest remained. The author lived in the county, where she and her work enjoyed high regard.

Hugh Trembath purchased his copy in Truro. It stirred memories, and then came something else........ to stir fears, to prick at a conscience. At long last there was work for the methane tankers. First one, and then the other, they were unchained from their moorings and tugged to the docks for a dust off, and a seaworthiness check....... and away they went, onto the high seas. Those berths below the ferry were not for immediate re-occupation. Here was an opportunity to lift the mooring buoys with their chains and their anchors. An overhaul was long due. There were spares to drop in their place.

The winches were brought up, and the hardware was heaved to the surface. The first two came cleanly, but not the third. A snagging was felt, and a dragging, a tearing, a snapping, and, as the end of the chain emerged, twisted thereon was a car door.

After a close police examination it was established to have been part of a commonplace Ford Escort Mk2, that this one had been red painted, and that it had been submerged for about ten years. A decision was required as to whether what remained on the bed needed to be raised. A police diving team was summoned, and what came was a specialist three man squad, attached to Special Branch. They worked at still water, launching their heavy-duty inflatable from Tolverne at high tide and at low. Hugh Trembath looked down from the Trelissick Garden, watching nervously. Sky and water were grey, and between all seemed of brooding monochrome, ever the medium for shadowy suspense. With Manderley there had been the bones in the wreck; with the Motel, Bates' Motel, a car was hauled from the swamp. Fiction, that was. For Carwinion the indictment would be real. He wrung his hands. What would they find? What would eventually emerge? He could only wait.

But nothing did emerge. Findings were reported, and a short statement released. The rest of the vehicle had been located on the bed, and identified as one that had been stolen in Birmingham. Closer details....... the date of the theft, the name of the registered owner, these were not released. There were other items of scrap strewn along the passage floor, and a general view was taken. Such detritus was bothersome to raise. It could stay. A minor case of car theft could be closed. Beyond that there was no indication of foul play.

Thatcherism might now be history, and likewise the Cold War. The Democrats, ascendant in Congress, could even be looking good for a return to the White House.......the world moves on, but rather more slowly for Carwinion. The Trembaths could be assured. They had friends still, 'friends' in high places.

THE END

Geographical note.

All of the countries, cities, towns, and villages mentioned in the story existed at the relevant times. The Carwinion Estate is imagined and the landscape to the north of Trelissick has been re-sculpted to accommodate its properties. Percuil Yard, Chapel Meadow, and the Pendower Cafe are likewise imagined. If an existing feature or business is mentioned it might be that the actual view therefrom of the surroundings differs from that described.

Historical note.

'Pandora Inn' is historical fiction. All, save four, of the speaking characters are fictional. They occasionally discuss people who have lived, or who are living. Their views on them will often contrast. No one person's views are those of the author. The four non-fictional speaking characters are the late J Edgar Hoover, his colleague, Nicholls, Mr Ken Downes, and the late Mrs Mildred Bruce. Each led a colourful life. All might have been invented by Upton Sinclair, or perhaps even by Nevil Shute!

Of the politicians mentioned, all who attained Cabinet rank were or are living people. Randolph Churchill was an MP. Ida Copeland was an elected MP, as is Tam Dalyell. Sir Edward Trembath (who speaks) is invented.

A number of actual businesses are mentioned, examples being the King Harry Ferry, the Pandora Inn, and Plymouth's Sunday Independent. All characters associated with any mentioned business, whether as employee or employer, are fictional and any resemblance they might have to real living persons will be coincidental.

The RFA, the Coastguard Service, the police, and the Ambulance service are examples of actual services mentioned. All characters associated with any mentioned service are fictional and any resemblance they might have to real living persons will be coincidental.

The British India shipping line did, I believe, operate a ship named the Kampala. The firm was taken over and the ship was disposed of long before the '82 Falklands conflict. I did see the actual vessel that was used as a military hospital when, in '85, she was brought to the Fal after subsequent service as a troopship.

She was laid up off Tolverne. The spectacle helped stir my imagination. I have my *Kampala* similarly positioned. None of my characters are intended to represent any person who served or was treated on the actual hospital ship. Any resemblance or similarity is coincidental.

To frame a historical context, I quote from the works of a number of actual writers. Two mentioned in the story are Kenneth O. Morgan and Clive Ponting (each recommended to anyone with an interest in the Labour Governments formed by Clem Attlee and Harold Wilson.) Mr Ponting will ever be associated with Tam Dalyell MP and the Belgrano. A character in my story suggests that rather than leaking 'Official Secrets' he was unknowingly passing on disinformation, that he was being manipulated so as to suppress a more disturbing truth.

If I'd been a juryman, and I'd suspected this, then I too would have disregarded the directions of the trial judge.

Writers need fuel. For me it has been passion, sparked by the Murrell case. No Judith Cook, no *Pandora Inn*......thank you Judith Cook.

Lord Birkenhead's biography of Walter Monckton, and N.S. Norway's autobiography, are essential to my yarn. I am particularly indebted to the Lady Juliet Townsend and A.P.Watt Ltd for their assistance. I suspect that there is much more to emerge on Walter Monckton, and on N.S. Norway...... and likewise on Nevil Shute!

Acknowledgements.

I gratefully acknowledge the assistance of the following:-

'The Guardian', for permission to use part of Pete Bowler's article on the *Lancastria*.

John Keegan and 'The Daily Telegraph', for permission to use part of 'The British Century'.

Gerald Howson (author) and John Murray (publishers), for permission to use part of 'Arms for Spain'.

The Lady Juliet Townsend, for permission to use part of her late father's biography of Walter Monckton.

Penguin UK, for permission to use part of 'The Spanish Civil War', written by Hugh Thomas.

Judith Cook (author), for permission to use parts of 'Who Killed Hilda Murrell' (New English Library) and 'Unlawful Killing' (Bloomsbury).

Kenneth O. Morgan (author) and Oxford University Press (publishers), for permission to use parts of 'The People's Peace'.

A.P. Watt Ltd (on behalf of the Trustees of the Estate of the late N.S. Norway), for permission to use part of 'Slide Rule'.

Mrs Heard of Mylor for permission to use her picture of a working boat.

The Author

Lliam West was born in Liskeard in 1949. He attended the Church School and the old Grammar School. After studying in Reading he moved to London, where he taught, before returning to his home town to continue the family business. This was sold up in 1985, enabling him to devote time to the care of his two sons and elderly father while his wife returned to her career.

For one with an abiding interest in political history and current affairs these were extremely interesting times.... the Murrell case was then something of a *cause celebre* and, even in sleepy Cornwall, it was still possible to find and talk to survivors of the *Lancastria,* and to political refugees driven from Franco's Spain. Mature students study (at evening class and college) then intervened and it wasn't until the purchase of a PC in 1998 that the long incubated ideas started to become the initial draft of *Pandora Inn.*

As well as Shute *(lonely Road)*, particular influences on his story telling are Doyle *(Micah Clarke),* Sinclair *(World's End),* Spring *(Fame is the Spur),* and Goddard *(Past Caring).*

For inspiration he has Cornwall.....and also there is Judith Cook.